A VIEW
FROM
THERE

A VIEW FROM THERE

ANGELA SLAUGHTER

TATE PUBLISHING
AND **ENTERPRISES**, LLC

Published by Tate Publishing & Enterprises, LLC
127 E. Trade Center Terrace | Mustang, Oklahoma 73064 USA
1.888.361.9473 | www.tatepublishing.com

Tate Publishing is committed to excellence in the publishing industry. The company reflects the philosophy established by the founders, based on Psalm 68:11,
"The Lord gave the word and great was the company of those who published it."

Published in the United States of America

ISBN: 978-1-68142-656-3
1. Fiction / Christian / General
2. Fiction / Romance / General
15.05.25

To Grandma, who went to be with Jesus in 2005, and who believed I could do anything. Every single day my heart aches for you—to hear you tell me you love me, to laugh with you. You were my rock, my place of shelter, my best friend. My life was beautiful because you took me in your arms and called me yours when you didn't have to. I can't wait to see your face again.

And to Grandpa, who met Jesus in November 2013. You were the strongest, most honest, greatest man I have ever known. No one could ever convince you that I didn't hang the moon. I hope I have made you proud. I love you so much. Please know you were always my hero. Always, always.

Chapter One

*I have noticed in all the serious
circustances of my life that nature always
reflected the image of my soul. On days
filled with tears, the heavens cried
along with me; on days of joy the sun
sent forth its joyful rays . . .*
-St. Thérèse of Lisieux

Kate Canton sat motionless in her Range Rover, never happier to see the inside of her garage. A minute passed. Then two. With effort, she unlocked her grip on the steering wheel and exhaled, half in release, half in exhaustion. She'd made it home.

The events of the week played over again in her mind. The phone call, the long drive alone, the hospital. The tubes that looped around and into her mother's body, the beeping machines, the doctors who gave their bleak prognosis. Kate pictured the faces of her family and friends already in tears, waiting to mourn. She recalled the fear and helplessness that threatened to crush her and then, two days later, her mother's face when she'd opened her eyes and lived.

Kate glanced in the rearview mirror and grimaced at her reflection. Her long brown hair was pulled up in an untidy ponytail, and her makeup-less face was pale and tired. The trip from Atlanta, Georgia, to Millsville, Arkansas, had taken nearly fourteen hours because of a storm somewhere in Tennessee that slowed but didn't stop her. She'd driven through sheets of rain and hail and could barely see the interstate, but she'd been determined to make it home to her husband's arms and the safety and comfort she'd find only there.

Gray would be asleep in their bed, and Kate's eyes brimmed with tears of relief. The nightmare was over. She was home. Her mother was alive. And Gray was just inside.

She grabbed her purse from the passenger seat and opened the door to the ding-dinging of the silver SUV with keys still in the ignition. The garage was cold, and she quickly made her way inside the house and into the dark kitchen. She placed her purse on the granite countertop, careful not to wake her sleeping daughter or startle her husband, neither of whom were expecting her until the following evening. She hadn't planned on leaving early, but her mother's condition was stable and her daughter had come down with the flu. She'd kissed her mother's forehead and promised to return with little Jane Ellen as soon as she was feeling better.

"Goodbye, Katherine," her mother had said. "Remember, if you run into those storms, don't be afraid to stop and find a place to rest. Eventually the clouds will pass, and you can start again."

Kate swallowed as she slipped off her shoes. Her mouth and throat were dry. She grabbed a bottle of water from the refrigerator and, after a lengthy gulp, she stumbled back a step and leaned against the counter. The room swirled around her and her stomach rolled—a reminder she'd forgotten to eat since morning. The dizziness faded as quickly as it came, and she set the water on the counter and tiptoed toward the living room.

Her feet sank into the soft carpet and a faint light glowed beneath the bedroom door and along the edge where it was cracked open just an inch. Her heart leapt. Gray was awake, probably still working. She smiled and almost skipped toward the door. She reached for the knob when an unfamiliar voice—a female voice—spoke from within. Kate withdrew her hand and leaned closer to the door, her green eyes growing large. Her heart pounded in her chest, and she pushed on the door just enough to peer inside.

The nearly naked blonde woman snuggled closer to her husband under the white sheets and kissed his bare shoulder. "I never expected to spend the night in this bed."

Gray laughed, his hair disheveled and damp. "Don't get used to it. She'll be home tomorrow."

The blonde pursed her lips. "You promised you'd tell her, Gray. This week."

"How was I supposed to know this would happen? Her mother almost died for God's sake."

Kate's body went numb. She turned away from the door and leaned her back against the wall, paralyzed, barely able to breathe.

"It could've been worse, you know?" Gray said. "If she'd have died, I'd have had to go all the way to Arkansas for the funeral and deal with the affairs. Who knows how long I'd have been stuck there? And I couldn't have told Kate about us right after losing her mother. Surely even you would've found that heartless."

Kate's body began to shake. The queasiness in her stomach returned, and the room again spun around her. She leaned harder against the wall for balance.

The blonde sighed. "I'm just so tired of waiting. It's been nearly six months, and you said—"

"Shhh." Gray placed his index finger against her lips. "Not long now, baby. I promise. Why don't we just enjoy this while we can?"

Six months. The remaining air escaped Kate's lungs.

Even the pounding of her heart couldn't drown out the sound of their bodies moving under the sheets and the echo of their kisses. Kate closed her eyes, but the air would not come. Her lungs cried out for it. She opened her eyes, but her sight was gone, replaced by blackness. The floor beneath her rolled like a storm-tossed sea. Vomit rose in her throat, and she lunged toward the kitchen, grasping the backs of the furniture with each step.

She fell onto the sink and gagged, but her stomach was empty except for the water she'd drunk just before. It was all that came up, and she spit it from her lips. Slowly the blackness disappeared from her vision, and she gazed into the sink at two empty wine glasses lying side by side.

The house resounded with the loud ringing of the telephone, and Kate jolted upright. Another ring. She wiped her mouth with her hand and shrank back into the shadows of the kitchen. The clock on the stove read 2:17 a.m. in glowing orange numbers.

Another ring.

"No, don't get it. Let Rosa," the blonde begged.

"Rosa's been asleep for hours."

Two more rings, then the click of the answering machine and Gray's no-nonsense voice coming from its small speaker. "You've reached the Cantons. Please leave a message after the tone."

After a long beep, Kate's Aunt Modean spoke amid static and bustling background clatter, her southern drawl anxious

9

and troubled. "Gray, darlin', are you there? Pick up, dear, if you can hear me." There was a long rustling pause followed by a troubled sigh.

"Okay, then," Modean continued. "Honey, it's Aunt Modean in Arkansas. Kate's on her way home. She left a day early to surprise you and Jane Ellen. Ruth got better, see, and . . ." She exhaled into the receiver. "But her mama's gone. Ruth's gone. It was sudden, and they don't know why yet. It happened about ten minutes ago. Please call me, darlin'. Please."

Kate stood still in the darkness of the kitchen, her limbs no longer shaking, her head no longer spinning. The queasiness was gone from her stomach. Gray and the blonde in her bed disappeared into the nothingness that engulfed her body, and the black void swirled around her like a vacuum, violently erasing her from where she stood, swallowing her heart, and sucking away everything that was Kate Canton until there was nothing. She slid down the kitchen wall and landed on the cold tile floor below. She no longer existed.

***

After the funeral was over, a couple dozen of the three-hundred plus who'd attended stood around Ruth Boudrow's gravesite to show their respects one final time. Kate sat beneath a portable funeral tent in a velvet-covered chair between her favorite cousin, Truitt, and their Aunt Modean. After four teary-eyed old ladies finished the last verse of "Amazing Grace," the elderly pastor dismissed the service in prayer. With his amen, as if on cue, thunder rolled and small drops of rain began to fall here and there. The departing mourners stepped faster toward the cemetery gate and the shelter of their vehicles.

Truitt stood and grasped Kate's arm. "If I ever make it to heaven, I'm gonna ask God why it always rains on the day of a funeral."

Kate attempted a smile.

"You need a minute?" he asked.

Kate nodded. Truitt helped Aunt Modean from her chair then whispered into the funeral director's ear. The man nodded and gathered his men to leave before stopping to whisper to Kate, "Take as long as you need. We'll be in the church with Mo and Truitt."

When Kate was alone in the cemetery with the casket and the open grave, she stared at the beautiful burgundy-colored box that held her mother's body. More thunder resounded from the sky, and lightning flashed in the distance. From behind her came the sounds of starting engines and tires driving over pea gravel, until all fell quiet except for the rain hitting the top of the tent.

She looked over her shoulder. No one in sight. She stood and walked around the casket, waiting on steel beams to be lowered into the earth. The wood was shiny and smooth, and Kate ran her fingers across it. How wrong it seemed for something so beautiful to be buried deep beneath the ground, away from the world and everyone in it.

And then the rain came. It pounded down on her tired body, soaking the new black dress she would never wear again. Her legs felt weak and began to shake, but she looked up to the sky, undaunted by the mounting storm. The heavy drops stung her cheeks and mingled with the black mascara that ran from her eyes. Her chin began to quiver, and the knot in her throat rose high.

She'd remained elegant and poised since her arrival in Millsville. Her family and friends, and even some people she'd never met, commented on her kindness and strength. Many said she reminded them of Jackson, her father, who'd died when Kate was only nine years old. "A picture of grace," they'd said.

Only Aunt Modean and Truitt knew about Gray and the other woman and how Kate's world had come crashing down around her in one unforeseen, merciless instant. But Millsville was small, and gossip spread with unrivaled intensity. Chatter about Gray's absence at the funeral was already making the rounds among Millsville's most scandal-savvy citizens. Soon, everyone would know.

In Gray's place, there had been an ornate, oversized flower arrangement addressed to the Boudrow Family from Debbie's Flowers and Gifts. While Kate hadn't expected him to attend the service, she'd anticipated a phone call or, at least, a note—if not to her, to Jane Ellen. But there'd been nothing. Only a card that read simply, *With sympathy, Gray Canton.*

Kate shuddered, and she wondered if the memory of that night on the cold kitchen floor or the icy October wind were to blame. Alone amid the graves, her sobs came on like waves without ceasing. Not since that night had she cried. Not since that night had she felt the desperation—the kind that choked her—that she did there, next to her mother's casket. She'd been too busy caring for Jane Ellen and preparing the funeral to wallow in the self-pity that was rightfully hers.

But her quivering legs could no longer hold her. She fell to her knees on the wet ground and covered her face with her hands.

"Mama, you can't leave me now. Please!" She caught her breath between sobs and dug her fingers into the soft earth on either side of her. "Please," she said, this time to the rain. "Please. Wash me away."

A strong hand clutched her shoulder from behind. Startled and humiliated, she glanced backward at a young man with black, wavy hair, wearing an expensive dark suit. She didn't recognize him, thank God. A funeral home attendant, she decided.

"Please, just one more minute." She wiped at her tears.

He squeezed her shoulder. "We can't understand his ways, Kate." His voice was deep and gentle. Still, it annoyed her.

Kate closed her eyes and took a deep, exhaustive breath. She'd endured three days of generic, though well-meaning, words of sympathy from family, friends, and complete strangers. The man's attempt at comfort rolled off her like the rain.

***

Inside the church, a little girl stood on tiptoe and peered out a tall window. Her grandmother would appear at any moment to hurry her to the car—she hated driving in the rain. Still, the girl wanted to see them. The rain was falling hard, in sheets and gusts that made it hard to make out the three figures standing in the cemetery. She squinted then rubbed her eyes. One had gone, and there were only two. The little girl sighed, disappointed. He had gone as quickly as he'd come.

***

Kate politely faked a smile. She was considering standing and shaking the man's hand in a pathetic formal introduction when someone else caught her eye.

Several graves away, another man was kneeling at a tombstone. His dark brown hair and overcoat dripped with rain, but he was unmoved. His stare pierced through her, and she wanted to look away, though something in his eyes would not allow it. His expression was solemn, but his eyes churned with agony and anger. They screamed at her, *You don't belong here!* Lightning flashed overhead, and the man looked up at the sky.

Kate studied the features of his attractive face, wondering if she should recognize him. He looked back at her, his glare even more hateful than before. Then, without a word, he stomped out of the cemetery gate and disappeared into the fog and rain.

Lightning cracked again, followed by a booming clap of thunder that shook the casket on the beams next to her.

"I'm sorry," Kate said, climbing to her feet, preparing again to introduce herself to the young man standing behind her. "How rude of me—"

"Kate!" Truitt shouted, running toward her with an umbrella.

Kate turned in a circle, but the man who'd touched her shoulder was gone.

Truitt reached her, panting for breath, and held the umbrella over her with one hand while pulling her to his side with the other. "C'mon. This storm's gettin' worse."

He wrapped her quivering, muddy hands around the handle of the umbrella and draped his jacket over her shoulders. The black lines of mascara stretched down her cheeks, and he rubbed at them with his thumb.

"I'm a mess." She wiped her hands on her dress.

"You're beautiful. As beautiful as I've ever seen you." Truitt took the umbrella again and pressed his lips firmly against her forehead.

Kate let him lead her out of the cemetery and to the long, black funeral car where Aunt Modean waited. Before climbing in, she looked back over her shoulder for either of the men but saw no one. Aunt Modean patted Kate's knee as she settled next to her in the car.

"You hang in there, darlin'. We're takin' you home."

Chapter Two

With a loud squealing of tires, the young woman's long, slender body was catapulted from her sleeping position on the backseat to the floorboard of the stranger's car. She grimaced in pain and listened. They'd stopped. Two hours before, when she'd talked the man named Robert into giving her a ride, he'd been alone. But she definitely heard two voices conversing, loudly, heatedly. Another man had joined them while she'd slept.

Her heart pounded as the second man exited the car and slammed the door, followed by more yelling outside the car. The smell of week-old vomit rose thick from the grayish carpeted floor mats of the ancient Honda and attacked the woman's nose.

"Sorry, Esther," Robert mumbled. "I'll be right back." He opened his door and climbed out of the vehicle after his friend.

Esther pushed herself back up onto the torn, vinyl seat with some effort. She was alone in the car, and she peered through the window to see Robert and the other man standing just inches away. She caught the words "love you." Then, "You'll never understand me." And, "Maybe we just need a break." They flailed their arms at each other, and the shouting match stretched on.

Robert, a young man of about twenty, reached for the other man's hand, but the other man pulled away, crossed his arms, and pouted. A lover's quarrel, the woman deduced, and without an end in sight. She sighed, and a lump rose in her throat. Home. She just wanted to go home. Robert's boyfriend stomped away, and Robert, teary-eyed, followed.

Esther pulled the sleeves of the leather jacket over her frozen hands as the Honda's heater pumped cool air into the backseat. Headlights approached from behind, and she drew her hood around her face. Then she lowered herself back down onto the seat and held her breath until the car drove past.

***

After a short drive, the funeral car pulled into Modean Wilkes's driveway. Several people stood waiting on the front porch.

"Who are they?" Kate asked.

Modean looked out the window. "Oh my Lord. That's Harold and Bessie and the Mayhans with more food."

"More food?" Truitt almost shouted. "We've got enough food in there now to feed half of Benton county as it is."

Modean ignored him. "I'll bet Bessie made her squash casserole and fried chicken." She turned to Kate. "I know you ain't got much of an appetite, sugar, but Bessie's casserole is heavenly. You just gotta try it."

The car came to a stop, and Modean scurried out to greet her friends.

Truitt leaned close to Kate. "Try the casserole. Stay away from the chicken."

Kate crinkled her brow as Truitt stepped from the car and helped her out after him.

"Trust me." He held the umbrella above them as they walked toward the porch and whispered, "Bessie and Harold kill and pluck their own chickens. Neither of them can see a thing. And I mean, not a thing. Last time I ate Bessie's fried chicken, I picked feathers out of my teeth for days."

Kate winced. "Casserole. No chicken."

"There you go. Repeat it over and over to yourself if you have to." Truitt stepped onto the porch to join the guests and lowered the umbrella. "Bessie! Harold! There'd better be some of your famous fried chicken in that basket!"

***

Kate slept little that night in Aunt Modean's upstairs bedroom and awoke early the next morning to the smell of fresh brewed coffee. She turned over in bed and smiled at the peaceful face of her sleeping child. Jane Ellen was seven, a small replica of Kate with her long brown hair and greenish-gray eyes. Kate listened for a minute to her daughter's steady breathing and wondered how she'd tell her they weren't going home to Daddy. Only three days earlier, she'd explained how Grandma Ruth went up to Heaven and wouldn't be coming back. Jane Ellen hadn't said much, but she'd cried in her mother's lap most of the day.

Kate leaned in and kissed Jane Ellen's warm forehead. Then she slipped out of bed and into a pair of furry pink slippers before making her way downstairs to Modean's kitchen. Kate was surprised when Modean wasn't in her usual chair at the kitchen table and was on her way to check the living room when she found a note taped to the refrigerator.

> *Truitt,*
> *Ms. Cora Beth is sick. Gone to see her. Be back soon.*
> *Check on Kate and JE.*

Kate set the note on the table and poured herself a cup of coffee in an *I Love Elvis* mug, complete with The King's silhouette in bright rainbow colors. She wrapped herself in a purple afghan and retreated to the front porch swing after a glance at the calendar told her it was Saturday.

Saturday mornings in Millsville were always the most exciting day of the week from late spring through early fall, as the town gathered in the square for the renowned Millsville Farmers' Market. People from miles around converged on the small town each year during market season to purchase the best fruits, vegetables, plants, herbs, and crafts in the state. Some years before, the market had appeared in an issue of *Southern Life* magazine, and a writer and photographer had come all the way from Chicago just to take pictures and talk to the townsfolk. Even Aunt Modean claimed to have been quoted in the three-page article, although the quote had been attributed to "a lifelong Millsville citizen," and many other residents claimed the same.

As a child, Kate had enjoyed the hullabaloo of the market—the booths, the smells, the bustling people, and how the air on Saturday mornings just felt different, filled with anticipation and delight. Kate and her mother had shopped those stands together Kate's entire life, and she wanted to be there among the crowds and produce and smells.

She set her jaw. That day, she would leave the shelter of Aunt Modean's house and venture into town. Partly for her sake, and partly for Jane Ellen's.

The screen door slammed beside her and out walked Truitt in a wrinkled T-shirt and orange striped pajama pants. His wavy blonde hair, normally styled to perfection, was without product and in a state of confusion atop his head. His deep brown eyes were pink and swollen, and a large, red indentation covered his left cheek. Kate laughed. She couldn't remember the last time she'd seen him not flawlessly groomed. Even at the funeral home three nights earlier, two young women had swooned over him, though he'd seemed not to notice. For a moment Kate had been appalled at the girls' attempts to flirt during her mother's funeral visitation. But as she watched Truitt greet visitors with an affectionate hug or handshake, tall and powerfully built in his suit and tie, she couldn't blame them.

Truitt rubbed his eyes and yawned. "It's freezin' out here."

"Get a blanket," Kate said.

Truitt returned inside the house, and the screen door slammed behind him again. Seconds later, he emerged wrapped in a colorful, handmade quilt.

"I fell asleep on a book." He pointed to his cheek.

"I can see that."

"What are you doin' up so early?"

"Don't most Millsville residents get out of bed at the crack of dawn?" Kate asked.

"Most Millsville residents are senior citizens."

Truitt took a seat beside her on the swing and stole the cup of coffee out of her hand. He took a sip then settled back, holding the quilt around his shoulders. "So, really. How are you?"

She drew her legs up onto the swing and rested her chin on a knee. "Better. Being here makes me better."

"So you're stayin'?"

She shrugged. "This is where I've always wanted to be. With you and Aunt Mo, and Mama and Jane Ellen."

"And your angry Cuban nanny." Truitt sipped the coffee.

Kate laughed. "You'll get used to Rosa. I just couldn't leave her with Gray. And she isn't angry." She grabbed her cup back from him.

"She probably hasn't forgiven me for walkin' in on her in the shower yesterday."

Kate grimaced. "Yeah, I heard about that."

"You'd think lockin' doors would've been a priority in Cuba."

"You'd think."

Silence settled between them. Somewhere in the distance a car horn blew three times, and a dog barked in response.

"Did I tell you it was Rosa who got Jane Ellen and me out of the house the night I found Gray with . . ." She swallowed. "The night Mama died? Gray never knew I'd been there until he talked to Aunt Mo the next day."

"Does she have family?"

"Her mother and sister live in Santa Clara. We're her only family, really. Although, she never cared for Gray."

"Ahhh. See? I'm already beginnin' to like Rosa. I never much liked Gray myself."

Kate stared into the distance. "I did."

Truitt put his arm around her. "Well, I hear Larry Joe down at the car clinic just divorced his sixth wife and is back on the market."

Kate rolled her eyes and scooted away from him. "Truitt, good grief."

"I'm just sayin'. There's got to be somethin' special 'bout a man who's gotten six women to marry him."

"Speaking of marriage, isn't it about time the most handsome bachelor in Arkansas gets himself hitched? Or do you plan on living with Aunt Mo forever?"

"Now, why would I go get married and completely shatter all of Millsville's suspicions that I'm a"—he glanced side to side then cupped his hand next to his mouth—"a homosexual."

"Truitt!"

He laughed. "Okay, okay, not everyone thinks so, but definitely Ms. Ella and Ms. Emma."

"The twins? They're still alive?"

Truitt shushed her with a finger to his lips. "See that yellow house over there? They moved there three years ago. Them and that dang cat. They're always around, just poppin' up when you least expect it."

"Cat? Don't tell me Mr. Gregory Peck is still alive!"

"He's fifteen years old. Not a tooth in his head. Completely deaf. And he stinks like road kill."

"And I suppose you're still his vet?"

"Don't think I haven't considered puttin' that poor creature out of its miserable existence. But believe me, he deserves every second of it."

"You must have shot him with your BB gun a hundred times when we were in school."

"Or more."

Kate laughed. "And now you're in charge of his health and well-being."

He shook his head. "Ah, life's mockery."

Kate nearly choked on the hot coffee. "Remember the time—"

"Shhh, shhh." Truitt sat up straight, his cool expression transforming to alarm before her eyes.

Kate looked up to see two old women, arm in arm, making their way up the sidewalk.

"Yoo-hoo!" they called, somewhat out of unison. One was carrying a large paper bag and the other held an oversized wicker purse. They were dressed identically, in white pants with large cuffs at the ankles, pink jackets, and pink T-shirts underneath that read *Market Queens* in big white letters outlined in sparkling silver rhinestones. The twins sported matching hairstyles—tight, platinum curls sprayed to perfection—and on their lips, a light frosty pink lipstick to match the excessive amount of rouge on their cheeks.

"Well, good morning, Ms. Ella, Ms. Emma. Come on up here." Truitt rose from the swing and hurried down the front steps to serve as the twins' escort onto the porch. An impenterable fog of Avon Musk and White Rain hairspray hovered around the women and threatened to suffocate Kate where she sat.

"Don't you both look lovely?" Truitt said. "Surely you must be on your way to some high-class social function open only to Millsville elite."

"Oh, Truitt Boudrow, you just stop that right now." The one holding the purse giggled with delight and slapped at his hand.

The twins shuffled over to Kate and sat on either side of her on the swing, each taking her by a hand. Kate tried to hold her breath, but her best efforts were no match for the musk. Somehow she managed a smile.

"Katherine, darling," began the one on her left, "you must know how terribly much we adored your mama."

"We loved her so," the other said.

"But surely you agree she was more than ready to meet your daddy in the clouds of Heaven, and I feel she is finally at true rest."

Kate paused to make sure the volley of words had subsided. Satisfied it had, she nodded. "Yes, I do agree. And I appreciate you both saying so."

"Oh, isn't she just beautiful?" one twin blurted. "That long, brown hair and eyes as green as the grass in spring. Your mama always used to say she should have put you in pictures so the whole world could enjoy that beautiful face."

Kate couldn't imagine her mother saying that.

The other twin nodded. "It's no wonder this little town of ours couldn't hold on to you longer."

Truitt put his hand on the shoulder of one of the twins. "Ms. Ella," he said, enunciating the name and tilting his head toward Kate. "Are my eyes deceiving me, or did you leave Mr. Gregory Peck at home today?"

Kate made quick mental note. *Ms. Ella to my right. Ms. Emma to my left.* Truitt winked at her.

"You know, Dr. Truitt, I don't believe Mr. Gregory Peck is feeling at all well today. He didn't eat his tuna fish, and he's been lagging behind all morning." She stood up and yelled down the street. "Mr. Gregory Peck! Here kitty kitty!"

"We may need to bring him to see you on Monday," Emma added. "He always eats his tuna."

Out of the bushes next to the porch hopped a feeble, overweight cat with blackish brown patches of fur arranged in

24

no particular pattern over a mostly bald, pinkish body. Drool dripped from the corner of his mouth, and the tip of his tail looked as though it had been shredded, possibly caught up in the blades of a fan. He appeared terribly annoyed that he'd been left behind and let out a pitiful, screeching *meow* directed at his two owners.

"There you are, darling!" Ella hurried down the porch steps and scooped him up into her arms. Kate recoiled and had to look away when Ella kissed him repeatedly on the mouth.

"Truitt, darling. Do you suppose Mo would mind if we borrowed a bowl of water for Mr. Gregory Peck? He seems winded."

"Certainly not." Truitt opened the door for Ella to carry the cat inside.

Emma followed close behind. "And perhaps some cheese, since he didn't eat his tuna this morning."

When the twins were out of earshot, Truitt whispered, "Imagine testin' that thing for worms."

Kate covered her mouth and giggled.

Emma reemerged onto the porch. "Where is Mo today? Still at Cora Beth's?"

"I believe so," Truitt answered.

"Well, Sister and I thought she might like to go with us to the market today. You know, this is the last market day of the season." Emma turned to Kate. "We'd love it if you'd come, too, dear. It would help get your mind off things."

Things. Kate wondered what they'd heard.

"I'd love to come, Ms. Emma. Jane Ellen and Rosa are still sleeping, but when they wake up, maybe we'll meet you there."

Ella came out of the house, holding the cat. The screen door slammed behind her, startling Mr. Gregory Peck, who leapt from her arms and tore across the street. "Oh dear," she said and went after him.

Emma patted Kate's shoulder. "We'll see you there, then, sweetie. Eightish?"

"You can't miss us!" shouted Ella from the road. "We're the booth with the pink awning and the sign that says 'Market Queens.' " She pointed to her shirt with pride.

Emma planted a loud wet kiss on Truitt's cheek. "See you Monday, dear."

And then they were gone.

Truitt reclaimed his seat next to Kate and wiped at his cheek with the afghan. "It was Ella who kissed the cat, right?"

Kate wrinkled her nose.

"You think every small town has an Ella Sue and Emma Lou DuBois?" he asked.

"If they don't, they should. What do you think was in that paper bag?"

Truitt shrugged. "The rest of Mr. Gregory Peck's tail?"

Kate laughed hard and fell onto her cousin's shoulder. Truitt put his arm around her. "This is where you belong, Kate. Where people love you and want to take care of you. You're gonna like it here."

Kate gazed down the oak-lined driveway. The cool wind picked up and blew her hair into her face, and she brushed it away from her eyes. The previous day's storms had passed, and the sky was clearing.

"I already do."

Chapter Three

Where shall I go?
What shall I do?
-Scarlett O'Hara

With twenty minutes to spare before their rendezvous at the farmers' market with the twins, Kate pulled into the church parking lot. Jane Ellen scurried out of the Range Rover and hit the ground running.

"Stay where I can see you!" Kate looked around. Everything seemed the same as it had been the day before—the same smells, the same sounds. The same sadness hanging thick in the air, tearing at her lungs with each breath.

Though she'd decided on a long-sleeved blue T-shirt and jeans, she couldn't shake the feeling that the previous day's black dress remained wrapped about her body beneath it all. She felt under her T-shirt just to be sure it wasn't hiding there, but her fingers found only skin. She recalled watching the dress fall from her fingertips the night before to land in a crumpled heap at the bottom of Aunt Mo's trashcan. Its designer was famous, its price tag staggering, but its purpose had been a dark one. The dress was not beautiful. She hated that dress.

A scene from *Gone With the Wind* sprang to mind—Scarlett O'Hara, young and beautiful, forced into mourning beneath mounds of black velvet and longing to free herself from the captivity to which unexpected death had sentenced her. Like Scarlett, Kate struggled beneath a blackness, something cold and sad and unrelenting. She felt beneath her shirt once more.

Jane Ellen found a rusty teeter-totter beside the church and climbed on, rocking side to side. "Mama, look at me!"

"I see you, honey!"

Kate wondered how long it had been since a child played there. The church building seemed run-down, unused. Even the sanctuary lacked the luster she remembered from years before, when the pews used to glow, the carpets smelled fresh and new, flowers decorated the stage, and the stained glass sparkled brilliantly in the sun. She'd been so young then—a girl, just like Jane Ellen—but so much had changed. Everything had changed.

Jane Ellen had been anxious to deliver a picture she'd drawn for her grandmother the night before. Kate held the colorful crayon drawing in her hand and walked toward the steps of the church. She could almost see her father's white Bronco parked in its usual spot next to the steps and, inside the church, him poised tall behind the wooden pulpit, Bible in hand, preaching to rows of regulars decked out in their Sunday best. To Kate it was still his church, even if death had stolen him away from her too soon. And away from them.

The pews had been full in the old days, of young and old, black and white, wealthy and poor. Mainly poor. Back then, at least to her, they'd all been the same. She remembered climbing onto the stage, singing in the choir when she was too young to read the words in the hymnal, standing on the pew beside her mother and waiting for her father to mention her name as he so often did. She'd gotten too much attention from the old folks who slipped her butterscotch drops and peppermints while her parents weren't looking. She still loved butterscotch drops.

Kate looked up at the tall wooden doors. She missed that church. Even as a child, she'd felt something inside its walls, something alive in those long-ago services at Millsville Baptist. Something indescribable that emanated from the faces of the congregants and hung like an unseen mist in the air above the pews. A joy. A peace. They sang about it in their songs. *"I have found his grace is all complete. He supplieth every need. While I sit and learn at Jesus's feet, I am free, yes, free indeed."*

The old men and women would stand with great effort during testimony services, and they'd speak of painful losses of loved ones and agonizing injuries and conditions. Yet in the same breath, they'd praise their God for his mercy, the same way her mother had when her father died.

Kate ran her fingers over the door's rough wood. Without anger or resentment, and in the very face of anguish and death, the old ones had thanked God. Though their bodies were weak, none could pry the hope from their solid, unyielding grasps. Hope was all they'd had, and it was theirs for the keeping. Kate had never forgotten them. She knew most of them must have been gone by then, but she wished for the chance to sit among them once again, feel their arms around her, ask them a million questions, learn from them, and share in their hope.

Her eyes brimmed with tears, and she looked toward the cemetery at her parents' graves, side by side. After so many years apart, they were together again. While nothing at all made sense in Kate's life, at least that did.

She pulled her jacket tighter around her and looked back toward the teeter-totter, but Jane Ellen was no longer there. She scanned the cemetery and the church parking lot then ran down the steps and around the side of the church.

"Jane Ellen!" Her heart pounded as her eyes searched in every direction. "Jane Ellen!"

"I'm right here, Mama!"

Kate turned to find Jane Ellen's small face peeping over a tombstone deep within the cemetery. The little girl waved then disappeared behind the stone once again. Kate breathed a sigh of relief and walked quickly toward her. As she neared her parents' graves, she remembered the drawing in her hand.

"Jane Ellen, don't you want to leave your picture for Grandpa and Grandma?"

"Come look, Mama!"

Kate lay the drawing next to their graves and lingered a moment. She kissed her fingertips and placed them gently on top of the cold stone. Then she smiled and swallowed hard. No tears. Not then.

Jane Ellen called again, and Kate went to meet her, sitting in front of a rounded tombstone.

"Look at the pretty lady, Mama."

The stone cut was from dark marble. Unlike the markers around it, this one was shiny, impeccably clean as though recently polished. In the middle, just below the name, was a large, oval-shaped picture of a woman. Her long, blonde hair flowed just past her shoulders onto a light blue V-neck sweater, and a string of pearls hung around her neck and matched her perfectly white smile. Her eyes were big and brown and danced with life and undeniable joy.

Kate almost smiled as she kneeled beside her daughter. She read the name aloud. "Anna Caroline Bauer."

"Anna," Jane Ellen repeated.

Anna was beautiful, and neither of them could look away

from her face.

" 'Nineteen eighty-two to two thousand and twelve,' " Kate read. " 'You are missed, Dear Angel. Your grace and beauty will forever be.' "

"What happened to her?" Jane Ellen asked.

"I don't know, sweetie."

"Is she in Heaven with Grandpa and Grandma?"

Kate was contemplating an answer when footsteps sounded from behind them. She jumped to her feet and grabbed Jane Ellen's hand. Standing just a foot away was the man who'd scowled at her the day before, his current stare even more cold and piercing. Kate glanced down at Anna's stone, then across the cemetery to her parents' graves. She and Jane Ellen were standing right where the man had stood in the pouring rain the day before. She clutched Jane Ellen close.

The man had traded in his tailored suit for an old pair of jeans and a dark jacket, and together with an unshaven face, his presence was intimidating. He glared at Kate.

"We were just admiring the gravestone." She motioned to the picture of the young lady. "She's beautiful. Did you know her?"

The man turned his attention to Jane Ellen, and his rock-hard expression softened. Kate's mind raced, but she could think of nothing else to say. Then Jane Ellen took a brave step toward the grave and pointed.

"Her name was Anna."

The man's lips spread into a slow smile, and the eyes that had shot flaming arrows at Kate turned bright.

"Are you Jane Ellen?" the man asked. His voice was strong, but somehow just as tender as his eyes.

Jane Ellen nodded up at him.

"I knew your Grandma Ruth," he said.

Jane Ellen's eyes grew large. "You did?"

The man nodded. "I did."

When he looked back at Kate, his sincerity faded in an instant. Then he smiled at Jane Ellen one last time before turning and walking toward the cemetery gate. Kate watched him for only a moment before bending down to Jane Ellen.

"Hey sweetie, why don't you go play on the teeter-totter again?"

"Okay!" Jane Ellen ran past the man and out the gate before him.

"Excuse me!" Kate said, much too loudly, as she approached the man from behind. He stopped and looked over his shoulder, his narrowed eyes brimming with bitterness. She extended her hand. "I'm Kate Canton."

He looked at her hand, then back up to her face.

She resisted the urge to roll her eyes. "I think I saw you yesterday, here in the cemetery. At my mama's graveside service. You said you knew her?"

His face softened again, and he glanced out toward Ruth's grave.

"Have we met?" Kate asked.

"No."

His indifferent tone mocked her, and silence fell between them again. Jane Ellen was singing "Somewhere Over the Rainbow" from the teeter-totter. Kate fidgeted, and the man stared at her with disdain.

"Well, okay, then," she said.

He turned and walked away, and she heard him mumble,

"Nice to meet you, Kate Canton."

Kate stood alone in the cemetery as the man disappeared around the side of the church. She wanted to scream at him, to return to her roots and give him a piece of her southern mind. How could he hold her in such contempt when he admitted never having met her?

She hoped she'd never see him again. And yet, despite his nasty attitude and deplorable lack of good manners, there was a warmth concealed somewhere deep behind his cold, striking face. Kate looked back over her shoulder at the tombstone of Anna Caroline Bauer.

Surely Aunt Mo would know the whole story, and no one could tell a story better than Modean Wilkes.

Chapter Four

*There is no season when such pleasant
and sunny spots may be lighted on, and
produce so pleasant an effect on the
feelings, as now in October.
-Nathaniel Hawthorne*

The Millsville Farmers' Market opened promptly at 7 a.m. every Saturday morning, June through October, but the line of eager buyers began forming around 6:30. The crowd members were usually cordial enough to one another, though each secretly vied to be the first inside the gates for the best choice of any particular market product. In June, the rush was for strawberries. Several vendors supplied them, but Virgil Wilson was widely known to produce the best berries in the state.

Virgil, a ninety-one-year-old widower and veteran of the United States Marine Corps, had seen battle in both Japan and the Philippine Islands during World War II but often joked he'd never seen fighting more fierce than on the first day of strawberry season. On that day, grown men and women would scratch and claw their way to his stand, grabbing as many berry-filled crates as they could carry. "It's a different kind of war," Virgil would say, "but war just the same."

In July, the hot market items were blueberries, green beans, potatoes, cucumbers, tomatoes, and of course, sweet corn. Like the run on berries in June, the rush for fresh corn could be treacherous. Mayor Tate Mills, who'd opened the farmers' market gates for thirty-five years, traditionally moved out of the way a little faster on the first day of corn sales. Market patrons would congregate before the large red cattle gates, chattering with nervous excitement, their eyes boiling with determination as each one resolved to be the first to Nettie Jacobs's little yellow stand. "Get your cane ready, Mayor, we're comin' fast!" they'd yell. "Open up and get outta the way! It's corn day!" But the old mayor needed no reminding. The looks on their faces were indication enough he'd better move fast.

The excitement of August was for onions, carrots, peppers, peaches, purple hull peas, nectarines, and the ever-popular Millsville watermelons. September and October brought brussels sprouts, every imaginable variety of winter squash, gourds, decorative corn, and of course, pumpkins. On this October day, the market was alive with fall décor. Hay bales, scarecrows, and intricately carved jack-o-lanterns were scattered among the rows of vendor stands and signaled that the harvest had come to Millsville.

Kate got lucky and found a parking spot close to the front gates. Jane Ellen bounced with anticipation, twirling her ponytail in her fingers, a habit she'd picked up from Kate, and stared out the window.

"Here we are," Kate announced.

As they walked through the front gates, Mayor Mills, already too tired to stand though it was only 8:15, handed Jane Ellen a green, okra-shaped balloon from his perch in a plastic lawn chair. "Welcome to the Market, cutie pie."

A hundred people or more were crowded around the vendor booths, set up in a U-shape around the Millsville town square. The surrounding street was blocked to traffic, but no one seemed to mind the temporary inconvenience. On non-market days, the Millsville square was peaceful and quaint with its large fountain and penny-filled wishing pool in the center, and the tall statue of Colonel Trampus Mills, a town founder and Civil War hero, keeping watch close by.

Kate sniffed the air. At one booth, they were brewing apple cider in a large cistern-shaped pot, creating an aroma that drifted on the cool breeze throughout the entire square, while another vendor served free popcorn balls to the children. People chatted in small groups, or watched their children have their faces painted or play on hay bales. The produce selection wasn't much to look at, so competition was at a bare minimum as the market customers mourned the last day of the season.

"Why hello there, Kate," called a voice from nearby. Kate turned to see Nettie Jacobs, waving from inside her little yellow booth.

"Hello, Ms. Nettie. How nice to see you again," Kate said, taking Jane Ellen's hand and walking over to the booth. Nettie hugged her with large, sympathetic eyes.

"It was a lovely funeral, wasn't it? How you doin', sweetheart? I been thinkin' about you since Ms. Ruth passed. Every time I drive past that big ol' house of hers I can still see her sittin' on that front porch." Nettie shook her head. "I'm tellin' ya it don't seem right for her not to be there." She took hold of Kate's wrist. "Oh, I hope you don't sell that place. Nobody without Boudrow blood should be livin' there." She rolled her eyes. "Oh Lord, just listen to me. That's none of my business, is it?"

Kate smiled and patted Jane Ellen's head. "Thanks, Ms. Nettie. And don't worry. I could never sell Mama's house."

A cell phone rang from deep within Nettie's pocket, the ringtone an outdated, monophonic version of the University of Arkansas fight song. Nettie jumped, startled, then dug inside her blue jeans. "My first grandbaby's about to be born. They've been callin' me from the hospital every few minutes with the latest. S'posed to be a boy." She put the phone to her ear. "Hello? Oh good. Good." She looked back to Kate and whispered, holding the phone away from her mouth, "I just couldn't miss the last day of the market."

"Kate! Jane Ellen! Over here, dears!" Ella yelled through the crowd.

Kate waved goodbye to Nettie and led Jane Ellen to the booth where the twins were working with an elderly black woman Kate didn't recognize.

"You made it!" Emma exclaimed, handing a bag filled with orange and yellow squash to a customer. "But where's Rosa?"

"She stayed to help Aunt Mo do some cooking. Vegetable soup, I think," Kate said.

Emma clasped her hand to her heart. "Modean Wilkes's vegetable soup. Heaven on Earth!"

"Your booth is beautiful, Ms. Ella, Ms. Emma. This pink is just the perfect color for it."

"Thank you, dear! Are you enjoying the market so far?" Emma asked.

Kate tried not to stare at the purple plastic tiara sitting crookedly atop Emma's head.

"Well, we actually just got here—"

"Isn't it exciting?" Ella almost shouted, wearing her own neon pink crown. "There is just nothing more exciting than a market Saturday morning. Too bad this is the last day of the season. Did you see our flowers, dear?"

Kate eyed the array of fragrant blossoms. "How could I miss them? They're gorgeous."

Emma picked up a long-stemmed red flower. "These here are marigolds. There's some yellow ones over there. Those are zinnias. These over here are dahlias, and those are sunflowers, of course. Today the sunflowers are going like hot cakes!" Emma gasped to catch her breath, then started waving ferociously. "Modean!" she yelled.

Aunt Modean was excusing her way through a huddle of old men to the Market Queens' booth. At age seventy-three, Aunt Mo was the picture of health, despite being fifty pounds overweight. A slightly raspy voice was the only evidence she'd smoked until her forties when her husband, Uncle Lou, had died of lung cancer. Mo's hair was white with streaks of dark gray and always pulled tightly into a bun on the back of her head, secured snuggly with bobby pins. Her everyday attire consisted of polyester pants, running shoes, and a long-sleeved, button-up top, no matter the season, and she most always wore a brown canvas backpack in lieu of a purse.

Jane Ellen leapt into Modean's arms. Modean, though far from frail, took a giant step backward and let out a loud, "Oh!"

"Aunt Mo! I went to see Grandpa's grave today at the cemetery, and there was a man there who knew Grandma Ruth. And he knew me, too!"

Mo stumbled to recover her balance. "Is that right? Well, who was he?"

Jane Ellen shrugged. Kate lifted her daughter out of Aunt Mo's arms and set her back on the ground. Aunt Modean breathed a deep sigh and flopped down into a folding lawn chair. "I'm not as young as I used to be."

The twins scurried about as a line of customers grew, stretching five people back from their booth. As the old women frantically grabbed whatever items their customers requested and packed them away in pink plastic bags, they both turned, neither watching where they were going, and collided into one another. The other woman working the booth tended to them and, after some bickering and finger-pointing, the twins were back to serving their waiting patrons.

Modean chuckled and shook her head. "They take this stuff as serious as a heart attack. It's their whole life right here. Did you see those durn crowns? Market Queens. Ha! I suwannee." She rolled her eyes.

"The market is really something," Kate said. "I didn't realize how much I'd missed this place."

"Oh, I could never forget. It's as much a part of me as anything else I know." Modean looked to Jane Ellen, who was leaning on the arm of her lawn chair. "Did you know your old Aunt Modean was born and raised right here in Millsville? Back when dinosaurs roamed the Earth."

Jane Ellen giggled, and an old man looked up as he crept by with his cane. "Couldn't get rid of ya if we tried." He smiled and hobbled past.

Modean batted at the air behind him. "Oh, you hush, Vernon Jenkins! And get on outta here!" She turned back to Kate. "Now, who was this man in the cemetery Jane Ellen was tellin' me about?"

Kate sent Jane Ellen into the booth to help the twins then looked at Aunt Mo. She could see his face clearly in her mind, and the same anxious, uneasy feeling returned. "He was handsome in a rugged sort of way. Dark hair and eyes. He didn't tell me his name, but he was at the grave of a woman named Anna Bauer."

Aunt Mo gave her a sympathetic smile and nodded. "That's our Pastor Malcolm."

"Pastor!" Kate exclaimed so quick and loud she surprised even herself. The twins and their customers snapped their heads in her direction and stared.

Modean shook her head and chuckled. "You'd never know it by lookin' at him. Or even talkin' to him. I know. That's our Malcolm."

"You must be thinking of someone else, Aunt Mo. This man isn't a pastor. He's rude and disrespectful and—"

"Broken up," Mo finished. "He's just broken, dear." She squirmed in her chair. "And you sure ain't gonna like this next part. Malcolm Bauer is the pastor of the Millsville Baptist Church. Well, technically, I guess. Still says it on the sign out front anyway."

"Millsville Baptist?" Kate's eyes went wide. "No. Not Daddy's church!"

Modean shook her head. "It's a long story, Kate."

Jane Ellen, who'd been helping the twins fill bags with produce and flowers, bounced into her mother's lap. "Mama, can I have some money for candy? Ms. Beulah wants to take me."

"Ms. Who?" Kate looked up at the smiling face of the old black woman working the booth with the twins.

"That's Beulah Macon," Aunt Mo whispered. "Don't you remember her?"

Kate returned the woman's smile and waved. "I guess not."

"She knew your mama and daddy. She used to cut hair at Ms. Lucille's beauty shop before Ms. Lucille passed on. She cut your daddy's hair. Even cut it for the funeral. She's gone to church with your mama and me for years."

"Can I go, Mama?" Jane Ellen begged. "Please?"

Kate looked back at the woman who stood waiting with her hand outstretched to Jane Ellen. "Okay. But hold Ms. Beulah's hand."

Aunt Mo reached into her pocket, pulled out a dollar bill, and handed it to Jane Ellen. "Here you go, darlin'. But whatever you do, don't go buyin' anything sweet now."

Jane Ellen cocked her head to the side. "Aunt Mo!"

"Well, maybe a piece of candy or two."

Jane Ellen gave Mo a quick hug and ran to take Beulah's hand. Kate watched them walk away.

"She'll be fine with Beulah," Aunt Mo said. "That woman's raised one child of her own and helped raise a passel of other people's kids all her life. Right now she's got her great-grandchild livin' with her. She's nine or ten, I can't remember which. They call her Beulah Two."

"Beulah Two?" Kate took a seat in a lawn chair next to her aunt.

"I know it sounds funny, but she's a little sweetheart. Her mama's name is Esther—that's Ms. Beulah's granddaughter. But nobody knows where she is. Last I heard she was livin' somewhere 'round Memphis, doin' drugs and walkin' the streets. Who knows what else. You see her 'round here every now and then. Sometimes she takes off with Beulah Two and worries Ms. Beulah to death. But she always brings her back." Aunt Mo sighed. "Lord knows what that child goes through

41

when she's with her mama. Anyway, poor Esther named her Beulah Two after her grandma."

Kate scanned the surrounding booths and spotted Jane Ellen and Beulah sampling a bowl of kettle corn.

"You know, Ms. Beulah knows Pastor Malcolm better than anybody 'round here. You should hear those two go at it. She stays on him pretty rough 'bout the way he does things. They get into these scripture-quotin' matches. Both of them got more scripture memorized than I've forgot in my lifetime."

"But a pastor, Aunt Mo? He seemed so angry. I just can't believe—"

"Kate, darlin'." Mo leaned toward her and spoke firmly. "Not everybody has your strength. Most people don't. They get mad. Bitter. Look at the world all different. When they lose somebody they love, they lose hope, too. And without hope, there ain't much to keep goin' on for. They just give up on themselves and everybody else. That's what Malcolm did."

"What happened to him?"

Mo sighed as though revisiting an unpleasant memory. "Two years ago his wife got killed in a car accident right outside town on the main highway. People say she was drivin' out to the church to meet Malcolm. She hit a tree head-on. Made it to the hospital, but she died pretty quick."

"Anna Caroline Bauer," Kate said.

"Beautiful girl. The two of them were just made for each other. So happy. I heard they'd been tryin' to have a baby. Some people say she was pregnant, but nobody knows for sure. You know how people talk."

Jane Ellen returned with a white paper sack full of kettle corn. "Mama, Ms. Beulah says I can come play with her great-granddaughter sometime and go to church with them. They live by the river and go fishing for catfish, but catfish don't really look like cats. That's just what people call them because they have whiskers."

Beulah hobbled her way back to the booth and stood over Jane Ellen with her hands resting on top of the little girl's head. "This baby's welcome at my place anytime."

"I really appreciate—" Kate took a step back. Just past Beulah, standing three booths away and staring at her was the young man who'd offered her comfort in the cemetery at the funeral the day before. She'd only glanced back at him while sobbing at her mother's grave, but she knew it was him. His hair was wavy and black, and he wore the same dark suit. Kate wondered if there was another funeral in town.

She hadn't noticed his eyes the day before, but that day, everything about him was composed around those eyes. Their intense, unusual shade of blue penetrated through her, even from a distance. Kate blinked. Had he been watching her? He smiled and held up a brussels sprout as if he'd simply been browsing the booths.

"We can't understand his ways, Kate." That's what he'd said to her.

Kate reached up and touched Beulah's arm. "Ms. Beulah, do you know that man?"

Beulah leaned on her cane and turned herself around, stepping in front of Kate and blocking her view. Kate jumped to her feet. "Right there!"

She pointed toward the booth, but he was already gone. The box of brussels sprouts remained, but the only person nearby was the old bearded man who sold his produce there.

"You mean Frank?" Beulah asked.

"No, no. There was a man standing there just a second ago. I don't know where he went, though." Kate scanned the market in all directions. "He was wearing a black suit. He had black, curly hair. I saw him in the cemetery yesterday. I think he works for the funeral home, and . . . I need to apologize to him." She sighed and sat back in the lawn chair next to Aunt Mo. "He was just there. That's so strange."

Beulah stared down at Kate then turned back and gazed at the place where Kate had seen the man. "Not so strange, child. Not so strange at all."

Chapter Five

Death is not the greatest loss in
life. The greatest loss is what
dies inside us while we live.
-Norman Cousins

Beulah's invitation to dinner came a few days later. Kate still didn't feel much like socializing, but she knew Jane Ellen would be thrilled to play with Beulah Two. As she drove, Kate decided she'd refrain from asking Beulah about Pastor Malcolm Bauer, but she couldn't help but hope he came up in conversation.

Kate and Jane Ellen bounced up and down in the Range Rover's seats. "Whoa!" Jane Ellen laughed. "This road is bumpy!"

Kate kept her eyes on the road ahead and surveyed her surroundings. They had to be getting close. The dirt road that ran beside the river looked the same as it had when she was a girl. Kate remembered the many visits she and her mother had made down Old River Road to her grandfather's house. She barely remembered the old man—he'd died when Kate was only three—but she could see the house clearly in her mind. When she could get around to it, she'd drive further down the rough and rutted road and see if the old place was still standing, though she doubted it.

"Is that Ms. Beulah's house, Mama?" Jane Ellen asked.

"I think so." Kate pulled into the dirt driveway and killed the engine.

"They've got real chickens!" Jane Ellen pressed her face against the glass as two scrawny roosters ran past her window on the nearly grassless lawn.

Kate stepped from the vehicle, and the two of them walked toward the tiny white house with a rusty tin roof and screened-in porch. A set of long wind chimes hung from either side of the roof and clanged softly in the breeze, and two large ferns in red clay pots sat next to the front porch steps. Kate thought the house looked a hundred years old, like something from a movie.

The front door opened and out stepped Beulah. "Hurry up on in here, girls! Supper's waitin' and about to get cold!"

Kate and Jane Ellen climbed the steps and entered the porch, where a young girl stood against the doorframe. She was tall for her age, skinny, and dressed in a floral-print dress and green and yellow tennis shoes. Her black, frizzy hair was pulled into a ponytail on the side of her head and tied off with a yellow band. At first glance, a faint smile lit the girl's face, but as Kate met her eyes, Beulah Two looked down to the floor and her timid grin vanished.

Kate took a step closer. "Hey there, Beulah Two."

The little girl fidgeted but answered, "Hello."

"My name is Kate, and this is my little girl, Jane Ellen. Your grandma invited us to have dinner with you tonight. I was thinking maybe you and Jane Ellen could play afterwards. How does that sound?"

"Really good," Beulah Two said politely, still staring at the floor.

Jane Ellen bounced on her toes. "Have you got catfish?"

Beulah Two looked up at Jane Ellen. "Uh-huh. Out in the

river."

"Maybe we could catch some."

A smile spread across Beulah Two's small face. "Okay."

Beulah laughed behind them. "Ain't nobody goin' catfishin' before we eat dinner. Or after neither! Y'all come on in here. Let's eat."

After a meal of fried chicken, cornbread muffins, pinto beans, fried okra, fried potatoes, and tomatoes and cucumbers, Kate pushed her plate away and slumped back in her chair. "Ms. Beulah, that's more than I've eaten in weeks. It was delicious."

Beulah smiled. "Your Aunt Modean been tellin' me you ain't been eatin' enough to keep a cat alive. 'Bout time somebody done got some food down you."

"Mama, can Beulah Two and me go play now?" Jane Ellen asked, still chewing a piece of chicken.

"If it's okay with Ms. Beulah."

"It's fine with me, child. Put on your sweaters first, though. And don't you girls go down by the river! Or nowhere close!"

Jane Ellen jumped from her chair and grabbed Beulah Two by the hand. "We won't! Let's go, Beulah Two!"

Beulah Two took one more gulp of her buttermilk, leaving a white moustache across her face, and bounced off after her new friend.

"Come sit on the porch with me," Beulah said to Kate. She used the table to help herself from the chair, and Kate thought for a moment the entire thing would tip over, food and all.

Kate took her glass of sweet tea and followed the old woman onto the porch. Beulah plopped her large body into an old brown loveseat sprinkled with small rips and tears. Kate picked an oak rocking chair with a dingy yellow cushion.

Beulah smiled. "Evenin's out here can be so peaceful. Sometimes me and Beulah Two sit out here 'til dark just listenin' to the river sounds. Tonight's nice, but in the summertime, the katydids and frogs and crickets all sing together. Like their own little choir."

"You must enjoy having Beulah Two here."

"In my heart, she mine. Her mama, Esther, was mine, too. Esther's mama, my daughter Maxie, died of breast cancer when Esther was just fourteen years old. Esther come to live with me and just went wild, drinkin' and smokin' and druggin'. Lord know what all else. I did everything but hog-tie her and drag her to church with me, but she ran off a few months after I got her. Lived a crazy life down in Memphis, sellin' herself to men for money and drugs. Two years after she run off, she come back with a little baby and ask me if I'd take her."

"She was only sixteen?" Kate asked.

"Almost seventeen. And still wild as the wind. I took that baby from her and raise her like my own. That is, 'til Esther come back when Beulah Two was about four. She took her from me. And there wasn't nothin' I could do to stop her neither. 'Cept pray. And I did pray."

"What happened?" Kate asked.

"Couple years later she brung her back to me. But it wasn't the same child."

Kate listened and watched Beulah's old black eyes brim with tears. "They hurt that baby, them folks Esther stayed with. Hurt her in every way you can imagine, and in ways you don't never want to neither." Beulah wiped a tear that escaped down her cheek.

Kate felt careless for asking such a personal question but

before she could apologize, there was a burst of laugher from the girls in the backyard. Then Beulah laughed, too.

"Does my heart good to hear that baby laugh."

"Ms. Beulah, she is so very lucky to have you."

"Oh, no, honey. You got it backwards. There ain't nothin' I ever done in my eighty-four years on this here Earth good enough to deserve that baby. Ain't no luck about it neither. I got blessed with somethin' most nobody nowhere ever will. That child's special." Beulah took a deep breath and slapped the arms of the rocking chair with a sly smile. "Now," she said, "what you wanna know about our Pastor Malcolm?"

Kate raised her eyebrows. Modean and her big mouth. "Well, um, I," she stuttered. "Well, I guess, I'm just surprised he's a pastor. That's all."

"You an' everybody else 'round here. Malcolm's had it bad the last few years."

"His wife's death?"

"Sweet Anna. I can still see her walkin' up them porch steps bringin' Beulah Two a baby doll after she come home from Esther's. Had to be just a few days before she died."

Kate stopped rocking. She bit her lip and leaned forward. "Tell me the story, Ms. Beulah. Aunt Mo told me a little, but she said you know him best."

Beulah sighed. "Malcolm only talked 'bout it once, and that was when I went to see Anna at the funeral home. Right before he changed. He told me she called him that mornin' at the church. She was all excited about somethin' and wanted to tell him after school—she taught third grade in town. Said she didn't wanna tell him over the phone. When she didn't show up by four o'clock, Malcolm went out lookin' for her. He must've come up on the accident right as they was loadin' her in the ambulance. So he seen her all bleedin' and busted up. Police say she swerved to miss the Foster boy on his bike and hit a tree. She lived 'bout three hours after they made it to the hospital." Beulah exhaled loudly. "And Malcolm's never been the same since."

"How do you mean, he's never been the same?"

"He just gave up on God. That simple. Oh, he still come to church on Sunday mornin's wearin' his Sunday clothes, but he just sits on stage. Never talks. Barely even looks up or moves anymore. And when it's over, he leaves out the side door. No 'bless you,' or 'how you doin',' or 'kiss my foot.' Just gone."

"Well, why don't you just find a new pastor?"

"Another preacher? Oh, we can't get rid of Malcolm. He'll come 'round. And if he don't, I guess we'll just keep singin' our old songs and havin' our testimony services 'til we all die off. There's only 'bout twenty of us now."

"Only twenty?"

"Mm-hmm. Down from 'bout two-hundred when Anna got killed. We'd bought some new land just outside of town on the main highway and was about to build a new church buildin'. That little one just couldn't hold us no more. But then the wreck happen, and we had to go and sell our new land to that weasel of a man, Mackey Johnston. He's the pastor at the church that sits there now, Millsville Grace Chapel. But I guess I shouldn't say ugly things about people."

Kate remembered passing the large white structure on the way to town the day before, and she nodded.

"It just break my heart to think 'bout Malcolm and his pain and what he could've done and almost did for this little town,"

Beulah said.

"Has anyone tried to talk to him?"

"I done talked to him 'til I'm blue in the face! I tell him if the Lord want us to keep livin' in the past, he'd've put eyeballs in the back of our heads instead of the front. I quote scriptures, shame him, praise him, but he know all I got to say. 'Til he make peace with the Lord in his own way, ain't nothin' nobody can say or do to help him."

"Ms. Beulah," Kate said, then pressed her lips together. She took a deep breath. "How did he know my mother?"

"Oh, your mama loved Malcolm! And she had a lot more patience with him than I do. She'd go see him after Anna died and bring him things. We all did. But he just seemed more easy with Ruth. Not so mad. She even let him stay in that house up the road for a couple months, 'cause he just couldn't go home to where he lived with Anna."

"Grandpa's old house? I thought Mama sold it a long time ago."

"Oh no. She still own it. Guess you do now. She even did repairs not too long ago. Looks real nice. Malcolm only stayed there a few months before he moved."

"Where does he live now?"

Beulah shook her head. "You wouldn't believe it. Ever notice that little wood shed behind the church? He fixed it all up, and now that's where he stays. He keeps up the cemetery, mowin' and such. Church pays him for that, but that's all he'll take money for."

"Why does he stay?" Kate asked. "If he's so miserable here in Millsville, why doesn't he just leave?"

"Because we won't let him leave, child! Oh, he done tried.

Tried and tried. But if he leave this place, there ain't no hope for him. He ain't got no family 'cept all us. This is where he needs to be. We know it. God know it. But since he barely talk to us and he don't never talk to God, he just confused. And truth is we need him just as bad as he need us." Beulah chucked. "Oh, we all just a buncha old folks. Millie and Taylor Ward, they younger—in they fifties—but most of us are old. Don't you tell Mo I said so. 'Cept for us, everybody else went other places, mostly over to Millsville Grace. Can't blame 'em, I guess. But we can't give up on him. Malcolm always knew how to show us we still mattered—that we was special. Not just old junk nobody wanted no more. He used to run himself to death comin' to see sick folks in the hospital or in they houses. Now, he never come."

"Have you spoken to him recently?" Kate asked.

"Yesterday." Beulah scowled. "I went to see him at the shed. He was workin' on his lawn mower and wasn't too happy to see me, but I didn't care. I told him I had a new verse for him." Beulah cleared her throat and quoted as though she were an actor on a Shakespearian stage, " 'Stand at the crossroads and look. Ask for the ancient paths. Ask where the good way is, and walk in it, and you will find rest for your souls.' "

"Jeremiah?"

"Mm-hmm. And you know what he said? Dropped his tools, looked me square in the eye and quoted me the rest of the verse, changed up a little. 'But I say, I will *not* walk in it!' " Beulah pursed her lips and shook her head in small jerks. "Mm, mm, mm. That boy know his Bible front to back. We went back and forth with scriptures for a while, then Beulah Two come in. That baby's the only person I ever seen can make Malcolm smile every time. And Beulah Two don't like any man but Malcolm. And that's a fact."

"He was nice to Jane Ellen, too. We saw him in the cemetery on Saturday."

" 'As water reflects a face, so a man's heart reflects the man,' " Beulah quoted. "There's good there. A whole lotta good. Even if he does his best to hide it. You can be sure it's there."

Beulah Two's feet clomped up the porch steps, and Kate jumped, spilling iced tea from her glass onto her jeans. She put her hand over her heart and laughed. "Beulah Two, you startled me."

"Grandma said you seen a man at the market. I seen him, too."

Kate looked to Beulah who was staring back at her with a knowing smile. "The man with the black curly hair? And black suit? I don't understand, sweetie. You saw him at the market?"

"No, I seen him with you out in the cemetery at Ms. Ruth's funeral. And I seen him with Malcolm. Twice now."

"The man who works for the funeral home knows Malcolm?" Kate looked back and forth from Ms. Beulah to the little girl, her forehead creased in confusion.

"He don't work for the funeral home, Ms. Kate."

From the nearby tire swing, Jane Ellen yelled for Beulah Two. Beulah Two took a slow step forward and put a small, boney hand on Kate's knee. "That man's an angel. A good one."

Her black eyes stared into Kate's, and the chimes next to the porch clanged as the breeze picked up. Beulah Two smiled, and for the first time, any trace of fear or uncertainty was gone. Kate looked deep into the girl's small face and felt she could get lost there.

Jane Ellen called again, and Beulah Two shot off the porch to meet her friend. Kate turned to Beulah, and the old woman was grinning.

"I told you, didn't I? That baby's special."

Chapter Six

Life is just a blank slate; what matters
most is what you write on it.
-Christine Frankland

Kate entered the Millsville Animal Clinic to the welcoming *ding dong* of the front door. A young woman with curly red hair looked up from behind the counter and surveyed her up and down.

"Can I help you?" she asked with a thick southern drawl.

"I'm looking for my cousin, Truitt Boudrow."

The girl rose from her chair, cocked her head to the side, and narrowed her gaze. Her eyes fell resentfully upon Kate's brown leather Louis Vuitton bag. She sniffed then disappeared into the back without a word.

Kate waited and peered through a small, round window in the door behind the desk but could see nothing. The redhead was gone. She took a seat in the clinic's waiting area, picked up a six-month-old copy of *The Pet Planet*, and pretended to be interested.

To her left, an old man struggled to keep his grip on a squirming black and white rabbit with one of its tiny feet bandaged completely. The man glanced at Kate and smiled a toothless smile as the animal nearly hopped out of his feeble hands. Kate smiled back.

Across the room, a mother and her little girl whispered to one another while keeping a close eye on their German shepherd puppy, who sat at their feet gnawing playfully at his leash. The little girl laughed and pulled at the leash, beginning a tug-of-war match with the little dog.

The smells of the waiting room invaded Kate's nostrils, and in an instant she felt nauseous. She covered her nose with her index finger against the overpowering antiseptic fumes and other indistinguishable animal scents, and strained to see if the redhead was anywhere in sight. Seeing no movement through the window of the door behind the desk, she fidgeted on the cushioned bench. The front door was only a few feet away, and she considered lunging for the handle. Fresh air waited just on the other side. She wrapped her fingers around the handle of her bag beside her, but just as she began to stand, the receptionist returned.

"Dr. Boudrow wants you to come on back here." The girl smacked her gum and motioned Kate over with a slight nod.

Kate chewed the inside of her cheek. The smell had to be worse back there. She looked around at the others in the waiting room. The old man stroked his rabbit's furry ears, and the little girl and her mother continued whispering happily. Kate sighed and gave the redhead an uneasy grin. She followed her behind the counter and down a hallway. On both sides, dogs barked and howled, cats wailed, and somewhere far away a bird screeched and squawked. Kate cringed and held her hand over her nose and mouth.

"Here you go," the redhead said, almost politely. She opened a metal door and stepped back for Kate to walk inside. Kate peeked in the small, colorless room to see Truitt standing over a white poodle lying on a table.

"Hey there, you," he said.

The redhead closed the door behind Kate and the clicking of her heels faded down the hall.

"Hey yourself." Kate eyed the motionless animal. "Is he . . ."

"No, no. This is Doodlebop. He's just sleepin'." Truitt took the poodle's small head in his hands and turned his lifeless face toward Kate. "Say hello, Doodlebop. Rrruff! Rrruff!"

"Truitt!"

Truitt laughed and laid the dog's limp head back on the table. "He's fine. Doodlebop's Roy George's dog. You remember Mr. Roy."

"He used to own the car wash?"

"Still does. Doodlebop's been comin' to me for years. Loves me. Lets me give him a complete physical, including shots. Not even a whimper. But let me try to clip this old boy's toenails, and goodbye, Doodlebop. Hello, Cujo."

"You put him to sleep to clip his toenails?"

"Did you wonder why my receptionist wouldn't set foot in this room?"

Kate widened her eyes and took a step back toward the door. "Anyway, Tru, the reason I came by is, I was wondering if maybe you'd go to Mama's house with me today. Around noon."

Truitt looked up from Doodlebop's paw. "You haven't been out there yet?"

"I tried once or twice but never even made it in the driveway."

"Well, no one's rushin' you, Kate. If you're not ready, we can—."

"No, no. It's time. It's been nearly two weeks since Mama's funeral, and, well, that little bedroom at Aunt Mo's just isn't big enough for me, Jane Ellen, and Rosa. I can't stay there forever."

Truitt smiled wide, and Kate slapped a palm to her forehead. "Oh no, Tru. I didn't mean for it to sound that way. *You* can stay at Aunt Mo's forever. It's just, I can't. I—"

"Relax! I'm not ashamed of the place I call home. It's not exactly a bachelor pad, but it has its perks."

"Like Aunt Mo's breakfasts every morning?"

"And buttermilk pie."

Kate cupped her hand over her mouth and nose again. "I don't know how you stand this smell."

Truitt leaned down to Doodlebop's floppy ear. "Don't listen to her, boy. She's a city chick."

"So you'll go with me? To Mama's?"

"Of course I will. Hey, by the way, did you see all those messages on the fridge from Boyd Walker?"

"I've tried to call him back but can't seem to catch him in his office," Kate said with one foot out the door.

"Lawyers are always hard to catch. I'm sure it's about Aunt Ruth's will."

She nodded. "Something else I haven't felt like dealing with yet. I'll swing by his office after we leave Mama's."

"Okay, but that's one stop you'll have to make on your own. Boyd Walker hates me."

Kate paused with her hand still on the door. "What? Didn't you play football together in high school? I thought you were friends."

Truitt grinned. "We were until I took his little sister out to dinner a few times."

"Linda Lou? Isn't she, like, thirteen?"

"She's twenty-four! Twenty-three when we went out. She's good-lookin', but a few peas short of a casserole if you know what I'm sayin'. Guess when I didn't call her back she got pretty mad at me. Who knows what she told Boyd."

Kate shook her head. "Heartbreaker."

Truitt chuckled and clipped another of Doodlebop's nails. "See you at noon."

***

Beulah Two lay on her back in a patch of dead grass behind her grandmother's house. She watched two white, fluffy clouds float side by side then converge into a heap, forming what looked just like a giant ice cream cone. The sky was a brilliant shade of blue, and the clouds were thick like the meringue she helped her grandmother make for pies. They swirled about, coming together, breaking apart, making elephants, clowns, whales, trees, sailboats, teddy bears, even a castle that split down the middle, it's halves forming two dancing birds.

And then she saw him. Next to one of the birds. A face, a body, two powerful wings. Finally. She waved to him, satisfied, and fell asleep.

***

At noon, Truitt pulled his Jeep into the driveway of Ruth Boudrow's home just as Kate stepped from her Range Rover. They met on the sidewalk and exchanged smiles, and Truitt took her hand without speaking.

The house stood large and majestic as it always had. They stared up at the white, two-story home with its four columns along the front porch that, oddly enough, seemed taller that day than in Kate's childhood.

Built in the 1890s, Ruth Boudrow's home had gone through its share of repairs and renovations but somehow always maintained its original splendor. Kate's father, Jackson, had bought the long-neglected home for his new bride in the early 1970s, and the couple had immediately set about restoring it. Soon after, the house had reclaimed its reputation as one of the most beautiful homes in the county and drew much attention for its historical significance.

Jackson and Ruth lived and loved there until Jackson died of pancreatic cancer in 1990 at the young age of forty-six. Afterward, Ruth never again spent money renovating the home. Instead, she kept it exactly as it had been when her beloved Jackson was alive. On occasion, she offered it to the Millsville Women's League for tea or some social event, and several times the home had been featured in the local paper and even a national magazine or two. But to Kate, it was simply home.

From the corner of her eye, Kate spotted Ruth's neighbors of nearly thirty years, Mr. and Mrs. Harper, sitting on their front porch in rocking chairs and looking her way. Kate smiled and waved. The old couple, well into their seventies, whispered to one another and finally waved back.

Kate squared her shoulders and ignored the lump in her throat. "I'm ready when you are."

Truitt squeezed her hand. "You know, you got enough of Aunt Ruth in you to keep her around this place forever."

Kate wiped a tear that, despite her best efforts, had escaped down her cheek. She pictured her mother standing on the front porch, waving wildly as she always did when Kate visited. Kate could see her, cradling Jane Ellen in her arms, kissing her again and again, then hurrying everyone inside for sweet tea and oatmeal cookies. Kate was lost in the memory when Truitt bounded up the front steps to the door and grabbed a large lock in his hand.

"Looks like a realtor's lock," he said, tugging at it. "What the heck?"

Mr. and Mrs. Harper retreated inside their house, and Truitt and Kate exchanged glances. Kate walked over to a window and peered inside. Her heart sank. "The furniture's gone. Everything's off the walls. Everything!" She turned horrified eyes on Truitt. "What's going on?"

A silver convertible screeched up the road and peeled into the driveway. "Kate!" the driver yelled as he brought the car to an abrupt stop.

Despite having lost most of his hair and having gained about forty pounds, Boyd Walker looked the same as she remembered from high school. He exited the convertible and hurried toward them gracelessly, his white, button-up shirt soaked with sweat under the arms, the sleeves rolled up to his elbows. Kate met him at the bottom of the front porch steps.

"I've been tryin' to get a hold of ya all week," Boyd said, out of breath, his accent even thicker than Truitt's. "I've been by Mo's three times since Monday. Just came from there, and Mo told me where y'all—"

"You know about this?" Kate asked, her eyes narrowed. "Aren't you supposed to be my mother's attorney?"

Truitt joined Kate at the bottom of the steps, and Boyd half nodded to him. "Truitt," Boyd said with a scowl.

"How you doin', Boyd?" Truitt's phony attempt at pleasantries dripped with sarcasm.

"Kate, I need to talk to you about Ruth's last will and testament." Boyd pulled a blue handkerchief from his back pocket and wiped sweat droplets from his brow. Kate wondered how he could be sweating in such cool weather.

"Why is there a lock on Mama's house?"

"Come on back to my office with me. I'll explain it all to ya there." Boyd stuffed the handkerchief back into his pocket.

"No, Boyd. I want to know right now."

"Hey, hey," Truitt said, putting a hand on Kate's shoulder. "C'mon now. Don't get all worked up. There's obviously been a mistake, and Boyd's gonna take care of it for us. Let's just go to his office and hear what he's got to say." Truitt shot Boyd a stern glance from behind her.

Boyd got into his car and slipped on a pair of outdated aviator Ray-Bans. "Follow me."

***

The Walker Law Office was located in a two-story yellow-brick house just off the square. With only three employees—a secretary, a retired, sixty-year-old legal assistant who came in once a week, and his mother for all other miscellaneous tasks—Boyd had done well for himself since barely graduating from Ole Miss Law School.

Boyd fidgeted with his keys in the lock. Finally the door opened, and he ushered his guests inside. He pulled a cushioned chair out of its place in the hall and placed it in front of his desk. After clearing the clutter from the desktop, he motioned Kate toward the chair. "C'mon and have a seat."

Truitt looked around the room for another chair and found

one for himself in the corner.

"Now," Boyd said, eyeing Truitt, "since this is a personal matter. Maybe it would best if we had this discussion in private."

Truitt pulled his chair up beside Kate and dropped down in it with a grin.

Boyd's sigh was almost a growl. "In other words, Truitt, go wait outside!"

"Not a chance, Boyd," Truitt said.

"What's your problem?"

"My problem? You're the one who acts like you wanna sucker punch me every time we pass on the street."

"Maybe that's because I do." Boyd rose to his feet behind the desk, his round cheeks growing redder by the second. "Now get on outta here like I already told you!"

Truitt stood, too. "Is this about Linda Lou? Look, I don't know what she told you, but—"

"Oh, she told me plenty. And if we weren't in the presence of a lady—excuse me, Kate—you might just get that sucker punch. In defense of my sister's honor!"

Kate raised an eyebrow at her cousin. "Honor?"

Truitt laughed. " 'Wait a minute, mister. I didn't even kiss 'er. Don't want no trouble with you.' "

Kate rolled her eyes and sighed. Leave it to Truitt to quote '70s rock lyrics in a crisis.

Truitt looked to Kate then back to Boyd with a wide smile. "Get it? Lynyrd Skynyrd? Linda Lou?"

"I know the durn song." Boyd gritted his teeth. "And if memory serves, there's somethin' next about a loaded forty-four."

"Boys, please!" Kate jumped to her feet. "Enough!" The

men stared at her and finally lowered themselves back into their seats. "I want Truitt here, Boyd. He's family."

Boyd conceded with a halfhearted nod.

"Now why is Mama's house locked up?" Kate asked and sat down.

Boyd sighed and leaned back in his tall, brown leather chair, the most expensive purchase in the office. It creaked and whined under his weight. "I've been Ruth's lawyer for three years now, and I was as surprised by this as you are."

Kate shook her head. "That is my mama's house, and I have every right—"

"It's not your house," Boyd said softly and lowered his head. "And legally, you don't have the right. I'm sorry."

"I don't understand."

Boyd reached into a drawer beside him and withdrew a thick, brown folder with a white label that read *Ruth Boudrow* and placed it on the desk in front of him. "Your mama was very specific. There's no mistake." He thumbed through the folder. "We spent lots of time together last year, Ruth and me. She wanted to make sure I understood her wishes. Make sure I had it straight, I guess. Almost like she knew—"

"Get to the point," Truitt said.

"The house ain't yours, Kate," Boyd told her bluntly. "It's been sold to the town. You know, that place you grew up in is over one hundred years old—a Millsville historical site. Supposedly Colonel Trampus Mills himself lived there at one time. The town's turnin' it into a museum of some sort. The mayor's on cloud nine."

"That's what Mama wanted?"

"It's all right here in her own handwriting. I've got it all typed up, but she wanted to make sure I had an original copy of it all written and signed by her. Ain't that just like Ruth?"

Kate slumped back in her chair and stared at the folder.

Boyd cleared his throat. "There's some money in an account at Sullivan Bank. All the information's there in the folder. Some money's been set aside for Jane Ellen's college tuition, but the rest is there waitin' for you. I know you and that husband of yours got your own money, but it's a nice amount. Mr. Jackson's life insurance and all, plus the money from the sale of the house." Boyd squirmed in his chair.

"What? What's wrong?" Kate asked, her eyes growing moist.

"All her belongings—furniture, clothing, appliances, knickknacks, et cetera—have been given to several charities around here, mainly the women's shelter over in Washington County." Boyd glanced at Kate and his expression softened. "Per the deceased's—Ms. Ruth's—specific request."

"And that's it?" Truitt asked. "It's all just gone? Given away?"

"Not all of it. There's several boxes and things I packed up for Kate myself."

"Yourself?"

"Well, it's not usual practice. But Ms. Ruth . . . Well, I did it more as a favor, I guess. She asked me if I'd make sure Kate got certain things, and I agreed."

"What sort of things?" Kate asked.

"Pictures, letters, an old baseball cap of your daddy's, some quilts. Sentimental things, I guess. She had most of it already boxed up in the basement with your name on it."

Kate took a deep breath. "I'd like to have them now."

"I already took them out to your granddaddy's old place out on Old River Road." Boyd leaned closer and rested his arms on his desk. "She left it to ya. The house and everything in it. It's all yours." Boyd dug through the folder again and pulled out a sealed, white envelope with the word *Kate* scrawled across the front in her mother's handwriting. "I don't know if this explains anything, but she asked that I give it to ya."

Kate reached for it. The room stood still, but her head was reeling.

"I'm real sorry, Kate. I know this is all a shock," Boyd said.

Truitt put his hand on her shoulder.

"It's okay, Tru, I'm fine. This is what Mama wanted."

"I'll make copies of everything and have the boy who's workin' for me this summer run it out to Mo's tomorrow mornin'." Boyd stood and shook her hand. "I don't know why your Mama did things like she did 'em. But I know Ruth, and she thought about this long and hard. There's a reason to it. You can be sure of that."

"Thank you, Boyd. I appreciate all you did for Mama."

Boyd nodded as Kate stood. Truitt followed her toward the door then stopped short and turned back to Boyd.

"Gimme three steps?" he said.

"Get out, Truitt!"

***

Malcolm sat on Beulah's couch with a cup of black coffee in hand. Beulah had parked herself across from him in an old recliner, her lap and legs covered with a small quilt. Neither quoted scripture. Neither attempted to pick a fight. Beulah studied Malcolm's gaunt face and dark circles beneath his eyes and offered him a piece of pie for the third time, possibly fourth. Again, he declined.

Beulah Two stirred in the bed in the next room, and Malcolm leaned forward to steal a look at her through the doorway. She moaned and rolled from her back to her side. He'd come to bring her a new jigsaw puzzle—five hundred pieces of broken-up Eiffel Tower, waiting to be reconciled by the little girl's hands. When he'd arrived, Beulah had told him where to find her. He'd scooped her up from the grass beneath the clouds, and she'd seemed weightless in his arms, like a life-size paper doll. He'd held her tight against his chest to make sure the gusts of wind didn't carry her away. As he'd laid her down onto the bed, her dark eyes had fluttered.

"Guess what I saw up in the clouds?"

"An angel," he whispered.

Beulah Two smiled. Then she sniffed and rubbed her cheek before rolling over in sleep.

Malcolm had decided to wait out her nap, but already an hour had passed with no sign of her waking. Beulah threw off her quilt and used the arm of the recliner to push herself to her feet.

"I'm gonna fix you somethin' to eat. You just wastin' away, Malcolm. And I ain't gonna sit 'round here and watch you do it."

Malcolm considered another protest but instead surrendered to the powers of Beulah Macon. He *was* hungry. And tired. So tired. He crossed his arms and leaned back onto the couch. As Beulah filled a pot with water and placed it on the stove,

A VIEW FROM THERE

Malcolm's eyelids blinked, then fell shut.

***

The drive along Old River Road seemed more violent than it had the day before, when Kate and Jane Ellen had visited Beulah. A bump here. A dip there. Another brutal bump. Rosa held tight to the box of cleaning supplies she'd smuggled from beneath Modean's sink but finally gave up and seized the grab handle above her window, her black curls springing with each jolt. Kate drove over a large rock, and the bottles of disinfectant sprays and sponges bounced out of the box and into Rosa's lap.

Kate cringed. "I'm sorry!"

Rosa muttered something in Spanish, and Aunt Mo reached up from the back seat and patted her shoulder. Truitt stared out the window and tried not to laugh.

Twice the road came close enough to the riverbank for them to catch a glimpse of the slow-moving water. Jane Ellen smiled, her face pressed against the glass, as they passed Beulah's to the right.

"Are we there yet?" Jane Ellen asked for the tenth time.

Kate pulled off the road and down a small gravel driveway before bringing the vehicle to a stop. They all climbed out of the Range Rover, their eyes staring straight ahead. Instead of the rundown house of her memory, a charming cedar-siding home sat in its place, complete with a wrap-around porch and a tall, river rock chimney.

After a long silence, Rosa shrugged and shifted her box of cleaning goods. "Much better than I expect."

Kate reached for Mo's arm. "Are you sure we're at the right

68

place?"

Modean shook her head. "Mm, mm, mm. That mama of yours."

***

Malcolm scraped up the last of his macaroni and cheese with his fork, leaving a small piece of fried ham alone on his plate. He wiped his mouth with a paper towel and took a long gulp of milk, finishing off the glass. Beulah sat across from him at her kitchen table, pleased with her victory. She leaned forward and cut a piece of chocolate pie and tossed it onto his plate.

"No, I can't. I'm stuffed, and I need to get back."

"Oh yes you can. Eat." She cut a piece for herself, too, and glared at him. Malcolm sighed and sank his fork through the three-inch-deep meringue into the thick chocolate, all the way down to the buttery crust.

"She was talking about angels again today," he said.

Beulah chuckled. "She always talkin' about angels, ain't she? Nothin' wrong with that."

"Except she thinks she actually sees them."

"How do you know she don't?"

Malcolm chewed and swallowed his bite. "She keeps telling me she's seen one with me. And yesterday, she told me she saw the same one with Kate Canton."

"Mm-hmm."

Malcolm watched Beulah's face and waited for something more than "Mm-hmm." She chewed her pie. Malcolm gritted his teeth.

"I'm just saying that with all she went through at Esther's, all this angel talk worries me. Make-believe isn't the answer. I know you don't think she needs counseling, but maybe—"

"The last thing you need to worry 'bout is that baby. She's fine. Worry 'bout yourself if you need somebody to worry 'bout. But you leave her be."

Malcolm sighed and leaned back in his chair. "Can you please pass the milk?"

***

While the others perused the grounds, Kate explored the inside of the house. She strode through the living room, where the floral couch and chairs she remembered were gone, replaced by stunning, rustic wood furniture. In the kitchen, the outdated, harvest-gold appliances were gone, and shiny, new, white ones with stainless steel handles stood in their places. The dingy, patterned wallpaper that had once adorned every wall had been torn down, and the walls were coated in fresh paint in soft, muted tones.

Kate headed down the hallway and peeked into the smaller of the two bedrooms. The old wrought iron headboard and rickety dresser and vanity had been removed. Instead, there was a tall cherry headboard with matching armoire and vanity, all brand new and smelling of freshly cut wood.

Further down the hall she found the larger bedroom—her new bedroom—and looked around. There was no bed, just a large chest of drawers and a white wicker rocking chair. Her eyes roamed the space where the bed would have been, and she furrowed her brow then shrugged.

Throughout the house, all the ancient pictures and

decorations were gone from the walls. Nothing so much as a clock above the door or trinket on a shelf. She stared at the wide, smooth expanse of paint and sat down in the corner to run her hand across the floor. As with the rest of the rooms, the orange shag carpet she'd known as a girl was gone, replaced by dark hardwood floors.

Outside, the few remaining crickets brave enough to withstand the cold weather were already beginning to sing, just as they'd sung at Beulah's the day before. Their song was a sad one, as though they knew winter was coming to chase them away. Kate's eyes brimmed with tears.

Gray. She wanted him. She wanted her home. And her mother. Her tears ran freely, carelessly, from the corners of her eyes.

With shaking hands, she pulled the letter from her jacket pocket and opened it for what seemed the hundredth time, hoping to find its contents had changed. The envelope was the same off-white with her name written in her mother's handwriting in dark blue ink. The page inside was folded the same, neat and crisp. It made the same sound as she unfolded the corners. And, as each time she'd stared at it before, the page was blank. Not a word. Not a scribble. Empty as the walls of the house around her. Empty as her heart.

Truitt tapped on the bedroom door before entering. She didn't bother wiping her eyes.

"No bed?" he asked.

"No bed."

He took a seat on the floor beside her. "May I?"

Kate handed him the paper. "I was hoping Mama would explain why she gave her house away. Why she wanted me to have all this instead. But she must have gotten confused and put the wrong page inside. I just don't know."

Truitt handed the letter back to her. "Or maybe she said exactly what she wanted to say."

Kate shook her head. "What do you mean?"

"Aunt Ruth gave you a blank page. Look around. Doesn't it remind you of somethin'?"

She scanned the bare walls. "This house."

Truitt reached into his pocket and pulled out a Millsville Animal Clinic pen and placed it in her hand. "It's a blank page, Kate. You can keep sittin' here, starin' all day at that letter, but it won't change a thing. It's up to you to write your own story now." He wrapped his fingers around her hand and pressed the pen to the top of the page. "You're the only one who can decide what to write. Not Gray. Not Aunt Ruth. Maybe she knew you'd be needin' this place someday. Somewhere to heal. To find your strength."

"But how could she have known?"

Truitt shrugged and leaned back against the wall next to her. "It's Aunt Ruth we're talkin' about here. You keep lookin' through her stuff, and you'll probably find Jesus's private cell phone number. Maybe a personal email between the two."

Kate laughed. And cried. From somewhere within the house a door slammed and Jane Ellen squealed. Aunt Mo hummed a familiar hymn, and Rosa removed refrigerator drawers with a thud. The crickets continued their song, and the world kept spinning. A world of change and fear and uncertainty—of doubt and disillusion. A world without Gray and her mother. And a world where her daughter needed her.

She glanced down at the letter and the pen in her hand.

72

Chapter Seven

> *There's a river somewhere that flows*
> *through the lives of everyone.*
> *-Roberta Flack*

Malcolm's alarm clock droned on until at last his groping fingers located it and sent it sailing across the room. His head emerged first from beneath the heavy blankets, and he sat up in bed. A cold chill ran through his body—the fire in his wood stove had gone out sometime during the night. He groaned, remembering what day it was, and pulled the blankets back over his head. Nine minutes later, the alarm clock resumed its screeching. Malcolm ran his fingers through his hair. Sunday again.

***

Kate sat on the steep bank of the river, watching the water slip past. A Sunday morning breeze picked up and blew her freshly brushed hair into her eyes. She smoothed it back and held her cup of steaming coffee close to her chest for warmth. The crisp air cut straight through her jeans, and the white sweatshirt was no match for the cold. She closed her eyes and breathed in the steam from her coffee.

A week after moving into her grandfather's house, the place already felt like home. Even Rosa had settled nicely into Jane Ellen's room. Her small cot sat in the corner next to Jane Ellen's bed, the wall next to it decorated with a wood-framed painting of the Virgin Mary, a gold crucifix, and a colorful tapestry depicting da Vinci's Last Supper. After an exhaustive search and a full interrogation of many in Millsville's Spanish-speaking community, Rosa had decided to attend a Catholic church in neighboring Tontitown and even commissioned a ride from a Hispanic couple she'd met in the grocery store a few days before.

Kate had plans to attend the Sunday morning service at Millsville Baptist with Aunt Modean, though she was less than thrilled about seeing Pastor Malcolm Bauer again. She did, however, look forward to spending time with Beulah and other members of the congregation who'd been friends of her mother. Something about being inside the church walls brought her comfort, and she needed all the comfort she could get.

The faint sound of voices floated to her on the wind. Kate set her coffee on the ground and stood as two figures emerged from around the river bend—Beulah and Beulah Two, holding hands and singing. Beulah smiled when she spotted Kate waving to them.

"Oh my, my! Didn't mean to scare you, child!"

"Not at all," Kate said. "I was just enjoying your song."

Beulah laughed. "Well, now you just lyin'. 'Cause neither one of us can sing a lick." She patted Beulah Two's shoulder, and the little girl grinned.

"Do you two ladies need a ride somewhere?"

"Naaah," Beulah said. "We just two fools out walkin'. Every Sunday mornin' me and Beulah Two go for a little walk down the riverbank, just down to the old bridge and back. We talk and pray. And sing!" She nudged Beulah Two, and the little girl looked back up at her. "Guess we better keep our volume down now we got neighbors."

"No, no. It's lovely. I like that song. Was it Father Abraham?"
Beulah Two nodded.

"That one's her favorite. 'Cept these old bones ain't much for the motions no more. Say, girl, what in the world are you doin' out here so early, standin' in the cold?"

Kate bent to retrieve her mug and swallowed a large gulp of coffee. "I can't seem to get enough of the river. It makes me want to just sit right here and watch the water move."

Beulah looked down river. "My mama lived on this river all her life, in the very same house we live now. Even when the cancer done eat her all to pieces, she wouldn't go nowhere but here. She always used to say the river was so peaceful to folks 'cause it don't got no doubts. No worries. It knows where it's going, and it's sure to get there sooner or later. And it don't wanna go no place else." Tears brimmed in the old woman's eyes. "Well, speakin' of goin', we best be goin' home, Beulah Two. These ol' legs ain't gonna make it no further. Let's turn back. We got to get ready for church."

Kate waved and called after them, "See you there!"

Beulah Two turned back for one last wave, and then the two of them walked away side by side.

Kate directed her attention back to the river. *"No doubts. No worries. It knows where it's going."* A playful squirrel jumped from limb to limb in a tree on the opposite bank and knocked a twig into the water below. As though it didn't mind the fall, the twig joined the water and floated out of sight.

Where am I going? Kate wondered. She'd received no word from Gray. Only a rumor Aunt Mo picked up from the beauty shop that he and the blonde had recently visited his parents' home on the outskirts of Millsville and been given an icy reception. Still another report held that Delta, Gray's older sister, was also visiting their parents and having a grand time heaping shame and unabashed condemnation on her brother and his lover. Kate had met Gray's sister only once but determined quickly that Delta Canton was a plain-speaking, no-nonsense woman. Married twice and divorced twice, enormously successful, fiercely independent, and not at all fond of her brother, Delta had no problem with confrontation, and Kate reasoned her part of the rumor was probably true.

"Kate!" called a voice from far away. She dumped what was left of her coffee onto the cold ground and ran up the hill toward the house and across the dirt road. Truitt's Jeep was parked catty-corner in the driveway, and Truitt was standing on the front porch.

"Hey!" Kate called just as Rosa opened the door from the inside. Rosa's round face was nearly as red as the leather purse she held over her arm. She wore a matching black and red checked dress and glared at Truitt, her nostrils flared and her hand on her hip.

Truitt waved to Kate then squared his shoulders. "Hey there, Rosa. I didn't mean to disturb you. I was just—"

"Jane Ellen still sleep. Bang bang bang wake her up!" Rosa beat her fist against the air.

"I'm sorry. I didn't mean to—"

"You find Ms. Kate?"

"Yes, ma'am. I didn't—"

Rosa shut the door in Truitt's face.

"Wow," he sighed. "She's just precious."

Kate laughed. "She'll warm up. What brings you out here

so early?"

Truitt stopped at the hood of his Jeep and took Kate's shoulders in his hands. "I need a favor."

She narrowed her eyes. "What kind of favor?"

He leaned in close. "I need you to go to church with me."

"Well, I was going to go anyway."

He nodded. "Right. But I need to go with *me*. To Millsville Grace."

***

An hour later Kate was sitting on an ultra-cushioned pew at Millsville Grace Chapel. She cut her eyes at Truitt who sat next to her, straining to catch a glimpse of a blonde woman seated two aisles up and to the left. Kate shook her head. For a moment she'd wondered if her cousin had suddenly come down with a serious case of religion. She should have known it involved a woman.

Truitt leaned forward to get a better look at Blonde Beauty, and Kate rolled her eyes. She grabbed a handful of his Ralph Lauren button-up and yanked. He fell back against the pew with a thud.

"You owe me," she whispered.

Truitt grinned and leaned forward again.

Kate looked around the church, on the property Millsville Baptist had purchased and lost to Pastor Mackey Johnston and Millsville Grace. She eyed Pastor Mackey, sitting in the middle of the stage in his baby-blue suit and tie, smiling at the choir's performance of "How Great Thou Art." His narrowed eyes and the slight smirk on his face made him seem almost smug. He moved his tiny hands, pseudo-conducting the choir from where he sat. Beulah had called him a weasel, and he nearly resembled one.

Tall, stained glass windows and lavish tapestries covered the walls, and ornate, gold lighting hung from the ceiling above. On the wall behind the pulpit stood a magnificent lighted cross. Below it, the choir, a group of about a hundred or so men and women dressed in navy blue robes, swayed side to side in unison, some clapping softly to the beat while others held their hands at their sides. Their voices were melodic and beautiful—except for one. Kate quickly spotted the off-key culprit.

She was in the third row of the choir loft, probably fifty-five years old with long, wiry white hair. Her glasses were thick, making her eyes seem much larger than they were, and dangly, beaded earrings whipped wildly about her cheeks with every awkward jerk of her head. As the choir moved on to an upbeat version of "Nothing But the Blood," the woman raised her arms to the sky and clapped her hands hard and loud, all while swinging her hips to the beat of the drum and singing as loud as her voice could carry. The women on either side of her scowled, exasperated.

Truitt nudged Kate and pointed out the woman with a grin, but he wasn't the only one who noticed. Pastor Mackey grimaced from his perch on stage, his cheeks red and his shifty eyes fiery. Somewhat discreetly, he twisted in his chair and whispered to the man seated next to him. Seconds later, that man got up and made his way to the choir director and spoke in his ear. With one sweep of the director's hand, accompanied by his severe glare, the white-haired woman's joyous expression faded. She dropped her hands to her side and swayed with the rest, her head hanging low and her voice hushed.

After the service, Kate waited outside in the parking lot while Truitt "accidentally" bumped into Ms. Beautiful with the long blonde hair, brown eyes, and legs that seemed never to end. Kate wondered if she'd ever see Truitt again.

Gazing across the parking lot at the mingling church members, Kate spotted Boyd Walker and waved. "Boyd!"

Boyd excused himself from a huddle of men and made his way toward Kate, examining her tan turtleneck and knee-length navy skirt every step of the way. "Hey, there, Kate." He extended his hand.

Kate took his sweaty palm in hers and tried to seem unaffected, then casually wiped her hand on her skirt afterwards. "It's good to see you again. I've been meaning to call you."

"What can I do for ya?"

A cold wind swept through the crowd, and Kate hugged her arms close to her body. "Well, I've been going through some of Mama's things—the boxes you brought by—and I can't find my daddy's Bible. Mama always kept it in a small brown box. I've searched through everything at least twice, and it's nowhere to be found."

"Hmm. You know, seems I remember somethin' about that Bible, but I just can't think of it right now. You sure she still had it at the time of her death?"

"Absolutely sure. She had it with her in the hospital the night I left . . . the night she passed away."

Boyd shook his head. "I'll check her file again, but you got copies of everything I got."

Kate's face fell, but she nodded. "Okay then. Thanks, anyway. If you think of anything, please give me a call."

"Sure," Boyd said. Then he cringed as Truitt descended the church steps behind her. "I'll see you later." He smiled and hurried back into the crowd before Truitt had a chance to greet him.

Truitt was grinning from ear to ear, his dimples glaring. He took Kate's arm and escorted her to the Jeep before opening her door and closing it behind her. Once he'd climbed in himself, he put both hands on the wheel and looked over at her, beaming with pride. "Her name is Vaughn Spencer, and we're havin' dinner Thursday night."

Kate rolled her eyes. "Like I said, you owe me. So, how did you meet Ms. Vaughn Spencer?"

Truitt started the engine. "You mean, *Doctor* Vaughn Spencer."

Kate stifled a laugh. "Pardon me."

"She ran over a baby armadillo and brought it by the clinic after hours. I almost didn't even answer the door. We were all locked up, but I heard her outside cryin' and went to check it out. Good thing I did."

Kate grimaced. "Did it die?"

"Did what die?"

"The armadillo!"

"Oh, yeah. She ran over its head with a Honda. It was DOA." Kate shook her head. "I've heard enough."

***

Esther peered out the window of her motel room, wearing large, dark sunglasses. Every noise made her jump. Every footstep passing outside her door made her nauseous.

Hitchhiking with Robert and his boyfriend had taken her most of the way home, but her destination was still nearly seventy-five miles away. She left the window and flipped through the phonebook with trembling hands then made a call to a local bus line. She hung up and took a deep breath in a futile attempt to calm her nerves. If only she had a cigarette.

The thunderous ringing of the telephone filled the room, and Esther nearly screamed. Her body shuddered. She stared at the phone and its blinking red light while the ringing continued, loud and violent. Finally she reached for the receiver, closed her eyes, and listened.

"No, I'm sorry," she said. "You have the wrong room."

Esther replaced the receiver clumsily and fell onto the bed in a crying heap.

***

"Okay, y'all. Let's dig in." Mo passed the large pan of meatloaf she'd prepared for after-church lunch to Kate first.

Truitt held a scoop of mashed potatoes in front of Jane Ellen. "Want some of these, Jane E?" The little girl nodded, and Truitt plopped them onto her plate with a splat.

"Aunt Mo, there's nothing in the world like your meatloaf and mashed potatoes," Kate said and swallowed her first mouthful of ketchup-smothered meatloaf.

"You mean ketchup loaf?" Truitt asked.

"This is how I always eat Aunt Mo's meatloaf."

"How do you even know there's meatloaf under there?"

"Oh, hush now, Truitt," Mo scolded then turned to Kate. "Thanks, honey. I knew it was your favorite."

"And thanks again for taking Jane Ellen to church with you this morning. She said she had a great time."

Truitt reached across the table. "Could you pass the ketchup, Aunt Mo? If there's any left."

"I said hush, Truitt. Now, what I want to hear about is this Ms. Vaughn Spencer."

Truitt chewed his green beans and shot a small squirt of ketchup on top of his meatloaf. He pressed his lips together to hide his smile, and Jane Ellen looked up from her mashed potatoes.

"Mama said Truitt likes all the pretty girls with blonde hair."

Truitt shook his head in disbelief, and Mo and Kate erupted in laughter.

"Did Truitt like the lady in the cemetery?" Jane Ellen asked.

"What lady, darlin'?" Mo asked.

"Anna. She's got blonde hair, too. Remember her picture, Mama?"

"Yeah, baby," Kate said. "I remember."

"Anna Bauer?" Truitt asked. "Now she was a pretty lady." He leaned toward Jane Ellen and kissed her cheek. "But everyone knows I'm crazy 'bout a brunette."

"You knew Anna Bauer?" Kate asked.

"Not really. She used to bring her yellow lab into the clinic. I think his name was Gus. Guess Malcolm got rid of him when she died." He salted his potatoes and took a bite. "I just ran into Malcolm last week."

"Did you talk to him?"

"No. I said 'hey' but he just kept on walkin'. Like always."

"Sounds like the good pastor." Kate held out her hand toward Truitt. "Ketchup?"

"There's no way you can put more ketchup on that poor meatloaf."

Kate narrowed her eyes.

Truitt grabbed the ketchup bottle off the table and held it tight against his chest. "No. I can't let you do it."

"Truitt Boudrow, give me—"

"Give her the ketchup!" Mo ordered.

Truitt obeyed with a sneer. Kate smirked and snatched it from him, heaping more of the red paste onto her meatloaf.

Mo poured some gravy on her mashed potatoes from a green and yellow gravy boat. "Seems you've taken quite an interest in Pastor Malcolm," she said, her eyes fixed on her plate.

Kate looked to Truitt, who had suddenly stopped chewing, then back at Mo. "You mean me?"

"He's certainly interesting," Mo said. "Good lookin', too. I can see why—"

"No!" Kate nearly choked on her biscuit and attempted to swallow before speaking again. "No. I mean . . . he wasn't even nice to us, Aunt Mo."

"He was nice to me," Jane Ellen said.

Truitt ducked his head and failed at concealing a smile.

"Your mama sure thought a lot of him," Mo added.

Kate finally swallowed the rest of her biscuit. "Maybe that's why I'm . . . curious."

After an awkward silence, Truitt lifted his sweet tea toward Aunt Mo, inviting her to clink glasses. "She's curious, Mo."

Kate nodded and raised her glass, too, her cheeks flushing pink. "Curious."

A VIEW FROM THERE

***

As the sun sank behind the trees later that evening, Kate sat in the very spot she'd been when the day had begun. The river seemed quieter, moving slower than it had in the early morning. She listened for the song of the crickets, but the cold weather had sent them elsewhere. Some had even made their way into her house in search of warmth, sending Rosa into fits trying to massacre them with an old boot and a spray bottle of unidentified blue fluid.

All was silent on the riverbank except the sound of flowing water, and though it was peaceful, the tide of emotions in Kate's heart thrashed about. Every fiber of her being ached for Gray, and thoughts of his betrayal threatened to drown her spirit. How she missed her mother, needed her, longed to be in her arms. Kate's shoulders slumped, her muscles tired. The familiar lump rose in her throat, and her eyes stung with tears.

The ground was cold, and she crossed her arms in an attempt to shield her body from the chilly air blowing off the water. A large, bright red leaf floated by in the current then got stuck in some debris near the bank a few feet away. Several other brilliantly colored leaves meandered by, blown into the water by the autumn breeze, along with a couple of water bugs that swam right past. But the big red leaf remained, tugging this way and that, unable to break free. Kate watched it struggle until her eyes could no longer focus through her tears. She took her face in her trembling hands and sobbed for the first time since the day of the funeral.

Gentle arms hugged her from behind, and Kate turned to find her Aunt Modean. Mo kissed her cheek and wrapped a blanket around her shoulders. "I just came to leave you some more papers Boyd Walker's boy dropped off at my house. Rosa said you were out here."

Kate shook her head. "I just don't think I can do this. I don't know how I can go on."

"Hush now, girl. This ain't the end for you. It's a new day. A brand new life."

Kate cried harder and rested her cheek on Mo's shoulder. "I don't want a new life. I want Gray. And I want Mama." She gasped for breath. "The world—it just keeps going on all around me, but I've stopped. I've just stopped."

Mo patted Kate's wet cheek with a gentle hand. "Ah, baby girl. I wish I could take all your pain and throw it down there in that river. Let it float on away. But you know I can't do that."

Kate nodded and sniffed, wiping the tears off her cheek.

"Here's one thing you can know for sure, though," Mo said, looking out over the water. "The pain that's runnin' through you right now is just like that river. Sometime or another it's gonna flow right on through everybody." She tilted Kate's chin up and peered into her red, watery eyes. "What you gotta remember is, you don't drown by fallin' in the water. You drown by stayin' there."

Kate looked back at the water, scanning for the trapped leaf, but it was gone. Her eyes searched downstream and caught barely a glimpse of the tiny red dot before it disappeared from sight, moving with the current and other leaves and water bugs and stuff of the river. Moving until another obstacle stood between it and where it was going.

"I want to believe he still loves me. Do you think there's a chance?"

Mo sighed. "Honey, I think that boy needs a good kick in the you-know-where. And even then, he just is who he is. Who he's always been. And no amount of kickin' or talkin' or anything else's gonna change that."

Kate buried her face in Mo's chest and let the tears flow again. "But I love him, Aunt Mo. He's supposed to love me, too! Why can't he love me?"

Mo held Kate until her sobs slowed, then subsided. The old woman took a deep breath then let it out slow. "Honey, I know this ain't a good time, but I guess it's as good as any, and I can't leave without tellin' you. You're gonna have to know sooner or later."

Kate raised her head and wiped her eyes.

"I came out here because there was a note stuck to the top of those papers Boyd sent. Said somethin' about him not findin' out anything about that Bible."

Kate wiped at her nose with her sleeve. "Daddy's Bible. I've been looking for days, but I can't find it anywhere."

Modean blinked, the wrinkles growing deeper beside her mouth.

"You know where it is?"

"Yeah, honey, I know. And you ain't gonna like it."

Kate sat up straight and raised her eyebrows.

"She gave it to someone."

"Gave it to someone? That's not possible. She knew how much that Bible meant to me. Who did she give it to?"

Modean shook her head and exhaled hard. "Malcolm Bauer. She gave the Bible to Malcolm."

Chapter Eight

*Since every death diminishes us a
little, we grieve—not so much for
the death as for ourselves.
-Lynn Caine*

On Saturday morning, Kate stood at the door to the shed Pastor Malcolm Bauer called home. She squared her shoulders and whispered to herself, "You can do this. That's your Bible, and you're going to go in there and tell him that. Knock on the door. Right now. Just knock on the—"

The door flew open with a loud creak. The pastor who looked nothing like a pastor had one arm through the sleeve of a blue button-up shirt and held a plunger in his other hand. He barely noticed her before they bumped shoulders and she was knocked back a step. He slipped his other arm into its sleeve and covered his bare chest. Kate had seen him twice before, but standing there in the morning light with his tousled damp hair, powerful chest, and deplorably bad attitude, she froze. Though she'd spent most of the night rehearsing a short yet direct speech, his eyes—beautiful, angry eyes—stared into her, crippling her concentration.

She swallowed hard and said, "I need to talk to you." It came out not nearly as forceful as she'd rehearsed.

He finished buttoning his shirt while she averted her eyes to the shed and waited, both of them pretending not to notice the overwhelming awkwardness.

"My father's Bible. My Aunt Mo said Mama gave it to you."

He stared at her a moment then walked toward his pickup, leaving her standing alone. "I don't see how that's any business of yours."

Kate's jaw dropped, and she followed him. "It's my business because it belonged to my daddy. I want it back."

Malcolm threw the plunger and it landed in the back of the truck with a thud. He rummaged through a rusty toolbox next to the cab. "Sorry. Can't help you."

"You can't help me? What does that mean? You don't have it, or—"

"I have it." He let the tool box's lid bang shut then opened the pickup's door and got in.

Kate stepped between the door and the truck before he could slam it in her face. "Look, I get it. You don't like me."

He scoffed. "You don't know anything about me."

His face was so close to hers, Kate could feel his warm breath on her cheek. "I know you have something that belongs to me." She stood up straight, glad he couldn't see her legs shaking.

"I have something that belonged to your mama, and she gave it to me. I would say that makes it mine."

He tugged on the door, and Kate stepped back. He pulled it shut and started the engine, and she watched him through the dirty window, half enraged and half desperate.

"Please! Just tell me what I can do!" she shouted.

He rolled his eyes and cranked down the window.

"Tell me what I can do to get it back," she said.

He gripped the wheel and stared out through the windshield. "Where were you all those nights she sat by herself in that big old house, feeling about as alone as somebody can feel?"

"I . . ." She blinked, stung. "I visited her as much as I could."

"Well from what I hear around town, you're getting your taste of it, Kate Canton. Your very own taste of alone. And from what they say, you're getting a double dose. But that's how life goes now. Isn't it?"

Kate clutched the window's edge and leaned closer. "You're right, I don't know you. But you don't know me either, and I don't care what you think of me. I just want the Bible."

"Like I said. I can't help you."

He pulled away and Kate stepped back, waving off a puff of exhaust.

***

Beulah leaned her tired body against the kitchen sink and washed the last glass in the lukewarm, not-so-soapy water. Beulah Two took the glass from her and dried it with a damp dishtowel.

"My, my, girl. For just you and me, we sure had lots of breakfast dishes," Beulah said.

Beulah Two put the glass in the cabinet then gazed out the window above the sink. "Grandma, somebody's out there."

Beulah pushed the shabby yellow curtain aside and peered out. "Hmm? Probably somebody lost and wantin' directions. I ain't never seen that car before." She hobbled back and squeezed out the cloth into the dirty dishwater. "Honey, will you wipe off the table? I'm 'bout to give out."

"Mama," Beulah Two said, her voice soft and troubled.

"What'd you say, girl?"

Beulah Two stood frozen at the window. "It's mama."

Beulah took a slow step toward the glass and watched as the car drove away and Esther walked toward the front porch, wearing a brown jacket and large sunglasses with a bag in each hand and a cigarette between her lips. Beulah looked down at Beulah Two, and the girl stared up at her with fretful eyes.

"Don't you worry, child. It's gonna be all right this time."

Beulah Two tore from the room while Beulah remained at the window, waiting. The porch's screen door screeched open then slammed. Then the front door closed, and slow footsteps fell behind her and stopped.

"Hey, Grandma."

Beulah closed her eyes.

***

As Truitt drove through downtown Fayetteville, Kate tried to remember exactly how he'd convinced her to accompany him to the Bikers and Barbeque Festival. She'd attended the event two years earlier with Gray and was not exactly thrilled about reviving old memories. But Truitt had insisted on getting her out of the house, and Rosa too quickly volunteered to watch Jane Ellen. Kate had decided it was a conspiracy, although she couldn't figure out how Truitt had talked Rosa into a partnership.

Bikers and Barbeque took place once a year in October on Dickson Street, the eclectic entertainment district in Fayetteville. The night before, Kate had caught a local news reporter doing a live broadcast from the event and knew exactly what she was in for: loud music, even louder bikes, and hundreds of thousands of people.

Truitt found a parking spot that wasn't a parking spot beside a Mexican restaurant near Dickson, and Kate got out and followed him toward the sounds of the festival. She sighed. The last place she wanted to spend her Saturday evening was in a crowd of strangers, but when Truitt turned to see if she was still behind him, she faked a smile.

Hundreds of motorcycles lined Dickson Street. Truitt was instantly in awe and began using words like *sick*, *sweet*, and *awesome*. The sun was setting, and Kate pulled off her sunglasses and put them on top of her head. She ran her hand over the shiny chrome handlebar of one of the bikes, and Truitt glared at her the same way he had when they were seven and she touched one of his newly shined Hot Wheels. She withdrew her hand and crossed her arms. She was ready to go home.

After fifteen minutes of motorcycle gawking, Truitt retreated in the direction of the food vendor booths in search of funnel cake. Kate found a protruding tree root not too far from an empty stage and took a seat. Feeling cold and unsociable, she leaned against the tree and pouted, thinking of her encounter that morning with Pastor Malcolm Bauer.

To his credit, his dark hair and eyes and strong mouth made him fairly good-looking. His sturdy jaw was in need of a shave, though, and his bitterness overshadowed all of it. She decided to avoid him at all costs and conceded with sadness that she'd probably never see her father's Bible again.

Truitt pushed through the crowd holding the powdered-sugar-covered funnel cake on a flimsy white paper plate. He plopped down next to her.

"Dig in," he said. "Careful, though. It's hot."

"No thanks. Not hungry."

"C'mon. Rest and food. Two basic human needs you've

been neglectin' for the past three weeks."

Kate growled, but she gave in and broke off a piece of the cake. The second it touched her lips, the nausea hit that had been plaguing her on and off since her mother's death. She chewed and swallowed anyway under Truitt's watchful eye.

"Attagirl. How about for dessert I buy you one of those giant turkey legs?"

Kate had just witnessed an oversized man in much-too-short cutoffs devouring that particular enormous, greasy gut-bomb. She nearly gagged. "No thanks."

Truitt laughed and filled his mouth with a huge piece of funnel cake. Just then a busty brunette bounced toward them in a straw cowboy hat, Daisy Dukes, and a tight pink T-shirt. She shrilled something that sounded like Truitt's name then fell to her knees beside him and grabbed him around the neck. Kate barely caught the funnel cake before it fell from his hands to the ground. The brunette let him go and punched playfully at his shoulder.

"Truitt Boudrow! Where in the world have you been?"

Truitt fidgeted. "Amy. Wow. I haven't seen you since—"

"The Cotton Bowl in Dallas. New Year's Y2K. What a time that was! Have you been hidin' from me?"

"I . . . No, I . . ." Truitt stammered and wiped powdered sugar off his top lip.

"Oh, you gotta see Stacy!" the brunette shouted. "She's home from Tulsa for the festival. She's gonna die when I show her who I found! Truitt Boudrow in the flesh!"

Amy jumped to her feet and pulled Truitt off the ground and into the crowd. He shot a fearful look back to Kate.

"I'll be right back. Stay put."

Kate watched him disappear into the sea of strangers. She set the funnel cake on the ground beside her and blinked back tears. There was no escape—she was stuck until he returned. She hoped Stacy wouldn't be as excited to see Truitt as her friend predicted, or that Truitt wouldn't be excited to see her.

A local band took the stage next to her, where a waiting crowd was gathering with cheers and whistles. A skinny man with long gray hair and a red bandana tied around his forehead stepped to the front of the stage with an electric guitar and began the intro to "Sweet Child O' Mine." He was no Slash, but the crowd went wild just the same.

Kate scrambled to her feet, funnel cake in hand, and retreated several yards away behind a cotton candy booth where few people were gathered around. Just as she settled on a nice patch of ground, she spotted four drunken festivalgoers who'd moved their dance party only a few steps from her. Two of the intoxicated strangers—a man and woman, both heavy and sweating in tight jeans—attempted to dance the two-step, each with a beer in hand.

Kate sighed. Two-stepping to Guns N' Roses. If Truitt only knew what he was missing.

The song had almost ended when a woman's familiar face caught Kate's eye in the crowd across the street. Her long, stringy white hair was pulled back into a ponytail, and her blue robe had been replaced with green cutoff overalls and a red short-sleeved shirt, but the jerky, awkward movements of her head were the same. Her long, beaded earrings bounced about as they had the Sunday before, in the choir loft at Millsville Grace. She began talking to a man whose back to Kate, and then her eyes filled up and she dabbed at them with a tissue.

The man put his hand on her shoulder, and the woman threw her arms around him in an abrupt embrace. Preoccupied, Kate didn't notice the nearly 300-pound man next to her before he two-stepped onto the tip of her finger.

She wailed in pain, grabbing the injured finger in her other hand and holding on tight until the pain began to subside. The man, nearly too drunk to stand and much too drunk to notice his blunder, danced on, this time to "Free Bird." Kate scooted several feet away, taking Truitt's funnel cake with her. Her finger still throbbing, she searched the faces across the street for the choir lady and found her just as the man with her turned to leave.

Kate's eyes grew large, and she jumped to her feet to get a closer look. There was no mistaking him. Pastor Malcolm crossed Dickson and passed within feet of her, wearing the same blue button-up shirt he'd pulled on that morning. His face was solemn, not a hint of expression as he walked through the people and out of sight behind a used bookstore.

Kate looked back at the woman, and she was smiling again. Kate furrowed her brow as the dancing drunk performed a ridiculous spin move, and his foot caught on nothing at all. He fell hard into Kate's legs, and she hit the ground stomach first, then face. The drunk stranger sprawled out on top of her, and in an instant his partner rushed to his side and heaved him off. He sat up, dazed, beer still in hand, though half its contents covered the backs of Kate's legs and behind.

Kate didn't move. Every inch of her body ached, particularly her mouth that was starting to fill with blood. She pushed up on her gashed hands, lifted her head, and spotted the funnel cake upside down a few feet away. Pain shot though her side, and she lowered herself back onto her stomach and moaned. A pair of hands slid around her waist, and she grabbed the unseen arm for support, allowing whomever it was to pull her to her feet.

"Are you okay?" asked the good Samaritan, his hand on her back.

Kate froze. She'd know that pronounced voice, that expensive, signature cologne anywhere. A warm trickle of blood escaped out the corner of her mouth down her chin, and she raised her head to face her rescuer. "Hello, Gray."

Her husband's blue eyes grew wide, and he quickly removed his hand from her back as though just realizing he was touching a hot stove. He took a giant step back next to the blonde whose mouth gaped open.

"Kate," he finally managed. He looked at the blonde and back to Kate again. "I didn't expect to see you here."

The drunk man's girlfriend strode over, soaked in sweat from all her dancing, and her breath nearly sent Kate back to the ground. "You okay, honey?"

Kate peeled her eyes from the beautiful woman gripping her husband's arm with long, French-manicured nails. "I think so."

"Well, you're bleedin'!" With some effort, the drunk woman dug a damp handkerchief out of her jeans pocket and dabbed it at the corner of Kate's mouth in awkward movements. "I'm so sorry about Bud. He's a clumsy dang drunk, but he feels real bad about fallin' on ya like that."

Kate glanced at Bud, who was sitting on the ground in his dirt-smeared wifebeater. He stared glassy-eyed toward the stage at wannabe Slash and the band, smiling and chugging his last drops of Michelob. Kate pushed the handkerchief away and tried to not think about why it was damp. "I'm fine, really.

Thank you." The woman shrugged and went back to tend to Bud.

Gray whispered something to the blonde, and she retreated in a huff. He waited until she was out of sight then stepped toward Kate again. His ash-blonde hair was messier than usual, and she wondered if he was sporting a new style or if the breeze was to blame. He wore dark jeans and a tan sweater that must have been new. He was the most handsome man she'd ever seen.

Gray took her hand and led her to the corner of the cotton candy booth for what little privacy could be found. His stare was piercing, and she hoped he didn't notice her catching her breath.

"I'm sorry, Kate," he said.

She touched her fingers to her mouth. "It's just a busted lip."

"No. I'm sorry about everything. Your mom, Jane Ellen." He sighed. "Us."

She wanted to respond but couldn't concentrate on anything but his warm hand on hers.

"I never meant for any of this to happen," he continued. "I never wanted to hurt you."

Kate nodded and looked down as he gently wiped more blood from her lip with his thumb. Her knees went weak and she fought the urge to fall into his arms.

"I want to make this right," he said.

Her heart thudded. He squeezed her hand tighter and leaned closer to her face. Kate swallowed hard, and the sounds of the festival fell silent around them. She watched his lips, waited for him to say something more. She could forget his mistakes. Take him back. Start over.

"I know you can't forgive me yet." His eyes were moist, and his voice cracked. He exhaled to compose himself. "But I want this thing with me and Kristen to be okay with you and Jane Ellen."

She withdrew her hand, feeling as though she'd been punched in the chest.

"Kristen," she repeated, and she was surprised how easily the name rolled off her tongue.

"I love her, Kate." He bit his lip and fidgeted. "I'm going to marry her. Soon." His words stung harder than her fall minutes before. She looked away into the crowd to keep from yelling at him, kissing him, hitting him, holding him.

"Did you hear what I said? I'm asking you for a divorce."

Kate blinked. In a dark corner of her mind she saw the word Kristen in big red letters, all caps, flashing like a neon sign outside a seedy motel. She pictured Jane Ellen's innocent eyes searching for a reason why her life was suddenly different. Then the noise of the festival descended again, and the world was moving once more.

"Get away from her!" Truitt knocked Gray aside with his shoulder. He took Kate by the arm and eyed her bloody face. "No. He didn't . . ."

"Truitt, I was only trying to help her," Gray said.

"He's telling the truth," Kate said. "Now can you please just take me home?"

Truitt turned to Gray. "I don't need another reason to tear you apart, Canton."

Gray took a step backward. "I didn't know she would be here. I wouldn't have come."

Truitt let go of Kate and stepped toward Gray until they

were nose to nose. He gritted his teeth and the muscles in his jaw tightened and released. "You never deserved her. Not in the beginning and sure as hell not now. Don't you ever touch her again!"

Their eyes were locked in a heated stare until Kate pulled her cousin back and began walking away.

"Don't make this harder for us, Kate," Gray called from behind them. "You'll hear from my lawyers within the week."

Kate closed her eyes and let Truitt lead her to the Jeep.

***

Malcolm Bauer made the short walk between his front steps and the backdoor to Millsville Baptist Church. He was exhausted from a long day made even longer by an unexpected trip to Fayetteville for "church business." The throngs of people at the festival had annoyed him, but even strangers were easier to deal with than Millsville folks. No stares. No whispers. No hugs or pity. He shoved his key into the lock and listened to the familiar click then stepped inside the dark sanctuary. He felt along the wall until his fingertips found the switch and he flipped on the lights.

All was silent inside the church. He took a seat in the front row and stared at the pulpit. It stood solid and glared back, taunting him. You don't belong here, it sneered. They'd been through this before, but this evening Malcolm was too tired to care. Besides, he knew, when compared to the great leaders of Millsville Baptist's past, he was insignificant if not a downright embarrassment. He looked down at the worn-out Bible in his hand that read Jackson Boudrow in small gold letters at the bottom right-hand corner.

Jackson Boudrow's daughter was not the kind of woman he'd imagined. She was strong. Determined. Beautiful, even. But she wasn't getting the Bible back.

The cell phone in his pocket vibrated then rang. He dug it out and checked the caller ID. Nate Bell, probably needing the toilet fixed again. Or maybe the sink, or perhaps a light bulb needed replacing. He set the phone beside him and waited until the ringing stopped. Then he closed his eyes and let his head fall back. The silence of the sanctuary comforted him as always. He sat motionless, soaking in the precious solitude, until he felt he was no longer alone. Anger filled him instantly and, this time, unexpected tears stung his eyes. He stood and clenched his teeth in the empty sanctuary then shook his head in frustration.

"Why can't you leave me alone?" he yelled toward the rafters. "Just leave me alone!"

Malcolm stood and stormed out the door, nearly knocking Beulah off her feet on the other side. He grabbed the old woman around her shoulders until he was sure she was steady. Then he took a step back and wiped his eyes before noticing her own troubled expression.

"Beulah Two?" he asked.

Beulah's black eyes were moist and red, and she leaned heavily on her cane. "It's Esther. She's back."

Malcolm's already pounding heart raced double time. "She doesn't want to take her again."

Beulah shook her head. "No, I don't think so."

"Then why's she here? Does she need money again?"

"I think she's runnin'."

"From what?"

"She won't say." Beulah leaned forward and whispered as though unseen ears were listening. "But she scared, Malcolm. Scared to death, and that makes me scared, too."

"I'll come talk to her."

"No need," Beulah said. "I done brought her to you."

***

It was getting dark out. Truitt had dropped her off hours before, but the encounter with Gray plagued Kate's thoughts and played over in her mind without ceasing. Rosa and Jane Ellen were already sleeping—she could hear their steady breathing down the hall from her place on the couch. She rocked forward and back in small, jerky movements, her hands in her lap, staring at a blank television screen.

He loved someone else. He'd looked her in the eyes and told her so. The hope that had sustained her, the possibility her family could survive, was no more. They were gone. Her mother. Gray. Forever gone.

"Mama."

She mouthed the word as a sharp pain shot through her stomach. She wrapped her arms around her waist until the ache subsided. The clock on the wall showed 9:30 p.m. She glanced toward Jane Ellen and Rosa's room, still rocking, still fidgeting. Another pain.

"Mama," she said, aloud this time, frantic and afraid.

She sprang to her feet and lunged for the keys on top of the coffee table. In an instant she was outside, running to the Range Rover. Her white tank top and thin pajama pants were no match for the cold air ripping at her skin, though she barely noticed. There was no time to change or even slip on a pair of shoes over the white ankle socks already wet and brown from the dew-covered ground.

She drove too fast over the bumpy dirt road, past Beulah's, to the main highway, then she drove even faster. She stared straight ahead, past the headlights into the darkness. Her eyes were dry. Her determination left no room for tears.

Six miles later and just half a mile from her destination, the Range Rover jerked. Then again. And again. The red low-fuel light was glowing and she wondered for how long. The engine died, and with some difficulty she pulled to the side of the highway. She threw open the door, didn't bother shutting it, and ran through the dark down the lonely road. Her lungs felt like they would burst, and her side and legs cramped. Her feet ached with each step, but she pressed on.

She tripped near the cemetery fence, but somehow she maintained her balance and threw open the gate. She gasped for air as she fell to the ground near the tombstone that read Boudrow in dark, carved letters. She was sweating and freezing, her teeth chattering. She moaned, holding her chest above her wildly beating heart. Slowly she rolled to her back on top of her parents' graves. Another pain ripped through her stomach, and she hugged her body with her bare arms.

"Hey, Mama," she whispered, blinking up at the stars above. "He's gone." Tears pooled in the corners of her eyes then streaked off her cheeks onto the cold ground. "I saw him tonight."

She rolled onto her stomach and pressed herself as close as she could to the body somewhere far below. Consciousness ebbed away as warm blood began to soak her pajama pants, unnoticed.

"Mama? I'm right here. Please hold me."

***

Malcolm walked Esther out of the church and escorted her to the dilapidated Pontiac where Beulah had been waiting for an hour and a half. He looked at the young woman, his eyes sincere but his brow furrowed.

"Are you absolutely sure you're not in any danger?" he asked for what had to be the twentieth time.

Esther nodded. "I'm sure."

"And you promise me again you haven't done anything illegal."

"I promise, Malcolm. I told you. I've changed. I just wanted to come home."

Malcolm exhaled and relaxed his shoulders a bit. He was not inclined to trust her, but it was late. They were both tired, and poor Beulah had to be freezing. He helped Esther into the car.

"We'll talk again soon," he said. If she was hiding something, he would find out.

Malcolm went back to lock the church door and then walked toward the shed, glancing toward Anna's grave as he always did before retreating inside. He barely noticed the still figure lying in the cemetery as a cloud moved slowly across the full moon.

He squinted and crept toward the cemetery gate. The cloud slipped away, and the cemetery brightened. Malcolm's eyes grew wide.

He ran through the already-open gate and fell to his knees at Kate's side then rolled her onto her back. Her eyes were closed, her body cold and wet. Without a word and with little effort, he scooped her limp body into his arms.

Chapter Nine

The Lord gave, and the
Lord hath taken away.
-Job 1:21a, KJV

Kate's eyes fluttered and opened. She blinked hard and slowly focused in on a framed picture of a man's face. He was probably seventy-something with gray hair and beard and dark, sad eyes. The eyes seemed vaguely familiar, but she didn't recognize the man or the wall his picture hung on. She tried to move her arms but they, along with the rest of her body, were tucked tight beneath a heap of heavy blankets. Her head throbbed with a brutal, relentless ache, and her limbs were weak and sore. Then the pain came again. It tore through her stomach like a dagger, and she whimpered.

Using all her strength, she managed to wriggle free from under her coverings and sit up. A damp washcloth fell from her forehead into her lap. She took it in her hands and examined it then looked around.

The room was dark. A dim lamp sat next to the bed and provided the room's only light. She squinted and made out a chest of drawers beneath a dirty window and a rocking chair just steps away, none of it familiar. She placed the washcloth on the nightstand beside her and tried to get up, but the room spun fiercely around her. She closed her eyes and laid her head back on the pillow. Vomit ascended in her throat, and she swallowed hard until the urge passed then opened her eyes again. The old man in the picture stared at her.

A voice began speaking from somewhere beyond the walls, but she couldn't make out the words. She tried to sit up again but the nausea returned with a vengeance, and once more she closed her eyes and pressed her lips together as tight as she could then covered her mouth firmly with her hand.

A door opened and closed. Footsteps. The pain in her stomach returned, and this time, the vomit was not staying down. She leaned over the bed and heaved. The thick mess splattered onto the floor with a sound that made her gag even harder. When at last she caught her breath, she reached for the washcloth, but it was gone.

Then a cold cloth was pressed against her forehead and a hand pushed her back toward the pillow. She opened her eyes and stared into the face of Malcolm Bauer. His expression was grim, but not angry. He wiped her wet lips with a tissue, quick but tender, then placed the washcloth in her hand.

"Just hold on, okay?" he said. "I called Truitt. He's on his way."

Kate's heart pounded. She remembered the festival and the glowing low-fuel light. She remembered the running and the pain in her stomach.

Malcolm walked a few steps away into the darkness of his home and returned with a large towel, then threw it on the floor over the vomit.

"I'm sorry," Kate said.

He spread wide the corners of the towel with his boot, then left the room once more. Kate shook her head and tried to disappear. She thought about making a break for the door but was afraid she would throw up again. If humiliation could kill, she would already be dead.

"Drink this."

Malcolm was beside her again. She opened her eyes as he lifted a glass of cool water to her lips.

Her hands were shaking when she took it, and the cubes clinked and clanged against the side of the glass. Kate waited for him to walk away, but he remained, watching her drink. She swallowed with difficulty then raised her eyes to him. His eyebrows were crinkled, his expression anxious and concerned. When she was finished, he took the glass from her and returned it to the sink, rubbing his head with his knuckles.

Another pain tore through her stomach, and she prayed Truitt would be there soon. Malcolm walked to a window beside the front door, pulled back the curtain, and peered outside into the darkness.

"Thank you," Kate said.

Malcolm turned his head toward her without letting the curtain fall. The washcloth peeled away from her forehead and dropped onto the bed.

"You're gonna be fine, okay? Truitt will be here any minute."

Kate squinted. Of course she would be fine. She was just tired and upset about seeing Gray. Stress had gotten the best of her. That was all. She opened her mouth to tell him so when the pain in her stomach caused her to pitch forward. She moaned and grabbed her stomach. Malcolm hurried to put his hand on her back and leaned down to her face.

"Kate? Kate, stay with me."

When the pain subsided, Kate looked up at him. His eyes were large and scared. She wanted to tell him she was fine, but the room was rocking like a ship at sea. Darkness fought to overtake her vision, and she reached out for him. Her fingers found his cheek, and he took her hand.

The door burst open. Truitt yelled her name, then Aunt Mo mumbled something and was answered by someone else whose voice Kate didn't recognize. Someone lifted her body into the air, but she couldn't move or speak. Then she felt the cool, wet blood soaking her pajamas. With her remaining strength she turned to glance back at the bed where she'd been laying and saw a great flash of red before all went black.

***

Beulah Two stood beside the couch where her mother had been sleeping for hours. It was nearly 11 p.m., and the little girl should have been in bed long before. Instead, she studied her mother's face—the light brown skin, the long black eyelashes, the small, flawless nose and mouth. In a slow, smooth motion, she leaned in close to feel Esther's breath in her face. She closed her eyes and inhaled it.

Beulah limped into the living room from the bedroom wearing a long blue nightgown. "What you doin' up, baby?"

Beulah Two raised herself away from the couch, and Beulah sighed.

"Let her sleep, child. Your mama's tired. She needs her rest. Now you come on back to bed."

Beulah disappeared into the darkness of her bedroom, and Beulah Two looked back to Esther. She saw their faces—Esther's friends, boyfriends, acquaintances, strangers. They swirled about in her mind, laughing, taunting, coaxing. They reached out for her with large, forceful hands and hot breaths.

They were always somewhere in the shadows, and Esther's return home had brought them with her.

But still, Beulah Two watched her mother sleep and smiled. Esther's face seemed peaceful, happy. Esther was the most beautiful thing she'd ever seen.

***

Kate awoke in a hospital bed. Her hand ached, and she raised it to see an IV tube leading from it to a clear bag catching an unidentified dripping fluid. In a chair next to her sat Truitt's new blonde friend in a white doctor's coat. She was sleeping and looked as though she'd been there for hours. The woman stirred then jumped to her feet and leaned over Kate's bed.

"Hey there," she said, her voice so sweet it was almost melodic.

Kate rubbed at her eyes. The pain in her stomach was gone.

"My name is Vaughn. I'm a friend of Truitt's. I've been taking care of you tonight."

So Ms. Blonde Beauty really was a doctor. Kate might have laughed if her mouth hadn't been so dry. Vaughn held up a white foam cup with a straw for her to drink. After a few sips that made her nauseous, Kate whispered, "What happened?"

Vaughn leaned down close. She chewed her lip and took a deep breath. "Kate, did you know you were pregnant?"

A wave of ice rushed through Kate's body. Her heart thudded, and for a moment she forgot to breathe.

"Pregnant? No, I—"

"I'm so sorry," Vaughn said, taking Kate's hand. "You had a miscarriage last night. But you're going to be fine."

Kate stared as Vaughn talked of blood transfusions, procedures, and medications. Her perfect mouth moved with soft and apologetic words followed by detailed explanations of her treatment so far. But Kate heard nothing. A single thought filled her consciousness and blocked everything else.

"How could he?"

Vaughn stopped talking, her mouth frozen open mid-word.

"How could he?" Kate repeated, tears filling her eyes.

Truitt walked into the room holding a Starbucks cup. "You're awake." He smiled and hurried to her bedside. "It's about time, too, Sleepin' Beauty."

Vaughn stopped him with a touch on his arm. "She's asking about her husband."

Kate reached for Truitt's hand as tears streamed off her cheeks. "How could he? How *could he*?"

Truitt took her in his arms and held her close as she sobbed into his chest.

"She's not talkin' about Gray."

Chapter Ten

He does as He pleases with the powers
of heaven and the peoples of the earth.
No one can hold back His hand or say to
Him, "What have you done?"
-Daniel 4:35, NIV

The large brown envelope from Young, Burke, and Kirby came on a Tuesday. Kate pulled it from the mailbox and stared at it a long while before closing the box and making her way back inside the house. Rosa looked up from her pile of laundry and froze.

They'd all been making a fuss over her since the miscarriage—Truitt, Modean, and especially Rosa. Mo came by at least once a day, Truitt sometimes twice. The day before, he'd come bearing flowers from the twins' greenhouse and a large sampling of breads, jams, and homemade butter from Beulah. Even Vaughn had dropped by once to check on her, but the two had ended up talking mostly about Truitt.

Kate walked to a tall shelf next to the kitchen door and placed the envelope as high up as she could reach. When she turned around, Rosa was right there behind her. Kate jumped, her hand fluttering to her chest.

"You okay, Ms. Kate?"

Kate flashed a bright smile though her stomach was churning. "Please stop worrying about me, Rosa. I told you, I'm fine."

The phone rang, and Rosa answered. After a few seconds

she held it out toward Kate. "It is Mrs. Canton, Gray's mother."

Kate closed her eyes, took a deep breath, then brought the phone to her ear. "Hello, Margie," she said.

Margie began with the usual "how are you" and "how's your family" then launched an apology for Gray's absence at Ruth's funeral and, of course, for the affair. They hadn't raised him that way, she said, and Kate knew it was true. Margie referred to Gray's new love interest as a *tramp* and a *gold digger*, among other names, then professed her love for Kate and promised she would always be part of their family.

At length, Margie got around to asking if Jane Ellen could come visit for the weekend. Levi's—Mr. Canton's—love of bowling had gotten the better of him, and he'd bought the little girl a child-size, glittering, pink bowling ball with her name etched in sparkling silver letters. The two of them could not wait to take her to the bowling alley to try it out. Kate agreed to deliver Jane Ellen to them on Saturday morning and pick her up again Sunday afternoon. Margie was thrilled, but before hanging up she spent several more minutes apologizing again for her son. She was crying by the time she said goodbye.

Kate hung up the phone and glanced at Rosa, who was staring at her out of the corner of her eye.

"No, I'm not telling them about the baby," Kate told her flatly. "They're good people. They don't need anything else to feel guilty about."

***

Nate Bell, a seventy-four-year-old retired mail carrier and widower of nearly three years, sat alone at his kitchen table.

The bowl of canned chili tasted horrible, but he couldn't stand the thought of another meal from Susie's Café. He crushed a handful of saltines into the hot chili, hoping to improve the taste, and stirred it with his spoon. As he waited for the crackers to soften, he took a healthy drink of milk and glanced up at the clock. Another long and lonely day was finally coming to a close, and Nate could not have been more grateful.

The visit from Pastor Mackey Johnston that morning had been a nice surprise and reprieve to the day's monotony. Any company was nice, as it happened so rarely. Nate took a huge bite of chili and crackers and chewed slowly. Had his wife, Evelyn, been alive, she'd have wiped his face tenderly with her napkin. Instead, Nate went to bed that night with dried chili smeared across his chin.

***

Malcolm stepped from his pickup into Beulah's front yard. The air was cold, normal for early November in Northwest Arkansas, and he zipped up his jacket all the way to his neck before diving his hands deep into the pockets. It had been almost a week since the surprise return of Beulah Two's mother, Esther, and Malcolm couldn't get his conversation with her out of his head. He wanted to believe Esther's story but couldn't shake the feeling there was something she wasn't telling him.

He hurried to the front porch and opened the screen door. It slammed shut behind him before he noticed Beulah Two, sitting on the floor in a heavy coat, a partially completed jigsaw puzzle before her with its many small pieces strewn to her left and right. Her eyes lit up when she saw him and, without a trace of nervousness or timidity, she smiled. Malcolm smiled back.

"Another puzzle, huh?"

The little girl nodded.

"Five-hundred piece?"

"Seven-fifty."

Malcolm sat down next to her on the cold porch floor and picked up a puzzle piece. "Another angel?" he asked, examining the completed sections. She'd finished one wing and a portion of the other.

"Mm-hmm," she said.

Malcolm tried without success to make his piece fit with another. "You seen any lately?" he asked.

"I already told you I seen one with Ms. Kate." Beulah Two said, focusing on the puzzle. "He's the same one I been seein' with you. "

Malcolm studied her as her eyes darted from puzzle piece to puzzle piece. He never believed her when she talked of her angels, but he also knew she would never lie.

Beulah Two looked up at him and smiled again. "Will you tell me 'bout Ms. Anna and the lightnin' bugs?"

Malcolm exhaled. He must have told her the lightning bug story at least fifty times, and she could, no doubt, tell it better than he could by then. But Beulah Two took the puzzle piece from his hand and tossed it back in the pile then settled back and waited. He shook his head, smiling.

"Before Anna and I were married, when we were just dating, I decided to surprise her with a picnic dinner in a field not far from here."

"At night," Beulah Two added.

"Yes, a nighttime picnic. I laid out a blanket with paper

plates and enough Chinese food from Madame Woo's to feed ten people."

"B'cause you wanted to make sure you got somethin' she liked."

"Right. It was June, and instead of lighting candles, I spent hours catching hundreds of lightning bugs. I put them in glass jars and set them all around the blanket."

"But Ms. Anna didn't like it."

"No. See, when she was a little girl, her older brothers taught her how to catch lightning bugs. One night she caught so many that the jar of bugs was bright enough she didn't even have to turn on her nightlight. She set the jar beside her bed and watched them move and glow until she fell asleep. What her brothers forgot to tell her was that she needed to poke holes in the top. When she woke up the next morning, all those lightning bugs were dead at the bottom of the jar. So when she saw all the ones I caught, flying around in all those jars, trying to find a way out, she just couldn't stand it."

"And you let 'em all go!" Beulah Two shouted.

"We opened every jar, and all the lightning bugs flew right off into the sky." He paused, looking out the porch screen. "It looked just like the stars were dancing, right above our heads."

"You never told me that part," Beulah Two said. "About them lookin' like stars. You never said that before."

Malcolm smiled. "Well, they did. Almost like they were stars we just set free, and they flew right on up and found their place in the sky where they belonged."

Beulah Two giggled.

Malcolm stood to go into the house and noticed another completed puzzle sprawled across the floor next to Beulah's rocker. "What's that?"

"That's a puzzle I did yesterday. It's a pretty mountain, but I can't finish it right now. There's a piece missin'."

Malcolm stared at the picture of a snowcapped mountain and tall, surrounding cedars. Near the center was a small hole where the missing piece should be, its absence throwing off the entire scene.

***

Jane Ellen bounced in the passenger seat as Kate drove toward the Cantons' home. In her seven years of life, Jane Ellen had spent only one night with her grandparents and was too young to even remember it.

"Are we almost there?" she asked, the grin never fading from her face.

"Almost."

Kate delivered her daughter as promised on Saturday morning, and the two were met at the elder Cantons' front door with a heavy, round gift, wrapped in blue paisley paper and topped off with a bright red bow. Jane Ellen kissed her mother goodbye then disappeared inside the modest brick home for promised chocolate chip cookies and Kool-Aid.

Five minutes later, Kate arrived in downtown Millsville and pulled into a small, unpaved parking lot behind Boyd Walker's law office. She felt under her seat and removed the envelope from Young, Burke, and Kirby. She examined it only a moment before grabbing her purse and heading for Boyd's front door.

Boyd sat alone behind his desk, no employees in sight. He was wearing a blue and canary-yellow polka dotted tie, though the knot was loose, and the top two buttons of his shirt were unfastened. The office was freezing, the thermostat sitting at a cool sixty degrees though the temperature outside was barely forty-five. He looked up as the door opened and beamed at her.

Kate smiled back. She was wearing a white button-up shirt, brown blazer, and dark jeans. Her hair was down, and she'd even felt well enough that morning to put on makeup. Boyd's eyes looked like they might pop out of his head.

"I'm sorry I didn't make an appointment," Kate told him.

He stood and shook her hand a bit too eagerly. "No problem at all. Please have a seat."

She handed him the envelope but did not sit.

"This arrived for me at home on Tuesday. I believe they're divorce papers from my husband's lawyers."

Boyd took the envelope and looked it over. "It hasn't been opened."

"No. I'd like you to do the honors. Then you can let me know what they're proposing in non-legal terms and give me your advice. Of course, I'll be paying you."

Boyd raised his eyebrows. He set the envelope on his desk and gave her a sympathetic smile. "Is Monday soon enough?"

***

Beulah Two had completed her puzzle and moved on to reading a book about insects on her grandmother's bed. Malcolm sat on the couch next to Beulah and sipped a cup of coffee. It was nearly one o'clock in the afternoon, an hour after his arrival, and still no sign of Esther. Beulah said she'd left for a walk that morning and hadn't been back since. Both she and Malcolm were beginning to worry, and his suspicions that she was hiding something were mounting with every passing second.

He and Beulah looked to each other as the porch's screen door slammed. Seconds later, Esther walked in wearing her grandmother's long black coat and Beulah Two's green beanie.

Esther's eyes grew wide. "What? What's wrong?"

"Where in the world were you, girl?" Beulah asked. "You had us scared to death."

"I told you I was just going for a walk. I met a woman named Rosa Morales. She works for a family just down the road."

"Kate's Rosa?" Beulah asked.

"I think so. Why are you both looking so mad?"

"Honey, we're just worried 'bout you is all."

Malcolm studied her every movement, and she looked at him and bit her lip. "I speak some Spanish," she said. "My roommate's mother was Cuban. I swear I was just talking with Rosa. You can ask her if you want."

Malcolm's expression softened, and he turned to Beulah. "Do you think you could give us a minute?"

Beulah nodded and joined Beulah Two in the bedroom to read about ladybugs, though she kept the door open just a crack.

Malcolm motioned for Esther to have a seat. She removed her coat and took Beulah's place in an old recliner, across from where Malcolm sat on the couch.

"Esther, no one's accusing you of anything, but you have to know, because of what's happened in the past, you make everyone around here a little nervous."

Esther lowered her head and pulled off the cap. "I know that."

Malcolm scooted to the edge of the couch and leaned forward, his elbows on his knees. "If there is anything else you need to tell me, anything at all, I need to hear it. Right now."

Esther's dark eyes went moist. She raised her head and gazed at him. Words formed on her lips, and Malcolm took a breath. Pain and fear swirled in her eyes and seemed to surround her like a cloud of smoke. She paused, then shook her head and looked to the floor. "I told you everything."

***

On her way back from Boyd's, Kate drove toward the church. She parked next to the cemetery and took a deep breath. The old church house loomed tall in front of her, and she climbed out of the SUV and ascended the steps to the front door. She pulled hard on the old handle but, as expected, the doors were locked tight. Undeterred, she walked back down the steps and turned over a large rock that sat beside the bottom step—the hiding spot her father had used. There the old key lay, and Kate took it in her hand and made for the door again. The key turned easily in the lock, and she entered the cold sanctuary.

The door closed behind her, taking the daylight with it. A few rays of sun seeped in through the windows, making the cross behind the pulpit visible.

Kate's bottom lip trembled as she stared at it.

"How could you?"

***

Malcolm returned home from Beulah's to see Kate's Range

Rover parked in front of the church. He hadn't seen Kate since that night at the hospital, where he'd stayed with Modean and Truitt until word had come that she'd be okay. Since then, their paths hadn't crossed.

He scanned the cemetery, but she wasn't at Ruth's grave. He looked over at the church and squinted toward the front door, which was slightly ajar. He jogged over and poked his head inside. It was dark, and he didn't see her at first. Then a movement caught his eye at the foot of the stage beneath the cross. She was on her knees before the pulpit, her face almost touching the floor—her sobs echoing off the rafters and filling the room. Malcolm chased away the notion that the sound of her tears rang beautiful in the place. In just six weeks' time, life as Kate had known it was lost forever, stolen from her mercilessly by the same God to whom she prayed.

With lightning speed, Malcolm turned away and hurried back outside, his heart beating wildly against his chest. He'd almost made it across the parking lot when the church doors squeaked open behind him.

"Malcolm! Wait!"

He stopped and turned as she approached, wiping at her wet eyes.

"I haven't had the chance to properly thank you for what you did. You saved my life, and—"

"Did you forgive him?" he asked.

"Excuse me?"

"In there just now. Did you forgive him?" He stepped closer to her, something in him churning, building. He clenched his jaw and shook his head. "He takes away your mother, your husband, and your child, and just like that, everything's okay?

In an instant he obliterates your life, and you can just walk in there, get down on your knees, and forgive him?" His face burned red, and he was breathing hard.

"No. No, it's not okay. I don't understand it, and maybe I never will."

Malcolm stepped forward until their noses almost touched. "So it's just like the old song. It is well with your soul, huh? Well, it's not well with mine. Don't you get it? He does things his way. He doesn't care about you or what you need. He takes when he feels like it. And you . . . God! You're so naïve, Kate."

She flinched, and he realized he'd never called her by her first name. "Is that what you tell those poor old people?" she asked. "The ones who walk in those doors looking for hope Sunday after Sunday? It's your responsibility to be there for them. They need you, but you're too busy feeling sorry for yourself to notice! You've abandoned them!"

"They don't need me. They only want to hear how their God watches over them—that he's loving and kind. But I'm done making them believe he's good and all the works of his hand are good. Because they're not. These people believe he takes care of them. That he's always near them. Well, he's not always near them!"

He grabbed her arm and pulled her toward the cemetery fence then stopped abruptly and pointed toward a nearby tombstone. "John Ashton. He was eighty-two. He fell in the snow last winter and froze to death before his wife found him."

He pulled her alongside the fence and pointed out another grave with an enormous tombstone. "Faith, Shelby, and Jacob Thompson. They were riding home from Susie's Café with their daddy when a deer ran into the road. The van flipped five times.

Faith and Shelby were ten-day-old twins, and Jacob was two. Their parents were told last year they couldn't have any more kids."

He waved a hand toward another grave. "Lee Hubbard. Seventy-five years old. He was burning a pile of leaves in his backyard when he fell and caught on fire. His wife Macie's in a wheelchair. She tried to get to him but couldn't. Instead she watched him burn to death in their own backyard."

Even in the dimming light of dusk, Kate could see the wildness of his eyes as he took hold of her shoulders with both hands.

"Is that well with your soul? The God you just forgave watched it all happen. He sat back and watched it! Just like with Anna, and just like with Ruth and your baby." His voice grew louder with each word, and he pointed toward the church. "I'm not going in there to tell those people he's good and he loves them and protects them. Because all I see is a God who singles out the old and the helpless. I see a God who could save them but doesn't. I'm supposed to tell them to keep trusting? To keep hoping?" He shook his head. "I will not lie for him a day longer!"

Kate stood frozen. Malcolm wanted to let go of her but couldn't will his body to move. His heart pounded as he studied her face. When the tears began to pool in his eyes, he released her and disappeared inside the shed.

Chapter Eleven

We dance round in a ring and
suppose, But the Secret sits in
the middle and knows.
-Robert Frost

Sunday morning, Kate sat in the sanctuary of Millsville Baptist Church, this time on an uncomfortable pew between Beulah and Rosa. The choir, a group comprising seven senior citizens, stood in two short rows on stage and sang the fourth and final verse to "Land Where Living Waters Flow."

Kate glanced at her watch then down the row to Beulah Two, who fidgeted on the other side of Beulah. Despite the little girl's best efforts to keep up with the lyrics and remain attentive, even she was about to doze off. The choir had opened the service and been on stage for forty-five minutes already. The troop was tired and ready to sit down. If their weary faces and weighty postures weren't indication enough, their exhausted voices, barely distinguishable over the congregation's singing, was proof.

For the hundredth time, Kate glanced up on stage to Pastor Malcolm Bauer, who sat, almost hiding, behind the choir, his head lowered and his eyes fixed on the book in his hand, not so much bored as inconvenienced. His hair was combed nicely, but his face was unshaven. He wore khaki dress pants, a brown button-up shirt untucked with no tie, and worn-out dress shoes. No suit, as one might expect from a pastor, but an ensemble much improved from his everyday attire.

Kate hoped to catch a glimpse of his eyes. She wasn't sure why. But Beulah had assured her the pastor took no part in the services, and this one would be no exception.

When the song finally ended, the relieved choir members closed their hymnals and began to exit the stage when an old woman in the first row struggled to her feet, wearing a blue floral dress, panty hose, and white, Velcro tennis shoes. "Nina!" she called toward the stage.

Nina, the blue-haired choir director, stopped in her tracks and looked up. The choir member behind her bumped hard into Nina's back. The woman behind him did the same until all seven singers formed a small pileup on stage, blocked from their exit by Nina's large rear end.

The old woman in the floral dress swallowed hard and spoke in the loudest voice she could muster, though it was raspy and weak and everyone in the room strained to hear. "Could you please do 'Amazing Grace' before y'all sit down?"

Nina's tired expression instantly vanished, replaced by a wide, sympathetic smile. Her eyes grew wet, and she nodded. "Well, we sure can, Ms. Ruby."

The old woman returned a fragile smile, her head shaking rhythmically from what seemed to be Parkinson's or another like disease, and she took her seat with great care. The choir members returned to their positions without being instructed and flipped through their hymnals.

"Page one-hundred-and-two! Let's do the first, second, and last verse," Nina called out to the congregation. "Y'all sing this one for Mr. Clyde."

The pianist pounded out the familiar tune with renewed

vigor, and Beulah leaned close to Kate. "That's Ms. Ruby Williams. They buried her husband, Clyde, last week. Stroke, I think. He'd been in terrible shape for years. They would've been married sixty-nine years in January. Long as I can remember, that man requested 'Amazing Grace' every Sunday. They sang it at the funeral."

Kate tried to look away from the old woman but couldn't tear her eyes from her. She felt a lump rise in her throat as Ruby, alone on her pew for the first Sunday in sixty-nine years, swayed back and forth to the familiar melody, her eyes closed. Her trembling lips mouthed the words. "The Lord has promised good to me. His word my hope secures. He will my shield and portion be as long as life endures." She raised a tiny quaking hand toward the sky and breathed a short prayer.

Kate looked again to Malcolm. The pastor sat as before, frozen, unaware or indifferent to the scene playing out before him.

The hymn ended, and an awkward silence followed, apart from the sound of the aged choir members shuffling off stage. Then Brother Jake Luther, a seventy-year-old chicken farmer and the church's only remaining deacon, stood and addressed the congregation in his best blue denim overalls. "Well, we're sure glad y'all came today." His words were abnormally unhurried. Just as slowly, he pulled a crinkled tissue from the pocket of his overalls and blew his nose. "Anybody got any announcements?" he asked, still wiping.

A woman near the back called out, "Y'all remember next Sunday's potluck. Everybody bring somethin' and stay for lunch."

Brother Jake nodded. "Remember this."

In the silence that followed, Kate turned to look around at everyone else looking around.

"Well, if that's all, I'll dismiss us in prayer," Jake said. His prayer was painstakingly long, his words slow and deliberate. Kate opened her eyes before the final "Amen" just as Malcolm stood and stole out the stage door.

"Told you so," Beulah whispered to Kate. "Does it the same every Sunday. Just up and leaves."

Kate was ready to up and leave, too. The service had been painful, if not excruciating, to endure, and though the few remaining members of Millsville Baptist were doing the best they could to salvage what was left of their vanishing church, Kate knew the doors would soon close for good. The thought both saddened and infuriated her. Her father's church, dead, as Malcolm Bauer sat on the sidelines watching, perhaps waiting, for it to happen.

"Ms. Kate, I'm going to the car," Rosa said, already out of the pew and heading swiftly toward the front doors. Kate sighed and watched her go. Rosa had frowned through the entire service, and Kate felt terrible for having suggested she accompany them after missing her ride to the Catholic church in Tontitown. Before Kate could follow after, Beulah took her by the arm and began introducing her to every elderly person in sight, some Kate recognized from childhood and some she didn't. Kate greeted them all with a hug and indulged their wishes to reminisce about her mother.

Fifteen minutes later, Kate made her escape out the church doors, but Rosa was nowhere in sight. Only three vehicles remained in the parking lot—the Range Rover, Beulah's Pontiac, and Brother Jake's yellow pickup truck.

Kate descended the steps and opened her mouth to call out for Rosa when a movement near the corner of the church building caught her eye. She stopped short and watched Rosa and Pastor Malcolm, standing near the side of the church, engaged in quiet conversation.

The two were face to face, with Rosa's back toward her. Malcolm spoke in a hushed tone, and his expression—what she could see of it behind Rosa's curly black hair—looked concerned. Rosa nodded and whispered quietly. Kate stood motionless and strained without much success to make out their words.

Beulah exited the church doors, holding tight to the handrail with one hand and grasping Beulah Two's shoulder with the other. Brother Jake followed close behind and pulled the tall wooden doors shut behind him with a loud thud. Malcolm looked up and caught Kate's stare. He whispered a final word to Rosa then walked away toward his shed.

Kate wasted no time hurrying to Rosa's side. "Is everything okay?" she asked.

Rosa clutched her purse and walked toward the Range Rover. "Yes, Ms. Kate. Everything is good."

Kate followed, jogging just to keep up. "Are you sure? Did he say something to upset you?"

"No. No." Rosa shook her head hard. "He's a good man."

"You're certain?"

"It was nothing." Rosa opened the door to the Range Rover. "Now, what do I make for lunch?"

***

Esther poured herself a steaming cup of coffee and sat down at her grandmother's kitchen table. She'd opted not to attend the morning church service with Beulah and Beulah Two, alleging a splitting headache as her excuse. And it had been the truth. Even as she sipped the coffee, Esther's temples pounded, reminding her of the pain that had plagued her most of the night. Four ibuprofen, two aspirin, and a cold pack had been no match for its strength, and though the morning had brought some relief, the throbbing persisted.

The house was chilly, the wood in the fireplace barely burning. Esther shivered and pulled the sleeves of her plain, gray sweatshirt down over her hands. Sleepless as the night had been on account of the headache, something more was to blame for her unrest. Since arriving at her grandmother's, she'd felt safe, hidden away from circumstances and memories that were behind her. But the morning gave way to a different feeling. She sensed it in the air around her, as though danger hid behind every chair, every door, waiting to take hold of her. She shuddered then stood and looked out the window at the dead, brown leaves blowing in the breeze. Try as they might to hold on to the dry limbs, the wind tore them from the safety of their lofty homes. They twirled and twisted in their descent, and Esther imagined them screaming all the way down to the cold ground.

***

Malcolm slammed the door of his pickup truck and stepped out onto Nate Bell's driveway. Frustration mounted as he approached Nate's front door and knocked much too hard.

Seconds later, Nate opened the door and scowled.

"Took you long enough to get here. Don't you ever answer your phone?"

Malcolm bit his tongue, an action he seldom attempted. "I was in church, Mr. Nate."

"Yeah, yeah. You were in church. I know." Nate opened the door wide for Malcolm to enter then turned and walked back into the house. It was a typical greeting, and Malcolm was not surprised.

"Do I need my tool box?" Malcolm called after him.

"Well, what do you think? My garbage disposal's broke! If you'd answer your phone you'd know that!" The old man kept walking toward his kitchen and mumbled a curse word under his breath. Malcolm closed his eyes and gritted his teeth then returned to his truck for the toolbox.

Nate was waiting for him in a chair next to the kitchen sink and frowned at him again as he entered the room. "I thought you fixed this thing the last time."

"So did I." Malcolm flipped the disposal's switch to the sound of a low buzzing.

"Hear that?" Nate asked.

"I hear it."

Malcolm flipped off the switch and sank his hand deep inside the sink through the drain. Nate fidgeted in his chair and watched in silence. Then he stood, removed a piece of cold cornbread from a container across the room, and sat back down. A few bites later he retrieved a gallon of milk from the refrigerator. Neglecting a glass, he reclaimed his seat next to the sink and took a large gulp straight from the jug. "I sure can't make this stuff the way Evelyn could."

Malcolm looked up just as Nate took another bite of the cornbread. "Ms. Evelyn was a good cook."

"I've been going to Susie's Café just about every day for lunch." Nate's tone turned soft and reflective. "Guess I'd rather eat here at home, but I just don't feel much like cooking."

Malcolm nodded, his eyes never leaving his work on the disposal.

"I ate breakfast there this morning. Susie's got the best sausage gravy I ever tasted. Evelyn never made sausage gravy. She made chocolate gravy. Best chocolate gravy you ever put in your mouth. Whole lot better than what you get at that diner in town by the fire station. Folks say that's the best, but they never tasted my Evelyn's."

Malcolm felt a dishcloth wrapped around the blades of the garbage disposal and tugged at it. *C'mon*, he urged, growing more uncomfortable with the conversation by the second.

"Didn't really enjoy it today, though. At Susie's, I mean." Nate took another drink from the milk jug. "Food was fine. But some boys from out of town were in there being loud and mean to Susie. You don't see that much around here."

Malcolm yanked the dishcloth once more, and it released its grip on the blades. "Out of town?" he asked.

"Well, I ain't never seen 'em around here. They were cussing all loud like, and one even pushed his plate of food right off the table onto the floor. Busted it all over the place, then told Susie it was her fault and told her to get him another one. Thugs. That's what they were."

Malcolm set the torn, soiled dishcloth on the countertop. "There's your problem."

"Just a rag caught up in there? Well I'll be!"

Malcolm washed his hands in the sink.

"You know, come to think of it, those boys at Susie's were asking about Ms. Beulah's girl. What's her name?"

Malcolm froze. "Esther?"

"Yeah, yeah. Esther. Wanted to know where she lived."

Malcolm dried his hands on a fresh towel and knelt beside the old man. "What did they look like?"

"Well," Nate began, his brow furrowed. "They were all young boys, maybe twenties or thirties. All of 'em were thugs. Tattoos, clothes too big. The black boy had a bunch of gold teeth."

"How many were there?"

"Teeth?"

"Men, Mr. Nate! How many men?"

"One black and two white. One of the white boys had a tattoo of a snake on his wrist. The black boy did most of the talking. He's the one that made the mess with his plate. John Peters finally had all he could stand and ran 'em off. John's a big man, you know. They said they didn't want no trouble and just left. Didn't pay Susie a dime for the food."

Malcolm grabbed his toolbox. "That should fix the disposal."

"You might talk to Susie!" Nate called as Malcolm neared the front door. "They were asking her all sorts of questions!"

Malcolm let the door slam shut as he ran down the porch steps, leaving Nate alone again.

***

Rosa and Kate ate their vegetable soup in silence at Kate's kitchen table. Even after a full interrogation on the ride home from church, Rosa maintained her silence concerning her private conversation with Pastor Malcolm. She insisted it was nothing, but Kate didn't buy it for a second. She sat across from Rosa and sipped her soup. Rosa did the same, avoiding eye contact.

Their silence was broken by the sound of the front door opening and Jane Ellen's voice shouting, "Mommy!"

Kate dropped her spoon in the soup and ran to greet her daughter. Jane Ellen threw her arms around her and barely took a breath during the narrative of her time spent at the Canton home, beginning with the threesome's exploits at the local bowling alley.

Kate waved to Truitt, who'd followed Jane Ellen into the house. He collapsed onto the couch, dug for the remote in the cushions, and found a football game on TV. When Jane Ellen was finished with her story, Kate hugged her again then plopped her back onto her feet.

"Thanks for picking her up for me, Tru. Did she talk your ear off?"

"Not any more than usual." He poked at Jane Ellen, and she giggled and ran into the kitchen where Rosa scooped her up and kissed her repeatedly on the cheek. Then Rosa sat her down at the table to eat some soup.

Kate sat down next to Truitt.

"Heard anything about the divorce?" he asked.

"I'm supposed to meet with Boyd tomorrow. How are things with you and the good doctor?"

"We have a date on Friday."

"I really like this one."

He smiled. "Yeah. Me, too."

Three heavy knocks fell on the front door, and Kate stood and looked out the window. "It's Beulah and Beulah Two."

Much to Rosa's dismay, Jane Ellen ditched the soup and bolted into the living room as Kate opened the door. She threw her arms around Beulah Two and pulled the little girl inside. Both girls erupted into giggles and disappeared into Jane Ellen's bedroom.

"I know I shoulda called," Beulah said. "But we was drivin' by, and I thought it'd be just as easy to stop."

"Come on in, Ms. Beulah," Kate said, taking her by the arm and helping her through the doorway.

"No, no, I can't stay. I was just wonderin' if maybe Jane Ellen could come play with Beulah Two this afternoon. You probably miss her after she's been with Gray's folks all night, but there's somethin' botherin' Beulah Two today. I don't know what it is, and she says it's nothin', but I know that child well as I know myself, and somethin's got her all troubled. I'm sure it's got to do with her mama showin' back up like she did. I just thought maybe Jane Ellen could help get her mind off things."

"Aunt Mo told me about Esther coming home," Kate said. "I hope it will be a good thing this time, especially for Beulah Two."

"So do I. Oh Lord, so do I. I think Beulah Two's just worried. And she too young to be worried. I never see her as happy as I do with your Jane Ellen, so I thought maybe you'd let me take her home with us. Just for a little while."

Kate hesitated, but in the end she couldn't say no. "Jane Ellen!" she called. "Come here, sweetie." After the girls skipped back into the room holding hands, Kate asked, "How would you like to go play with Beulah Two for a few hours?"

"Yeah!" Jane Ellen and Beulah Two bounced up and down.

"I sure do appreciate it, Kate." Beulah looked past Kate to Rosa, who was standing in the doorway of the kitchen. "Well, hey there, Rosa. I heard you got to meet my Esther. Didn't you?"

Rosa nodded then turned and disappeared into her bedroom.

***

The door dinged as Malcolm walked into Susie's Café in downtown Millsville, just off the square. Only one middle-aged couple sat in a booth near the back, eating their chicken fried steaks and chatting. Malcolm took a seat beside the cash register at the bar, and Susie emerged from the back in her usual attire of blue jeans, black Crocs, a long white apron smeared with the special of the day, badly dyed red hair pulled back into a tight ponytail, and a blue-ink pen resting snuggly above her ear. She smiled a weary smile then removed the pen with a sigh and pulled a small notebook from her pocket.

"Hey there, Brother Malcolm. What'll you have today?"

"Dr. Pepper to go," he said and pulled two dollar bills from his wallet and lay them on the counter.

"Easy enough." She turned and grabbed a white foam cup from the top of a tall stack behind her and filled it with ice.

"I heard you had some trouble in here this morning," Malcolm said after the noise of the ancient ice machine subsided.

"You must've been talkin' to Mr. Nate." Susie shook her head in disgust. "Just a few out-of-towners passin' through, I guess. Thought they'd stop in and have a little fun at my expense."

"Are you okay?"

"It shook me up a little. Lucky for me, Big John Peters was sittin' right there in that booth eatin' his grits and bacon. He got all up in their faces, and they left. Sort of surprised me they gave up so easy."

"Nate said they were asking you questions."

Susie tilted her head and tucked the pen above her ear. "Yeah. Sorta strange now that I think about it. They were askin' about Esther Jones, Ms. Beulah's granddaughter. I told 'em I ain't seen that girl in years, and I ain't. I heard she's been out in Memphis, and I guess that's where they knew her from. I saw their Tennessee plate when they drove off."

Malcolm's heart began to pound, and a chill ran the full length of his back. "What were they driving?"

"I didn't get a good look at it, but it was a real fancy black car. Four-door."

"Can you think of anything else they said?"

"They asked where Esther used to stay when she was here, and I told 'em I just didn't know. I think they knew I was lyin'. That's when one of 'em dropped his plate on my floor and when Big John had all he could stand. I sure wasn't gonna tell 'em where Ms. Beulah lives, Brother Malcolm."

"No. You did the right thing. Thanks, Susie."

***

After an hour and a half of watching a football game she couldn't have cared less about, Kate rose from the couch and picked up her jacket. Truitt, who'd been asleep for the past twenty minutes, opened his eyes and lifted his head off the arm of the couch. "What's the score?" he asked in mid-yawn.

"The red team is ahead by seven."

"Where're you goin'?"

"To get Jane Ellen at Ms. Beulah's. It's almost four."

Truitt scratched his head and yawned again. "C'mon. I'll take you."

Kate climbed into Truitt's jeep and hugged herself tight. The vehicle's soft-top was no match for the cold wind tearing its way inside. Truitt cranked the engine and turned down the radio. "Sorry. She won't heat up just goin' to Beulah's and back," he confessed, backing onto the dirt road.

The sound of a blaring horn and skidding tires caused Truitt to slam on his brakes. He and Kate looked up just in time to see Malcolm Bauer's pickup slide past them, tires locked, into the ditch. Kate's hands were frozen to the dash. Her heart nearly exploded in her chest, and she struggled to catch her breath.

"What the heck is he doin'?" Truitt jumped from the Jeep and hurried to the truck. As he approached the tailgate, Malcolm threw the pickup into reverse. Truitt leapt out of the way as the truck's tires threw gravel high into the air before the pickup jerked its way back onto the road. Malcolm threw open the door and jumped out.

"What are you doin'?" Truitt shouted. "You almost killed us! And me, twice!"

Kate hopped out of the Jeep and walked toward them. Malcolm passed Truitt without a glance and met Kate in the middle of the road. Her heart hadn't yet recovered, and the look on the pastor's face startled her all the more.

"Where's Rosa?" he asked.

"She's in the house. Sleeping, I think."

"Have you seen Ms. Beulah today?"

"Yes, she came by earlier to pick up Jane Ellen."

"Jane Ellen? She's at Beulah's?"

"Yes. Playing with Beulah Two. What's going on?"

Malcolm's expression twisted into a grimace. "I have to go."

Kate grabbed his arm. "No! What is going on? Tell me."

"They may be in danger."

"Danger? Who?"

"Esther. Ms. Beulah. Anyone in that house."

Kate's legs began to shake. "I don't understand."

"There's no time to explain. I have to go!" Malcolm ran to his pickup and took off toward Beulah's. Truitt took Kate's hand and pulled her toward the Jeep. "C'mon, Kate. Hurry."

Kate forced her legs to move and glanced up to see Rosa standing in the doorway, her hand over her mouth. Kate ran back toward the house, and Rosa was crying when Kate grabbed her by the arms.

"Rosa, you know something. Tell me what's happening!"

"Oh, Ms. Kate!" Rosa sobbed. "I should have told you."

"Told me what? Told me *what*?"

"Ask questions later, Kate!" Truitt shouted. "Let's go!"

Kate stared at Rosa a moment longer then turned and ran to the Jeep.

***

Malcolm sat on Beulah's front porch, rocking steadily in an old rocking chair. He was still out of breath when the black Chrysler 300 pulled into the driveway but tried desperately to appear relaxed. Only seconds before, Beulah had been raking leaves in the front yard while Jane Ellen and Beulah Two played nearby. The rake now lay haphazard next to the small pile of leaves, and all were concealed safely in the house. Malcolm glanced at the shotgun propped against a small table beside him. His hands were shaking, and he gripped at the arms of the chair until his knuckles were white.

The men exited the car and walked toward the house, one black and two white, just as Nate Bell had described. The black man walked a step ahead of the others—the leader, Malcolm decided. As they drew closer, Malcolm stood, his hand just inches from the gun.

"What can I help you boys with?"

The man in front smiled broadly, revealing four gold teeth across his upper plate. "We just wanna talk." They kept walking, nearing the porch.

"You can talk from there." Malcolm said.

The men stopped and stared at him. The leader surveyed him from head to toe, and Malcolm knew he was gauging his nerve. The staring match continued for several tense seconds, and then the man threw back his head and laughed before stepping again toward the porch.

The shotgun was in Malcolm's hands in seconds. He raised it high and aimed through the screen at the stranger. "I said, you can talk from there."

The man's smile vanished. He held up his hands and took a large step back. The other two did the same, and Malcolm noticed a tattoo in the shape of a snake on the taller one's wrist. "Hey, man," the leader said. "All right. All right. Don't go gettin' in over your head now."

Malcolm's hands were trembling as he did his best to play it cool. The door behind him opened and Beulah stepped out with a large hunting rifle aimed directly at the men. The two henchmen took several more steps backward. Their leader remained unmoved.

"Hey, c'mon now." The man lifted his hands higher into the air. "I said I just wanna talk." His agitated tone worried Malcolm.

"Then talk," Malcolm said.

"I'm lookin' for somebody. A girl. Esther Jones. Folks in town tell me she used to live around here."

"She doesn't live here," Malcolm answered. "Now if that's all you came for, it's time for you to go."

The man's friends looked back and forth between Beulah and Malcolm but didn't dare move until their leader moved first. Instead, he took a small step forward, staring deep into Malcolm's eyes.

"I think she does live here. I think you're lyin'."

"I'm the only one who lives here," Beulah said. "Esther Jones ain't been seen 'round here in years. Now you boys go on back where you came from and leave an old woman alone."

Beulah Two opened the door and stepped onto the porch between Malcolm and her grandmother.

"Get back in the house," Malcolm whispered. "Now, Beulah Two."

But the little girl didn't move. She fixed her eyes on the man near the porch, then cocked her head to the side and set her gaze just behind him.

"Only one who lives here, huh?" The man looked to Beulah Two. "You live here, too. Don't you, little girl?"

Beulah Two didn't blink. Her expression was intense, fearless. Even as he addressed her, her stare remained fixed behind him, as though she saw something no one else in the yard could see. The man studied her, and his countenance changed from one of boldness to discomfort under the little girl's gaze.

"Hey! I'm talkin' to you, kid!" He turned and looked behind him over his shoulder. "What are you lookin' at? What's wrong with you?" He looked to Malcolm. "What's wrong with her?"

Malcolm held the gun and cut his eyes toward Beulah Two, then back to the stranger. "Beulah Two, back in the house," he said.

Truitt peeled his Jeep into the driveway just yards from the Chrysler and opened the door. His own shotgun in hand, he raised it with authority toward the men. Kate bailed from the passenger's side and ran up the porch steps past the three strangers. She threw open the screen door, grabbed Beulah Two, and hurried her into the house.

The men near the car were shuffling from foot to foot. One of them stepped forward and gestured toward the leader. "Hey, man—"

"You, shut up!" The man cursed and silenced him before turning his attention toward Truitt. "What is this?" he asked with a nervous laugh. "I got a senior citizen and now a pretty white boy pointin' a gun at me?"

Truitt smiled and motioned with the shotgun. "Nice grill, Flavor Flav."

The man chuckled again but was not amused. "All right. We're leavin'."

The other two men opened their car doors while the leader squared his shoulders and bowed his back toward Malcolm. "If she's here, we'll find her."

"I told you," Malcolm said. "She doesn't live here."

"And I told you I know you're lyin'." Anger boiled behind the stranger's dark eyes as he glared at Malcolm. Finally he turned and joined his friends in the car. They sped down the driveway, leaving a heavy dust cloud in the air behind them.

Malcolm and Beulah lowered their guns. Truitt threw the shotgun over his shoulder and joined them on the porch. "Can anybody here tell me what the heck is goin' on?"

Malcolm turned and walked into the house. "No. But I'm about to find out."

Inside, Kate sat on the floor behind the couch, holding Jane Ellen and Beulah Two in her arms. Malcolm found Esther cowering under the kitchen table. With one fluid motion, he grabbed her by the arm and dragged her out as she squealed. He stood her up with her back against the counter. Her body quaked and was covered in a sheen of sweat.

Adrenaline and anger surged through Malcolm. He tilted her chin and forced her eyes to meet his own. "Start talking."

Chapter Twelve

Honesty is the best policy.

Beulah sat just outside the bedroom door, nodding off to sleep. For hours she'd strained to hear the conversation within, but her hearing wasn't as good as it used to be. Twice she'd stood to enter the room but withdrew again to the chair on both occasions. Malcolm had been firm in his warning. Under no circumstances was anyone to open the door.

The clock on the wall struck 11 p.m. Kate lifted her head from the arm of the couch, surprised she'd nodded off. Jane Ellen cuddled next to her while Beulah Two lay curled up across from them in Beulah's old recliner, both girls fast asleep. Kate slipped Jane Ellen's head from atop her leg and rose from the couch.

Beulah finally drifted off, and Kate paused to gently push her head off her chest and back against the wall to a more comfortable position. Beulah snorted and sniffed, and her head fell forward again. Kate sighed and stepped over to the bedroom door. She pressed her ear firmly against the wood but heard nothing except Beulah's thunderous snores.

Two hours had passed since Malcolm had sequestered Esther inside. Kate's frustration swelled. She reached for the knob when voices on the porch caught her attention. She withdrew from the door and peeked through the front window. Standing in the dark were Aunt Mo and Truitt, talking with a man in a black uniform and a shiny gold badge. Kate recognized him as

Clinton Davis, a longtime family friend and the county sheriff for as long as she could remember. Kate glanced toward the bedroom door one last time before joining the group on the porch.

Sheriff Davis looked up as the door opened and tipped his hat to Kate as any good sheriff would. "Good evening, Kate."

"Hello, Sheriff Davis."

"I was just saying goodbye. You good folks need to get some sleep. It's probably close to midnight by now."

Mo removed the afghan from her shoulders and wrapped it around Kate. "Thanks for comin' out, Clinton. We sure appreciate it."

"Wish I could do more. It's real good to see you, Kate. Sorry it had to be under these circumstances."

The sheriff nodded to the women, shook Truitt's hand, then showed himself off the porch to his car.

"What did he mean by 'Wish I could do more?' " Kate asked. "Didn't they find them?"

"There's nothin' the cops can do," Truitt told her. "They didn't break any laws. We're the ones who pointed the guns at them. Plus I called him Flavor Flav."

"But they came here for Esther."

"Esther hasn't said a word. Malcolm's still in there with her. She's too scared to talk."

Mo put her arm around Kate's waist and hugged her. "Now don't you worry, honey. Everybody in this town knows about those boys by now, and they're mad as heck about it. Everybody's on the lookout. That includes Clinton and his boys. If they come back, it won't be two seconds before the cops know about it."

The door behind them opened again and Malcolm stepped out onto the porch. He glanced at the others only a moment before turning his attention directly to Kate. "I think you and Jane Ellen should stay with Mo for a few days."

"You don't think they'll be back, do you?" Aunt Mo asked.

"I don't know, but it's too secluded out here. We're a good fifteen minutes from town with no other houses anywhere close. I'll be staying here with Ms. Beulah 'til this all dies down."

"Did Esther tell you anything?" Truitt asked.

"No, but she will." He looked to Kate again. "It'd be a good idea to keep yourself and Jane Ellen away from here for a while."

Kate nodded.

"Don't forget the story," Malcolm said. "Those boys came all the way from Memphis looking for Esther, but no one has seen or heard from her in years. Not even Ms. Beulah."

"And we're sure no one saw her comin' into town?" Mo asked.

"Pretty sure. And she hasn't been anywhere since. Except for us and Rosa, and now the sheriff, no one else knows she's back."

Mo took a step forward and hugged him around the neck with both arms. "Thank you, Malcolm."

Malcolm went rigid in her embrace.

"I'll go get Jane E." Truitt entered the house, and Mo followed. Kate started in when Malcolm took her by the arm.

"Rosa knows more."

"She says she's told us everything."

"And do you believe her?"

Kate examined his weary, bloodshot eyes. Though his face

reflected a courageous resolve, she recognized the fear and frustration beneath. Malcolm looked down at his hand still wrapped around her arm and let go.

Kate finally shook her head. "No. I don't believe her."

***

Kate tossed and turned all night and awoke early the next morning to the smell of Aunt Mo's pancakes. Mo's guest bed was comfortable, but Kate missed her house and the small mattress on the floor in her own room. Not a day had passed that Rosa hadn't asked when Kate would be purchasing a new bed. But Kate didn't mind the floor, and bed hunting was far from her highest priority.

Her stomach churned at the thought of food so early in the morning, and she covered her face with the thick blanket to shield her nose from the pancake smell. Soon, memories of the night before met her in the darkness beneath the blanket. The faces of the three strangers. Beulah holding a gun as able and courageous as a soldier going into battle. Esther shivering under the table, paralyzed in fear, her eyes glazed and lifeless as though she were already a corpse. Beulah Two, held in Kate's arms there on the floor behind Beulah's couch. But she hadn't trembled as Jane Ellen had. No tears had fallen from her eyes. She'd been strangely unmoved, relaxed even. And Malcolm—Kate's hero and adversary. She rubbed the crease on her forehead, then instead of considering it a moment longer, she drifted to sleep again.

***

Esther stood in a blue bathrobe beside her open bedroom window and smoked a Marlboro Red as Beulah Two walked in.

"Hey there, baby. Early for you to be up."

Beulah Two closed the door behind her and took a seat on the bed. Esther held the cigarette in her trembling hand and closed her lips around it, deeply inhaling then releasing the smoke toward the window.

"Grandma and Pastor Malcolm say I can't go outside for a while, so I have to smoke in here. I'm trying to quit, though." Esther pointed to a white patch on her upper arm.

Beulah Two looked down at her lap and played with her hands. "That man that was here . . . the one who talked to me. He's a bad man."

Esther extinguished the cigarette on a small saucer that was substituting as an ashtray. "Yes, honey. I think he is."

"He did somethin' bad?"

Esther sat down on the bed next to her. "I've been trying hard to do the right thing by you, Beulah Two. I know I made lots of mistakes. But for a long time now, I've been trying to do good. Trying really hard. It just seems like trouble always finds me."

Beulah Two wrapped her arms around her mother's waist and hugged her tight. Tears streamed down Esther's cheeks, and she smoothed the little girl's hair with her hands.

"I keep wondering how somebody as messed up as I was could make something as perfect as you. And you know what?" She turned Beulah Two's chin up to hers. "It doesn't have a thing to do with me. You're straight from Heaven, Beulah Two.

Not because of your mama. But in spite of me."

***

Aunt Mo shook Kate until she surfaced from beneath the blanket. "My word! I thought you'd smothered yourself. Scared me half to death!"

Kate rubbed her eyes and sat up. "I must have fallen back asleep. What time is it?"

"It's 9 a.m., honey, and Malcolm's here wantin' to talk to you."

Kate jumped from the bed and disappeared into the bathroom. After a few minutes she descended the stairs in her pajama pants and a Razorback sweatshirt she'd stolen from Truitt days before. Malcolm sat alone at the kitchen table with a glass of orange juice while Mo talked on the telephone in the living room. Kate paused on the last step, and Malcolm turned and looked at her then stood.

"I didn't mean for Mo to wake you."

Kate pulled her hair into a ponytail as she entered the kitchen. "It's fine. Did you find out something?"

"She's still not talking. That's why I'm here. I think whatever it is Esther's not telling me, she told Rosa. I need you to find out what she knows."

Kate shook her head. "Rosa's been so upset since yesterday. She hasn't even come out of her room."

"Well, when she does, do what you can. I have a feeling this isn't over." Malcolm took one last sip of juice. He walked toward the door but turned back in the doorway. "I should've told you before. I'm sorry about . . . the baby."

Kate looked up. His face was tender, honest. "Thank you," she said.

He nodded and walked out.

***

Kate walked up the sidewalk toward Boyd's office and saw him peering through the window and straightening the collar of his shirt.

"Good mornin'!" he said when she entered. "I was hopin' you'd make it in today."

She sat down in front of his desk and rested her purse on her lap. "Well? Do you have that information I need?"

Boyd leaned back in his tall leather chair and picked up a thick folder. "I do. And I think you'll be pleased. More than pleased." A huge smile spread across his chubby face. "You're set, Kate. I don't know about this husband of yours. I can't understand what kinda man would do what he did to you. But he's either consumed with guilt over it or else he's the most generous man on Earth. What they're proposin' here is unheard of."

"What do you mean?"

Boyd lay the folder down on his messy desktop, turned it around to face Kate, and pushed it toward her, pointing to a highlighted number. Kate's eyes widened, and she looked back to Boyd.

His toothy smile was even wider than before. "See what I mean?"

***

Truitt took a bite of his turkey sandwich and looked over Kate's papers, strewn across the table at Susie's Café. "This is what Gray's gonna be sendin' you per month?"

Kate picked up a french fry. "That's just for Jane Ellen." She pointed to a number listed farther down the page. "That's a one-time payment made to me once the house sells. Plus he's giving me the Range Rover. And Rosa gets to stay with me."

"Wow. Guess those mass torte cases have been workin' out for him, huh?" Truitt continued to chew. "Are you sure that's not a typo?"

"I don't think these guys make typos. I'm still going to look for a job around here. Jane Ellen will be starting school after Christmas, and I'll be needing something to do."

"And what did Gray say about Jane Ellen?"

"I have full custody. He doesn't want to see her, Truitt. There's no mention of visitation, and I'm sure that wasn't an oversight."

Truitt handed the papers back to her. "No. These boys seem pretty thorough."

Susie approached their table with the same tired look as always. "Any dessert for you kids?"

"How about some blackberry cobbler?" Truitt asked with a flirtatious smile.

"Sorry, Truitt. Nate Bell just took off with the last of it."

"Apple cobbler?"

"Comin' right up." Susie disappeared behind the counter.

"With ice cream!" Truitt called.

"Nate Bell?" Kate asked. "That name sounds familiar."

"It should," Truitt said. "He's been around here forever. His wife, Evelyn, used to help out the twins with their greenhouse and gardens before Ms. Beulah. She died a few years ago. Ever since, Aunt Mo's tried to take care of him. He's pretty resistant to folks, though. The only person I've ever seen him talk to is Malcolm, and that's because Malcolm uses the old garage behind his house as a wood shop."

"What does Malcolm need with a wood shop?" Kate asked.

"Well, Malcolm makes furniture. The best in the state if you ask me. He made all the pieces that are in your house. Aunt Ruth had him busy for months. Didn't you know?"

Kate shook her head. "I had no idea."

"Anyway, after Evelyn died, Nate went all bitter. His health started goin' downhill. Malcolm and Mo used to try to get through to him. That is until Malcolm's wife died. Then Malcolm stopped goin' by to see him, and Nate stopped goin' to Malcolm's church. Now he goes to Millsville Grace. I hear Pastor Mackey goes by to see him quite a bit but spends more time talkin' him out of his money than talkin' about God."

Susie returned with the hot cobbler and set it in front of Truitt. He thanked her and sank his fork into a steaming chunk of apple. Kate looked out the window and caught a glimpse of an old man crossing the street holding a small foam container.

Truitt followed her eyes outside. "There goes my blackberry cobbler."

***

Aunt Modean shut the lid to the washing machine with a bang and breathed a tired sigh. Her mind was troubled with thoughts of the strangers, not to mention her constant concern for Kate and Jane Ellen after losing Ruth and Gray, and a baby. She could hear Jane Ellen upstairs playing with her dolls and smiled at the music of the little girl's laughter.

Mo closed the door to the small washroom and headed toward the kitchen. As she passed by the bathroom she heard a muffled sobbing from within. She paused and pressed her ear against the door. "Rosa?" she called. "Rosa, is that you?"

"I'm fine, Ms. Modean," came Rosa's reply, followed by more sobs.

Modean turned the knob and slowly opened the door. Rosa sat on the floor near the sink. Her eyes were red and swollen, and she held a large bundle of toilet paper in her hands.

"Rosa! What on Earth is the matter with you?" Modean hurried to her side, and Rosa wept all the harder. "Now, calm down, honey." Mo put her arms around her and patted her back. "You just tell me what's troublin' you."

Rosa wiped her nose with the toilet paper and looked up at Mo, colossal tears streaming down her face. "I put Ms. Kate and Jane Ellen in danger. It was my fault."

"Now, you know better than that. Those boys came outta nowhere. You couldn't have known. It's not your fault."

"But it is. I never should have let Ms. Kate send Jane Ellen to that house."

"You can't blame yourself. You couldn't have known."

Rosa stopped her crying and grabbed Modean's hands. "But I did, Ms. Mo. I did know."

***

Nate Bell's home sat on a corner surrounded by a wire fence that at one time had been considered decorative but had ended up rusted and broken down by weather and time. Kate followed Truitt's directions and pulled into the driveway. Sure enough, behind the charming, yet aged, little brick house stood a small garage-like structure. Kate looked around but didn't see Malcolm's truck. Smoke drifted from the top of the garage, signaling someone was inside. Kate parked the Range Rover in the driveway and headed toward the door.

She knocked once, and the unlatched door opened on its own. She walked inside and stopped short. Surrounding her was piece after piece of handcrafted furniture. Tables, hutches, bedroom furnishings, desks, dressers, chests—all made from hardwoods like cherry, oak, and maple, and all unique and beautifully crafted. Kate ran her hand across an intricate carved pattern adorning the side of a tall china cabinet and noticed a couch across the room that almost matched the one in her own living room.

A crashing noise echoed throughout the space, and Kate jerked and took a step back toward the door. She waited and heard more bustling. "Hello?" she called. "Mr. Bell?"

She took a few cautious steps toward the noise when Malcolm stood up from behind an unfinished shelf. Both jumped at the sight of the other, and Malcolm pulled the earpieces from his ears.

"I didn't mean to startle you," Kate said.

Malcolm glared at her, the graciousness from the morning replaced by his characteristic look of irritation. Though it was a look Kate recognized, it surprised her, and she frowned.

"Did you talk to Rosa?" he asked.

"Not yet. I've been running errands in town. I actually stopped by because I'm looking for a bed for my house, and I thought since Mama had you make some other pieces for her, you might possibly . . ."

Malcolm dropped the sander from his hand and walked across the room to a tall sleigh bed made from oak and finished in a dark cherry stain. He plucked off a small yellow tag taped to the headboard and brought it over to her. Kate took it and read it aloud. "Sold. Ruth Boudrow."

"I just haven't had a chance to deliver it yet. It's paid for."

Kate looked down at the tag again then back to him.

"Unless you don't like it."

Kate shook her head. "It's perfect."

"I can bring it out this afternoon on my way to Ms. Beulah's. Unless you've moved it I know where the spare key's hidden."

"I didn't know there was a spare key."

"Third rock to the right of the first rose bush."

Kate nodded. "Yeah, that would be great."

Malcolm's cell phone vibrated on the small table where he was working. Kate took the cue as time to leave and walked back toward the door, examining Malcolm's handiwork to her left and right. Had she not seen it for herself, she'd have never believed him capable of creating such beautiful things.

At the entrance to the shop, she reached for the door when Malcolm stepped up behind her. "Let's go," he said. "That was Modean. Rosa's ready to talk."

Chapter Thirteen

> *Truth is like the sun. You can shut it out*
> *for a time, but it ain't goin' away.*
> *-Elvis Presley*

Kate, Malcolm, and Esther sat in silence in Beulah's living room, Malcolm in the recliner, and Esther and Kate on the couch. Every so often Esther glanced to the floor or out the window, but Malcolm never took his eyes off her. She squirmed under his stare and crossed her arms. Then she settled deeper into the soft cushions of the couch and wished they would swallow her up.

Her grandmother appeared from the kitchen with a cup of hot coffee and set it on the table in front of Malcolm then stepped back and scanned the room. She looked from Malcolm to Esther, then back to Malcolm again before retreating into the kitchen.

The squeaking of the porch's screen door filled the room, and Modean entered with Rosa close behind. Esther sat up, and her eyes widened, watery and pleading, frozen on Rosa. Rosa's cheeks and nose were red, and she wiped at them clumsily before letting go of Modean's arm and joining Esther on the couch.

Rosa's lip quivered. A tear escaped down Esther's cheek and fell into her lap, and Rosa took Esther's trembling hand and held it tight. "You must tell them," Rosa said.

"Have you—"

"No," Rosa assured her. "That is for you."

"But you promised."

"That was before the men came. You think not talking is protecting your family, but you are wrong. You must tell Pastor Malcolm what you told me."

Esther swallowed hard and fought the urge to run. Her secret was still safe, but it was only a short reprieve. She closed her eyes and tried to remember why she had confided in Rosa in the first place. It had been a moment of weakness. Her secret had been eating her alive, and Rosa had looked at her with soft eyes and a willingness to listen. Though they had only just met, the words had spilled from Esther's mouth like water from a faucet. Esther rubbed her temples and wondered how she could have been so stupid.

Rosa stood and looked down at her with compassion but spoke direct and firm. "If you do not tell him now, I will." She turned and left the room, joining Beulah and Modean at the kitchen table, leaving Esther alone with Kate and Malcolm.

Esther exhaled and leaned her head back onto the couch. She took her face in her hands and wanted to cry, but she was far beyond tears. She wanted to run but knew of nowhere as safe as where she sat. Peering through her fingers, she saw Beulah sitting at the kitchen table, her eyes shut and her lips murmuring a rapid prayer. Esther focused on the old woman's hands clasped together on the table, her knuckles white as she clenched her fingers together.

"We want to help you, Esther," Kate said. "Let us help you."

Esther removed her hands from her face and sat up again. She turned toward Malcolm, who stared into her with blazing dark eyes that demanded answers and would accept nothing less than the truth.

"I think somebody wants to kill me." The words left Esther's lips before she could stop them.

Beulah ceased her prayer and looked up.

Malcolm crinkled his brow. "Why would someone want to kill you?"

Esther's eyes filled with tears. "I don't know."

Malcolm shot to his feet and lunged toward her. He grabbed her by the shoulders and shook her. "Look around this room! Every person in here could be in danger because of you. You almost got your own daughter and grandmother killed yesterday. Don't you dare give me 'I don't know!' I'll kill you myself before I let any of these people get hurt because of you!"

Tears poured from her eyes, and her bottom lip trembled along with her hands and legs. She gazed up at him, afraid but resolute. Beulah held her breath. Rosa reached across the table and took the old woman's hand while Modean looked away.

"I know you don't have a reason to trust me," Esther said between sobs. "But I swear to you, Malcolm! I don't know!"

Malcolm studied her face then released her and made his way back to the chair. "Start at the beginning and tell me everything."

***

After a long cigarette break in the front yard that did nothing to calm her nerves, Esther sat down on her grandmother's couch. She stared at the floor and bit at the inside of her cheek until she tasted blood. Someone put a glass of cold water in her hand, and she looked up as Kate touched her shoulder and smiled reassuringly.

"Take your time," Kate said then sat beside her.

Esther nodded and almost smiled back when she spotted Malcolm in the recliner, his eyes narrowed and his gaze more piercing than before. Her grandmother sat to his right in a wooden chair she'd pulled in from the kitchen, and Modean and Rosa were at the kitchen table. Esther lowered her head again and noticed the wet spot on the carpet below.

Kate took the glass of water from Esther's trembling hands and set it on the coffee table in front of them. Malcolm leaned forward, his hands clasped together and his elbows resting on his knees.

"All right. Let's hear it."

Esther wiped her hands on her jeans. Her heart pounded, and her stomach ached. She opened her mouth but the words refused to form. Tears pooled in her eyes and panic mounted with each breath, and she had to dig her fingers into her thighs to keep from bolting from the room. She heard the creaking of her grandmother's chair as Beulah pushed to her feet and hobbled toward her. Kate stood and relinquished her seat then helped the old woman down to the cushions of the old couch next to Esther.

Beulah heaved a sigh and took Esther's hand. "Look at me, girl. We all got a past full of ol' junk we wish we didn't have. We all done bad things. You ain't the first one. But as soon as you walked in that door right there a few days ago, I knew you'd changed. You ain't the same Esther from before. So whatever all that junk is you keep tryin' so hard to hide, it ain't as bad as you think cuz it did somethin' to you. Somethin' good. My mama, your great-grandmama, used to say, 'Life's like a big ol' wind. It strips us down to the stuff that's too strong to be blown away so we can see who we really are . . . the true us.' This is who you are, honey. This is the true you. Now I'm gonna sit right here beside you cuz no matter where you been or what you done, you're mine. And I'm gonna take care of what's mine."

Esther studied her grandmother's face and felt her strength build. She took a long, deep breath and squared her shoulders toward Malcolm. "All right. What do you want to know?"

"Everything," Malcolm said.

Esther swallowed. "About four years ago I was in trouble in Memphis."

"What kind of trouble?" Malcolm asked.

"I got myself arrested, and not just once. Mostly for drugs." She glanced at Beulah. "Once for prostitution. I spent some time in prison . . . almost three months. Once I got out, they gave me a hundred hours of community service. My parole officer told me they were looking for volunteers at St. Luke's, a church downtown that runs a food bank and soup kitchen on Monday and Wednesday nights. And that's where I met Father Francis."

"Who's he?" Malcolm asked.

Tears stung Esther's eyes, and she blinked them away. "Father Francis Martin. He was the priest at St. Luke's. He knew what I'd done . . . the kind of person I was. But he treated me like I mattered. And for the first time in forever, I started thinking that I might."

Esther squeezed her eyes shut and rubbed at her forehead. "After I finished my community service, I kept volunteering at St. Luke's. Father Francis helped me get my GED, and I enrolled in classes at the junior college. I got an apartment with a couple of girls I met at the church, Olivia and Beth. They were good girls, and they liked me . . . something I wasn't used to." She laughed. "I was working at the zoo, thanks to Father Francis calling in a favor to a friend. I'd been clean for almost two years and even spoke a few times in a recovery group at the church. I was finally doing things right, you know? Finally being someone I could be proud of." She leaned over and rested her head against Beulah's. "Someone Grandma could be proud of."

Malcolm sighed. "That's great, Esther, but what we need to know is why those men came here for you."

"You said you wanted to know everything," Esther said. "I'm telling you everything."

Malcolm nodded, waiting.

"A few days ago," Esther said, "I was working at the Monday night soup kitchen at St. Luke's. It was a cold night, and more people than usual showed up. We ran out of food and had to turn a bunch of them away. I volunteered to lock up for the night, and after everybody left, I went to lock the sanctuary and found Father Francis talking to a man. I figured he was one of the people who hadn't gotten any food because he seemed real upset, but they were in the front row and I was in the back by the door and couldn't understand what they were saying. Then Father Francis noticed me and walked back to where I was to say good night. I asked who the man was, and he told me he'd come to church for prayer and confession. I looked up to the front of the church, and the man was looking back at us, watching. I'd never seen him before, and I can't explain it, but there was something about him that made me nervous. I told Father Francis I wanted to stay until they were done, but he insisted I go. I didn't want to leave Father Francis alone with him. But I did."

She wrung her hands together. "My apartment was close, but I didn't have a car and had to walk. Father Francis always worried about me walking in the cold. He led me to the door and took off his jacket and put it around me." Esther pointed to a brown leather jacket hanging on a hook beside Beulah's front door. "That jacket there."

Esther reached for the glass, her hand shaking harder than before, and took a long sip of water.

"I started home, the whole time thinking I should've stayed. I even almost went back, but it was so cold, and I just wanted to get home. I don't know how far I'd gone, maybe a hundred feet, when I heard gunshots. Three, one after the other. And I knew. I just . . ." Her chin trembled. "I ran back toward the church and saw two men pulling another man into a car in the parking lot. It looked like the guy who'd been talking with Father Francis, but it was so dark. He was trying to fight, but they threw him in the backseat of the car and sped off right past me. I ran inside the church, and there he was." She sniffed and shook her head.

"Who?" Malcolm asked. "There *who* was?"

"Father Francis," she said. "He was on the floor, on his back in the center aisle." Tears spilled down her face. "He'd been shot. There was blood everywhere. I've never seen so much blood."

Beulah took the water glass out of Esther's hand and set it on the table. Then she wrapped both her hands around Esther's and held them tight.

Malcolm's eyes widened. "Who shot him?"

Esther wiped at her cheeks and shrugged. "I don't know. I told the police about the man in the church and the men in the car. I was at the station for hours, and by the time I got home it was nearly morning. My roommates were out of town, but when I went to put my key in the door, I saw someone moving inside the apartment and Beth's little dog was barking. I thought maybe one of them had come home early, and I was about to go in when a man—" She swallowed hard and shivered. "First he wasn't there . . . and then he was. Standing right beside me."

"The man from the church?" Beulah asked.

"No," Esther said. "This man was young. Handsome. He put his hand on my wrist and stopped me from turning the key. Then he just looked at me like he knew me. Like he knew what had happened."

"Did he say anything?" Malcolm asked.

"He said . . ." Esther closed her eyes and recalled the voice she'd never forget. "Run. He told me to run."

"And you did what he told you?" Malcolm asked. "You didn't know him, but he said 'run' and you took off?"

"Yes," Esther said firmly. "I caught a taxi to Beale. There'd been a concert at the Pyramid, and I figured Beale was as good a place as any to disappear into a crowd. I'd only been there an hour or so when I felt something buzzing in the pocket of Father Francis's jacket. It was a cell phone, and it was ringing. I don't know why I did, but I answered it. Nobody said anything at first, then somebody . . . a man . . . he said my name."

"Wait," Malcolm said, "Whose phone was it? The priest's?"

"I don't think so," Esther said. "He always kept his phone in his front pants pocket. I'd never seen this one before."

"Then whose was it?" Malcolm asked. "And how did the man who called know your name?"

Esther shrugged. "That's what I don't know. The man asked

where I was, but I was so scared I didn't say a word. Then I heard some rustling and another man must've taken the phone from him. He said he was a detective and I might be in danger. He said he needed to come get me right away and asked where he could pick me up. I didn't know what to believe, I was so scared. And then . . . I heard Beth's dog barking. They were in my apartment."

Beulah gasped. "Oh Lord."

"I tossed the phone in an alley and hid in the back of one of the bars. I overheard a guy at the table next to me talking about his long drive back home to Oklahoma. He was nice, and we talked for a while. I convinced him to give me a ride, and he took me as far as Fort Smith and even gave me money for a motel and bus fare. The next morning I took the bus to Millsville, then caught a ride from an old man to Grandma's."

Malcolm leaned back in the recliner. "This doesn't add up, Esther. Who were the men in your apartment and what did they want from you?"

Esther shook her head. "I don't know. I called my roommates from the motel, and they said when they got home the next morning the place had been torn apart. Like someone had been looking for something, but nothing was missing." She swallowed. "Except the dog."

Malcolm closed his eyes and rubbed his forehead. "Okay. Assuming the men in your apartment were the same men who saw you leaving the church, how could they've known where you lived?"

"I'm not sure. A big crowd showed up at St. Luke's after the police got there. Some people were just curious about all the commotion, but most were folks from the community. They knew Father Francis. And me. If someone wanted to know where I lived, almost anybody there could've told them."

Malcolm jumped to his feet and grabbed the back of his head with his hand. "C'mon, Esther! What were they looking for? What'd they want? You've got to know!"

Esther shook her head. "I don't. I swear I don't."

"Why didn't you just go to the police?" Malcolm asked.

"Do you think they care about what happens to me? Or that they'd have believed a word I had to say, with my record?"

"Then that's it? You're telling me that's all you know?"

"That's it, I swear," Esther said. "Malcolm, you've got to believe I'd never have come back here if I thought anyone would come looking for me. I'd never put Beulah Two or anyone else in danger."

Malcolm kicked at the coffee table, and the glass of water tumbled onto its side. "But they did. They did come looking for you. And God knows what would've happened if I hadn't been here!"

Esther sobbed and nodded. Beulah pulled her closer until Esther's wet cheek rested on her shoulder.

"All right, Malcolm," Beulah said. "That's enough."

***

Beulah Two and Jane Ellen had spent most of the day playing in Modean's backyard and had nearly completed building their lawn chair fort when Truitt announced it was time to take Beulah Two back to her grandma's.

From the moment she walked inside her grandma's house, Beulah Two had sensed something bad—something heavy in every room. Though her grandma assured her everything was fine, Beulah Two hadn't been able to shake off the feeling that it wasn't, and she'd wondered what had happened there while she'd been out playing.

Hours had passed since her grandma had tucked her into bed, but Beulah Two hadn't stayed there long. Instead she leaned on the wall next to her window, staring up at the dark sky, bursting with more stars than she'd ever seen. She raised her hand toward the window and pressed her palm against the cold glass. Then she closed her eyes and imagined herself up there with the glimmering stars, far above her grandma's house and the trees—above everything. That familiar longing to leave the ground wrapped itself around her heart, and she leaned her cheek against the glass.

The floor creaked outside her door, and she lunged back into bed. She buried herself beneath her quilt and squeezed her eyelids together as tight as they'd go. The knob turned and the door opened, and Beulah Two froze, listening to her mother's steady breathing from the doorway. Then the door closed again, and her mother was gone.

Beulah Two opened her eyes and threw back the quilt. The stars were calling to her again.

***

At 11:30 p.m., after hours of tossing and turning in Modean's guest bed, Kate gave up on sleep. Thoughts of Esther and the priest and the men in Beulah's yard ran on a loop through her mind and stole her rest.

A gentle knock fell on her door, and she jerked upright and

yanked the quilt up around her chin. The door creaked open, and Truitt stuck his head inside. "Kate?"

"Truitt! You almost gave me a heart attack."

"Sorry," he said. "Malcolm's outside. He wants to talk to you."

Kate's eyes widened, but she pulled a robe over her T-shirt and shorts and met Malcolm on the front porch in the bitter cold night.

"Sorry to come so late," he said.

"It's okay. I couldn't sleep either."

Malcolm stuffed his hands deep into the pockets of his coat. "Look, as long as Esther's here, Ms. Beulah and Beulah Two are in danger, not to mention anyone in that house. I called the sheriff and told him all about what Esther said tonight, but his hands are tied until something actually happens, and by then it may be too late. So I've been thinking." He exhaled, his warm breath like smoke in the frigid air. "How well do you know your sister-in-law, Delta?"

"Delta Canton?" Kate crinkled her forehead. "I don't really know her at all. We only met once or twice. She came to the wedding, and I think we saw her once on Thanksgiving. Gray always said she wasn't much for family events. Why?"

"Go get dressed," he said. "You two are about to get reacquainted."

Chapter Fourteen

Big wheel keep on turnin'.
Proud Mary keep on burnin'.
Rollin', rollin', rollin' on the river.
-John Fogerty

While Levi and Margie Canton spent the weekend in Branson, Missouri, their oldest child, Delta, packed the last of her belongings from their house in Millsville and prepared for her return home to Houston. Her visit had already lasted longer than she'd planned and, though Millsville and the accommodations of her parents' home were far from the luxurious life she knew in Houston, the company of her parents and the welcoming nature of the townsfolk comforted Delta's ever-lonely spirit.

A week had turned to two, then three, and then Margie had begun making plans for a Christmas with her daughter at home—an event that hadn't occurred since before Delta left Millsville with her first husband at age seventeen, nearly thirty-five years earlier. Delta simply hadn't had the heart to decline her mother's invitation. Or the courage. Instead, she'd decided to sneak away while her parents took in the bluegrass shows of Branson. Her note was written. Her bags were packed. Her plane would leave at 6:45 the next morning.

It was late, but Delta couldn't sleep. She'd just settled onto the front porch swing with a cigarette dangling from her long fingers, tipped with shiny red nails. She was wrapped in an ankle-length fur, and while she hadn't left the house all day, nor had even the intention to, her hair and makeup were done to perfection.

At fifty-one, Delta Canton looked her age, or maybe older, even though her second husband had prompted and paid for several plastic surgeries—two she admitted to, one she vehemently denied. Still, she was an attractive woman and working on husband number three, a wealthy real estate agent in Houston. He'd insisted she come home for Christmas, because he had a surprise for her. Delta hoped it came with a question and at least five karats.

The lights of the SUV blinded her at first, and she stood with her hand blocking her eyes from the beams. Malcolm climbed out of the vehicle first.

"Hey, Delta."

Delta snuffed out her cigarette on the porch railing and descended the steps with a beaming smile. "Malcolm Bauer!" She put her hands on his shoulders and held them firmly.

"I heard you were in town," Malcolm said.

"I heard you were, too. Can't say I'm surprised you're still hanging around this place." Delta noticed her other guest and squinted. "Kate?"

Kate walked around the Range Rover and extended her hand. "Hello, Delta. It's been a long time."

Delta ignored Kate's hand and threw her arms around her in an abrupt hug. "I'm so sorry about that brother of mine, honey." She pulled away but held tight to Kate's arms. "That's not how my mama raised him. He surprised all of us with what he did. And we all know it takes a helluva lot to surprise me!"

Malcolm cleared his throat. "Delta, I'm sorry to just show up like this, but we need to talk to you."

"Sounds serious," Delta said.

A gust of wind whipped passed them, sending a shiver up

166

Kate's spine. She shot a quick, anxious glance at Malcolm, who didn't notice. But Delta did.

"Well, come on. It's freezin' out here." Still gripping Kate's arm, Delta led them toward the house. "I'll make us some coffee, and we can talk. Good Lord. If I'd have known I was gonna have company, I woulda got myself all dolled up."

***

Three hours later, Kate rocked on the front porch swing, wrapped in a quilt, when Delta came outside with her cigarette.

"Malcolm's asleep," Delta told her. "Bless his heart. He looks worn smooth out."

Kate smiled and tried to shoo away memories of swinging on Margie's front porch with Gray. Delta took a seat next to her and exhaled a thick puff of smoke into the air. "He's a good man, you know?"

"Who?" Kate asked, still lost in thoughts of Gray.

"Malcolm. He's rough around the edges, but heck if he don't have a right to be. Even still, he's a good man."

"I don't mean to pry," Kate said, "but how do you two know each other?"

Delta took a long drag on her cigarette and smiled as she exhaled. "Would you believe we met in church?" She laughed. "I was stayin' with Mama and Daddy. It was right after Keith, my first husband, left me. I was a mess. Mama talked me into goin' to church with her. That was back when she went to Millsville Baptist. Now she goes to that new big church . . . somethin' Grace, I think." Delta rolled her eyes. "Anyway, I can't remember a word of Malcolm's sermon, but after it was over, and everybody left, I couldn't move. Almost like I was glued to that pew. Malcolm walked off the stage and just sat down next to me. He didn't say a word for the longest time, and I didn't either. He just sat and listened to me bawl like a baby. Afterwards he invited me to lunch with him and his wife."

"Anna?"

"They'd only been married a few months. I'll never forget. She made spaghetti and meatballs and burned the bread." She smiled. "After lunch, Malcolm and I talked at his dinin' room table for hours, him tryin' to convince me of God things, and me bein' too stubborn to believe a word of any of it. But all the same, he helped me that night more than anyone's ever helped me in my life. I had a pocket full of pills and every intention of goin' to bed and not ever wakin' up again." She sighed. "But I didn't go through with it. And it was because of Malcolm."

Kate looked out into the night. "That's not the Malcolm Bauer I know."

"Sure it is," Delta said. "He's just buried up under all his sufferin'. Almost like he laid down in a grave next to Anna. Only difference is, he can get up anytime he wants and she can't. Yes ma'am, he may be buried up, but he's still Malcolm. A man with a heart like that don't change. Can't change! We've all seen him try. But there he sits in that house, the same Malcolm all those years ago."

Kate let the words settle on her, uncertain she could ever believe them. "What happened between you and Keith?"

Delta put out her cigarette on the arm of the swing and tossed the butt into a small tin trashcan next to her. "Did Gray ever tell you that Daddy grew up in the Mississippi Delta?"

Kate shook her head.

"No? Doesn't surprise me. Gray never took an interest in family stuff like that. Anyway, they say the delta begins in the Peabody Hotel in Memphis and ends at Catfish Row in Vicksburg. It's supposed to have some of the most fertile soil in the world. Daddy's family lived near Greenville, Mississippi. Our grandpa worked for one of the county's biggest cotton farmers, so Daddy pretty much grew up in the fields. He always told me stories about how much he loved it there."

Delta's smile faded. With shaking hands she attempted to light another cigarette but was unsuccessful and shoved her hands back into her pockets. "He named me after that place," she said. "Delta. One of the richest, most fertile regions in the world."

Delta looked at Kate and forged a painful grin. "Keith left me 'cause he wanted children. And I couldn't give 'em to him."

Kate reached for her hand, but Delta quickly grabbed another cigarette and this time lit it on the first try. She inhaled it powerfully then blew the smoke high into the air. "A woman named Delta as barren as a desert. Daddy should've named me Sahara." She chuckled, a bitter sound.

"I'm so sorry, Delta."

"Now don't you feel sorry for me. My second husband certainly didn't want kids, and the next one's already got five of his own. Still payin' child support on three. Some things just aren't meant to be. Me and babies . . . Things didn't turn out like I planned, but life has a funny way about itself. And we, well, we just keep rollin' on."

Delta stood and walked to the edge of the porch, leaving Kate alone in the swing.

"What's that song?" Delta asked. She started to hum

softly, then louder, until the hums turned to words in a melody. "Rollin', rollin', rollin' on the river."

She threw back her head and startled Kate with an unexpected roar of laughter. "C'mon!" Delta nudged Kate's shoulder. "Rollin', rollin', rollin' on the river." She imitated Tina Turner's twisting hand motions as best she could and moved her hips to the silent beat.

Kate laughed, too, and couldn't help herself from joining in. She stood and danced next to Delta, singing the only words she knew. "Rollin', rollin', rollin' on the river. Rollin', rollin', rollin' on the river."

Malcolm's sudden appearance in the doorway brought Kate's impromptu performance to a sudden halt, but Delta kept swaying and humming.

"We need to go now," Malcolm said. "I need to take Kate to Mo's. Then I'll be back."

Delta nodded. Then she turned and took Kate's hand. "You will always be welcome in this family, Kate Canton. I oughta be shot for not gettin' to know you before now, but just because my brother's an idiot don't mean anything for you and me. You're my sister. You hear me? Gray was never so lucky as the day he met you. You take care of that sweet girl of yours and remember what I said. We gotta just keep rollin' on. If not for us, for the people who need us."

Malcolm turned away, looking uncomfortable, then hurried to the Range Rover.

Kate hugged Delta and then followed Malcolm off the porch. At the bottom step she turned back. "Thank you, Delta," Kate said.

Delta blew her smoke into the air then extinguished the

cigarette on the rail. "Now don't you worry 'bout Esther. She'll be fine at my place in Houston. It'll give y'all some time to sort out all this mess, and it'll give me some company. Besides, I'd probably jump off a cliff if Malcolm Bauer asked me to." Delta laughed.

Kate lowered her head. "No. I meant thank you for tonight— the way you treated me like I'm still family."

Delta propped a hand on her hip. "Well, last I checked sisters are still considered family."

Kate smiled and joined Malcolm in the car.

Chapter Fifteen

Go on, take the money and run.
-Steve Miller Band

At 8 a.m. on New Year's Eve morning, Kate stepped into Aunt Mo's guest room where Jane Ellen lay sleeping. She stood still, listening, waiting until the sounds of her daughter's steady breathing could be heard above the noises of downstairs. Kate smiled and backed out of the room, glancing briefly at the mattress on the floor where Rosa used to sleep.

She closed the door and leaned against it. It had been nearly two weeks since Rosa had boarded the plane back home to Cuba. Kate had spent days trying to change her mind, but Rosa had insisted she wanted to spend Christmas and the New Year with a sick cousin in Santa Clara. Still, Kate understood it was guilt that had sent Rosa away. She'd been unable to forgive herself for keeping Esther's secret and the consequences that had followed. As Rosa's plane had taken off, Kate had had a feeling she might never see Rosa again.

Kate's eyes were wet when Truitt found her at the top of the stairs.

"Hey!" he said. "I have a surprise for you."

"It's too early in the morning for surprises, Tru."

"Yes, but it's New Year's Eve. Rules change on holidays." He looped his arm through hers and pulled her down the stairs.

"Okay, but I need to change clothes."

"No need. Where we're goin', nobody cares what you look like."

***

Pastor Mackey Johnston hung up his cell phone with trembling hands and leaned his head back on the tall seat of his car. He cursed loudly and, in a sudden fit of rage and panic, banged his hands on the steering wheel over and over until his palms ached. A drop of sweat rolled down his nose and landed in his lap.

When the outburst subsided, Mackey studied his reflection in the rear view mirror. He pulled a handkerchief from his pocket and wiped the drops of perspiration from his forehead and cheeks. He smoothed his hair with his sweaty palm then straightened his collar and tie.

Nate Bell appeared behind the screen of his front door and waved to the pastor. Mackey waved back. He cleared his throat and checked his reflection again. One more deep, calming breath, and he opened the car door with an oversized smile. Nate grinned, looking pleased as usual to have the company.

***

Kate stood with her eyes closed outside an undisclosed location, wearing a pink hoodie and thin plaid pajama pants tucked inside tall brown boots. She promised Truitt she wouldn't peek, but that had been five minutes ago. He'd left her there, alone and freezing and having not the slightest clue where she was. As the seconds ticked by, she decided one little peek couldn't hurt, but just before she had the chance to steal a look, Truitt took her by the arm and slapped a gloved hand over her eyes.

"Cheater."

He led her inside, and warm air engulfed her. She breathed it in.

"You could have at least let me grab a coat," she said.

The sounds began from somewhere in the distance. A meow. A bark. A squawk. She tugged on his hand and opened her eyes. "Your clinic?"

"I told those guys to be quiet, but they're not much for cooperation."

"What are we doing at your clinic on New Year's Eve?"

Truitt placed his hand over her eyes again and began leading her toward the back. "I told you. It's a surprise."

Kate walked blindly and held tight to Truitt's arm, animal noises all around them, until finally he stopped and dropped his hand.

"Okay. Open your eyes."

Kate blinked at a cage containing a large, unkempt dog with big, dark eyes and a wet, black nose. She looked to Truitt, and his smile spread from ear to ear.

"Surprise!"

She furrowed her brow, and the dog whined and inched closer to the front of the cage.

"This is Lynyrd." Truitt knelt next to the dog's face. "Named after the greatest band of all time. He's got some German shepherd in him, but he's mainly mutt. Do you like the name Lynyrd? Because we threw around Van Zant for a while, too. You could shorten it to just Van. Or even Zant. I think Lynyrd sounds—"

"Truitt!"

"Okay." Truitt's tone softened. "An old guy brought him in

about a month ago. He found him down by the dump. Somebody probably got tired of him and just dropped him off. He was half-starved to death and somethin' had beaten him up pretty good—another dog or coyote. We patched him up, and here he is."

Lynyrd pressed his nose through the holes in the cage and whined again.

Kate shook her head. "He looks very sweet, but why did you bring me here?"

Truitt stuck his hand through the cage, and the dog licked it and growled playfully. "Lynyrd needs a home, Kate."

Kate turned and headed for the door, but Truitt beat her to it.

"Listen, okay? I know you're not a dog person. I know that. But it's a win-win situation for the both of you. With you and Jane Ellen leavin' Mo's and movin' back out to your house tomorrow, you need some extra protection. Lynyrd here's like a free security system. With fur."

"Esther's gone. No Esther, no need for protection."

Truitt went back to Lynyrd and rubbed his ears in silence. Guilt. Kate knew the scheme.

"Didn't you try taking him to the pound? Maybe someone would adopt him from there."

"He's been there for weeks. I told them to call me when his time was up. They called yesterday."

Kate tilted her head back and moaned. Truitt stood, and Lynyrd pawed at the cage. The dog's eyes, pitiful and pleading, fell upon Kate. He used to belong somewhere. He'd been someone's pet until they'd grown tired of him and moved on. She knew how he felt—abandoned and afraid, wondering what to do next. She knelt next to him and rubbed his wet nose.

"Will he fit in the Jeep?"

***

Malcolm sat in his truck in Nate Bell's driveway and watched as Reverend Mackey Johnston of Millsville Grace waved goodbye to Nate then backed away in his navy Cadillac. Mackey was too preoccupied with his cell phone to notice Malcolm as he passed, and Malcolm was glad he didn't have to exchange a disingenuous nod or wave. The two had met only once, and the heated encounter had ended with Mackey's vowing to call the police on Malcolm for terroristic threatening.

The Cadillac pulled onto the highway, and Malcolm wished he'd punched the man when he'd had the chance. No doubt Mackey had been reminding Nate to increase his tithe this week, as he did every week. Nate already gave much more than he should—or could—but Malcolm had decided years ago that it was none of his business. If Mackey Johnston could talk him out of his life's savings, that was Nate's problem.

Malcolm got out of his truck and knocked on Nate's door. Nate peeped out the screen and scowled then opened the door. "I called you yesterday."

"I had some things to do," Malcolm said.

"Yeah, yeah. Come on back here. My light won't come on in my refrigerator."

"You probably just need a new bulb." Malcolm stepped inside and wondered why Nate hadn't asked Mackey to fix it. He caught up with Nate in the kitchen and noted the open bleach container on the counter as the smell assaulted his nose. "What's with the bleach?"

Nate's front half was stuffed inside the refrigerator, his rear end sticking out. "Aw, I was trying to do some cleaning. Evelyn used bleach to clean everything. But the darn stuff stings my hands."

Malcolm took hold of Nate's hand and held it up to the light. It was wrinkled and spotted with age, and covered in several large, red spots. His other hand looked even worse. "Nate, these are chemical burns. You can't touch the bleach directly to your skin. You should've been wearing gloves."

"I don't remember Evelyn ever wearing gloves." He yanked his hand away.

Malcolm pulled a dishtowel from an open drawer and wet it in the sink. "Wrap this around your hands. I'll go get you some Tylenol from the medicine cabinet, and we probably need to call a doctor."

Nate held the wet towel only a moment before hurling it back into the sink. "No."

Malcolm stopped in the doorway. "These burns could be serious. Just do what I asked and wrap your hands, all right?"

"I said no." Nate stood indignant against the refrigerator.

"Nate—"

"Why do you care about these old hands? Huh?" Nate held them toward Malcolm. "You been renting that woodshed from me for years. Before that, you were my preacher. But every time I need you, you always got something more important to do. Don't you think I know how it pains you to knock on my front door?"

Malcolm stepped toward him. "Listen—"

"No, I won't listen!" Nate backed away and almost stumbled. "I won't listen to a word. Time's passed for me to listen to you. I used to want you to say the things a man of God is supposed to when life gets bad. But you didn't have nothin' to say. Reverend

Mackey—he comes to see me every week. Sometimes twice a week. He listens to me. He reads his Bible to me. Sometimes brings me stuff from Susie's."

"He's after your money, Nate," Malcolm said.

"Maybe so!" Nate's eyes filled with tears. "But he comes to see me. And I don't got to ask. He comes and he sits and he listens. And that's more than you ever done for me. So, go on now. Get outta here. And don't you worry about coming back!"

Nate nudged past Malcolm and retreated into his bedroom before slamming the door behind him. Malcolm stood alone in the kitchen, his nose burning from the bleach.

***

Beulah found Beulah Two behind the house in her husband Curtis's old fishing boat. Curtis Macon had worked for the city's highway department for twenty-five years when he'd died of a heart attack in the early '80s, leaving Beulah alone with their daughter. The boat, Curtis's prize possession, had not seen water since.

Beulah Two sat in one of the rickety seats, holding a stray cat that Beulah had been trying to shoo away for weeks. The cat screeched and bolted at the sight of her.

"Girl, it's freezin' out here." Beulah twisted a long scarf around the little girl's neck. "Come on inside, honey. Grandma just stoked the fire for you. It's nice and warm in there."

Beulah Two smiled and stared into the distance.

"You thinkin' about your mama? Now, Beulah Two, you know she's in a safe place. You'll see her again. It's not like the other times when she left."

"I wasn't thinkin' about Mama, Grandma." The little girl lifted her gaze toward the sky. "I was wonderin' about Heaven. What do you think it's like up there?"

Beulah stepped over the edge of the boat, holding tight to the side, and sat down in the cold seat across from Beulah Two. "Well, I imagine it's nice and warm to start with."

Beulah Two giggled.

"And I imagine everybody's happy and smilin' all the time, 'cause they keep seein' people they know. And after that happy homecomin's over, they turn 'round and see somebody else they know, and get happy all over again." Beulah rubbed her achy hands. "And no more pain. No, ma'am. Not one. And no bein' sad 'bout stuff we can't fix neither. We just sit up there and look around, and there's just pretty every which way you turn."

"That's what I think, too." Beulah Two said. "And when you get there, do you think you'll get to see Grandpa?"

A smile spread across Beulah's wrinkled face. "Oh yes, I will, girl. He'll probably be fishin' on a boat just like this one out on the Crystal Sea. I'll have to stand on the shore and yell at him." She cupped her hands around her mouth and pretended to see someone across the yard. "Curtis! Curtis Macon, you better put down that pole and get on over here and see me!" She laughed. "Oh, you bet I'm gonna see him, girl. I can hardly wait."

Beulah Two giggled again. "I'm sittin' in his seat, huh? You used to sit right there, and Grandpa would sit here?"

"That's right. We'd fish for hours. Catfishin' was his favorite. He sure was good at it, too. Almost as good as he was at fryin' 'em. Mm, mm, mm, that man could fry up the best catfish you ever put in your mouth!"

"And Ms. Anna?" Beulah Two asked. "We'll get to see Ms. Anna again in Heaven, right?"

"And sweet Anna. She'll be there, too."

"And then Malcolm won't be sad no more."

Beulah sighed. "I imagine not."

Beulah Two looked back to the sky with longing eyes. "I think I'd like to go there."

"I think I would, too, sweet girl." Beulah reached across the boat and grabbed the little girl's hand. "I surely would."

***

Truitt and Vaughn huddled close together on the edge of Aunt Mo's couch. Kate sat across from them on the loveseat, snuggling with a freshly washed Lynyrd the Dog. All of them, Lynrynd included, stared at the Connect Four game in the middle of the coffee table. Truitt slowly extended his hand and dropped a black checker into the grid. Vaughn moaned.

"Ha!" Kate yelled and added her red checker on top of Truitt's. "Connect four!"

Truitt fell back onto the couch in disgust. "I quit. I hate this game. And you're all a buncha cheaters."

Vaughn rubbed his shoulder. "Maybe next time, Truitt."

"Didn't you say that just before Jane Ellen beat him for the fifth time?" Kate asked.

Truitt threw a pillow at Kate's head, though it missed its target and hit the dog. Lynyrd twitched his ears and left Kate's lap for the safety beneath the kitchen table.

Vaughn yawned. "I'm not sure I can make it until midnight, guys. It's not even nine o'clock, and I'm already exhausted."

"Oh, you have to stay 'til Aunt Mo gets back," Kate said. "New Year's Eve hot chocolate is a Boudrow Family tradition."

Truitt looked at his watch. "She should be home from the twins' house any time. She went over to help them take down their Christmas lights. Another yearly tradition."

"They still do that?" Kate asked.

Truitt nodded. "The twins supervise while Mo does all the work. Then they eat homemade gingersnaps and drink spiked eggnog until Ms. Emma and Ms. Ella pass out and Mo sneaks back home."

Vaughn laughed, and Kate rolled her eyes.

Truitt set up a new game of Connect Four and smiled. "Come to think of it, maybe the three of us should head on over to *their* party."

***

Mo sat at the twins' kitchen table, eyes closed, rubbing her temples. Emma Lou sat to her left, Ella Sue to her right, and Mr. Gregory Peck purred contentedly at her feet, stinking to high heaven. The twins had been bickering for over half an hour over the critical matter of nutmeg. Or rather, the lack thereof. But the harmless banter was quickly turning into an all-out battle.

Emma argued it was Ella's yearly duty to purchase nutmeg for the eggnog. Ella, however, maintained she was merely in charge of the gingersnap ingredients, and the only spice that fell under her jurisdiction was ginger. Furthermore, nutmeg was part of the eggnog, and eggnog duty belonged solely to Emma. Mo's headed pounded.

"Sister, if you will recall, each and every year, you purchase the spices and ingredients for the cookies, while I tend to the eggnog items," Emma said.

Aunt Mo sighed. Ella sat tall in her chair and laid her hands ever so properly on the table. "Tell me, Sister, when did nutmeg cease to be an eggnog item?"

"It is a spice, and you always purchase the spices."

"I have never purchased the nutmeg."

"Yes, you have."

"No, I haven't."

"Yes, you—"

"Ladies!" Aunt Mo stood from the table and took a deep, exhaustive breath. "I have nutmeg at home. I'll just run across the street and get it. I won't be gone two minutes."

"Is it McCormick brand?" Emma asked.

"Oh yes, Modean, it must be McCormick brand. Not that no-name, cheap brand you use."

Modean grabbed the twins' car keys off a hook by the back door. "Fine. The store doesn't close 'til nine. I'll take your car and make it there in time. And when I get back, you two had best be done fussin'."

Ella and Emma had no time to object before Modean hurried to their garage and climbed into the car. Peace and quiet at last. She locked the doors just in case she'd been followed, pulled out of the driveway, and headed down the road as slowly as possible. The longer her reprieve from the twins and Mr. Gregory Peck's stench, the better. She tuned the radio to the local oldies country station. Loretta Lynn sang about the life of a coal miner's daughter, and Modean sang along.

***

Vaughn lay sleeping on the loveseat next to Lynyrd while Truitt and Kate watched Jimmy Stewart and Donna Reed dance the Charleston into a swimming pool. Kate had seen the scene at least twenty times before but laughed out loud anyway. Vaughn moaned and pulled the afghan up around her neck, and Lynryd snuggled closer to her side.

"Lightweight," Truitt said, looking at Vaughn.

Lynyrd's head snapped up. His ears perked toward the ceiling, and he let out a long, quiet growl. Vaughn bolted upright as Lynryd jumped to the floor and parked himself before the front door. The sound of footsteps resounded on the porch, followed by three firm knocks. Though Esther was gone, and all threat gone with her, caution and vigilance remained among them. Truitt walked to the door and peered out the glass.

"It's Malcolm," he announced.

Kate shivered, and her chest felt tight. She hadn't seen Malcolm in weeks. Not since the night with Delta—the night Esther went away. She'd thought of him many times, though, in particular on Christmas Day. She'd even summoned the courage to call him, but he hadn't answered. She hadn't been able to shake the image of him alone in his little shed on Christmas, his dead wife lying close by. She'd considered taking him a plate of leftovers, but Mo warned her against it. "Leave him be," Mo had told her. And so Kate had. Beulah had later said he'd dropped by her house on Christmas morning with a gift for Beulah Two but declined the invitation to stay for dinner.

Malcolm knocked again, and Truitt opened the door. He stood there in jeans, his army-green coat, and navy beanie.

Malcolm locked eyes with Kate but looked away just as quick. He pulled off his cap, leaving his hair a mess, and Truitt took a step back and motioned for him to come in.

"Sorry for not calling first," he said then turned to Vaughn. "Dr. Spencer, I know it's late, but I need your help."

Vaughn was already slipping on her shoes. "What is it?"

"Nate Bell got some pretty bad bleach burns on his hands this morning. I've been trying to call him for hours, but he won't answer his phone. He didn't want my help, but I think he'd listen to you."

Vaughn took off toward the kitchen. "Let me get my coat."

Lynyrd pressed his nose against Malcolm's leg, and Malcolm leaned down and scratched his ear.

Vaughn returned with her coat and said, "You know, I thought about Nate today when I heard about Pastor Mackey. I bet he took it pretty hard."

"Heard what?" Malcolm asked, and Kate and Truitt looked at each other, blank expressions on their faces.

"You didn't hear?" Vaughn asked. "It's all over town. Pastor Mackey's secretary couldn't get in touch with him today. She got so worried she called Sheriff Davis. They went to his church office, his house . . . Everything was gone. Apparently he was in a lot of trouble with some people over gambling debts. They think he stole a bunch of the church's money and left town."

"Oh no," Malcolm moaned. "No, no, no."

He threw open the door and ran to his truck. Vaughn followed. Truitt stopped at the door and turned back to Kate.

"I have to stay here with Jane Ellen," she said. "Go with Vaughn. Hurry."

***

Mo crept back toward the twins' home in the massive Lincoln. The white plastic sack containing the treasured nutmeg rested safely in the passenger's seat. She shook her head at the thought of the twins and couldn't wait to tell them the young lady behind the counter distinctively remembered that one of them, she knew not which, had come into the store earlier that week and purchased the same container of McCormick nutmeg, explaining that eggnog was simply not eggnog without the special ingredient. Mo laughed aloud and turned up the volume to the radio. She'd always loved Dolly Parton.

As she drove and sang, soft snowflakes began to fall on the windshield, making only a brief appearance before melting away. Mo smiled—the first flakes of winter. She almost didn't notice Nate Bell's house as she passed.

When it finally caught her eye, Mo gasped and slammed on the brakes.

Chapter Sixteen

Faith consists in believing when it is
beyond the power of reason to believe.
-Voltaire

Malcolm's headlights glared on the highway in front of him, and he turned sharply into Nate's driveway. He stomped the brakes of his pickup just before sliding into the side of Nate's house. Truitt and Vaughn braced themselves as their bodies lunged toward the dash.

Malcolm saw him first. "No. No. No." He leapt from the truck and ran through the yard as another set of headlights lit him from behind. Mo pulled the twins' Lincoln to a stop inches from the truck's bumper, and Truitt hurried to help her out of the car.

"I saw somebody up on the roof!" she shouted, near tears. "Is it Nate?"

Truitt took her by the arms. "Aunt Mo, I need you to go into the house and call 9-1-1. Tell 'em to hurry. Can you do that?" Mo nodded and scurried inside.

Truitt ran around Nate's house with Malcolm and Vaughn, and the three of them stared up in silence.

"Oh my God," Truitt said.

The snow fell fast from the sky, and Nate looked down at them. He was dressed from head to toe in a crisply ironed United States Army uniform, complete with several shiny medals on his breast that glistened in the moonlight. In his hand was a

Bible and a framed picture of his wife, Evelyn, when she was a girl, and secured around his neck was a thick, braided rope that ran several feet to the chimney and looped around it.

Nate looked toward the sky, and several flakes of snow landed on his cheeks and forehead.

"I took a bullet to the leg in Korea. Never did walk again without it hurting. I didn't get much from the government, but what I got I tried to save. When Evelyn got sick, it took nearly all I had to pay the doctors."

He lifted a shaking hand to his face and studied the mass of red blotches on his palms. "My hands hurt tonight. I couldn't write the check for Pastor Mackey, so I asked him to do it for me. He said he was needing some folks from church to donate to the youth ministry. Said there was kids needing people to sponsor them to go to camp out in Missouri. I told him I'd give two hundred dollars."

"C'mon, Nate," Malcolm said. "Come on down."

"He wrote it for fifteen thousand!" Nate's eyes were wild and scared. "He took all of it! He knew it was all I had!"

"Mr. Bell?" Vaughn took a step toward the house. "I just came by to look at those burns on your hands. Malcolm told me you might need some help."

"Oh, Malcolm told you, did he?" Nate laughed. "Malcolm don't know a thing about people needing help, not one damn thing. And he lied if he told you different! Now y'all get gone, I don't need an audience. Go, or I'll do it right here in front of you. I swear I will!" He slid the tip of his shoe closer toward the roof's edge.

"Nate!" Malcolm cried. "C'mon, Nate. I know you're hurt. I know what Mackey did, but you're gonna get your money

187

back."

"It ain't about the money! I thought he cared about me. But you were right, weren't you? Bet you came out here to say 'I told you so,' huh? Well, don't let this stop you. Go ahead and say it, you coward!"

"That's not why I came. I brought Dr. Spencer so we could help you."

"Help me?" Nate's voice trembled and cracked, and the tears steamed down his freshly shaven cheeks. "You're telling me you came here tonight to do what you ain't had the time or want-to to do in nearly two years?"

Malcolm hung his head. "Please. Just come down so we can talk."

"I don't need to talk no more," Nate said. "I thought that's what I needed. I thought I needed you to tell me God didn't forget about me. That he was still around and he was still good. I kept waiting and hoping you'd tell me that. But you didn't. I kept waiting to see if I could feel him around me, but I don't feel nothing! And now I know why. Because he ain't around me! He took her and left me here alone!"

"Nate." Malcolm pressed his lips together, ready to force the words from his mouth. "That's not true."

"It is true!" Nate took a large step forward, stopping just shy of the edge, and Vaughn buried her face in Truitt's chest. "He took my Evelyn and left me suffering in this house all by myself. There ain't no plan. Pastor Mackey was always talking about providence, whatever that means. He said nothing in life just happens by chance. But God taking Evelyn . . . there wasn't no reason. He wanted her gone, and he took her. Because he could. What kind of good God does that? He don't love me!

And he ain't here!"

Nate's body trembled. Tears and saliva dripped off his chin, and he stared down at Malcolm with turbulent, unpredictable eyes. Mo rushed around the corner from the front of the house and gasped when she saw the rope. She covered her mouth with her hand, and Vaughn put an arm around her waist and pulled her close.

"Nate, please." Malcolm stepped forward, away from the others.

"And he did the same thing to you!" Nate yelled. "Ripped Anna away from you without even blinking! Killed her, or let her be killed, and for what? I'll tell you. Because he *could.* There ain't no such thing as providence. You hear me? He ain't good! Good don't leave an old man to die alone and suffering. Good don't sit by and watch a man like you ruin himself out of grief. He ain't good. He ain't good!"

"Nate, they're gonna find Mackey, and when they do, we can put this whole mess behind us."

Nate tucked the picture of his wife under his arm and opened the Bible. His crying turned to deep sobs. "You ain't listening to me." He gripped several pages in his hand and ripped them from their binding. "I said he ain't good." He tossed the torn-up pages high into the air and tilted his tear-stained face toward the sky and wind and snow. "Did you hear me?" he screamed to Heaven in desperation, ripping the pages as fast as he could. "I said you ain't good! Damn you, God! Damn you! How could you?"

Then all went silent. Nate's mouth continued moving but made no sound. Truitt laid a hand on Malcolm's arm, and the cold wind whipped against his face, but all he could hear was

189

the steady beating of his heart. White wisps of paper fell like giant flakes of snow amid the small ones. Malcolm opened his hands and several pieces of the thin white pages landed in his palms.

He stared down at the words he'd once revered and held sacred, words he'd kept on a shelf, untouched since her death. Though the night was bitter cold, his palms felt as warm as if he held them to a flame and grew ever warmer with each tiny bit of paper that landed there.

"Do something." Truitt's grasp on his arm tightened. "I think he's about to do it."

Somewhere in the distance a siren blared, pulling Malcolm from his daze. The red glow of ambulance lights drew near, and adrenaline surged through his body. He wanted to scream. Or run. He could feel himself being pulled back toward his truck. He could see himself escaping. The ambulance would be there in seconds. He could drive away. Nate didn't need him. None of them needed him.

He wiped at his eyes and wondered how the tears got there. He needed to leave—the emergency personnel would get the crazy old man off the roof. Why was everyone looking at him?

The pages continued to flutter around him as Nate edged forward. Malcolm clenched his fists, ready to bolt, but he looked up instead.

"What if I was wrong?"

Nate stopped tearing the pages.

"What if I was so mad at him for taking Anna—" His voice broke at the sound of her name on his own lips, and he squinted away the tears. "What if all the hurt made me confused? What if I was wrong?"

"Don't you start that!" Nate yelled. "Don't you lie to me now!" He took another step toward the edge of the roof until both feet were halfway over.

"I'm not lying to you. I'm just asking you to consider that maybe you've been putting your faith in the wrong things. Me and Mackey . . . we're just men. We're gonna screw things up, and I'm not saying that gets us off the hook. We failed you, Nate, both of us, and that was wrong. But eventually even the best of men will fail you."

Nate shivered as the cold wind swept through his uniform. Malcolm wiped his eyes again.

"I think Mackey was right about providence," Malcolm said. "I think maybe there *is* a plan, like a great big map for every one of us. We start here and end somewhere up ahead. And the people we love sometimes go with us on the journey from start to finish, but sometimes they only travel with us for a while, like your Evelyn and my Anna. But until we get to the end, we just have to keep on going, even if it means we gotta do it alone."

"Don't you preach to me about keeping on going. You're not going nowhere!" Nate yelled. "You stopped a long time ago. Just sat right down where you were and stopped."

"I already told you I've failed! I haven't done much right for a long time. But this isn't about me. It's about you, and you're here for a reason. Evelyn's gone because it was her time. But time's not up for you. There's stuff left for you to do. More places to go. More people to love."

"I'm eighty-two years old," Nate said with a sob. "Nobody tries to help me. There's nobody to love me."

Mo shook her fist toward the roof. "Nate Bell, I tried to help you after Evelyn died. Lots of folks did. But you pushed me and everybody else away. It was you who turned your back on people, not the other way around."

Truitt took Mo's arm and gently pulled her back as tears streamed down her face.

The ambulance pulled in the driveway, lights flashing and sirens screaming. The doors opened and three paramedics ran toward them.

Truitt turned and held up his hands. "Hold up, guys. Wait."

"Nate?" Malcolm said. "I know it's hard to see the good in anything anymore. You wait for a miracle that never comes and wonder why God doesn't show his face when you need him the most. But sometimes you just have to trust without a miracle. That's what Evelyn did, right up to the end, and it's what she'd want you to do, too."

Nate dropped his face into his hands and sobbed. "But I can't find him."

Malcolm turned to Truitt and whispered, "Get up there."

Truitt ran around the house and came back with a ladder. He leaned it up against the gutter and made his ascent, a paramedic at his heels.

Nate raised his head and wiped at his eyes and nose with his sleeve.

"Nate, don't you get scared, okay?" Malcolm called. "You just keep looking at me. Truitt's gonna come help you get that rope off."

As Truitt gained his footing on the roof, Nate looked at him over his shoulder and his foot slipped. He swayed, his knees bending as he tipped first backward, then forward so far it looked like he might dive off headfirst. Vaughn gasped, and two paramedics lunged past Malcolm, their arms outstretched.

But Nate steadied himself, his eyes large and filled with alarm. He reached both arms out for better balance and lost his grip on Evelyn's photograph. The frame collided with the snow-covered rooftop then slid off the ledge and shattered upon impact with the frozen ground below. Nate glanced down at the shards of glass glistening with each flash of red from the ambulance.

Malcolm bent to retrieve Evelyn's picture from the demolished frame. He looked back to Nate and focused on the Bible still in his hand. Nate drew the half-destroyed book to his chest, and the words left Malcolm's lips before he could stop them.

"Faith isn't faith until it's all you're left holding on to."

Truitt stepped across the shingles and untied the rope from around the chimney. "Okay!" he shouted.

The paramedic on the roof crept to Nate's side and took him by the arm. Malcolm lowered his head and exhaled.

Mo approached him from behind and placed her hand on his back. "Malcolm?"

Malcolm looked up at her and blinked, then darted past her. He brushed by Vaughn and several other neighborhood folks who'd gathered in the yard and jumped into his truck. A police car came barreling into the driveway, narrowly missing Malcolm's truck as he made his escape onto the highway.

Chapter Seventeen

*Faithless is he that says farewell
when the road darkens.*
-J.R.R. Tolkien

Kate walked up the front steps with uncertainty. At the tall doors, she faltered and almost retreated to the safety of the Range Rover when a loud crash came from somewhere within the sanctuary. She pulled on the heavy door of Millsville Baptist and peered inside.

The stained glass window behind the platform was broken, and several hymnals lay scattered on the floor. Malcolm sat in the front row, alone, his body bent forward, his hands holding the back of his head. The podium lay on its side at the bottom of the stage, and a potted altar plant rested upside down on the carpet, soil and broken greenery all around

Kate clenched her jaw before slipping inside and up the aisle. When she was a few rows behind him, Malcolm turned, and their eyes met for only a moment before he resumed his position on the pew with his back to her again.

Kate took a seat in the row behind him. "Aunt Mo told me about what happened at Nate's." She swallowed and waited for a response that didn't come, then she closed her eyes and tilted back her head. "I don't know why I'm here."

"Neither do I."

Kate sighed. "Mo said you saved Nate's life tonight. You've been doing a lot of that lately—saving lives. First me. Then everyone at Beulah's. Now Nate."

Malcolm leaned back and stared at the empty stage. "Nate

Bell joined the army when he was eighteen," he said. "They sent him to Korea during the war and two months later they sent him home with a hole in his leg and nightmares that lasted for years. Evelyn had to wake him up and hold him like a baby almost every night until he cried himself back to sleep."

He spun to face her, his eyes red and filled with tears. "They gave him the medal of honor. The medal of honor!" he shouted. "But for two years I've done everything I could to ignore him like he was worthless. Like he was an annoyance!" Malcolm's voice shook. "If he'd died tonight, it would have been my fault. I talked him down not because I'm a hero but because I couldn't handle the guilt of his going through with it. Nate Bell was the only hero out there tonight. And he was right about me. I'm nothing but a coward."

The sanctuary was cold and still, and Kate could hear her heart pounding. "You may be a lot of things, but a coward isn't one of them. You try so hard to be invisible around here. But the truth is, people in this town need you. Just like Nate needed you tonight."

Malcolm slammed his fist down on the back of the pew, his face splotchy and the veins in his temple protruding. "The only thing Nate needed tonight was to never have known me. Maybe then he'd still have his faith, and he wouldn't have been up on that roof with a rope around his neck."

A loud boom resounded outside and filled the sanctuary, followed by another, then another. The two looked out a nearby window in time to witness the sky light up in a stunning explosions of reds, purples, and greens. Kate glanced at her watch. Midnight. The celebration of a new year had begun.

They watched in silence until the last firework vanished and the sky was peaceful once more.

"Look, I don't know what you expected to find here. But I'm tired, and I need to go home. It's already morning, and—"

"They're rejoicing." Kate smiled then bent over to pick up a Bible off a pew. She handed it to him before walking back down the aisle toward the door. With her hand on the handle, she stopped. "Psalm thirty. Green ink," she said. Then she opened the door and walked out.

***

Malcolm took a deep breath and exhaled with his eyes closed. He turned to look behind him, but Kate was already gone. He tried to recall Psalm 30, but his thoughts were clouded. He opened the Bible she'd handed him and flipped through it until he found the passage. He skimmed the chapter and shrugged then tossed the Bible back onto the pew.

"Green ink," she'd said. He rubbed his forehead then blinked and sat up straight. He jumped up and almost stumbled as he hurried from the church and out to the shed. Inside, he flipped on a lamp and found Kate's father's Bible on a shelf beside his bed. He tore it open and raced through the thin sheets before landing on Psalm 30.

His body froze as his eyes fell upon the faded green ink underlining the words.

Weeping may remain for a night, but rejoicing comes in the morning.

Chapter Eighteen

> *Millions of spiritual creatures walk*
> *the earth Unseen, both when we*
> *wake, and when we sleep.*
> *-John Milton*

As the weeks passed, Malcolm Bauer made himself invisible. He did not take his usual seat on the stage at Millsville Baptist. He did not make or sell furniture from the shop behind Nate's house. He did not show up at Susie's for a meal or visit Beulah and Beulah Two. Now and then his truck was spotted, parked in front of his shed next to the church, but only Nate Bell claimed to have caught a glimpse of him at all. Malcolm had been standing outside Nate's front door, but by the time Nate had opened it, Malcolm had been gone.

On the first Sunday in February, Kate looked around the sanctuary of Millsville Baptist as the choir members ascended the stage. A face here and there she didn't recognize made for at least ten new bodies occupying the pews.

Beulah leaned over to whisper much too loudly in her ear. "We're gettin' some of Mackey's folks from Millsville Grace, them bein' without a preacher and all. Guess they don't know we ain't got no preacher either." She chuckled.

Nina, the choir leader, wore a beaming smile, and the ancient pianist—a woman of about ninety—banged out a grand intro to "I'll Fly Away." Nina pointed to someone in the crowd and waved the person up on stage. Every head turned as a woman with white, wiry hair and thick glasses stood and made her way toward the front of the church. Kate recognized her from the choir at Millsville Grace, the same the woman she'd seen with Malcolm at the biker festival.

"Who is that, Ms. Beulah?"

"Name's Iris Glassman. She moved here last year from somewhere up north. Boston, I think. Works at the school cafeteria."

"I've seen her talking with Malcolm."

"Mackey and his bunch ran her off from Grace. Didn't think she was good enough for his highfalutin choir. When Malcolm heard 'bout how Mackey treated her, he told her she need to come sing in our choir where folks would appreciate her. Guess she finally decided to come."

Iris was already swaying and clapping, her giant earrings dancing about her face. Her presence seemed to revive the others on stage, and some tapped their feet or tilted their heads from side to side. Though the uncertainty and trepidation about Malcolm's absence weighed heavy on every heart, something was different about the first Sunday in February. And everyone sang.

***

Malcolm looked up at the sky and leaned against the back of the church building as music from the choir and the booming piano escaped through the old walls. He sensed it, too. Something different. Something that felt fresh, renewed. He closed his eyes and breathed it in.

***

That afternoon Kate settled in with a John Grisham novel next to Lynyrd on the couch—*her* couch. It had been nearly a month since she and Jane Ellen had moved out of Aunt Mo's. Kate had missed her little home by the river. She'd also developed an undeniable affection for the mutt lying next to her. She rubbed his head as she read, and Lynyrd moaned blissfully.

In the next room, Jane Ellen and Beulah Two played Barbies while jumping on the bed. But it was Sunday. A time of rest. And that's precisely what Kate intended to do, bed-jumping or no bed-jumping.

Lynyrd's ears perked up, and he raised his head off her leg with a quick jerk.

"What is it, boy?"

Lynyrd stared out the front window and let out a long, low growl. Kate put down her book and walked to the window. She scanned the yard and the road but saw nothing out of place. By the time she made it back to the couch, Lynyrd was happy again and ready for her to resume her position so he could resume his.

***

Modean and the twins finished their Sunday lunch at Susie's and glanced over the dessert menu.

"Susie dear!" Ella called. "Do you have any of that delightful bread pudding you had last week? Sister and I have not been able to stop talking about it since."

Susie wiped down a table then collected the three-dollar tip and tucked it inside her apron pocket. "Sorry, Ms. Emma. Only thing I got left is apple pie, peach cobbler, or banana puddin'."

"Oh, I'm Ella, dear."

"Sorry, Ms. Ella. One of these days I'll keep the two of you straight." Susie laughed. "Or maybe not. If I was gonna figure it out, I'd have done it long before now."

"You know you're gonna get the banana puddin', Ella," Mo said. "It's what you get every time. I don't know why we got to go through all the drama."

Emma nodded and giggled. "She's right, Sister. You do love Susie's banana pudding."

"Three banana puddins, Susie!" Modean shouted. "Oh, and I'll take the check."

"Well, isn't that lovely of you, Modean?" Emma said.

"Yes, very lovely," Ella added. "In fact, Sister and I have been talking about how pleasant you've been lately. Why, I haven't seen you so lovely since—" Ella gasped, throwing her tiny hand over her mouth.

"What?" Modean asked. "What's wrong with you? Are you havin' a heart attack or somethin'?"

Ella grabbed Emma's arm. "Sister, are you thinking what I'm thinking?"

Emma mimicked her sister's gasp, and they stared delightedly across the table at Modean. Susie brought out the puddings and placed them on the table in front of the three women.

"What?" Modean demanded.

The twins exchanged schoolgirlish glances. "You're sweet on someone," Ella said as a giggle escaped Emma's lips. Susie smiled and retreated as fast as she could from the booth.

"Good Lord! I ain't sweet on nobody! I suwannee, the older you two fools get, the crazier you get!"

The twins snuggled together on their side of the booth. In perfect harmony, they picked up their spoons and dug into their puddings with beaming smiles.

Modean rolled her eyes and grabbed her own spoon. She took a bite and yelled to Susie as she chewed, "And bring them their own dang bill!"

***

Jane Ellen and Beulah Two sneaked through the living room, but Kate pretended to be oblivious. The girls snickered and shushed one another much too loudly as they tiptoed behind the couch. After they counted to three, they sprang to their feet and yelled, "Surprise!"

Kate gasped dramatically and made her eyes as wide as they could go. But Lynryd wasn't pretending when he yelped as though he'd been shot and leapt off the couch. He scurried into the kitchen and to the safety beneath the table. The girls wailed with laughter. Jane Ellen fell onto the couch with her mother, and Kate tickled her sides as the little girl squirmed and squealed, "We got you, Mama!"

Kate looked up, and Beulah Two stood over at the front window, staring out. "Are you okay, honey?" Kate asked.

"Ms. Kate, can I go outside for a minute? I promise I won't go near the road."

"Well, sure. Just put your jacket on first."

Beulah Two pulled on her jacket as quickly as she could. "You wanna come, Jane Ellen?"

"No thank you," Jane Ellen said, skipping into the bedroom and picking up her Barbies again. Beulah Two shrugged and bounced out the door with a smile.

***

Four knocks fell on Nate Bell's front door. Since the incident on the roof, not a day had passed that someone hadn't stopped by with food or well wishes. Mainly food. Though embarrassed by the spectacle he'd caused, Nate loved the company. He smiled as he opened the door, and then his jaw fell open.

After a tense moment of silence, Malcolm held up a grocery bag. "I bought some sugar and cocoa. I doubt we can even get close to Ms. Evelyn's chocolate gravy, but I thought we could try."

Nate shook his head. "You keep me from strangling myself and now you wanna poison me?"

Malcolm smiled.

"Well, get on in here," Nate said. "We'll give it a go. Lord help us, but we'll give it a go."

***

Kate had almost drifted off to sleep with her book in her lap when she remembered Beulah Two outside. She looked to her watch. Almost 4 p.m. Beulah was making dinner for all of them and Kate had promised to be there with the girls by 4:30. She stood from the couch and glanced out the window.

And then she saw him—the familiar, handsome face. The dark-haired man from the cemetery the day of her mother's burial—the same man she'd seen at the farmers' market before he'd disappeared without a trace. He was standing next to Beulah Two beside the Range Rover, and then he looked up and met Kate's stare.

Kate couldn't move. His eyes seized her as though they had arms, reaching through the yard, into the house, and holding her where she stood. When he finally cast his gaze back to Beulah Two, Kate ran through the door and out to the yard.

In seconds she reached Beulah Two's side, and there was no one else. Just Beulah Two and Lynyrd, who'd escaped out the open door and ran in loops through the yard, sniffing at the ground. Kate scanned the road in both directions then turned in circles, searching for him. She knelt next to Beulah Two and gripped her arms.

"Where did he go?"

A wide, delighted smile spread across the little girl's face. "You mean you saw him, too?"

"Yes, I saw him. Where did he go?"

Beulah Two shrugged. "I don't know. Guess he had someplace else he needed to be."

Kate's heart was pounding. "Hasn't your grandma told you how dangerous it is to talk to strangers?"

"We wasn't talkin'. He was just standin' with me for a while. And he ain't no stranger, Ms. Kate. He's 'round here all the time."

Kate felt the hairs rise on the back of her neck and goose bumps form on her arms and legs. "What do you mean, sweetheart? Why is he here? What does he do?"

"He just watches, that's all," the little girl answered. "Can I go back inside and play with Jane Ellen now?"

Kate swallowed hard and released her. "Sure, honey. Go on in."

As Beulah Two scurried back inside the house, Kate scanned the yard once more. She was alone.

A VIEW FROM THERE

***

Malcolm washed the last pot in Nate's kitchen and set it next to the sink. Nate leaned back in his chair at the kitchen table and patted his full belly. "You sure surprised me tonight."

Malcolm towel dried the pot and dropped it into a drawer with a clatter. "As much as I'd like to take credit, that was my grandmother's recipe. I had it written down on the back of my hand."

Nate chuckled. "No, I mean you surprised me by coming here. After what I done, I—"

"Nate, the only one here who has anything to be ashamed of is me." Malcolm sat down in the chair across from him. "And I should've been by sooner."

Nate leaned toward him. "Tell me the truth. Did you mean what you said? You know what I'm talking about. Did you mean it, or were you just saying it to get me down off the roof?"

Malcolm exhaled, long and slow. "I wanted you down, Nate." He rubbed the back of his head. "But what I said, I meant."

Nate stared for a while, then broke into a smile. "Ain't there one more biscuit left? Well, bring it over here and pass the butter. We sure can't let a perfectly good biscuit go to waste."

***

Supper was over, and Beulah stood at the counter, slicing into a warm, thick apple cake. She set a large piece onto a plate and headed toward the table. Just as she reached Kate, the plate slipped from her grasp and shattered onto the floor.

"Oh Lord, these ol' hands don't wanna hold nothin' no

more."

Kate jumped up and grabbed the broom. "You just sit down, Ms. Beulah. Let me get this."

Beulah fell into a chair at the table, rubbed her hands, and moaned. "Arthritis done eat 'em up. The doctor in Fayetteville gave me some pills, but they don't do no good. They get worse when it's cold."

Kate swept up the last of the plate into the dustpan and dropped the pieces into the trash. She replaced the broom and took a seat beside the old woman. "Ms. Beulah, you've got to stop feeding me like this. That was the best chili I've ever had."

"Oh, you ain't as big as a minute. And you still ain't had your dessert. Let me go get it."

Kate reached for her arm. "I was wondering if I could talk to you about something first. Something that happened today with Beulah Two."

Beulah nodded.

"She was standing with a man outside my house today. The same man I saw at my mother's funeral, and the day after at the farmers' market. I ran out to see what he was doing there, but by the time I got to them, he was gone."

Beulah's forehead crinkled, and then she chuckled. "You mean to tell me you seen one of her angels?"

"No!" Kate said. "It was a man . . . in regular clothes. No wings. Just a man."

"And he just disappeared?"

"Well, yes."

"How many times is that you seen him now? Three?"

Kate counted in her head. "Yes."

"So what makes you so sure he ain't no angel?"

"Because people don't see angels, Ms. Beulah."

Beulah shook her head. "Didn't I tell you already? Beulah Two's special. She got a gift, that girl. I don't understand it, and I don't expect nobody else to neither. But if she says she's seein' angels, then I believe she's seein' angels. Maybe that's how she got through what happened to her when she was with her mama. I don't know. But it don't got to make sense to you or me or nobody else."

Kate raised her eyebrows. "So, you're telling me you think the man I saw today in my yard is an angel?"

Beulah leaned forward. "You tellin' me you think he ain't?"

Chapter Nineteen

The splendor of the rose and the
whiteness of the lily do not rob the
little violet of its scent nor the daisy
of its simple charm.
-St. Thérèse of Lisieux

Debbie Williams fell into bed after the grueling day of work. Her fingers were pink and sore and covered with tiny red poke holes from thorns. She rubbed at them and then fluffed up her pillow.

Debbie was a divorcée of five years. Her ex-husband, Sammy, had left her for a younger woman, who then promptly left him for a younger man just two short months later. Sammy had been repentant—he'd come home to Debbie with his suitcases and phony tears, but Debbie had never been one to forgive and forget. Though all she'd known since age sixteen was having babies, keeping house, and being Sammy's wife, Debbie had been harboring a dream.

Eight months later, Debbie's Flowers and Gifts had opened next to the hardware store on the Millsville square. Her business was small, but profitable. Debbie had already put one son through college, and the other would graduate from Arkansas State in the fall. She owned her car, plus a delivery van, and the mortgage on her house was paid in full. Debbie was proud of herself and had every right to be. She was a survivor.

The next day was Valentine's Day—Debbie's busiest holiday of the year. The week before, the number of orders and deliveries had mounted with every ring of the telephone, along with Debbie's stress level. Near panic, she'd summoned the help of her mother and aunt, along with her oldest son's girlfriend, Amy, who worked part-time at the shop during the week. Together, the team of four had worked from morning 'til night that day. When they'd finished, they'd been exhausted and weary. She'd bought her recruits dinner from Susie's and sent them home with orders to return by 7 a.m., promising the next day would be much, much worse.

Debbie let her head sink into the pillow and closed her eyes just as the phone rang. It was Amy calling from her bathroom floor with news that she was sick and wouldn't be able to make it in to help in the morning. Before she hung up, Debbie could hear her vomiting in the toilet.

Only minutes later, the phone rang again. This time, her mother explained that both she and Debbie's aunt were sick and pointed an accusing finger at Susie's fried shrimp. Debbie's hand fluttered to her chest in relief. She'd had the burger and fries.

She hung up the phone, her breathing going shallow and her forehead breaking out into a sweat. It would be impossible to handle the shop alone on Valentine's Day. Both of her sons were scheduled to make her deliveries, but she'd need someone to help fill orders and work the register. She chewed her nails and stared at the phone. And then she thought of a name.

***

Kate dropped Jane Ellen off at school and drove toward Debbie's Flowers and Gifts. The shop was still several miles away, but she could already smell the sickening sweetness of roses and carnations. Her stomach churned. She'd vowed to avoid Valentine's Day this year—to steer clear of heart-shaped boxes of chocolates, balloons, cards, and above all, flowers. But Debbie had called the night before and all but begged for help in the shop. Kate had known Debbie a long time, the way anybody "knows" anybody in a small town, but even though they weren't close, Kate hadn't had the heart to refuse her. Before hanging up, she'd willingly sentenced herself to a full day of working in the midst of all things red and pink and frilly. She fought back a heave.

***

Beulah Two found her grandmother asleep on the couch with a crossword puzzle in her lap and pencil in hand. The little girl sat down next to her and tried to slip the glasses off her face undetected, but Beulah's eyes blinked open. She smiled.

"Guess I dozed off again."

"Grandma, can I ask you somethin'?"

"Well, I was wonderin' when you was goin' to. You been walkin' 'round here all mornin' with somethin' on your mind. Uh-huh. Grandma knows when you worryin' 'bout things. Now what is it?"

"It's about Mama."

Beulah pulled Beulah Two to her side and held her close. "What about your mama, honey?"

Beulah Two fought back the tears that stung her eyes with as much bravery as she could muster. "I was just wonderin' if she's gonna come see me on my birthday this year."

"Girl, your birthday ain't 'til June! That's more than three months away."

"I know, but Malcolm said she had to be away for a while, and . . . well, Mama ain't never missed my birthday."

Beulah took the little girl's face in her hands. "And you know what that means? It means your mama loves you. If she can be here, she will be. You hear me?"

Beulah Two clutched her grandmother around the waist as a gush of tears ran down her cheeks. "I hope she can. I really hope she can."

***

Kate stared down at the infinite number of buttons on the prehistoric cash register. Debbie had already spent more time than she could spare giving her temporary employee an operating lesson. Kate had listened and tried to soak in the information but knew she was bound to do more things wrong that day than right.

Debbie wrapped her arms around Kate's shoulders in a warm hug. "You got no idea how much I appreciate your comin' in like this to help me out. I know this must be a rough day for you, what with you and your husband havin' troubles."

"Ex-husband," Kate said. The words felt shameful on her lips. "The divorce was final two weeks ago."

"Oh, honey, I didn't know." She glanced side to side then whispered, "You need a bye fire."

"Excuse me?"

"It's what you do when it's time to say 'bye' to somethin' or some*body* and get on with life without 'em."

Kate looked around the empty shop. "Why are you

whispering?"

" 'Cause it's not to be discussed in open company. It's a secret ceremony passed down through the women of my family for years. And it works, too, honey. I'm livin' proof."

"What do you do at a bye fire?"

"Shhh!" Debbie put a finger to Kate's lips as though the shop were bugged. "If you're ready, and I mean really ready to put that piece of your life behind you and get on with the rest, you be at my house next Wednesday night at seven o'clock. I'll explain it all then. Oh, and there's somethin' you've got to bring." She leaned over and whispered it into Kate's ear.

Kate's eyes widened in bewilderment, and then the phone in the back room rang, along with a cell in Debbie's pocket.

"Anyway, hon, no matter what you decide about comin', I'm real sorry about the divorce. And I know the last thing you must want to see right now is a room full of roses and giant balloons that say 'Be Mine.' " She rolled her eyes. "All that stuff still makes me a little sick to my stomach, and Sammy's been gone for over five years now."

Debbie coaxed the phone out of the pocket of her tight-fitting Lee jeans. Kate smiled and picked up a long-stemmed white carnation off the counter. "This just gives me something to do other than sit around and feel sorry for myself. I don't mind at all. Besides, I think it will be fun."

The phone on the wall next to the cash register chimed in loudly, bringing the total number of ringing telephones to three.

Debbie rolled up her sleeves. "Here we go. Hope you still feel the same way by the time we close. But I doubt it."

A VIEW FROM THERE

***

By noon, Kate had removed her shoes. Sweat beaded on her brow, and her hair fell free of her ponytail and hung loosely around her face. The steady stream of customers had dwindled, but Debbie warned her it would be only a small reprieve. The procrastinators would be arriving soon, the husbands and boyfriends who'd put off their Valentine's Day gift-buying until the last minute. They would scurry in, begging for whatever candy or flowers Debbie had left. Daisies, carnations, plastics, they wouldn't mind, just as long as they could leave with something in hand. It was the same year after year, and Debbie was ready for them.

She ordered pizza and paid the delivery boy while Kate tied a large red bow around a white teddy bear. The sad little thing had been sitting on a shelf all day, staring at her as she worked. Probably laughing to himself at all her blunders, she thought. Kate liked him anyway and decided she'd take him home to Jane Ellen.

The front door opened again, and in walked Nate Bell in a pair of denim overalls over a light blue button-up. Debbie greeted him with a mammoth hug. "How you doin', Mr. Nate? I been thinkin' about you."

"I'm good, real good. Just came in to pick up my order."

Debbie disappeared into the back room and returned seconds later with a large glass vase filled with a dozen white roses. "Just finished her up. This what you had in mind?"

Nate beamed. "That's just fine."

He dug into his pocket and pulled out his wallet, then handed Debbie a hundred dollar bill. "I still owe you for last week's delivery, too."

Debbie rang up the sale. "You need some help gettin' out to your truck?" she asked.

"No, I got it. Thanks a lot."

Nate took the vase in his hands with supreme care and walked out the door to his truck. Debbie peered out the window to make sure he made it safely then turned to Kate. "Now who on Earth is Mr. Nate buyin' flowers for? He hasn't set foot in here since Ms. Evelyn died. Now he's been in three times in two weeks."

"Sounds like Mr. Nate has a sweetheart." Kate smiled, straightening the bow on the bear.

Debbie sighed and pulled a large piece of steaming-hot pepperoni pizza out of the box. She took a bite and chewed as she spoke. "Nate Bell's a dying breed—a man who really knows what romance is all about. Not like the young folks these days. Virtual dating and text messaging. Do you know what my son bought his sweet girlfriend this year for Valentine's Day? An iTunes gift card. Without even a card or box of chocolates. Just handed it to her! Now ain't that somethin'? Where's the romance in that? That boy took after his daddy more than I care to admit. Poor thing."

Kate tore open a packet of Parmesan cheese and sprinkled it onto her pizza.

Debbie swallowed her bite and shook her head. "I'm tellin' ya, there ain't many of 'em left. I'm talkin' about men who know how to treat a lady like a lady. With respect and honor— and passion." Debbie raised her eyebrows. "Somebody who'd kill without blinkin' to protect her, but gentle as lamb when he's with her. Nope. There ain't many left."

213

Debbie averted her eyes to the large front window. She took another bite of pizza then sat up straight and brushed the Parmesan bits off her jeans. "Speak of the devil. Here comes one of 'em now."

Kate turned to look as Malcolm entered the store. She'd just stuffed her mouth full of pizza and sped up her chewing but was unable to swallow before he made it to the counter. His eyes widened when he saw her, and in an instant he turned his attention to Debbie and her stalker-like gaze.

"I'm here to pick up my order," he said.

"Well, sure you are, Pastor. It's in the back. I'll run get it. Kate, could you ring him up for two Valentine's specials?"

Kate finally swallowed and stepped over to the register. "I haven't seen you in a while," she said.

"I've been around."

She gave him his total, and Malcolm pulled out his wallet and handed her a credit card. Kate hadn't been successful in running a card all day, but she took it from him anyway and slid it through the reader, avoiding eye contact.

"Beulah and Beulah Two," Malcolm said.

"I'm sorry?"

"The flowers. They're for Beulah and Beulah Two. I try to do it every year."

"That's really nice of you."

The card reader beeped with the usual failure message. Kate sighed and slid the card again, praying for a miracle.

"I always go with the Valentine's special because I don't know much about flowers," Malcolm said.

"The special has roses and daisies, I think." She bit her lip. *Hurry up, Debbie*, she pleaded silently.

"Guess I can't go wrong with roses," he said.

Kate finally took her eyes off the card reader and looked up at him. "Roses are beautiful. But daisies are my favorite. They're simple. And perfect."

The reader beeped again. Error.

Debbie emerged from the back with two vases of pink and red roses intermingled with an occasional white daisy. Trailing high in the air behind her were two large, heart-shaped helium balloons that read *Be My Valentine* in white, cursive letters.

"Darn card reader not workin' again?" Debbie asked. "Dadgummit." She plucked the credit card from Kate's hand and swiped it hard and fast. "Oh, Kate! I forgot Malcolm's chocolates. Could you grab 'em? They're on the back table."

Kate gratefully obliged and escaped into the workroom. As the door closed behind her, her heart raced and she placed a hand over her chest. She spotted the two small boxes of chocolates on one of the worktables and retrieved them then gathered herself before heading back into the shop.

She looked around but didn't see Malcolm anywhere, and Debbie had another slice of pizza in her hand. "He said he had to go." Debbie shrugged.

Kate stood holding the chocolates and her eyes fell on the register. Lying across the keys was a single white daisy. She picked it up and held it to her nose.

Debbie gnawed on a crust. "I'm tellin' ya, a dyin' breed."

***

Before Debbie's Flowers and Gifts closed for the night, every flower and balloon had been sold, every box of chocolates purchased, and most every stuffed animal, large and small, cute and not-so-cute, had been snatched up by the procrastinators. The frantic stampede had begun around three o'clock and ended two hours later. Kate had battled the urge to climb onto the counter and shout, "Shame on you for waiting 'til the last minute!" But she was much too exhausted to yell, much less climb. And besides, that was their mothers' job.

Her feet and back hurt, and her fingers throbbed from being poked by rose thorns, all but four of them covered by bandages. She needed her bed. And a bath. Not necessarily in that order.

Debbie, herself worn thin, gave Kate a final hug and showered her with more words of gratitude. Kate grabbed Jane Ellen's teddy bear off the counter and stuffed him inside her purse as the shop's phone rang.

"We're closed!" Debbie yelled.

Kate laughed. "I'll get it. It can be my last act as assistant florist. She answered the phone as she had all that day. "Debbie's Flowers and Gifts. This is Kate."

"Kate, it's Truitt."

"Oh, hey. We're just closing up. Tell Jane Ellen I'm on my way—"

"Listen," he said, his voice strained. "It's Gray's father. He's had a heart attack."

Chapter Twenty

Although the world is full of suffering, it
is full also of the overcoming of it.
-Helen Keller

Malcolm sat on Beulah's couch. Beulah Two had just fallen asleep with her head on his arm, and he dared not move it. It had been weeks since he'd seen her face, and he'd missed her.

The television was much too loud, just like Beulah liked it. Malcolm had watched the episode of *Gunsmoke* more times than he could count, but it was better than getting an earful from Beulah. He could tell from the moment he'd stepped foot inside the house that she was mad at him, if not downright furious. Beulah Two had thrown her arms around him and thanked him over and over for the flowers and balloon. But Beulah's face had been hard. She hadn't offered him a smile, much less a thank-you.

Malcolm wondered if he might sneak out unscathed when he looked away from the TV and caught Beulah glaring at him. "She been missin' you," she said with a scowl.

Malcolm nodded. "I know."

"It ain't like you to stay gone so long. Ain't like you at all. First her mama, and then you. That baby don't deserve that."

"I know," he repeated.

Beulah glanced to the vases of flowers on the kitchen table. Her face relaxed a bit, but the frown remained. "She asked me about Esther today. Wanted to know if she was gonna come for her birthday. Ever since Beulah Two's been born, no matter where Esther was at or what she was doin', she showed up at

217

this house on that baby's birthday. Sometimes she was in a mess of a shape. How she even knew what day it was, I don't know. But she showed up."

"June is still months away."

"That's what I told her. But it's on her mind."

Beulah Two squirmed and changed positions with a slight whimper.

"So, do you like them?" Malcolm asked.

"Like what?"

He nodded toward the flowers. Beulah's mouth twitched then broke into a smile. Malcolm smiled, too.

***

Kate arrived at the hospital and hurried to the ICU, where Margie Canton and a few of her friends sat in the waiting room, all dressed in their bowling league shirts. At the sight of her, Margie flung herself on Kate and wept. Kate cried, too. She remembered all too well the nights of waiting in the same room—the fluorescent lights, the squeaky floors, the smell of medicine and cleaning fluid. She held Margie tight, unsure whether her own tears were for Levi or for her mother.

"We'd just left the bowling alley," Margie said, sniffling. "Levi bowled a two-eighty-nine! He opened the car door for me, and I waited, but he never came around to the driver's side. When I opened the door to check on him, he was face-down on the pavement." She buried her face in Kate's shoulder and sobbed.

A doctor approached and took Margie aside, and Margie nodded along as he spoke to her in whispered tones. Then Margie joined Kate and they sat down together on the uncomfortable vinyl bench while Margie relayed what the doctor had told her—that Levi had suffered a massive heart attack. He needed coronary artery bypass surgery and, while in most cases such a surgery was performed after the heart had had time to recover from an attack, in Levi's case surgery was required immediately to restore blood flow to his heart.

"His chances aren't good," Margie finished then slid off the bench to her knees and dropped her face into her hands.

Night turned slowly to morning, and Kate fell asleep in a small, cushioned chair in the corner of the waiting room. She awoke with a shooting pain in her neck and side then sat up and rubbed her eyes.

Margie was knitting at warp speed in the chair next to her, her face hollow as she'd kept it most of the night, following her collapse on the floor. Sunlight peeked through the blinds behind them.

"Any word from the surgeon?" Kate asked.

Margie shook her head.

Kate patted Margie's back. Then she stood, stretched, and ran a hand through her hair. Coffee. She needed some.

She reached for her purse and hoped she had a dollar for the vending machine. As she headed for the door, her eyes landed on Gray, asleep in a chair. She caught her breath and froze, watching his chest rise and fall as she had so many times before.

The door opened and the surgeon appeared in his green scrubs and hat. The noise stirred Gray, and he jumped to his feet. Margie lunged toward the surgeon and grabbed him by the hand. Gray nodded toward Kate, and she nodded back.

"Mrs. Canton, the surgery went well. Mr. Canton is in

recovery and doing fine. We'll be keeping him here for a while, but I expect him to recover fully. He's a lucky man."

Margie burst into tears and threw her arms around him, and the surgeon kindly hugged her and patted the back of her head. Gray stepped forward and coaxed his mother away to take her in his arms while Kate shook the doctor's hand and thanked him again.

Gray held Margie as she sobbed before he looked up at Kate and smiled. He mouthed the words "thank you," and she nodded. Her job was done. She grabbed her purse and walked out the door.

The elevator ride to the lobby seemed bottomless. When finally the doors opened, Kate willed her legs to carry her outside. Near the end of the long hallway, Truitt appeared around the corner with two cardboard coffee cups. Kate felt a lump rise in her throat and she hurried her steps. When she reached him, she put her head on his chest and felt safe as he wrapped his strong arms around her. Tears streamed down her face, free to flow at last.

"Is one of those for me?" she asked, pulling back and wiping at her cheeks.

"Yep."

She took one of the hot cups from his hand. "White chocolate mocha?"

"Extra whipped cream."

"You're a saint."

"No, *you're* a saint. Valentine's Day at Debbie's and an all-nighter at the hospital with your ex-mother-in-law? Mother Teresa's got nothin' on you, kid."

Kate laughed and sipped her mocha.

"C'mon. I'll take you to breakfast," Truitt said. The large automatic doors opened with a swoosh and a blast of cold air from outside, and Malcolm strode toward them from the parking lot. His face was cleanly shaven, and he was dressed in nice jeans and a dark wool coat and scarf. Kate wiped the remaining tears from her eyes, but he had already noticed.

Truitt extended his hand, and Malcolm shook it firmly.

"Good to see you, Malcolm."

Malcolm nodded. "I got a call about Levi. Is he okay?"

Kate's heart pounded again. "He's out of surgery and doing fine. Margie's still in the ICU waiting room if you'd like to see her."

"Thanks." He took a step inside the hospital then stopped. "Kate?"

She turned back to face him.

"Ms. Beulah told me about the man you saw with Beulah Two. Be careful."

Kate took in the serious look in his eyes then nodded. "I will," she said, and she and Truitt walked on.

"Wow," Truitt said. "That's the first time he's spoken to me in years. Almost reminded me of the old Malcolm."

Kate thought of the daisy in her purse as someone called her name from behind. She turned around to see Gray sprinting toward her.

"Great," Truitt moaned.

Gray slowed as he caught sight of Truitt and resumed his approach with caution. "Kate, can we talk for a minute?"

"No," Truitt answered promptly.

"It's okay," Kate said. Truitt narrowed his eyes at Gray, issuing a clear warning, then climbed into the Jeep and shut the door.

Gray led Kate a few steps away beside a parked ambulance. "I just wanted to say thank you for coming last night. Mom would've been up there all alone if not for you."

Kate shrugged. "Levi is Jane Ellen's grandfather. I wanted to be there."

Gray exhaled, his jaw working. "Jane Ellen is actually what I wanted to talk to you about. Do you think I could see her? Maybe take her to a movie? I'll be in town for a few days, and I was thinking it would be nice to spend some time with her."

"That's good to know."

Gray looked away and exhaled. "Look, I know how it looks, me not asking for a share of Jane Ellen's custody. But right now just isn't a good time for me and Kristen. You understand."

Kate clenched her jaw and took a deep breath of frigid air. "If you'd like to see her, I'm sure we can work something out. She's missed you."

"I've missed her."

Silence fell between them, and Kate hugged her body and tried to keep her teeth from chattering.

"There's something else I wanted to tell you," Gray said, his face solemn. "Kristen and I got married last weekend. We're going to have a baby in a few months. A girl. I wanted you to hear that from me."

Kate blinked, waiting for the sting, for the rush of grief to engulf her. She braced for the tears as another gust of wind thrashed about them, blowing her hair into her eyes. She brushed it away, looking into the face of the man she once loved and adored, but all she felt was the cold.

His brow furrowed. "Kate?"

"Oh. I'm sorry. It's just . . . It's really cold out here, and Truitt is waiting on me." She took a few steps backward toward the Jeep. "Jane Ellen will be thrilled to see you. Just give me a call."

She climbed into the Jeep and watched Gray staring at their taillights as they drove away.

"What was that all about?" Truitt asked.

Kate took a long sip of her mocha. "We were just talking about the weather."

***

Emma and Ella stood on Modean's front porch, peeking in through a window and whispering. Inside, Modean walked through the living room, and the twins ducked to either side of the glass. Modean rolled her eyes then threw open the front door.

"What in the world are you two doin' out here in the cold? Are you spyin' on me now?"

The twins looped their arms together and pushed their way inside. "We were just wondering if you did anything special yesterday," Emma said.

"After all," Ella said, "it was Valentine's Day. The day of love." The twins covered their mouths and giggled.

"You don't think I know what day it was?" Modean snapped. "I got more sense than the two of you crazies put together."

"Oh, Modean! Don't be so secretive," Emma said, pouting. "We know you're hiding something from us. Why, just in the past couple of weeks Sister and I have seen a delivery truck from Debbie's right out there in your driveway. Twice!"

"You *have* been spyin' on me! I oughta call the sheriff on the both of ya."

The twins scanned the room and it didn't take long before they spotted a large vase filled with a dozen white roses sitting on the dining room table. They gasped simultaneously. "Oh, Modean! Who are they from? You *must* tell us!" Ella shouted.

"Yes, yes, you *must*! We'll just burst if you don't!"

Mo ushered them back toward the door. "Well, go ahead and burst then, 'cause I ain't tellin' you nothin'!"

Footsteps fell on the front porch, and then Truitt and Kate walked in. "Well, hello, ladies." Truitt said.

"Don't 'hello' them," Mo said. "They're spies. And trespassers. And they were just leavin'!"

Kate eyed the flowers on the table. "Aunt Mo, are those from Mr. Nate?"

The twins, halfway out the door, whipped their heads around, their faces beaming. They lunged at Mo with hugs and squeals and, sandwiched between them, Modean moaned.

***

Malcolm sat next to Margie in the waiting room and listened as she recounted Levi's 289 bowling score frame by frame, followed by a brief description of his collapse in the bowling alley's parking lot. Malcolm managed an occasional "mm-hmm" and "okay" and was thankful Margie was doing all the talking. The thought of having to come up with words of comfort, or any words at all, made his stomach churn.

A man entered the room, and Malcolm recognized him at once. Gray wasted no time in extending his hand to Malcolm and interrupting his mother's narrative. "Hi. I'm Gray Canton."

Malcolm looked over Gray's face. He was handsome enough. His eyes were dark blue and serious, his nose strong and prominent. He smiled, revealing a dimple on his right cheek, but Malcolm couldn't muster a smile in return. He didn't like the man and found it impossible to pretend otherwise, but he stood and shook his hand much too firmly. "Malcolm Bauer."

"Gray, this used to be our pastor at the Millsville Baptist Church," Margie said. "Don't you remember Malcolm?"

Gray shook his head. "Can't say that I do."

"Malcolm here knows Kate. Don't you, Malcolm? He and Ruth were real close."

Gray raised an eyebrow, still smiling. "All right. Good to hear our Kate is settling in."

Malcolm almost sneered, and he gripped Gray's hand a little harder. "She's settled just fine. No thanks to you."

Gray withdrew his hand, and the staring match was on. Margie jumped to her feet between them and pulled Gray down into the chair beside her. "Gray, dear, your Aunt Helen came by earlier. She said to tell you hello. Her daughter—your cousin Kelly—is graduating from the U of A this spring, did you know that?"

Malcolm saw his chance to escape and took it after one long last glare at Gray Canton.

***

Kate and Jane Ellen drove back through town toward home. Both were exhausted and needed baths, not to mention sleep. Jane Ellen sat in her booster seat with a new doll Aunt Mo had given her, humming a tune that resembled a waltz while the doll danced this way and that. Kate watched her in the rear view mirror, trying to remember when her life had been that carefree—before her father had died and the world forever changed.

She dug inside her purse and pulled out the daisy, wilted and sagging, and held it to her nose. She'd thought of it throughout the day—at the hospital, at breakfast with Truitt, then at Mo's. She'd wanted to touch it, to see it, to hold it. But was it the daisy she'd been thinking of at all? The notion confused her, surprised her even, and she tossed the daisy back inside her purse and drove on toward home.

A mile later, something on the side of the road caught her eye, and she pulled over sharply in front of an aged farmhouse. Sitting in the yard was an old Ford Bronco, shiny white except for a few patches of rust, with silver lettering. Her pulse quickened. *It can't be*, she thought.

In 1976, her father had purchased a Bronco just like it and drove it until the cancer took his life. Ruth had parked it in the garage, and there it had sat for years until Kate went to college and Ruth finally got the nerve to sell it.

Kate glanced back to Jane Ellen, who had yet to notice they'd stopped. She sang with growing intensity as her doll danced and turned back flips in midair.

"Hey, sweetie. Sit tight, okay?"

Kate walked around the Bronco and ran her fingers along the side. She peeked in through the windows and saw the same tan interior she remembered as a child. She made her way to the other side and knelt next to the bumper. A smile spread across her lips as she placed her hand inside the dent made the day she and her father had slid off the road in the snow and collided with the neighbor's mailbox. She hadn't been wearing a seatbelt and had flown into the dash. Her forehead still bore the scar.

An old man stepped up behind her. His face was drawn and wrinkled, half covered in a stubbly white beard. His lips were pursed together hiding a mouth without teeth, but his eyes were kind and crinkled at the corners. "I'm tryin' to sell her," he said, his hands deep inside the pockets of his blue trousers. "She's been good to me. Nineteen seventy-six model. Drives real good. Air and heat still work fine."

"Would you mind my asking, where did you buy this?"

"I bought it off my brother-in-law back in ninety-nine. Not sure where he found her. Somewhere here in Millsville. I got it for my grandson, but he got himself a sports car when he went off to college. She's been sittin' here ever since."

Kate laughed out loud and put both hands on the hood.

"I'll let you take her for a spin if you want."

"I'll take it," she said.

"I'm askin' fifty-five hundred."

"Cash okay?"

Chapter Twenty-one

There is in every true woman's heart a
spark of heavenly fire, which lies dormant
in the broad daylight of prosperity, but
which kindles up and beams and blazes in
the dark hour of adversity.
-Washington Irving

Malcolm's drive down Old River Road had become a nightly
ritual. Each evening just before sundown, he'd drive past
Beulah's, scanning both sides of the road and making certain
everything was as it should be. And it always was. Quiet.
Undisturbed. Afterward, he'd head past Kate's to check out
her home, as well. Beulah might have been unconcerned about
the man Kate had seen in her front yard with Beulah Two, but
Malcolm didn't like it—angel or no angel.

As he passed Beulah's, the sun was setting, creating a sky
of reds and oranges. The lights were on in her living room
and kitchen, and he wondered what she was cooking and even
considered pulling in the driveway to find out. He was starving,
and the only thing in his refrigerator was a six-pack of Dr.
Pepper and a package of cheese slices. But he drove on. Susie's
Thursday special was fried catfish, hushpuppies, fries, and slaw,
but everyone in town knew it went quick. He glanced at his
watch and drove faster toward Kate's.

Her house loomed into view on the right. Her Range Rover
was gone and no lights shone from inside. Malcolm shrugged
and continued on, his mind fixed on Susie's catfish, when
a shadowy movement at the side of Kate's house caught his

eye. A person. A man, opening the kitchen window. Malcolm braked, and his truck skidded to the side of the road. He jumped out and pulled a rifle from the truck bed.

***

Emma and Ella hurried as fast as their legs would carry them across the street, down the road, and up Modean's front porch steps. Together they knocked on the door and exchanged an uneasy glance. Modean opened the door with her oversized vacuum circa 1988 in hand.

"Oh, so you're knockin' now, huh? Well, that's good, I guess."

Emma reached for Mo's arm. "We've been trying to call!"

"I've been vacuumin'. Can't ya see? What's a matter? You two look like you just seen a ghost."

"Mr. Roy called," Emma said. "He's been trying to call you, too. You know how he sits on that police scanner of his from sunup to sundown. Well, he heard just a few minutes ago that someone's been caught trying to break in over at Kate's."

Mo dropped the vacuum.

***

Kate's cell phone chirped, and she dug it out as she drove. "Hey, Truitt."

"Where are you?" Truitt asked.

"I just pulled onto Old River Road. Jane Ellen and I are going home to make Rice Krispie treats." Jane Ellen heard from the backseat and clapped her hands.

229

"Listen, I'm on my way there. I need you to stop at Ms. Beulah's and wait on me."

"Why would I do that?"

Truitt paused. "It's a long story, but I think someone's tryin' to break into your house. The cops are on their way."

"*What*?"

"Just stop at Ms. Beulah's and wait on me, okay?"

Kate hung up the phone and flung it on top of her purse. She floored the Bronco and, minutes later, slid into Beulah's driveway. Beulah hurried to the door as Kate waved Jane Ellen toward her.

"I'm so sorry, Ms. Beulah, will you take Jane Ellen inside? I'll be back as soon as I can." Without even waiting for a nod of confirmation, Kate rushed back to the Bronco and sped away toward her house.

She spotted Malcolm's truck on the side of the road as she pulled into her driveway. She stepped from the Bronco and eased toward the front door, her heart pounding. She could hear Lynryd growling within and thought of the man she'd seen standing in her front yard with Beulah Two. It was him. It had to be him.

Fear and anger surged through her as police sirens howled in the distance and Lynryd barked violently. She knew she should wait on the police, but instead she threw open the front door.

She caught her breath and stared, mouth open, eyes wide, until Gray finally yelled, "For God's sake, Kate! Get this dog out of here!"

Kate raised her hand to her mouth. A terrified Gray, pale and covered in sweat, sat perched precariously atop a tall bookshelf, books and broken picture frames scattered about, while a furious Lynyrd sat below, ready for the one wrong move that would send the stranger to within range of his waiting teeth.

Across the room, leaning casually against the living room wall, was Malcolm, a rifle propped against his legs.

"Gray! What are you doing here?" Kate cried.

A drip of sweat fell from Gray's nose to the floor. He rolled his eyes in exasperation. "I came to see you and Jane Ellen. Now can you please call off your bodyguard? And take that dog away!"

Kate rubbed her forehead. "How did you get in?"

Gray's hands trembled and the whole bookshelf shook. Lynryd stared up at him, poised and ready.

"I let myself in. I didn't think you would mind. And then that monster tried to kill me!"

Kate narrowed her eyes. "You didn't think I'd *mind*?"

Lynyrd snarled again followed by a terrifying woof. Gray shuddered and held on for dear life.

"I caught him breaking in through the kitchen window," Malcolm said. "And it's a good thing I got here when I did. Lynyrd was about to have him for dinner. Looked to me like he was snooping."

Kate's gaze fell on the gaping hole in the upper thigh of Gray's khakis, revealing a pair of white boxer briefs stained in red. The sirens drew closer, and a flash of blue lights filled the room.

"I wasn't snooping!" Gray shouted. "Kate, please!"

Kate bent low and patted the floor. "Come here, boy. Come on."

Lynyrd whined, torn between obeying his owner and tearing the intruder to shreds. He cut his eyes toward Kate, then back to Gray. Kate called to him again, and this time Lynyrd left his post and approached Kate to shower her face with kisses. Kate took him by the collar and led him toward the bedroom where she closed him inside, but not before hugging him and telling him what a good boy he was.

Gray was already climbing down when she returned. Malcolm hadn't moved, and neither had his rifle. A uniformed deputy entered the house, gun drawn, through the open front door, and Gray raised his hands high into the air.

"Pastor Malcolm, what's going on?" the officer asked.

"You'll have to talk to the lady, Luke. This is her place."

Gray looked from the deputy to Malcolm and back again. "What is this? You two know each other? Kate, please tell him who I am!"

"Ma'am?" the deputy asked. "Do you know this man?"

Kate crossed her arms and rolled her eyes. "Until two weeks ago, I was married to him."

After another glance at Malcolm, the deputy holstered his weapon, and Gray's shoulders sagged. He exhaled exhaustively, lowered his hands and leaned forward as if readying himself to vomit.

"But he has no business breaking into my home," Kate added.

"Come on, Kate. Our daughter lives here."

"But you don't."

"Ma'am, would you like to press charges?" the deputy asked.

Kate stared at Gray. He looked pitiful with his leg bleeding and his knees trembling. His best efforts to appear composed couldn't veil the fear and humiliation behind his eyes.

"No," she said with a sigh. "I don't want to press charges."

The deputy stepped forward and took Gray by the arm. "I'll escort you out, sir."

Gray allowed the officer to lead him toward the door but not before shooting Malcolm a look and cursing him under his breath.

"Wait!" Kate shouted, and Gray and the deputy stopped in the doorway. "Before you go, there's something I need from him."

Gray tilted his head back and groaned.

"What do you need, ma'am?" the officer asked.

Kate grimaced then pointed at Gray's feet. "His shoes."

Gray's mouth dropped open. "What? My shoes?"

Malcolm ducked his head and chuckled.

"That's an odd request, ma'am," the officer said.

Kate bit at her thumbnail. "It is, isn't it?"

Gray scowled at her, his nostrils flared and teeth clenched. "I don't know how I was ever married to you. You're as crazy as everybody else in this backwoods redneck town."

Kate walked slowly toward him and didn't stop until they were nose to nose. "And yet you're the one crazy enough to break into your ex-wife's house. Give me the shoes."

Gray laughed and straightened the cuffs of his shirt. "I'm ready to go, officer," he said and took a step out the front door.

The officer caught Gray by the shoulder and stopped him short. "Redneck, huh?" His mouth curved into a smirk. "Give her the shoes."

***

Kate walked up Debbie's front porch steps and rang the

doorbell. She clutched the paper bag close to her chest and wondered for the hundredth time what she was doing there. Music played loud from within—Janis Joplin's "Bobby McGee." Kate heard voices and knocked again, then footsteps approached and the door opened.

Debbie gasped. "You came!" She yanked her inside and hugged her then eyed the paper bag. "Did you bring everything?"

"I did the best I could, but—"

"Kate!" Delta nudged Debbie out of her way and came at Kate with outstretched arms.

"Delta? Margie said you were out of the country."

"Well, I was. But I came home quick as I could with Daddy being sick and all."

"But what are you doing here at Debbie's?" Kate asked.

"Girl, me and Debbie's been friends since kindergarten. We graduated together from Millsville High. Class of nineteen eighty-one. I was voted Most Likely to Wear My Skirts Too Short, and she was voted Most Likely to Climb the Water Tower with Sammy Williams."

Debbie and Delta roared with laughter and bumped rear ends. "She's stayin' here with me while she's in town," Debbie said. "Not what she's used to back in Houston, but I guess my meager accommodations will just have to do."

"Oh, hush up," Delta said and bumped her again. Debbie left the room with a chuckle, and Delta called behind, "Well, I certainly wasn't gonna stay at Mama's with Gray and his knocked-up Tanning Bed Barbie! Oh, I'm sorry, Kate. I probably shouldn't say stuff like that in front of you. If you haven't noticed, sometimes I just don't know when to keep my mouth shut."

Kate smiled. "It's fine."

"Well, we're all just sick about what happened tonight with that knuckle-headed brother of mine. I knew he was stupid, but what he did out there at your place takes him up a notch to certified idiot." Delta put her arm around Kate and led her down a hallway toward Debbie's kitchen. "Come on back here. There's someone else that showed up I think you might recognize."

Kate rounded the corner into the kitchen and came face to face with Modean. Mo froze, her eyes wide as though she'd been caught in the act of committing a crime. Kate raised her eyebrows. "Aunt Mo?"

"What on Earth are you doin' here?" Mo asked.

"Well, I, umm. I—"

"She's here for the same reason as you, Modean." Debbie sat down at the table with her Mountain Dew.

Kate looked around the room and confessed, "To be honest, I'm not sure I know why I'm here."

Debbie took her by the hand. "Aww, hon. 'Cause you're ready to move on. Aren't ya?"

"Yes. I am." She held up the paper bag. "But I still don't understand all this."

Delta startled them with a loud cackle. She pulled a pack of Marlboros from her pocket and headed for the back door. "Go on. Tell her, Deb. Tell her about your crazy Aunt Hildy and her bye fire rules."

"Shush, Delta! Everything in that bag is just part of the ceremony," Debbie said. "Now why don't you go in the back and change? I've still got a few things to get ready out here."

Kate obeyed and made her way into a guest bedroom. She

closed the door behind her and sat down on the bed's white, embroidered comforter with her paper bag in hand. There was a light tapping on the door, and then Mo peeped inside. "Can I come in?"

Kate motioned her in, and Mo sat down next to her on the bed.

"I'm sorry if I looked surprised to see ya." Mo said. "I got so scared when I heard someone was tryin' to break into your house. And then we found out who it was!" Modean rolled her eyes. "I guess you were about the last person I expected to run into tonight."

"What a night." Kate shook her head. "But let's not talk about Gray. I want to know how things are going with you and Mr. Nate."

Modean coughed, her eyes wide. Then she sighed, the corner of her mouth turning up in a smile. "Oh, I didn't want to make a big fuss about it. It started out me just takin' a few meals to him after the thing on the roof. And then he started askin' me to stay and eat with him. Then he started bringin' me flowers and gifts and takin' me out to dinner in Fayetteville. We even went to see a movie. I hadn't been to a theater in years!" Mo twiddled her thumbs. "I felt plumb silly at first. Me, datin'! I'm nearly seventy-four years old! But we had such a nice time. We'd just sit and talk like it was the easiest thing we ever done. And then I realized . . . for the first time since your Uncle Lou died, I didn't feel lonely when I got in bed at night and things got all quiet in the house. The dark didn't make me sad no more. Before, when I'd open my eyes in the mornins, a new day just felt like somethin' I had to do. Now when I wake up, I got a reason."

Kate took her hand. "Aunt Mo, you already had a reason!

You mean the world to me and Jane Ellen. And Truitt would be lost without you. So many people in this town need you. How could you ever feel lonely?"

"Oh, it ain't nothin' you did, sweet girl. It ain't nothin' nobody did. When Lou died, I think the biggest part of me died with him. I spent thirty years of my life with that man. And I've spent the last twenty-six without him. He was the love of my life, and I guess I figured if I moved on without him, I'd be lettin' him down. Not to mention, lettin' him go."

Modean stood up and unbuttoned her coat, revealing a long, blue, silk nightgown beneath. She tapped her foot and brought attention to the oversized men's work boots she wore. "But I'm ready now," Mo said.

Kate opened her bag and pulled out a new pink nightgown, the price tag dangling. "It's cotton. Do you think it'll do?"

Modean threw her head back and laughed. "Lord, girl, I hope so."

***

In the backyard, Debbie knelt beside a blazing campfire with Delta and three other women Kate didn't recognize. Brief introductions were made, and Kate wondered if they felt as silly as she did in their nightgowns and awkward footwear. The heat from the fire wasn't enough to keep Kate's bottom lip from quivering, but the others didn't seem to mind the cold. They stood near the fire, whispering among themselves, restless and waiting for Debbie to begin.

Delta puffed on a cigarette. She wore her long fur coat, a yellow nightgown peeking through from beneath, and a tall pair of men's boots like the rest of them. Her hair and makeup were perfect as always, but she chewed on her lip and looked at the ground. Then she caught Kate's stare and smiled with a shrug.

Kate sighed. If Delta was nervous, she should be, too.

Someone hit play on an enormous 1980s-style boom box, and a track that reminded Kate of the *Gone With the Wind* theme began to play. Debbie stepped forward in a floral-print, silk nightgown and a thick denim jacket. On her feet were brown leather boots, several sizes too big, that thudded with each step on the cold ground. She held a small, black book in her hand, its leather tattered and frayed, and at first glance, Kate assumed it was a Bible. Debbie opened its yellowed pages, and the women hushed and circled together around the flames.

Debbie surveyed the women with an intense gaze, the flames illuminating her face. The ceremony had begun.

"Ladies, tonight is about lettin' go. It's about sayin' goodbye to a part of your past that's got you stuck. If you're truly ready to take that step, raise your right hand and say, 'I am.'"

The women exchanged glances then held up their hands. One by one they repeated, "I am."

"Good," Debbie said. "Do you have the items I asked you to bring?"

Kate held the paper bag at her side. Mo dug deep into her pockets.

"Please remove the items and place them in front of the fire."

Kate stole a peek at Modean's pile—her Uncle Lou's watch, a red handkerchief, a pocketknife, and a gold wedding band. Kate gasped, and Mo glanced at her but looked away quickly.

Kate pulled her own objects from the bag—a dried red rose, a folded slip of notebook paper, a long dark feather, and an old hardback copy of Harper Lee's *To Kill a Mockingbird.*

"Faye, we'll start with you," Debbie said. "Please pick up the object you brought that means the most to you and tell us about it."

Faye, a tall, thin woman of about sixty looked as if she might pass out at any moment. She stared wide-eyed at Debbie, then gazed around the circle of women. She bent slowly and picked up a blue, button-up, short-sleeved shirt with the name *Al* embroidered in orange cursive letters on the breast. She held it across her body with shaking hands, displaying it for the others to see.

"This was my husband's work shirt. Well, one of 'em anyway. Most of y'all knew Al. He worked down at Hodge's Garage for seventeen years." She lowered her head, and when she raised it, her bottom lip quaked. "He got sick last year. Lung cancer. He fought it for six months before the good Lord took him home. This is the shirt he wore on his last day at the shop." She brought it to her face and buried her nose in the fabric. "It smells like sweat and his cologne." Faye began to sob. The woman next to her put a comforting arm around her waist and cried with her. "My sister asked me to move out to Dallas to be close to her and my family. I want to go, but I'm afraid if I do, I'll forget . . . I'm afraid I'll forget my life here . . . with him. I don't want to forget." Faye crumbled in tears.

"Thank you, Faye, darlin'." Debbie stepped over to her and hugged her close. She was wiping tears from her own face by the time she pulled away. "Delta, why don't you go next?"

Delta bent toward the ground and rose with a hundred dollar bill in her hand. "I had a fiancé until a week ago. He was loaded." She smacked her gum and inhaled the bill's aroma.

"This is what I'm gonna miss the most."

The group was silent until Modean let out a loud snicker. Then Faye giggled, too. Then Kate, and then the entire group erupted in laughter. Debbie rolled her eyes at Delta and waited until the women had regained their composure.

"All right, all right. Settle down, ladies. Kate, honey, why don't you go?"

A million butterflies flipped around in Kate's stomach. She gazed down at the items at her feet and made her choice. She picked up the notebook paper and unfolded it.

"This is a note my ex-husband left for me one morning several years ago. I found it in my favorite coffee cup after he left for work." Kate stared at Gray's handwriting on the page.

"Well, read it, honey," one of the women finally said.

Kate hesitated then cleared her throat. "It says, 'My beautiful Kate. The hardest thing I have ever done was getting out of bed this morning, letting go of you under blankets that were warm. Everything seems cold when you aren't with me. I wish I could live every second of the day with you by my side. It's where I belong, wherever you are, those warm places. I love you, Kate. P.S. I had a dream the baby was a girl. Love, Gray.'"

Kate felt the sting of tears but battled against them. "He left me for someone new this past October. I guess someone that makes him feel warmer." She laughed. "He asked me for a divorce, and it was final three weeks ago. Oh, and he was right. The baby was a girl."

Delta swallowed hard and took a deep breath. "Don't you make me cry, too, girl."

"Thanks, Kate," Debbie said. "You did good. Mo, how about you?"

Mo leaned into Kate. "Can you bend down there and get me that ring?"

Kate bent over, then hesitated, her fingers inches from the ring.

"Please, Kate."

Kate retrieved the ring and slipped it into Mo's hand. Mo examined it then held it up for the rest to see. The gold glistened before the flames.

"This is my Lou's wedding band. We bought it in 1958 for fifty-five dollars." She laughed. "That felt like a fortune back then. Guess it was to us. He put it on his finger and never once took it off, 'til they took it off him after the funeral." Tears formed in Mo's eyes and streamed down her red cheeks. "It's been sittin' in my jewelry box for nearly thirty years. I pick it up every mornin' and look it over. I imagine it on his hand. I remember every vein. Every line. Every wrinkle. I know how every nail looked, and the scar on his thumb he got from a barbed wire fence when he was just a boy." Mo stared at the band, her chin trembling. At last she looked up at the others. "Well, that's all I got to say."

Kate smiled at her, tears streaming from her eyes. Mo slipped her arm inside Kate's and gave her a reassuring nod.

When the last woman had finished sharing her memory item, silence fell over the group. The fire raged higher, stretching toward their memories scattered on the ground just out of reach, waiting.

Debbie stepped up onto a wooden box. The wind whipped at her long, brown hair as if it had been rehearsed, and she raised her arms toward the sky.

"Ladies, please take all your memories into your hands and

lift them high above the flames."

Kate helped Modean retrieve her objects off the ground. With trembling hands, Modean lifted them towards the fire, and the wedding band glinted in the light.

Kate looked around the circle at the others. She searched their faces as they held out their possessions as dear as breath, poised and ready to toss into the flames. She felt her pulse increase, and her eyes widened.

"On my count, ladies!" Debbie shouted. "One . . . Two . . ." She raised her arms high. One of the women whimpered. Another gasped. Then Debbie lowered her arms and stepped down from the box. "Ladies, please put your memories down and take a seat."

The women exchanged glances. Bewildered and relieved, they obeyed and lowered themselves to the ground—everyone but Delta, who propped her hand on her hip.

"Well, what in the world?" she cried. "Are you tryin' to give me a heart attack? I thought this was a bye fire! If we're gonna do this, let's do it already!"

Debbie stood tall and opened the book in her hand. "Sit down, Delta, and just listen for once."

Delta rolled her eyes but did what she was told.

Debbie took a deep breath and held up the book. "Ladies, this diary belonged to my Great Great Aunt Hildy Thomas. It's been passed down through the women in my family for generations, and I'm about to read a passage to you, written by Hildy herself over a hundred and forty years ago." Debbie gingerly flipped through several of the ancient pages, then cleared her throat.

" 'October twenty-ninth, eighteen sixty-seven. Last night I went to sleep listening to Ada cry, just like every night before.

It's been nearly six months since her fiancé was killed, but my child's suffering grows stronger with every day that passes. I had just dozed off when I heard the crackling of a fire below my window. I grabbed my coat and ran into the yard. I'll never forget the sight of her. Ada had built a fire and was standing there, staring at the flames like she was in a trance or had finally gone mad. She was wearing her silk nightgown and James's old work boots, and in her hand she held the wedding dress I made her last year.

" 'When I screamed her name, she told me to leave her be. But I didn't go. I stood with her a long while in the cold without saying a word, praying God would give me the words to say to my child, whose tormented spirit has endured more in her eighteen years than most could bear in a lifetime.

" 'I prayed and prayed, and when she raised the dress over the flames, I told her that in that dress, there was no grief. The grief is deep inside the pieces of her, and unless she was willing to throw herself into the fire, burning that dress wouldn't change a thing.' " Debbie glanced up at her captive audience then back down at the diary. " 'I told her, until now she carried around a spark in her like all good women do. We walk around with it inside us until dark falls pitch black all around, and then it sets itself ablaze so we can find our way. This is that time for her. It's her darkest hour, and she just found her fire. I told her that burning her dress wouldn't ease her pain and that the only thing that needed to end up in the fire was the boots on her feet. That James's footsteps wouldn't carry her anymore. Only her feet alone would take her where she needed to go.

" 'She stared at me for the longest time, and I thought at any moment she might step into the fire herself. Then she lay the dress gently on the ground and pulled the boots off her feet. She stood tall in front of the flames and threw first one then the other into the fire without a solitary tear. Before the night had gone, we danced and sang around the blaze like two crazy women. My child had found her fire.'"

Debbie looked up and closed the book. All around the circle, the woman sniffed and wiped tears from their cheeks. After a lengthy moment of silence, Delta stood and brushed off her behind.

"So, we ain't gotta burn this stuff?"

"You ain't gotta do anything, Delta, except realize that you got a fire burnin' in you. All of you! A fire that's blazin' 'cause it has to! And it's gonna light your way even in this dark you're walkin' through."

Delta dropped her face into her hands and let out a sob. Debbie hurried to her. Faye met her there, and both women held Delta in a tight embrace.

"Shhh, honey. It's all right to cry. You got every right to."

When Delta finally raised her head, revealing mammoth tears in her eyes and on her cheeks, she dug deep into the pockets of her fur coat and pulled out several hundred dollar bills. "I'm just so happy. I thought I was gonna have to burn all this money."

"Oh, Delta! Good grief!" Debbie pushed her on the shoulder.

Delta's eyes glistened with tears, but her red lips spread into a wide smile, and everyone laughed.

Modean bent, slipped off one of Lou's boots, and threw it into the fire, followed by the other one. Then she wiggled her bare toes on the cold ground. Faye followed with Al's boots, and one by one, the women tossed their boots into the fire. The kindled flames leapt toward the sky, their hunger quenched at last.

All eyes fell upon Kate, and she bent down, hoping no one would notice. But a snicker here and a giggle there signaled they had. Kate slipped out of both shiny, leather wingtips and held them up for all to see. She shrugged. "It was short notice."

The group exploded in laughter. Kate tossed the shoes into the blaze as someone cranked up the stereo. Janis sang "Piece of My Heart," and they danced like crazy women around the flames.

Chapter Twenty-two

Murder is terribly exhausting.
-Albert Camus

Kate glanced at her watch for the tenth time since arriving at Mo's. It was Sunday morning, and they were running late for church. Jane Ellen had gone ahead with Truitt and Vaughn at Vaughn's insistence, and they all were to rendezvous at Millsville Baptist at 10:00 a.m. It was already 9:55.

Modean finally emerged from her bedroom, rubbing her eyes and mumbling. "Dadgummit! I still can't find my glasses!"

"I've looked everywhere I can think of out here, Aunt Mo," Kate said. "But we really have to go if we're going to make it to church on time. We still have to stop and pick up the twins."

Mo shook her head. "Well, they gotta be around here somewhere. We'll tear the place to pieces when we get home from church. Let's go."

Kate and Mo hurried out to the Bronco just as Emma and Ella came walking up Modean's driveway. It was mid-March, and the air was crisp, but not cold. The twins wore crocheted shawls, both pink, and khaki dress pants with hot pink high heels.

"Yoo-hoo!" they called. "Here we are! We decided it would be better to meet you here."

Ella took a seat next to Kate in the front as Modean and Emma settled into the back. As Kate backed down the driveway onto the road, the Bronco rolled over something and landed with a dull thud.

"Oh, great," Kate said. "I hope that wasn't Jane Ellen's

soccer ball. I told her to bring it in last night."

"It's on my side," Modean said. "I'll check." She exited the vehicle, and in her absence Emma and Ella talked about the beautiful, sunny morning and how excited they were to visit Millsville Baptist again after attending Millsville Grace for so many years.

Kate checked her watch again and gritted her teeth, craning her neck to see if she could get a glimpse of Mo out the Bronco's rear window. Then Mo reappeared at the rear passenger side door. Her face was white, her jaw clenched. She stared dead ahead, clinging to her purse and breathing harder than normal.

"Well?" Kate asked.

"Just the soccer ball," Mo said.

"Poor Jane Ellen." Emma shook her head and frowned. "We'll just have to buy her a new one."

The twins resumed their conversation as Kate caught a glimpse of Aunt Mo's troubled expression in the rearview mirror.

***

Malcolm threw the green striped tie onto the bed. After several attempts at tying it properly, the tie had beaten him. He simply wouldn't wear one that day. He shrugged. The congregation hadn't seen him in a tie in years—the shock would probably be too much for them anyway.

He pulled on the navy suit coat and examined himself in the mirror. His pulse raced, and his palms were sweaty. Through the reflection, his eyes found the bookshelf behind him, where Jackson Boudrow's Bible rested. He turned around and grabbed it off the shelf. The book and its former owner usually sent waves of self-doubt surging through his body. Jackson Boudrow's shoes could never be filled—not by anyone, especially him.

But that day, thoughts of Millsville Baptist's former pastor gave him an inexplicable reassurance. He wondered again why Ruth had given the Bible to him when it should have gone to Kate, but he was more grateful to have it than ever. Malcolm tucked the Bible under his arm, picked up the tie, and walked out the door.

***

The church's sanctuary was over half full when Modean and Kate arrived with the twins. Jane Ellen, who'd been watching the doors for her mother, rushed up the center aisle and into Kate's arms. Kate hugged her tightly and stole a quick kiss on the forehead before Jane Ellen hurried back to her place between Truitt and Vaughn.

Modean and Kate found a seat on the opposite end of Truitt's pew. The twins sat directly behind them next to an old friend and longtime church member, Betsy Belmont, the former Women's League chairperson and professional gossip. The three began whispering and laughing at once and did not notice the choir members taking the stage and beginning their song.

Kate picked up a hymnal and flipped through the pages, looking for page number 279. It was a familiar tune, but she needed help with the lyrics. The choir sang at full volume, and Kate sang along. "Some glad morning we shall see Jesus in the air, coming after you and me, joy is ours to share. What rejoicing there will be when the saints shall rise, headed for that jubilee yonder in the skies. Oh, what singing, oh, what shouting, on that happy morning when we all shall—"

Modean elbowed Kate hard in the arm. Kate winced then turned wide eyes on her. Modean leaned toward her and spoke out of the side of her mouth. "Get. Truitt."

Kate peered down the aisle toward Truitt and counted seven people between the two of them. She turned back to Mo and shook her head, but Mo narrowed her eyes and nodded sharply. There was no use telling her 'no.'

Kate leaned forward as far as she could. Truitt was looking toward the stage, singing the words by heart. "Truitt," she whispered, and the woman seated beside her gave a quick twitch of her head. Kate tried again, this time a bit louder. "Truitt!"

Three more heads turned to look, but Truitt stared straight ahead, singing obliviously. Kate turned to Mo to report her failure when, over her head, Mo hurled a wadded-up church bulletin. The paper bomb soared down the pew and popped Truitt in the side of the face. Truitt lurched sideways and nearly fell out of his seat, and every head in the pew turned and looked directly at Kate.

Truitt leaned forward and raised his eyebrows at her. Kate leaned back and pointed to Mo, who was already mouthing something even Kate could not decipher.

"What?" Truitt whispered.

Mo tried again, intermittently cutting her eyes back toward the twins. Truitt shook his head and shrugged. The others in the pew were looking from Mo to Truitt as if watching a tennis match, some annoyed, others thoroughly entertained. The music stopped briefly, just long enough for Nina to call out another song number. The pianist fired up the keys again, and the choir resumed their singing.

Mo resorted to sign language. She held her hands in front of her face like claws and growled, pointed discreetly behind her, then let her head fall to the side with her eyes closed and her tongue lolling out. Truitt crinkled his brow and shook his head, and Modean's shoulders fell in exasperation. She lunged for her purse and handed it to Kate. "Pass it down."

Kate took the bag from Mo and let it plop into her lap, unprepared for its weightiness. She raised an eyebrow at Mo only to be elbowed again, this time in the side. Kate sighed and tapped the woman next to her on the shoulder. "Could you please pass this down?"

The woman scowled but took the bag, grimacing under its heavy weight, and passed it to the man beside her. Slowly but steadily, the purse reached Truitt. He took it in his lap and unzipped it as quietly as he could. The song was almost halfway finished when Truitt peered inside.

In an instant, he leapt to his feet with his arms in the air and landed in the aisle. The purse plummeted to the floor with a loud thud, and he shot Mo a terrified glare. Modean's eyes were wide, and she feverishly pointed at the purse. Truitt looked down at the furry tail poking out through the top and pounced, shoving it back inside before zipping the purse back together.

He stood again, and the music stopped, all eyes in the church upon him. Truitt froze, holding the purse close to his chest, and scanned the faces in the room. Then he threw his hands in the air and shouted, "Hallelujah! Now that is a song!"

Kate lowered her head and winced, and Vaughn stared in disbelief. Then the silence was broken by an old man in the back. "Hallelujah!"

Then another shouted, "Hallelujah!" and added, "Praise Jesus!" The church erupted in hallelujahs and applause, and the music started up again with renewed fervor. Truitt made his way out the back of the church, and Modean hurried close behind. Kate crept out of her seat and chased after them.

She pushed out the door to see Truitt pacing in the parking lot, staring at Modean with narrowed eyes. "Aunt Mo, why is Mr. Gregory Peck in your purse?"

"Because Kate backed over him on the way over here!"

Kate gasped and threw her hand over her mouth. Her knees went weak, and her bottom landed on the church step. "You mean it wasn't the soccer ball?"

Truitt unzipped the bag and waved the tail at her. "Does this look like a soccer ball?"

"You didn't know he was under the car, honey," Mo said. "Stupid cat. I don't know how he lasted this long."

"Mo!" Truitt shouted, grabbing her by the shoulders. "Why is he in your purse?"

"Because the twins were in the car with us! I didn't want them to see him when we drove off! I thought about tossin' him in the bushes, but I was afraid they'd see me do it! I had my purse in my hand, so I just stuffed him in!"

"Well, what am I supposed to do?"

"I don't know! You're the vet! Pronounce him dead or somethin'!"

"He's dead! Feel better?"

"No! 'Cause he's still in my purse!"

Footsteps clicked along the pavement, and the three of them hushed as Malcolm headed toward the church door. The pastor was wearing a sport coat and poorly tied tie. His hair was fixed neatly, and his shaven cheeks appeared fuller, not hollow as usual. He turned his gaze on them, the look in his eyes confused but pleasant, and somehow more alive than before.

Malcolm looked from Mo to Truitt and down to Kate on the step. "Is something wrong out here?"

"Kate killed Ella and Emma's cat," Modean spouted without wasting a second.

"Then Mo packed him up in her purse and passed him to me during 'Up from the Grave He Arose,' " Truitt said.

Malcolm's eyes fell back to Kate. She stood, meeting Malcolm face to face, and took his tie in her hands. "Been a while, huh?"

Malcolm smiled. "Is it that obvious?"

Kate maneuvered the tie into a perfect knot then smoothed it down with the palm of her hand and examined her work. "There. Much better."

It would be several more seconds before he tore his eyes from hers. "I'd better get inside."

Kate nodded and watched him disappear around the side of the church. Truitt and Mo stared at her, then Truitt waved his hand inches in front of her face. "Ummm . . . yoo hoo! Kate? Over here? Not sure what just happened there, but remember the dead cat in the purse? The one you murdered?"

"Oh, hush, Truitt," Mo said.

Truitt growled and scratched the top of his head as he formulated a plan. "All right. You two go back inside. Tell Vaughn I'll meet her back at Mo's for lunch. I'll go . . . dispose of the body."

"What will we tell the twins?" Kate asked.

"The truth," Truitt said. "But not now. I'll talk to them when

I get back. Let me handle it."

Truitt lay Mr. Gregory Peck onto the floor of the Jeep, and Kate took Mo's arm and led her back up the steps and into the sanctuary.

Back inside the church, Modean and Kate reclaimed their places on the pew. Kate gave Vaughn a reassuring nod while Modean whispered a lie to the twins about Truitt being sick. Then Kate and Modean leaned back onto the pew and exchanged a wary glance. Crisis averted. For the time being. The notion of admitting to Emma and Ella that their beloved cat was not only dead but flat as a pancake made Kate ill.

Kate recalled the thud of the Bronco rolling over what she'd thought was Jane Ellen's soccer ball. She cringed and tried to dispel the moment of impact from her mind when out of the corner of her eye she saw Modean waving to someone across the room. Kate turned to see Nate Bell on the other side of the church in a brown suit and tie, waving back with a wide smile. Kate couldn't help but smile herself.

From the stage, Nina announced the next song would be the last of the morning and called out number 135, "Standing on the Promises." As the pianist played, Kate caught her first glimpse of Malcolm sitting on the stage behind the choir members. It was his first Sunday back at church in weeks. He held her father's Bible and stared down at it as the choir members sang their hearts out. So far he hadn't deviated from his customary Sunday morning behavior.

Still, Kate looked around her and felt a tingling on her skin. There was an energy in the sanctuary, an anticipation on the faces of the people, an eagerness, as though they were at a Millsville High School football game, minus the cowbells and applause and signs. They sang louder, some smiling, some clapping, all waiting and wondering if this would be The Sunday.

They were cheering for him silently, deep in their hearts, pulling for him to stand up and say something, anything, to give them an indication that Malcolm—their Malcolm—had come back to them. Kate smiled and bit her bottom lip. *You can do it, Malcolm. Stand up. Just stand up.*

The song ended, and the choir exited the stage and took their seats. Malcolm's eyes were glued to the book in his hand. He did not stand, or speak, or even move. The hope hanging high above the crowd began to wane. His hands shook, and a sheen of sweat broke out on his forehead.

The silence stretched on, and finally old Brother Jake pushed himself to his feet from his spot in the front row and turned to address the crowd with a smile and nod. "Mornin'."

"Mornin'," they all replied.

"Well, who's got a testimony to share today?" Jake's speech seemed even slower than usual.

One by one, people stood and told a story or shared a scripture. Some talked of sickness. Some of happiness. Some wept. Some laughed. Almost everyone ended with, "Y'all pray for me and my family." But Malcolm kept his eyes on the book, stiff and unwavering. When the last person had shared, Jake stood again. After a single quick glance toward Malcolm, he addressed the congregation.

"We sure are glad to have all our visitors with us today. Y'all come back and be with us next week. I think Nina gave us our announcements this morning. If that's all, I'll dismiss us in prayer."

Malcolm jumped to his feet, and Kate nearly gasped out

loud.

***

Malcolm stepped toward the pulpit and gripped it with both hands, staring out at the crowd as they waited. He clenched his jaw and swallowed hard. His hands shook, rattling the pulpit, and his legs threatened to fail him. A lump rose in his throat, and his lungs refused to expand.

Seconds passed. A minute. Then, in the second row, Ruby Williams rose to her feet with great care and steadied herself with quaking hands. Her eyes met his, and she smiled a sweet, grateful smile. Malcolm's own eyes filled with tears. He hadn't called Ruby after her husband, Clyde, suffered his stroke and lay in a hospital bed for days. He hadn't gone to see her or taken her a meal. Hadn't offered to preach the funeral. Hadn't *attended* the funeral. Hadn't been by to check on her since. And yet there she stood, smiling at him as though she couldn't be prouder of her own son.

Behind Ruby, Willie Henderson stood. Wille's wife, Mae, had been in the nursing home for more than two years, and Malcolm had never been to visit her or the family. He'd never acted for one second as though he'd cared. But Willie stood for him, tall and certain. The old man smiled, and a fresh stream of tears ran down Malcolm's cheeks.

Throughout the room, people stood one by one, until every pew was empty. Someone in the back began to clap, slow and quiet at first, then loud and boisterous. The gesture was contagious and spread throughout the congregation, and Malcolm stood behind the pulpit and wept.

Chapter Twenty-three

A hero is no braver than an ordinary
man, but he is braver five minutes longer.
-Ralph Waldo Emerson

At Modean's kitchen table, the twins stuffed their mouths full of Mexican chicken casserole and green beans while Modean and Kate exchanged uneasy glances and picked nervously at their food. Poor Vaughn still had no idea what was happening or where Truitt had run off to, but the way she looked between Modean and the twins while keeping her lips pressed tight together gave Kate the impression she was savvy enough to figure out whatever it was required the utmost discretion. She chatted with Jane Ellen at the table and patiently awaited an explanation.

After lunch, the sisters declined dessert—Mo's homemade raisin pie. They were tired, they said, and ready for their Sunday afternoon nap. Moreover, Mr. Gregory Peck had not shown up for his breakfast that morning, and the twins were certain he was awaiting their return, probably pacing angrily at their back door. No doubt he was incensed and would let them have it at first sight.

Emma and Ella had almost made their way out of Mo's front door when Truitt walked in. He hugged them, apologized for missing lunch with the two most beautiful women in town, and showed them out. Modean stood as he entered the kitchen.

"Well? Did you . . . you know?"

Truitt walked to Vaughn and kissed the top of her head then plopped in a chair next to her. "It's done."

"What's done?" Jane Ellen asked.

Vaughn took Jane Ellen's hand. "Why don't we go play in the living room?" she asked then led Jane Ellen out of the kitchen.

"I buried him in the field behind the clinic," Truitt said. "I even put up a little stone if they ever want to go visit him."

"Thank God it's over," Mo said on an exhale. "When are you gonna tell 'em?"

Truitt stuffed a roll in his mouth and chewed fast. "Now."

Kate put her forehead on the table. "I can't believe I killed Mr. Gregory Peck."

"Oh," Truitt said with his mouth full of roll then finally managed to swallow. "You didn't kill him."

"What?" Modean and Kate asked together.

"I said Kate didn't kill him."

"You mean he wasn't dead?" Modean cried.

"Oh, he was dead all right. And he'd probably been dead all night. The only part of him that wasn't stiff as a board was his tail. I can't believe you couldn't tell, Mo."

"I didn't have my glasses!" Mo shouted. "You mean I carried a dead cat around in my purse for nothin'?"

"Afraid so," Truitt said, and Kate burst into laughter.

Mo sat down at the table and shook her head. "Oh, good Lord. I gotta get a new purse."

***

Levi Canton recovered from his surgery and was released from the hospital two weeks after the heart attack. A day later, Malcolm drove Delta to the airport while Delta divulged the intimate details of her family relations.

"You know Gray already went home to Atlanta with that new wife of his. He wanted to stay longer, but Kristen absolutely did not. Nope, she was adamant about goin' home, and the issue was not up for debate."

Malcolm nodded, half tuning her out. He didn't care to hear about Kate's ex-husband.

Delta sighed. "I'm actually a little sad to leave Millsville this time. Ain't that a first. But I need to get back and check in on Esther. Anyway, I been missin' that girl."

Malcolm pulled over alongside the curb at the departures gate. "All right, honey," Delta said. "I appreciate the lift." She gave him an immense hug, and Malcolm hugged her back. "You don't worry about anything in Houston, now, you hear me? I'm takin' good care of everything."

"I know you are," Malcolm said. "Not much longer now."

"Oh, there's no rush. I told you, I'm enjoyin' Esther bein' at my place. It's almost like I'm with family again."

"Thank you, Delta."

She nodded and gave him a ruby-red smile then picked up her leopard-print carry-on. "Talk to you soon."

Malcolm watched her ascend the escalator, and she was gone.

***

March turned to April and, with it, warmer weather arrived in Millsville. The flowers bloomed. Songbirds and insects came out of hiding. People emerged from the warmth and shelter of their homes into yards and gardens in desperate need of care.

The days grew longer. And Malcolm Bauer showed up for church every Sunday morning in his jacket and tie. Though he had yet to actually say a word, he was there.

Some church members called it a miracle. Others wouldn't set their hopes so high. After all, Pastor Malcolm sitting on stage without a move or a murmur was not the least bit unusual. But even the most ardent of skeptics couldn't deny something was different about him. His eyes had come back to life.

Even Kate had noticed something new, but it had nothing to do with his eyes. Since the day of Mr. Gregory Peck's demise and her moment in the church parking lot with Malcolm and the tie, Malcolm had been avoiding her. In fact, she could have sworn she saw him cross to the other side of the street when he saw her coming out of Robinson's Hardware a few days before. On Tuesday, she'd walked into Beulah's for dinner just as Malcolm had been walking out. She'd smiled and said hello, and he'd nodded and kept walking. On Sunday morning in church, she'd caught him looking at her, but before she could smile at him, he'd looked away and never looked back. As much as she wanted to believe his evading her was all in her head, it wasn't. That she was sure of.

On Wednesday afternoon, Truitt picked up Kate from Hodge's Garage. The Bronco had been making a clicking sound, and Truitt had convinced her to have it checked out. They stopped at Susie's for an early dinner, and Truitt was ecstatic to discover Susie's Wednesday night special was chicken potpie. He shoveled in the steaming chunks of chicken, vegetables, and Susie's homemade buttery crust as though he hadn't eaten in days but promised Susie he'd save room for dessert.

"So how are the twins?" Kate asked.

"Still in mourning. I've been by twice already this week. Both times they were wearin' black. And no, I'm not kiddin'. The garden's keepin' 'em busy, but they're still havin' a hard time. Malcolm was there last night. I heard he's been out visitin' folks again."

"Maybe so, but he's been avoiding me like the plague."

Truitt took another massive bite and spoke as he chewed. "C'mon, Kate. You know it's because you make him nervous."

"Nervous? What are you talking about?"

"You make things different for him."

"Different how? What do you mean?"

"I've seen the way he looks at you. We all have. He cares about you, and that means he thinks about you. And if he's thinkin' about you, he's not thinkin' about Anna. Grievin' her death is all he's known for years. You're changin' things for him."

Kate stabbed at her salad with a fork. "That's ridiculous."

"You know it isn't. Because you care about him, too."

"Can we please talk about something else?"

"You brought it up."

Kate growled. "You're impossible." She threw her napkin at him but missed. Truitt threw it back and hit his target. They were laughing and arguing by the time Malcolm entered the diner and approached their table.

"Truitt?" Malcolm began. "I need your help."

"Sure," Truitt said, wiping at his mouth and trying his best to pretend the pastor hadn't just been the topic of their conversation. "Is it an animal emergency?"

Malcolm stared at him then sighed. "Something like that."

Truitt stood and pulled a twenty out of his wallet for Susie.

"Kate's with me."

"Bring her," Malcolm said. "We may need all the help we can get."

Kate gathered her things and followed them out the door as Susie yelled, "Hey, Truitt! You promised you'd save room for my cobbler!"

***

Truitt and Kate followed Malcolm up to the doors of Butterfield Manor Nursing Center. They exchanged a curious glance as Malcolm pushed numbers into a keypad next to the side door of the facility. The door buzzed, and Malcolm pushed it open and stepped aside for Truitt and Kate to enter. An elderly woman was pushing a walker down the hall wearing a blue dress, red high-top Reeboks, and a Razorback baseball cap. She stopped to greet the visitors with a toothless smile before continuing at a snail's pace down the corridor. Malcolm walked ahead of them, and they followed.

As he rounded the corner toward a sign that read *Nurses Station*, a voice called from behind them, "Malcolm!"

They turned as an attractive brunette in her late forties, wearing pink scrubs and a name badge that said *Pam, LPN*, headed toward them. Pam looked exhausted and on the verge of a breakdown. She extended her hand to Malcolm, and he shook it with a sympathetic nod. "I brought Dr. Boudrow."

Pam gave him a relieved smile. She let go of Malcolm's hand and grasped Truitt's in a firm shake. "I'm certainly glad to see you, Dr. Boudrow. Do you remember Ms. Lucy? Lucy Stroud?"

Truitt squinted up at the ceiling. "Lucy Stroud? Well, yeah.

She and Mr. John used to bring their dog in to see me. But I haven't seen them in years."

"Mr. John passed away four years ago," Pam said. "Ms. Lucy has been with us for nearly two and half years. They never had children, and there's no family around here to speak of. She's in the late stages of Alzheimer's, and I've been taking care of her since she got here." Pam glanced at Malcolm.

"Truitt, Ms. Lucy remembers you," Malcolm said. "Well, she remembers you today, anyway."

Truitt shook his head. "I'm afraid I don't understand."

"Ms. Lucy's dog, Trixie, died of old age before Ms. Lucy came to live here," Pam told him. "But about a year ago someone brought her a toy dog. I guess they thought it was a nice gesture, but Ms. Lucy gets confused so easily. The toy moves and barks when you pet it and, well, Ms. Lucy became convinced that it wasn't a toy at all. At first we thought it would be a problem, but having Trixie back seemed to calm her. She started smiling again like she did when she first got here and even remembered things better."

"So she believes the toy dog is Trixie come back from the dead?" Truitt asked.

"Oh, she doesn't remember that Trixie ever died. Most days she doesn't remember her husband is gone. We made Trixie a little bed in the corner. Sometimes the nurses bring her doggie clothes and treats. Trixie and Ms. Lucy are a pair around here. Ms. Lucy doesn't go anywhere without Trixie on her lap. And that's our problem." Pam dug into her shirt pocket and pulled out two triple-A batteries. "Ms. Lucy used to let us take Trixie out every now and then for what we told her were walks. But since the Alzheimer's is progressing, she's become afraid people want to steal Trixie from her. She hasn't let her out of her sight in weeks, and Trixie's batteries died two days ago."

"She's convinced someone poisoned the dog and that she's dying," Malcolm said. "She's been in her room crying and belligerent since yesterday. She bit Pam's arm this morning."

Pam held up her arm to show the white bandage with the faint hint of red seeping through from beneath. "You should see the other nurse on duty. Lucy threw a shoe at him and busted his lip open. He had to have three stitches. She can't remember who we are, and that just makes her more confused and agitated. She's been screaming and scratching at everyone who goes in her room, not to mention throwing things. We haven't been able to give her her medications or take her to the bathroom." Pam sniffed and wiped at her wet eyes. "If word gets out, they'll have us restrain her or even transfer her to another wing. She'll lose her freedoms over there, and they certainly won't let her have Trixie." Pam pulled a Kleenex from her pocket and blew her nose. "I know I'm too attached, but Lucy is special to me. It's just not fair for her to be all alone."

"She mentioned your name this morning, Truitt," Malcolm said. "We think you may be the only one she'll let near Trixie, and if that's the case, you can try to change her batteries."

Pam put her hand on Truitt's arm as a tear slipped down her cheek. "I know all this must sound so silly to you, but—"

"Not at all." Truitt smiled and motioned for Pam to go ahead. "Lead the way."

***

Truitt approached Lucy's door with tremendous caution. He

tapped lightly, and the door opened with a slight creak. He could hear Lucy sobbing from her chair in the corner. Still undetected, he took a careful step inside and the old woman came into view, her white hair disheveled and her face drawn and wrinkled. A light blue shawl was draped around her shoulders, and a small, furry dog lay in her lap. Trixie was wrapped tightly in a pink baby blanket, and Lucy stroked her honey-brown ears.

"Ms. Lucy?" Truitt said softly.

Lucy looked up and her sad eyes went wild. She reached for a cup of water on the table next to her and threw it at him as hard as her feeble arm would allow. The flying foam cup made it only to the center of the room before splattering onto the floor, and a few drops wet the tips of Truitt's gray Converse shoes. Lucy picked up a book and raised it above her head, and Truitt threw up his hands.

"Ms. Lucy, it's Truitt Boudrow. Remember me? Dr. Boudrow from the Millsville Animal Clinic? I'm Trixie's veterinarian. I heard she's not feeling well, and I came to check on her. If that's okay with you."

Lucy froze then tilted her head to the side. "Dr. Boudrow?"

Truitt breathed a sigh of relief. He stepped toward her and smiled reassuringly. "It's good to see you again, Ms. Lucy. It's been a while since you've been into the clinic."

Lucy's expression turned soft and vulnerable. She reached for Truitt's hand and pulled him down next to her. Her swollen, pink eyes overflowed with tears, and her voice was weak from hours of weeping and yelling at anyone who breached her doorway. "Dr. Boudrow, they've killed her."

Truitt pulled a tissue from a box next to Lucy's bed and dabbed at her wet eyes. "No, no, Ms. Lucy. No one would want to hurt Trixie. If I could just have a look at her—"

"Oh yes, they poisoned her. They poisoned her, I know it!" Lucy's eyes went wild again. "The neighbors hate Trixie 'cause she barks at night and chases their cats. They think it's Trixie who digs up their yard, but it's not! It's the Laymons' cocker spaniel. I've seen him do it." Lucy sobbed. "But Trixie's a good dog, Dr. Boudrow. You know she's a good dog."

"Yes, Ms. Lucy. I know. She's a very good dog."

Lucy leaned forward and searched the room with her eyes. "Where is John? John would know what to do. John?"

Truitt maneuvered himself directly in front of Lucy with his hand on her knee. "I'll have a talk with the neighbors, all right? I'll tell them what a good dog Trixie is and promise them she won't bark at night anymore."

"And tell them I'll keep her inside so she can't chase those cats."

"I'll tell them. And I'll make sure they know she's not the one diggin' in their yards." Truitt patted her shaking hand. "Now, I need you to let me have a look at Trixie. It's not too late for her, but you have to let me examine her."

"But you can't take her away!" Lucy cried. "No, you can't take her!"

"I won't take her away. I'll just lay her right over here on your bed." Truitt stroked the toy dog's head. "Ms. Lucy, I promise to help her. But you have to let me take her over to the bed. Can you do that?"

Lucy glanced toward the bed, only steps away. Then, with wary hands, she wrapped the baby blanket even tighter around Trixie's furry body and handed her to Truitt with the greatest of care.

***

Malcolm and Kate stood outside Lucy's room on opposite sides of the hallway. Kate twirled her hair around her index finger and glanced toward the nurses' station for Pam, but she was nowhere in sight.

Malcolm leaned against the wall and stared at the shiny white floor. "So where's the Rover?"

She wrinkled her forehead. "Excuse me?"

"The Range Rover? What'd you do with it after you bought the Bronco?"

"Oh, right." Kate chuckled. "I gave it to the women's shelter in Fayetteville. Mama volunteered there sometimes. The only vehicle they had was an old van that was in the shop most of the time. They needed something reliable."

Malcolm laughed. "Well, a Range Rover should do it."

Kate laughed, too. "I would've loved to have seen Gray's face when he found out. He bought it brand new for my birthday last year."

They were laughing when a muffled barking sound came from within Lucy's room. Pam rushed down the hall toward them and skidded to a stop outside the door. She knocked softly and cracked open the door, and the three of them peeked in to see Lucy rocking Trixie as the little dog moved its head and tail and barked. The old woman was smiling from ear to ear while tears of joy streaked her cheeks.

She reached out to Pam as though she'd never forgotten or doubted her. "Oh, Pam, come see! Trixie is alive!"

Pam rushed to Lucy and wrapped her arms around her neck. "That's wonderful," she said through tears.

Truitt stood from his seat on the bed. "Ms. Lucy, I'm gonna go now. If you need anything at all, you just tell Nurse Pam here, and she'll let me know."

"Oh, thank you, Dr. Boudrow. I will!"

"And remember what I told you. It's important that Trixie get some exercise every day. The nurses have agreed to give her walks and take special care of her, so you let them do that, okay?"

"Oh, yes, I promise I will. And I'll tell John what you did for our Lucy. He'll be so pleased."

Truitt kissed the top of Lucy's head then left the room, and Malcolm and Kate followed him into the hallway. Truitt smiled, wiping at his eyes.

Malcolm reached out and shook his hand. "Thank you."

Truitt shrugged. "She's got nobody but that stupid toy dog. I give her five minutes of my day, and she thinks I'm a hero."

Malcolm gazed at him, then slid his eyes to the floor.

"But you were," Kate said. "Five minutes made you her hero."

Truitt glanced back at Lucy through the doorway. She was smiling and rocking Trixie to sleep with a soft lullaby.

Chapter Twenty-four

Outside the open window The morning
air is all awash with angels.
-Richard Purdy Wilbur

It had been nearly a month since Kate had visited her parents' graves. She pulled two pale yellow calla lilies and three white gerber daisies out of a vase in Debbie's floral cooler, looked them over, then wrapped them in tissue paper. Debbie walked through the front door as Kate pounded on the cash register's buttons.

"Good grief, it's windy out there today!" Debbie's hair was in a tangled mess atop her head, and she pulled a strand out of her mouth and did her best to smooth out the rest. "Thanks for helpin' me out today, honey. Hope I wasn't gone too long, but let me just tell ya, the tables I did for the Women's League luncheon are gorgeous!"

"I'm sure they are. I saw some of the hyacinths you used in the back."

"Aren't they somethin'? Have you ever seen such a pretty purple? Apparently purple is the official color of the Women's League." Debbie put her hand on her hip and rolled her eyes. "Little pretentious if you ask me. But I guess nobody asked me. What in the world are you doin' there?"

Kate banged on the stubborn keys. "I was trying to ring up these flowers I'm taking to Mama and Daddy's graves, but the five key is stuck again." She hit it hard, this time with her fist. Debbie grabbed her hand.

"Oh no you will not. I ain't takin' any money from you

after you came to my rescue and watched the shop for me this afternoon—not to mention every other time I've called. Don't you even think about payin' me. Now you just get on outta here." Debbie pushed her toward the door. "Shoo!"

"Thank you." Kate grabbed her purse and the flowers before pushing open the door.

"You tell your mama I said hello," Debbie called behind her. "We sure miss her around here."

"I will," Kate said and waved goodbye.

***

With sunset only minutes away, Kate walked through the cemetery toward her parents' graves. The wind whipped her hair in a frenzy about her face, and a strong gust blew one of the daisies from her hand. The flower flipped end over end across the grounds until it came to an abrupt stop against a tall tombstone. Kate considered chasing after it when a small whirlwind of dust flew into her face with a fury.

She closed her eyes and covered them with her hands. After the mini twister moved on, she opened her eyes to see Malcolm walking toward her, his dark brown hair flying untamed in the wind. He looked just as he had the first time she'd seen him—the day of her mother's funeral, when she'd been standing in that very spot. But instead of watching her with somber contempt as he had that day, he recovered her lost flower and held it out to her with an expression that was soft and gracious.

"Ruth loved daises, too," Malcolm said.

Kate nodded and took the flower from his hand. "And lilies."

"I cleaned their stone this morning." He glanced toward her

parents' gravesite. "I try to do it every few months."

"Thank you," Kate said. "I suppose I thought the grounds crew did that."

"I am the grounds crew."

Kate laughed then dipped her head, expecting him to walk away at any moment. Conversations were not Malcolm's strong suit, especially extended ones.

But he didn't walk away.

"Kate," he said, "I need to talk to you."

She willed her heart to slow down as she counted in her head the handful of times he'd used her name.

"I've been wrong about a lot of things lately, you being one of them. I made a lot of assumptions about you before we ever met, and I treated you unfairly." He glanced at the tombstone next to them. "Your mother . . . she was one of the greatest women I've ever known. And I never met Jackson, but—" He shook his head. "If out of nothing more than respect for them, I shouldn't have judged you the way I did. I was wrong. And selfish. And I'm sorry."

The sun had set almost completely, and the unrelenting wind continued to lash about them. Kate stepped toward him and, in a move that surprised even herself, she reached for his cheek.

The sound of Malcolm's name being called floated to them on the wind, and they turned to see Beulah Two standing at the cemetery gate with Beulah in the old Pontiac behind her. Kate dropped her hand and stepped back.

"They're here to see me," Malcolm said.

"Of course." Kate smiled. She wanted to say more, but the words hung on her lips, lost.

"We call Esther twice a week from my house. Just to be safe.

I have to tell Beulah Two that her mom can't come see her for her birthday in June. It's too soon for her to come back. It just doesn't feel right yet."

"Have you talked to Delta since she got back to Houston?"

"She said everything's fine. Better than fine. I think she'll be sad to see Esther go when the time comes."

Beulah Two yelled for Malcolm again.

"I'd better go."

"Sure. You go." Kate nodded and watched him walk out of the cemetery.

***

Kate sat on the ground by her parents' graves for nearly an hour. The wind grew fiercer by the minute, but she couldn't compel herself to leave. It had been too long since she'd spent time with them, and the place was calming. Quiet.

She pictured her father and imagined the way she'd felt in his strong arms just before he'd laid her into bed at night. Of the aroma of his cologne and the smell of leather on his hands from his Bible.

She thought of her mother and how the two of them would walk arm in arm through the farmers' market, carefree and enjoying each other's company more than anything the market had to offer.

But then, whether she liked it or not, her mind began churning with thoughts of *him*.

Kate lifted her eyes and spotted the dark tombstone only a few graves away. She stood and took one of the calla lilies with her, knowing her mother wouldn't mind sharing.

Anna Bauer's enchanting smile was frozen in time, as was her beauty. Her expression in the photo reminded Kate of an old movie she'd once seen. Anna's eyes were calling to the person behind the camera, needing him, loving him infinitely. Kate had no doubts the photographer that day had been Malcolm.

She stepped forward and lay the calla lily in front of the stone. She opened her mouth to speak but then felt the approach of someone behind her.

She whipped her head around, but no one was there. She turned her body in a complete circle. Though she saw no one in any direction, the unmistakable feeling that someone was near engulfed her. Goose bumps rose on her arms and legs, and she shivered.

She shook her head, trying to rid herself of the chills. Of course she was alone. She scanned the grounds again. No one.

A breeze blew against her cheek, but the air was unusually warm. She pressed her hand to her cheek and began walking toward the cemetery gate, but by the time she got there she was sprinting.

She'd just slipped her key into the Bronco when she heard the music coming from inside the church. Instead of climbing into her car, she climbed the stairs to the church. At the loud creaking of the door, Beulah Two looked up from the piano and stilled her fingers.

"Oh, don't stop," Kate said and made her way up the aisle to the stage. "I didn't even know you could play, Beulah Two."

The little girl wiped at her eyes and managed a weak smile. "It's the only song I know," she said, pecking out a few more notes. "Grandma taught me."

Kate sat next to her on the bench. "Well, it was beautiful."

She wrapped an arm around her as Beulah Two sniffed. "Oh, honey. What's the matter?"

Beulah Two's bottom lip quivered. "Malcolm says I can't see Mama on my birthday. But I always do. Always. She never missed even one."

"I know, sweetheart, but it's still too soon for your mama to come back here. Malcolm is just trying to keep you safe. You *and* your mama. You know that, don't you?"

Beulah Two nodded. "I ain't mad, Ms. Kate. I just feel like cryin'."

Kate wrapped Beulah Two's small body in her arms. "Then you cry, sweet girl. You just cry."

Beulah Two buried herself in Kate's embrace and sobbed, and Kate's eyes stung as she thought of how she'd be celebrating her own first birthday without her mother in September. Though it was months away, she already dreaded it.

On her last birthday, Ruth had sent her two dozen homemade double-chocolate brownies and a music box in the shape of a cotton bale that played "Dixieland." Kate had memorized the card.

Promise to share the brownies with Jane Ellen, but the music box is all yours. I found it at the market today. It's hard to believe it's been thirty-two years since I held you for the first time. You were such a beautiful baby, and you're even more beautiful today. I am so proud of the wife and mother you've become, and I love you with all my heart. Love, Your Mama

They'd talked for an hour on the phone that night, beginning with Ruth's octave-too-high version of the happy birthday song.

Kate smoothed Beulah Two's hair. She knew exactly how the little girl felt. Girls needed their mamas. Especially on birthdays.

"Ms. Kate?" Beulah Two asked, staring up at her. "You don't need to be scared of the bad angels."

Kate felt the goose bumps popping up on her arms again. "What do you mean, sweetie?"

"They can't hurt you. They only want to scare you, but you don't got to be scared."

Kate took Beulah Two's chin in her hand. "How do you know when you see an angel?"

Beulah Two gave her an excited smile, as though no one had ever thought to ask her before. "Well, I always feel 'em first. And when I feel 'em, I just start lookin' all around 'til I see. When I lived with Mama, I saw lotsa different ones. Good ones and bad ones. Mostly good ones. I didn't like it at Mama's, but the angels made me feel safe. Around here, though, I've only seen three different ones. I think they live here, too."

"What do they look like?" Kate asked.

"Just like us," Beulah Two said. "They don't got wings or long white dresses like in pictures. They wear clothes like everybody else does."

"And the bad ones?"

Beulah Two's smile fell. "I can't see their faces. They hide 'em like they're ashamed of what they do."

Kate bit her lip. "Have you ever . . . talked to an angel?"

"Just once. I don't know his name, but he's the angel I always see 'round here with you and Malcolm. He's my favorite." She smiled.

"The one who was with you in my yard?"

"Mm-hmm."

"And what did he say when he talked to you?"

She pursed her lips in thought. "All he did was ask me a question."

Kate hesitated, afraid to ask but too curious to let it go. "What did he ask you?"

"He said, 'You can see me?' "

Kate felt lightheaded, like she might fall off the bench. When she looked up, Malcolm was standing at the end of the first pew, watching them.

"C'mon, Beulah Two," he said. "Your Grandma's waiting in the car."

Beulah Two gave Kate a quick hug and hurried toward the church door. As she passed Malcolm he reached out to her. "Hey. Are we okay?"

Beulah Two smiled and hugged him tight around his waist. When she released him, Malcolm gave her a high five, and the little girl skipped toward the church doors.

Malcolm came to join Kate on the piano bench. "You shouldn't encourage her. It's not good for her to be making up stories. She has to learn to—"

"I believe her," Kate said. Her heart was pounding, and her arms and legs felt like heavy weights.

"What?"

Kate looked through the open doors out to the cemetery. "I said . . . I believe her."

Chapter Twenty-five

*Love is like wildflowers. It is often
found in the most unlikely of places.
-Author Unknown*

Modean couldn't sit still. She paced. She stared out windows. She vacuumed. She dusted. She called Vaughn, but Vaughn didn't answer. She did a crossword puzzle. She called Vaughn again. She paced some more and, above all, she worried.

She might have let it pass when Nettie Jacobs told her she'd witnessed Nate Bell being wheeled out of the hospital earlier that week and helped into Malcolm's truck by a nurse and Malcolm himself. But when the twins had added they'd seen Nate coming out of Vaughn's office, Mo had convinced herself of the worst.

Nate had been elusive over the past several weeks, mysterious even. Mo had only seen him twice, as opposed to every day, as they'd grown accustomed. Something was wrong, and Mo decided it was something horrible.

She picked up the phone to try Vaughn again when someone knocked on her front door. Mo's eyes widened when she saw Malcolm standing on her porch. His face was grim, and Mo felt faint.

"Modean," he said without an ounce of emotion, "I need you to come with me."

Mo wanted to cry. Instead, she went for her purse.

The two drove in silence over bumpy back roads in Malcolm's truck. Modean's stomach was in knots as she prepared herself. Nate had to be sick. Very sick. Probably cancer, just like Lou. It figured that, just when she'd found happiness again, death was about to steal it from her.

A lump rose in her throat, and she swallowed it away. It was time to be brave. If not for herself, for Nate.

Malcolm pulled the pickup to the side of the road in a location Modean didn't recognize. He got out and opened her door, and she took his hand and let him help her from the truck. Her eyes explored her surroundings but saw nothing but woods and dirt road.

Malcolm pointed toward a small gap in the trees. "Right through there."

Mo furrowed her brow, her heart pounding. Malcolm hadn't spoken a word since they'd left her house, and she knew asking questions would be futile. Her options were either go see what was beyond the trees or get back in the truck.

***

Malcolm watched Mo disappear into the trees and remembered a time when he'd led another woman to that place. He thought of the Chinese food and lightning bugs. And he smiled.

***

Only a few steps into the woods, the trees thinned out and opened to a field of yellow and white wildflowers. In the middle of the field, Nate Bell sat rocking in a white rocking chair, an identical chair sitting empty beside him.

Mo took her time walking to him, trying to read his blank

expression. Then he smiled and motioned for her to sit. Despite her best efforts, her eyes filled with tears.

"Nate, what's this all about? Nettie Jacobs said she saw you at the hospital, and the twins said you were at Vaughn's, too. Are you sick? Tell me right this second if you are."

Nate took her hand and looked out across the field at the flowers swaying in the warm breeze. "When Evelyn and I first got married, we always used to say we wanted to grow old together. We wanted to watch our grandkids play, watch the sun go down, rock in rocking chairs." He looked at Mo. "Well, we didn't have any kids. And I was just too busy and stubborn to watch a sunset or waste my time rocking in a chair. When Evelyn died, I gave up on all that. I gave up on everything. That's why I ended up on that roof."

"I told you we don't have to talk about that no more," Modean said with a shake of her head.

Nate patted her hand. "I didn't take care of myself, Modean. Evelyn always made my doctor's appointments, made me take my medicines, made sure I was eating right. When she was gone, I didn't do any of it, and I didn't care about doing it either. I didn't care whether I lived or died." He looked deep into her eyes. "But now I do."

Modean held her breath and braced herself.

"The twins and Nettie are right. I went to see Vaughn, and she sent me for some tests at the hospital. I needed to make sure about some things. And what I found out is, I got a long time to sit here and rock."

Modean blinked and almost choked. "You mean . . . you're okay? You don't have cancer? You ain't gonna die!"

Nate laughed. "Well, not today anyway."

Modean leaned into his shoulder and let the tears of relief flow. And then she socked him in the same shoulder. "Nate Bell, I've been a nervous wreck thinkin' you were dyin' on me! Don't you ever do that again! And why did you have Malcolm bring me all the way out in the boonies to tell me you ain't gonna kick the bucket? You coulda told me that much on the phone!"

Then Modean's eyes fell upon the diamond band in the palm of Nate's outstretched hand, and she hushed.

He reached for her left hand and brushed his thumb over it. "I had to know for sure I'd have a lot of time left to rock with you before I asked you to be my wife. And they told me I do. So, I'm askin' you, Modean Wilkes, will you marry an old man who loves you?"

Tears streamed off Mo's cheeks. "Yes. Of course I will."

***

Kate fumbled with the heavy key ring and attempted for the fourth time to lock the door to Debbie's Flowers and Gifts. It was a Friday, Debbie's biggest day of the week for deliveries, and Debbie was out making the rounds in her Ford pickup truck while her son employed the van.

Kate had successfully locked the door only once and decided it had been a mere stroke of luck, a massive fluke. She twisted and jiggled the key, turned it upside down, tried a different key. Then she sighed and took off her jacket and purse. A few deep breaths later, she was ready to try again.

"Why don't you let me help you with that?" Boyd Walker slipped his Ray Bans on top of his balding head and took the keys from Kate's hands. She sighed in relief and took a step back to let him work.

"I haven't seen you around in a while, Boyd. You must be keeping yourself busy."

He chuckled and jiggled the key. "A little too busy. If my caseload keeps pilin' up, I may have to hire a real secretary. Don't suppose you'd be interested."

Kate laughed. "Between this place and home with Jane Ellen, I keep myself busy enough."

Boyd pulled the key from the lock and yanked on the door. "There ya go." He handed the keys back to Kate.

"Thanks. I'm glad you just happened to be walking by today."

Boyd bit his lip and looked at her sheepishly. "Well, I'd be lyin' if I told ya I just happened by."

Kate slipped back into her jacket and pulled her purse over her arm. She glanced down at his feet as he shuffled them back and forth.

"I came to see if I could ask you a question. A personal one." He rubbed at his head under the sunglasses. "This is sorta hard for me. I haven't done anything like this in years."

Kate wanted to run. Or close her eyes. Or disappear. Anything to stop him.

"Thing is, I think I'm outta practice, and I'm sure I'm just gonna make an idiot of myself," he said.

"Boyd!" Kate shouted, cringing at how loud and abrupt it sounded. "Boyd, my husband just divorced me. I'm still trying to figure out what life looks like with just me and my child."

"I know!" Boyd said, his eyes lighting up. "That's why I knew you'd be just the person to talk to. You know exactly what she's been through and if I even got a chance with her."

"Her who?" Kate asked.

"Debbie! Aww, Kate, I think about her all the time. I drive past this place at least five times a day just so I can see her standin' behind the counter through the window. I've been in a few times, but she never seems to notice me."

Kate raised her eyebrows. "Debbie is at least twelve years older than you."

"I know it, and I don't care. She's beautiful and smart and, well, I just want to get to know her better—ask her out on a date maybe. And I thought since you know her pretty good, you might give me some honest advice. I know she's been real hurt by her ex-husband and that she's got life by herself down pat. But do you think she might give me a chance? If I asked?"

Kate flushed and chuckled quietly, ashamed she'd assumed Boyd's affections were directed at her. She smiled at him. "I think Debbie Williams would be a lucky woman to have you."

Boyd beamed. "You do? Well, do you think you might put in a good word for me?"

"It would be my pleasure."

***

When Kate pulled into Modean's driveway, Malcolm was unloading two white rocking chairs from the back of his pickup. He set them on Mo's porch and waved to her, and Kate eyed the chairs as she approached.

"Did you make these?"

He nodded.

"For Mo?"

He nodded again.

"I didn't know she needed new chairs." Kate dug into her purse. "Here, let me pay you for them."

Malcolm put his hand on top of Kate's to stop her. "You should go inside, Kate."

She raised her eyebrows. "Why? Is something wrong?"

"Just go inside. Mo's waiting for you."

Kate found Modean drying coffee mugs at the sink and crying. Kate rushed to her side. "Aunt Mo, what's wrong? What's happened? Is it Nate?"

Mo turned around with a beaming smile, her face streaked with happy tears. She held out her left hand, and Kate's eyes quickly found the diamond band. She gasped and took hold of Mo's finger.

"Nate?"

Mo nodded. "Mm-hmm."

Kate threw her arms around her and held her tight. "You're going to be a bride!"

Chapter Twenty-six

All persons are puzzles until at
last we find in some word or act
the key to the man . . .
-Ralph Waldo Emerson

Malcolm leaned against Beulah's doorframe as she pulled open the door.

"Is she okay?" Malcolm asked.

Beulah stepped aside and motioned for him to come in. "She's fine. A little sad, but she's all right. You didn't have to drive all the way out here just to check on her."

He followed her into the kitchen and took his favorite seat at the table.

"I was just about to pull some biscuits outta the oven. You want one?"

"If you've still got that blackberry jam you made last summer."

"Boy, you know I do." Beulah laughed.

On top of the table sat one of Beulah Two's puzzles, an old metal picture frame, and two rolls of blue wrapping paper. Beulah threw a dishtowel past Malcolm's face and it landed on top of the puzzle.

"Now, you ain't supposed to see that."

Malcolm pulled the towel off and stared at the puzzle. He recognized the snow-covered mountain surrounded by tall cedar trees on every side. But most of all, he recognized the missing piece in the center. Malcolm rubbed his hand across the empty space. "I've seen this."

Beulah threw the towel back over the puzzle and slapped at his hand. "Now, you just leave it alone. That baby's been workin' on this for your birthday, and if she wants it to be a surprise, then it's gonna be a surprise."

"My birthday?"

"Yes, your birthday. June second—that's a week away. You'll be thirty-five, in case you done forgot."

"I did forget."

"Yours is five days before Beulah Two's. Can you believe she's gonna be nine years old?" Beulah pulled the blackberry jam from the refrigerator and set it in front of him with a butter knife and plate.

Malcolm shook his head. "I wish I could do something about letting her see her mama, but it's still too soon."

"She knows that! She knows you just tryin' to protect us. She ain't mad at you, Malcolm. That girl loves you. Even when you ain't loveable." Beulah opened the oven and pulled out the pan of piping hot biscuits. Using her apron, she transferred the biggest biscuit to Malcolm's plate, and he broke it open and filled it with the thick, dark jam even as the steam rose.

Beulah patted his head. "But you been more loveable lately than you been in a long time."

"Thanks. I think."

Beulah laughed. " 'A happy heart makes the face cheerful.' "

" 'But heartache crushes the spirit,' " Malcolm said, finishing the verse.

Beulah went to the refrigerator and pulled out a tub of butter. "Lord knows you had your share of heartache. And more than that, too."

Malcolm chewed his biscuit in silence.

Beulah's mouth twisted into a smirk. "But I betcha don't know where that scripture came—"

"Proverbs fifteen, verse thirteen," he answered before she could finish.

Beulah roared with laughter. "Well, well. Guess I got some brushin' up to do. My, my. Where is that Bible?"

***

The sun was setting, and there was still no sign of Beulah Two. Malcolm had left hours ago, and Beulah considered calling him back over to help look for the little girl but decided to try yelling for her one last time. She shuffled off the porch and into the yard, looking in every direction. "Beulah Two!"

"Grandma!" Beulah Two ran toward her from the back of the house with an oversized smile planted on her face.

"Good Lord, girl! I was gettin' worried. It's almost dark out here. Where you been?"

Beulah Two was breathless. Her hands were cupped tightly together, and she held them up toward her grandmother. Her skin lit up with a greenish glow, then extinguished, only to light up again a few seconds later.

"Lightnin' bugs!" Beulah shouted. "They already out? Well, I guess it is nearly June."

"I been waitin' for 'em," Beulah Two said. "And tonight they finally came!" She opened her hands, revealing two small insects with long, black bodies and glowing green abdomens. They crawled from finger to finger, then to the center of her palm where they opened their wings and took flight toward the sky. Beulah Two giggled and watched until they flew out of sight amid the tall trees. She took her grandma's hand, still beaming with delight. "Now Malcolm can have his birthday!"

"Sounds like you been workin' up a plan." She nudged Beulah Two toward the porch. "Go on. You can tell me all about it in the house."

"Okay, Grandma, but you can't tell Malcolm. It has to be a surprise."

"If you say it's gotta be a surprise, then it'll be a surprise. Now, shoo! I never did like bein' out here after dark." Beulah scanned the yard then shook off a chill. " 'Specially not lately."

***

Kate found Truitt lying on a bench in the Millsville Laundromat. The small, white brick building had been around since she was a girl and hadn't changed at all since she'd last been inside. The owners were old, bordering on ancient, and trying to sell, but since the place had been on the market for two years without even a nibble, the couple was about to throw in the towel and close the laundromat's doors for good.

At least half of the washers didn't work and most of the dryers. The dollar bill changer hadn't functioned properly in years, and the owners remedied the problem by placing two baskets on the front counter—one filled with dollar bills, the other with quarters. It was a system based on honesty and, as far as they could tell, one that worked well.

Kate sat down next to Truitt and gave him a nudge. "Okay, I'm here. So what's the emergency?"

Truitt sat up and pointed at two large baskets filled with crumpled clothing. "Laundry."

"Laundry?"

"Laundry. I don't know anything about it. Washin', dryin', ironin', foldin' . . . I'm laundry stupid."

Kate laughed. "You're thirty-two years old. Why is this suddenly a problem?"

"Because I've never lived by myself a day in my life! I was just fourteen when Mom and Dad died. I moved right in with Aunt Mo, and she never let me touch the laundry. Now, with her and Nate gettin' married, I'll be getting a place of my own, and I've got to learn how to do my own laundry. And you're gonna teach me. Right now."

Kate whined and leaned back onto the bench. "C'mon, Tru. It's late, and I worked all day at Debbie's. I'm exhausted. Besides, you take most of your stuff to the cleaners anyway."

Truitt stood and picked up a handful of dirty clothes from one of the baskets and tossed them in a heap at her feet. "Suit yourself," he said. "I guess I'll just have to bring all this stuff to you from now on. Shouldn't be more than one or two loads a week. Maybe three if you count my scrubs from work. Hope you don't mind, but they can get pretty messy. Animal blood, urine . . . all sorts of bodily fluids actually. And the smell! Wow—"

"Fine." Kate sighed and started sorting colors. "But let's hurry. Susie's got poppyseed chicken tonight, and it goes fast."

"Everything goes fast at Susie's."

She picked up a pair of jeans and shook them out. "First rule of laundry, especially for men, check the pockets. You don't want to wash a pen or your wallet." She dug her hand into the front pocket of the jeans and pulled out a small gray box. Truitt lunged for it and snatched it out of her hand. Kate's eyes grew huge. "Truitt Boudrow, is that a ring?"

"Rule number one, check the pockets. Got it. Movin' on. Rule number two?"

"It is! You're going to ask Vaughn to marry you?"

Truitt threw his head back and rubbed it side to side on the wall behind him. Then he moaned. "I was. Last night I took her to dinner in Fayetteville. Afterwards we went to dessert on the square, and it seemed like the right time. There was music and lights and a carriage ride. And then I just couldn't do it. I froze up. I could barely talk much less get down on one knee. Besides, Nate sorta beat me to the punch and stole my thunder."

Kate couldn't keep from smiling. "You bought a ring. I never thought I'd see the day." She patted his knee and took the box from him. "Don't worry about finding the perfect moment. Just keep this close by and let the perfect moment find you."

"Aren't you gonna open it? See if I did good?"

"No. I think I'll wait to see it until it's on her hand."

"I can't promise when that'll be."

"That's okay. I'm not going anywhere."

Truitt handed her a striped, button-up dress shirt. "Not until you do my laundry anyway."

Kate elbowed him in the arm. "Vaughn's really great. It's funny she's the luckiest girl in Millsville and doesn't even know it yet."

"Just Millsville?"

"World is probably pushing it."

Truitt smiled. "Won't the twins be surprised?" he asked. "Me marrying a woman, and all?"

Kate laughed. "If Mr. Gregory Peck getting stuffed in Aunt Mo's purse didn't give them a heart attack, nothing will."

Chapter Twenty-seven

*Let go. Why do you cling to pain? There
is nothing you can do about the wrongs
of yesterday. It is not yours to judge.
Why hold on to the very thing which
keeps you from hope and love?*
-Leo Buscaglia

It was the last Saturday in May, and the Millsville square was
bustling with townsfolk. Two city workers dressed in dingy
white coveralls were painting the square's light poles a dark
gray while several others swung buzzing weed trimmers around
the bases of anything that would stand still. A woman with a
floral-print hat and matching gloves pruned hedges near the
statue of Colonel Mills. A man in overalls hosed down benches.
And a group of local 4-H students picked up trash in oversized
orange bags.

Kate watched the goings-on outside Debbie's window with
curiosity. No parades were scheduled until the fourth of July
and no festivals until the fall. She left her place behind the
counter and walked to the glass.

An old woman pulling baby's breath from Debbie's cooler
shook her head in disgust. "Won't be long now 'til the masses
descend."

"Excuse me?" Kate asked.

"The farmers' market. Next Saturday is opening weekend. I
dread it every year. Folks comin' from all over the place. Traffic
so bad you can't get anywhere," she grumbled. "I grow my own
fruits and vegetables anyhow. And they're a heckuva lot better

than anything you can buy over there, I'm tellin' ya. Just a lot of senseless fuss and chaos if you ask me."

Kate looked out the window at three men stringing up a large white sign between two oak trees in the middle of the square.

Millsville Farmers' Market. Open Every Saturday 7 a.m., June 7 – October 18.

"Oh, the market!" Kate shouted.

The woman scowled, replaced the baby's breath inside the cooler, and left the store in a huff. Kate barely noticed, her eyes affixed to the sign. The market. Only a week away. There was something renewing about its return, something that felt a lot like hope. Life kept going, moving, and so did she.

She was still smiling when the front door dinged again and Beulah limped in with her cane. Kate hurried to help her inside and greeted her with a mighty hug. "Ms. Beulah! What a surprise! What can I help you with?"

"A chair to start. My legs are done give out."

Kate dashed around the counter and found a folding chair then rushed it out to the old woman who promptly collapsed into it.

"Whew! I can't hardly walk across the floor no more." She was panting when she took Kate's hand. "I been tryin' to get a hold of you all week. Mo told me I could find you here."

"I'm so sorry, Ms. Beulah. We've just been so busy lately."

"Oh, don't you worry about it. I got you now. And just in time, too."

"In time for what?"

Beulah looked around the store. "You got another chair back there? This might take a while."

***

Dark was fast approaching, and with it the end to a relentlessly long day for Millsville Baptist's pastor. He'd spent the entirety of it locked away in Nate's shed, working on an armoire for Mr. Robinson of Robinson's Hardware, a fiftieth wedding anniversary surprise for his wife. He hadn't stopped for lunch or taken a break when Nate had brought him a Dr. Pepper and bag of stale cheese puffs. He hadn't even gone to the hardware store after he'd run out of bolts. Instead, he'd confined himself to the shed and his work with no interruptions. Except, of course, for Nate and the cheese puffs.

Malcolm had labored tirelessly on the armoire from dawn until dusk. His eyes were full of sawdust. His hands were tender and bore two blisters, one on his thumb, the other on his palm. At 8:15 p.m. he'd had enough and tossed his tools into the back of his pickup. It was time to go home, and not a moment too soon.

He'd kept himself too busy to think about the significance of the day, his thirty-fifth birthday, until he came to the stretch of road between Nate's and home marked with her memory. It was the place he sped past every day holding his breath—the place of the accident, the last place her eyes had seen. Next to a tall oak whose trunk was still scarred from the impact of her car stood the small white cross and a bouquet of blue plastic flowers. Malcolm always made a point never to glance in their direction, but as he headed home, his eyes drifted.

At the sight of the cross, memories of birthdays past— birthdays spent with her—came without ceasing. The fuss she'd always made about his special day, the cakes and candles and balloons, the house full of friends. The attempted, but never successful, surprise parties. The perfect gifts. The hugs and kisses and happiness. As hard as he pressed down on the gas pedal, the pickup truck wasn't quick enough to outrun the pain.

When he arrived home, he leaned his head onto the door and worked his key into the lock. His T-shirt was drenched in sweat, his arms, face, and hands covered in dirt and grime. He needed a shower—a cold one—and the comfort of his bed. With every blink, the tree and the cross flashed behind his closed eyelids. He needed to dive into bed, deep under blankets, to find sleep and an escape from the nightmare of being awake without her. He'd spent this birthday like every birthday since she'd died— alone and sad and wanting her.

As his key turned inside the lock, something called to him from within the church across the parking lot. There was no sound, but the urgency was intense and all too familiar. Malcolm shook his head and had almost made it into his shed when he paused and looked toward the church.

From what he could see, the doors were locked tight. No lights shone from within. Crickets sang in the background but couldn't drown out the call. He lowered his head and could almost feel the cool water of the shower rushing over his tired muscles.

Moments later he was inside the sanctuary, walking the center aisle to the first pew. The silence of the place was deafening.

"Not today," he finally said aloud. "I can't. Not today." Malcolm took his face in his hands and then rose from the pew. "I said I *can't*. I'm too tired to fight today." His voice cracked. "Not that you fight back. You just let it happen. I yell, and you just . . .You're always the same! You call me in here, and I scream, and you don't do anything! Well, do something!"

Malcolm sat back down on the pew. His eyes were moist, and his throat was dry. "I miss her. I miss her so much. And I miss . . ." He looked toward the rafters. "I miss . . ."

There was a shuffling of fabric in the row behind him, and he swung around to see Kate taking a seat. He quickly wiped his eyes. "We really need to stop meeting like this."

"I heard a rumor that today's your birthday." She leaned forward and set a small, wrapped gift on the pew beside him. "It's not much."

He picked it up and looked it over.

"Like I said, it's not much," she said. "Open it."

Malcolm was too embarrassed by the spectacle he'd just made of himself to refuse her. No doubt she'd heard him arguing with the ceiling. He peeled back the green bow and navy striped paper down to a small cardboard box. He opened it cautiously and pulled out a black and white photograph of a young woman. "Ruth," he said.

"She was sixteen," Kate told him. "It's the first picture Daddy ever took of her. They were at the drive-in for their first date. Mama said she nearly died of embarrassment when he pulled out the camera and asked her to smile. But she was so beautiful." Kate smiled down at the picture. "Anyway, Daddy always kept it in his Bible. But the last time I saw Mama, the night I left her in the hospital, I took it. I don't know why. I think I just wanted to keep her close to me until I got back to her. But it doesn't belong with me now. It belongs in Daddy's Bible. With you."

Malcolm shook his head.

"Page two-thirty," Kate said before he had a chance to object.

"The book of Ruth, chapter one. If you look close, you can see the yellow edges of the outline where it's been all these years."

Malcolm tucked the picture back inside the box. "Thank you."

Kate leaned back onto her pew and settled into the silence of the church as several minutes rolled past.

"I must have sounded crazy when you came in," Malcolm said at last. "This will be my fourth birthday without her. My fourth birthday alone."

"You're not alone now," she said, and he turned around to face her. "And it sounded as if you weren't alone when I got here either."

Malcolm's eyes grew watery, and he swallowed the sob that fought to escape into the open. "I don't want to hear him. I try to ignore it, but I can't get him out of my head. I can't walk into this sanctuary without hearing him whisper . . . just like you and I are talking right now. He wants me back here. He wants me to preach again, to be who I was." Malcolm shook his head. "But I don't know how to be that man. Not anymore. Not without her. I can't just let her go and move on like we never happened. Like she never happened." Tears finally fled his eyes and ran down his face. "She was so beautiful. She made everything beautiful. I can't let her go. I can't."

Kate leaned forward. Her hand hovered over his back, but then she pulled it away. "If she was so beautiful, then why do you hide her?"

Malcolm narrowed his eyes. "What?"

"You say she was beautiful, Malcolm, but you walk around here with her memory tucked away in your pocket. Everyone here lost her. They want to think about her with good memories and love, but all they can think is that the day they lost her, they lost you, too." Kate's own eyes filled with tears. "You'd rather hover over a grave and keep her in dark places than be the man she loved. I didn't know her, but I'll bet she would want you to let her shine, just like she did when she was here, and just like she would want you to shine, too."

Malcolm's hands were shaking. Emotions churned and swirled inside him like a mighty wave that would swallow him up. He watched the tears fall from Kate's eyes and wondered if the feeling in his chest meant he was furious, or confused, or thoroughly taken with the woman. One thing was certain—no one since Anna had spoken to him with such unbridled truth, not even the bold Beulah.

He wanted to walk out of the place, or yell at her, or laugh at her, but all he could do was stare until she stood and extended her hand toward him.

"Come with me," she said. "I have something I want to show you."

He hesitated only a moment before taking her hand. They walked up the aisle, and as they stepped outside into the darkness of the night, Beulah Two looked up from the bottom step. She jumped to her feet, her eyes dancing with anticipation, and ran up to take his other hand. "Happy Birthday, Malcolm."

"Beulah Two, what are you doing here so late? Where's your grandma?"

"She's here, too. We're all here."

Malcolm looked to Kate, then back to the little girl holding tight to his hand. Beulah Two smiled up at him, then pointed into the darkness. "Look."

Malcolm turned his gaze toward the cemetery. He squinted,

let go of their hands, and descended the steps. He crossed the gravel parking lot, gripped by the sight, and stopped at the cemetery gate. Tears flowed like streams down his face and onto his already damp T-shirt as hundreds of tiny green lights awaited him.

He could barely make out the dark figures standing among the tombstones. They were perfectly still, holding the restless specks of light. Malcolm opened the gate with a pounding heart and walked slowly through. He approached the closest of the figures, and the woman's shadowed face came into focus. Ruby Williams leaned over her walker next to the tombstone of her husband, Clyde, and in her quaking hand she held a mason jar containing a single lightning bug. It climbed and flew up the sides of the jar in desperation, frantically searching for freedom, before falling once again to the glass bottom.

Ruby smiled at Malcolm as he passed and, a few steps later, he came face to face with Nate Bell. Nate stood beside Evelyn's tombstone, holding his jar with a lone lightning bug.

"You told me once that I was here for a reason," Nate said. "You said Evelyn's gone 'cause it was her time and that I had more stuff to do and people to love. I believed you. And you were right." Nate choked back his tears. "Now it's your turn to believe the same thing."

Nate put a hand on Malcolm's shoulder, and Malcolm grabbed it and squeezed it tight. He swallowed the growing lump in his throat and caught sight of Beulah, standing just behind Nate among the three tombstones of her husband, Curtis, her daughter, Maxie, and a stillborn baby boy who'd died nearly forty years before. In her jar were three lightning bugs.

She smiled at him with moist, black eyes as he approached. "Beulah Two did this for you. We all did it for you."

Malcolm stood with her a moment then wandered away among the graves and people. He recognized their faces, remembered the loved ones they had buried. He looked out over the scores of tiny lights, glowing in the jars. So much heartache symbolized in their minuscule beams. And then he saw Kate, next to her parents' graves. In her jar, two lightning bugs spiraled together, glowing side by side.

He met her there and fought the urge to reach out and hold her, or maybe to let her hold him. Their eyes locked together, and he could almost feel the warmth emanating from her heart. "Kate . . ."

Kate nodded over his shoulder toward Anna's grave. He looked back and saw it, too.

"She's waiting for you," Kate said. "Go on. I'll be right here."

Malcolm hesitated. He took a breath then turned away from her and made his way toward Anna's tombstone. He passed others along the way, each holding to their lights. His heart raced, and then he was there.

At the stone bearing Anna's image, he fell upon his knees and lowered his face to the ground, sobbing as he had the day he'd left her there. Beulah Two placed her gentle hand on his back, and he raised his bloodshot eyes to her and leaned his back against the stone. The little girl held out a jar toward him, and the tiny insect inside crawled along glass bottom, searching for a way out. Its body illuminated with a beautiful green glow, and it flew to the top of the jar only to hit the metal lid. Malcolm reached out and took the jar in his blistered hand.

"Remember the story?" Beulah Two asked. "The one you told me 'bout Anna and the lightnin' bugs?"

Malcolm nodded. "Yes," he said, though he barely made a sound.

"You said Ms. Anna was sad when she seen all the lightnin' bugs you put in the jars, and then you and Ms. Anna opened up all the lids and let 'em go."

"Every single one."

"And when they flew out, they looked just like stars dancin' above your heads, like stars you just set free, and they flew up to the sky and found the place they belonged."

Malcolm's bottom lip quivered. Beulah Two hadn't forgotten a single detail. The lightning bug was climbing up the glass again, and Beulah Two knelt down beside him. "Do you remember?"

"I remember."

She took his hand and placed it onto the jar's lid. "Let her go then. That's what Ms. Anna would want. Let her fly right on up to the sky so she can be beautiful again."

Malcolm's hands shook. He stared into Beulah Two's small face, so innocent and bold. Her hand was frozen still on top of his, her dark eyes blazing warm. He looked out over the cemetery again. So many lights. So many lives. His vision blurred with tears, and he blinked them away to see a single spec of light float toward the sky. It rose higher and higher above the graves, flashing its green radiance, until it disappeared from sight.

Another tiny light flitted just above the tombstones before setting its course for the treetops. Then another. One by one, all across the cemetery, the lighting bugs were set free, and they filled the air above the onlookers on the ground.

Beulah gasped and placed her hand over her heart, and Nate found Mo at Lou's grave and held her close as they watched the flickering sky, side by side.

Beulah Two removed her hand from Malcolm's and stood up beside him. "Are you ready?"

Malcolm pushed himself to his feet. He looked down at the face of his wife smiling up at him from her tombstone. As in life, the sight of her took his breath away.

He twisted the jar's lid and dropped it on the ground then reached his fingers inside. The little bug quickly found them and crawled onto his ring finger. It meandered its way up to the place a silver wedding band once wrapped around, and it stopped, glowing.

Malcolm smiled. "Go on. Let them all see you."

The lighting bug spread her wings and took flight from his hand. Little by little she rose, circling and shining, until her light couldn't be distinguished from the glowing stars above.

Chapter Twenty-eight

Our dreams drench us in senses,
and sense steeps us again in dreams.
-Amos Bronson Alcott

Esther was back in Memphis, in St. Luke's Church. The place was dark as she felt her way along the edges of the pews. She called out, "Father Francis!" But the massive sanctuary returned only an eerie silence.

She moved forward, terrified of what crouched in the shadows. She could sense them watching her, was certain at any moment they would reach for her and pull her into the darkness. She could smell the sulfurous stench of murder on their breath. Her pulse raced, and she increased her pace, her hands trembling, grasping for the cold wood of the pews.

In an instant she was on the floor, her hands and face covered in the wet, sticky liquid that caused her to slip and fall. She tried to push herself to her feet but slipped again to her belly with a splat. A light shone from somewhere above and illuminated the sanctuary. Esther looked around her at the pool of thick, red blood. Father Francis lay next to her, his face ghostly white. His eyes were closed, his mouth slightly gaping.

She crawled to him, slipping and sliding in his blood, until she reached his side and threw her arms around him.

"Father Francis, they killed you!"

She sobbed without ceasing until she felt movement beneath her and the sensation of icy breath on her forehead. When she raised her head from Father Francis's chest, he was staring at her. She pushed herself off his body and scooted backwards across the aisle until her back hit the end of a pew.

His eyes gazed into her, dark and empty. Slowly he lifted his hand and pointed into the shadows of the sanctuary. "They're still watching."

Esther's body trembled violently, her face and hair soaked in his blood. "Who? Who's watching?"

A gray hand emerged from the darkness and grabbed her shoulder. Claw-like fingernails sank deep into her flesh like hooks. She tried to lunge forward but the hand pulled her onto the floor, dragging her under the pews. She scratched at the unseen enemy and kicked at the pews with her feet before letting out a blood-curdling scream. "Nooo!"

Warm arms wrapped around her and a soft voice shushed her gently. "Esther, wake up, honey. It's just another dream. It's only a dream."

Esther opened her eyes and searched the room. She felt her face and hair for blood that was not there. Her heart pounded deep in her chest, and she struggled for each breath. Finally her wild eyes met with Delta's.

"See?" Delta said. "It's just me. You're at home in your bed. It's me, Esther."

Esther buried her face in Delta's embrace and cried. Delta held her until her white cotton pajama top was drenched in tears. She smoothed Esther's hair again and again and hummed a tune until Esther's body began to relax. Her sobs slowed, then stopped.

"Are you okay, honey? That's the third time this week."

Esther wiped at her nose and nodded.

"Same one?"

Esther nodded again. "This time he opened his eyes and

talked to me."

"Who did?"

"Father Francis."

"Well, what did he say?"

"He said . . . " Esther swallowed. "He said, 'They're still watching.'"

Delta pressed her lips together. "Now, Esther, sweetie, it was just a dream. Just like all of 'em before were just dreams. You're safe here with me, hundreds of miles away from anybody who might want to hurt you. Besides, all that's behind you. And just look at all you got goin' for you now. School, your job at the coffee house, Marcus."

Esther couldn't help but smile at the mention of his name.

"That boy's crazy 'bout you, girl. I can see it in his eyes every time he looks at you. And so can everybody else, too."

"I don't deserve him, Delta. He's so good. Just all good, inside and out. I thought for sure after I told him about my past and all the stuff I did he'd take off."

"But he didn't," Delta said. "And he's not goin' to. He loves you. You gotta start lovin' yourself they way we all love you. That girl you used to be, she's long gone. And the new Esther . . . well, she's strong and smart and brave. Not to mention beautiful." Delta smiled mischievously. "And if she plays her cards right, she just might get to marry a sweet, handsome doctor."

Esther fell back onto her pillow. "I don't deserve to be in the same room with him, much less be loved by him." She looked up at Delta. "And I don't deserve you either. This house, the way you treat me . . . You've done so much for me."

Delta took her hand. "Now you listen to me. I have loved

every second of you bein' here. You are a gift to me, Esther Jones. A gift. And don't you be thinkin' any different. Now, you lay back down and go to sleep. You got a early mornin' class, and I gotta get my beauty rest. I sure don't need to wake up with bags under these eyes. I got enough problems beauty cream don't fix." Delta patted Esther's cheek and left the room.

Esther closed her eyes and pulled the sheets high around her neck. But sleep would not come. When the sun rose outside her window, the words were still echoing within her.

They're still watching.

Chapter Twenty-nine

*Deep into that darkness peering, long I
stood there, wondering, fearing . . .*
-Edgar Allan Poe

Malcolm drove down Old River Road on his nightly rounds. It was just past 10 p.m. and, as he'd predicted, every light was out at Beulah's. As usual, all was still and quiet on the grounds surrounding her house. Still he scanned the yard for a hidden threat. But just like every night before, he saw nothing out of the ordinary and drove on toward Kate's.

The music boomed from his radio—an old Rolling Stones tune. As his pickup approached Kate's driveway, Malcolm punched off the music and slowed. He saw nothing, heard nothing, but an eerie sensation began at the top of his head and coursed down his spine and into every part of his body. He pulled the truck to the side of the road and killed the engine.

The moon was hidden behind thick clouds, and the dirt road was dark apart from the headlights of the pickup. Malcolm examined the tree line on either side of the road, but there was no movement save for the gentle wind that swept through the treetops and rustled the leaves. Malcolm stood motionless in the middle of the road with the headlights at his back, unable to shake the feeling that someone, or something, was watching him.

"Hello?" he called into the darkness, but all remained hushed except for the rustling branches above. Malcolm returned to his truck and checked the bed, just to make sure his rifle was there. Then he climbed into the cab and started the engine.

As he steered his pickup past Kate's house, he considered pulling into the driveway to check on her and Jane Ellen. He hadn't seen her in a few days, since his birthday in the cemetery with the lightning bugs, and there was much to say. But not just then. Instead, he put more pressure on the gas pedal and drove toward home.

***

Kate tucked Jane Ellen into bed beneath a fuzzy Cinderella blanket and kissed her nose. "Now close your eyes and go to sleep. We've got a big day tomorrow."

The little girl reached for her favorite toy, a stuffed pink flamingo named Perry, and pulled him under the blanket with her. "Don't worry, Mama. I haven't told Beulah Two about her party."

"Good, because we want it to be a surprise."

"Don't forget, you promised to let me help blow up balloons in the morning."

"I won't forget. Good night, honey."

Jane Ellen nodded and hugged her flamingo tight. Kate turned off the light, closed the door softly behind her, and made her way back into the kitchen where a table full of flowers, balloons, and an assortment of party supplies awaited her.

She'd been planning Beulah Two's birthday party for weeks and was determined to make it extra special, given that Esther wouldn't be there. The last-minute preparations were coming along, and Kate was glad she'd delegated responsibilities earlier in the week. Beulah was in charge of making the desserts—Beulah Two's favorites, chocolate pies and oatmeal raisin cookies. Susie was to supply a plethora of barbequed meats, along with all the sides and fixins. Debbie had donated dozens of yellow daisies and even included tall crystal vases and piles of baby's breath for arranging. Truitt had been in charge of acquiring Beulah Two's favorite flowers, magnolia blossoms, to be used for the cake, and since Emma and Ella's prized magnolia trees produced the most beautiful blossoms around, he'd been sent to sweet-talk them out of as many as they'd part with. In the end, they'd agreed to nine—a sacrifice made only in honor of Beulah Two.

Everyone from the church had been invited to Beulah's for Beulah Two's surprise celebration, as well as various other friends and acquaintances from the town, including Debbie and Boyd. The couple had been spending much of their time together, prompting the Millsville gossip wagon to take off at full speed. Kate had tried to quash any chitchat from patrons in the flower shop, but Debbie had told her not to bother. Debbie didn't mind—she loved a good scandal, and being at the center of the talk only made her excited. Folks were passing by the flower shop window at a slower pace, everyone hoping to catch a glimpse of the longtime bachelor and much-older divorce caught in a lovers' embrace. Debbie had confessed she loved the attention and even felt like a small-town celebrity with all the whispers and stares.

With a daisy in one hand and a vase in the other, Kate settled in for a long night of flower arranging and party-favor assembly. An exhaustive hour later, all the flowers were perfectly arranged in the vases, and she lined them up in neat rows on the countertop and admired her efforts. Debbie would be pleased.

Next on the agenda was party favors for the kids. Kate gazed over the mountain of supplies—lip glosses, crayons, tiny puzzles, candy. Overwhelmed, she picked up a strand of purple ribbon and glanced at the clock. 11:15 p.m. Lynyrd shuffled into the kitchen and fell at her feet.

Kate reached under the table and patted his head. "You still up, too?"

The dog whined and sprawled out flat on the cold tiles. Both of them yawned, and Kate's eyes drooped. She needed caffeine.

The refrigerator was stocked after a recent trip to the grocery store, and she dug through it for a can of Diet Coke. The thought of coffee was tempting, but it was much too late at night. She bent low, peering through the groceries until finally she spotted the red and silver can at the back of the bottom shelf.

She grabbed it and rose from her crouch. Slipping her finger under the pop-tab, she caught a shadowy image passing through the living room out of the corner of her eye. The can fell from her hand onto the floor with a racket that sent Lynyrd bolting from beneath the table and overturning two chairs. He dashed into the living room and settled onto the safety of the couch.

Kate remembered the feeling she'd had in the cemetery a few weeks before, as though someone had been there— someone she couldn't see, but who could see her. She grabbed a pair of scissors off the kitchen table and crept toward the living room. Lynyrd looked up at her with sad, wet eyes, and Kate felt ridiculous. If Lynryd hadn't seen anything, then certainly there had been nothing to see.

Still, she scanned the room, holding her scissors in a combat-ready position. Then she heaved a great sigh and stroked Lynyrd's back, trying to ignore the unsettling chill in the air.

"C'mon, Kate," she said out loud. "You're exhausted and seeing things. Get a hold of yourself."

She'd just lowered the scissors and turned back toward the kitchen when Lynyrd's ears perked high into the air. The hair on his back bristled, and a low guttural growl rumbled in his throat. In an instant he was off the couch and staring out the window.

A cold chill ran up Kate's spine. She gripped the scissors until her hand ached and hurried from room to room, switching off lights until the house was completely dark. Lynyrd snarled, pawing at the door as Kate pressed her forehead to the window. The moon was shining, and she could make out her Bronco in the driveway, Jane Ellen's bicycle, and the trees in the distance. Then a cloud slipped in front of the moon, and she caught a hint of movement behind the Bronco before all went dark. She gasped. Lynyrd barked wildly.

Kate looked around for her phone before remembering she'd left it in the Bronco. She'd never installed a landline and suddenly felt like kicking herself. She rushed into the bedroom and, standing on tiptoes, reached up to the top of her closet. Her fingers found the small, black box, and she pulled it down.

She wasn't sure she could even remember how to load the pistol. It had been years since Gray had taught her. The bullets fell from her trembling hands, but after several attempts, she got the gun loaded and ready.

Lynryd paced back and forth in front of the door and whined to be released into the night. Then he went back to the window and growled again.

"Probably just a raccoon, boy," Kate said, trying more to convince herself than the dog. She peered outside, and the moon was shining bright once more. All was still, undisturbed.

She relaxed her shoulders and patted the dog's head. "We're just getting ourselves all worked up over nothing. I think it's time for us to get some sleep. What do you think—"

Lynyrd snarled and beat the window with his paw. Kate pressed her forehead to the window and saw it, too. Down the hill, near the tree line, a dark figure crouched low to the ground. Kate squinted and could barely make out the outline, but there was no mistaking its presence. Another cloud passed over the moon, and the figure stood and began walking toward the house as darkness cloaked the yard once more.

She ran into Jane Ellen's room, scooped the sleeping child into her arms, and carried her back into the living room. As Kate deposited her onto the couch, Jane Ellen opened her eyes.

"Shhh, honey," Kate whispered. "Be very quiet for Mommy. You sit still right here for just a minute. We're going to go to Aunt Mo's, okay?"

Jane Ellen nodded, her eyes only half open, and leaned back onto the couch.

Kate grabbed the keys off the hook on the wall and stuffed them into her pocket. The gun lay on the windowsill, and she picked it up as the cloud slipped off the moon and the yard lit up again. She peered through the glass, and the figure was gone.

"What's wrong, Mommy?"

"Shhh. Shhh. Shhh. Nothing, baby. You just sit very still and quiet."

A loud clatter came from the back of the house, and Lynyrd tore toward the sound, barking at the top of his lungs. Jane Ellen peered over the back of the couch.

"Who's in my room, Mommy?"

Kate lunged for her and pulled her to her bare feet. "Listen to me, Jane Ellen. When I open the door we're going to run to the car as fast as we can. Do you understand? As fast as we can." Jane Ellen whimpered and nodded, and Kate tucked the gun into the waistband of her jeans and dug the keys from her pocket. She took Jane Ellen by the hand and peeked out the window again. There was another loud clatter from the back, and she took a deep breath and threw open the front door. "Run!"

Jane Ellen's feet padded over the grass and gravel. When they reached the Bronco, Kate fumbled with the keys in the lock. She dropped them twice before recovering them and unlocking the door. Then she picked up Jane Ellen and tossed her inside.

Footsteps fell behind her, and she reached for the gun and swung around, ready to fire.

Malcolm threw up his hands. "Whoa! Kate! It's me!"

Kate dropped the gun and fell into his arms. Lynyrd barked from within the house then shot out the open front door and made a beeline for the backyard.

"What's going on?" Malcolm pulled away and retrieved Kate's gun from the ground.

Kate's hands and voice shook. "I thought I saw someone in the living room, and then Lynyrd started growling out the window. There was a man down there by the trees. I guess . . . it was you?"

"Down by the trees?" Malcolm asked, furrowing his brow.

Kate nodded. "Then he came toward the house, and then we heard something crashing in the back." She looked down and noticed the rifle in Malcolm's hand. Her eyes went wide.

"That wasn't me. Get in the car and lock the doors. Call 9-1-1." He grabbed her hand and wrapped her fingers around the pistol.

She obeyed and watched him disappear around the back of the house, his rifle ready. After calling the police, she held Jane Ellen until Malcolm reemerged from the darkness with Lynyrd at his side. Kate rolled down her window, and he leaned in.

"There's no one back there."

"Malcolm, I swear, I saw someone. He was standing just down the hill. I know I wasn't seeing things, and Jane Ellen heard the crash—"

"I believe you, Kate. That's why I came over here."

"You saw someone, too?"

"No."

Kate shook her head. "I don't understand."

"It was just a feeling when I drove past earlier."

Kate shivered and pulled Jane Ellen closer to her side. "Malcolm, what's going on?"

Malcolm looked out across the darkness of the yard. Police sirens wailed in the distance.

"I don't know."

Chapter Thirty

*Well, now it gettin' late on into the
evening and I feel like, like blowin' my
home. When I woke up this morning all
I, I had was gone. Now it gettin' late on
in the evening, man, now, I feel like, like
blowin' my home. Well now, woke up this
morning, all I had was gone.*
-Muddy Waters

By mid afternoon, Kate and her recruits, Debbie, Modean, Ella, Emma, Truitt, Vaughn, and Jane Ellen, had transformed Beulah's lackluster backyard into a picture-perfect party setting fit for the pages of a magazine. Ten long tables, borrowed from the Millsville Women's League, adorned the yard draped in white tablecloths and topped with arrangements of daisies and lines of flickering candles. White helium balloons rose high from the backs of chairs and Beulah's clothesline, and string lights ran from tree to tree next to rows of round paper lanterns.

Beneath a massive white tent, surrounded in flaming bamboo torches, sat the buffet table that overflowed with barbeque ribs, chicken, and pork, along with buns, sauces, potato salad, baked beans, coleslaw, and tomato and cucumber salad. Beulah's chocolate pies were piled high with fluffy white meringue, and mounds of oatmeal raisin cookies sat beside them. On each end of the buffet tables sat large glass dispensers filled with ice-cold homemade lemonade and sweet tea, and nearby a small, round table was loaded with party favors—crystal angels in yellow paper boxes surrounded by yellow and white M&M's, Beulah

Two's favorite candy in her favorite colors.

The crowd began to gather around 5:30 p.m., and at 6, they anxiously awaited the birthday girl's arrival. At 6:01, Malcolm led Beulah Two by the hand to the backyard where over sixty guests, young and old, stood poised and ready.

"Surprise!" they yelled at the sight of her.

Beulah Two's smile spread from ear to ear. She clutched Malcolm's hand and waved at the crowd who laughed and cheered and waved back. Beulah approached her, arms spread wide, and enveloped her in an enormous hug.

"Was you surprised, baby girl?"

Beulah Two nodded.

Jane Ellen grabbed Beulah Two around the waist. "It was a secret party!" she exclaimed, and the little girls giggled. "C'mon! Come see all the flowers!" And they disappeared into the sea of people.

Beulah took Malcolm's hand. "Thank you. She ain't never gonna forget this."

"This is all Kate," Malcolm said as Kate mounted a chair next to the buffet table. He smiled. "She did all this."

"Hello, everyone!" Kate yelled, and the crowd hushed. "Thank you for coming out to help us celebrate a very special day for a very special little girl. The only two requirements of the evening are to have a great time, and to eat too much of Susie's barbeque!"

The people erupted in claps and cheers, and Kate stepped down. Muddy Waters, Beulah's favorite blues artist, sang "I Feel Like Going Home" over the speakers. Several guests grabbed a partner and danced, including Truitt and Vaughn, followed by Modean and Nate.

Beulah Two looked out over the people and laughed, then pulled Jane Ellen into the crowd to dance.

***

Esther's eyes were red and swollen from a day of crying. She hadn't left the house or had a bite to eat. Her stomach groaned and ached as she prayed for the hours to pass quickly.

When Marcus knocked on Delta's door with two white paper bags full of Thai food, Esther flew into his arms.

"I gave her away. I left her. For years, I didn't want her!"

Marcus's eyes widened and he glanced at Delta.

"And now she's all I want," Esther sobbed. "I just need to hold her and tell her I'm sorry. I'm so sorry. It's her birthday, and I'm not there."

Delta wiped her eyes and walked out of the room, and Marcus dropped the bags of food to the floor and held Esther tight in his arms.

***

Kate signaled for Truitt and Malcolm to bring out the cake. She put her hands over Beulah Two's eyes as everyone sang "Happy Birthday to You." When it ended and the applause and cheers began, Kate removed her hands, and Beulah Two gasped and threw her hands over her mouth.

In front of her a sat a three-tiered, white cake covered entirely in magnolia blossoms, and on the very top, a tall crystal angel stood powerfully with his wings outstretched toward the sky. The little girl stared at the angel's resolute eyes and mighty jaw.

314

"Hey, I know him!" she said.

"Go on, sweetie," Beulah said. "Make a wish and blow out your candles."

Beulah Two closed her eyes, leaned over the magnolia blossoms, and breathed in. "They smell just like lemonade," she said. Then she blew until every flickering flame of the nine candles was extinguished. The guests whistled and applauded.

***

Through the cheering crowd, Malcolm spotted Sheriff Davis sitting in his patrol car in front of Beulah's house. Malcolm strolled over, and the sheriff rolled down his window.

"Hello, Preacher."

Malcolm nodded. "Sheriff. Anything?"

"Nope. We found a few shoeprints around Kate's house, but that don't tell us much. I've had officers patrolling out here all day, but there's been nothing unusual to report. We've had an increase in robberies near the county line. Maybe somebody got wind of the kind of money Kate's got and thought they'd try to see what they could make off with."

"Is that what you think?"

"That's what I hope."

"Yeah," Malcolm said. "Me, too."

"I'm gonna keep watch out here 'til your party's over."

"Thanks, Sheriff. I'll be staying here with Ms. Beulah for the next couple of nights. Just to be safe."

"And Kate?"

"She and Jane Ellen are staying at Modean's."

"Good idea. Can't be too careful."

A VIEW FROM THERE

***

At 10:30 p.m., the last of the guests left Beulah Two's party with bellies full of barbeque and a blues beat ringing in their ears. Beulah was worn out and getting herself ready for bed in the house. Outside, Beulah Two and Jane Ellen played a game of chase while Kate, Malcolm, Vaughn, and Truitt picked up trash and gathered the remnants of the celebration.

Truitt slapped at his arm for the twentieth time that night. "Dang mosquitoes!"

"We're almost finished, Tru," Kate said. "If you'll just help me load these tables into the back of Malcolm's truck, we'll be done for the night."

Malcolm cut in front of her and took the edge of the table out of her hand. "I've got it."

Kate smiled and backed away while the two men lifted the table and headed toward Malcolm's truck.

"Ah!" Truitt shouted, dropping his end and causing Malcolm to lose his grip and stumble to the ground. Truitt paced in quick circles, pawing at his back.

Vaughn hurried toward him. "What's wrong?"

"Mosquito!" Truitt yelped. "It got me! The thing had to be the size of a buzzard! Did you see it?"

Malcolm, still on the ground, lowered his head and propped his arms on his knees. Kate started toward him to see if he'd hurt himself, but then his shoulders started shaking with a chuckle.

It was soft at first, barely distinguishable, just before he threw his head back and laughed aloud. Kate put her hand to her mouth. She'd never heard his laugh or seen such a big smile on his face. She blinked, unable to look away.

Beulah Two stopped running and stared at him. A smile spread across her face, and a giggle escaped her lips. Kate laughed, too. Then Vaughn and Jane Ellen. Soon they were all on the damp ground, rolling with laughter, while Truitt did his best to reach the spot on his back where the giant mosquito had attacked. No one even noticed when it started to rain.

***

Delta pulled the comforter up around Esther's waist and sat beside her on the bed. Esther smiled and took Delta's hand as the tears fell.

"She knows," Delta said. "Everything in your heart that you want to say, she already knows."

"I've never missed her birthday."

"You'll see her soon. And when you do, you can give her that big present over there you keep starin' at. All this mess will blow over, and you can start a brand new life with her."

Esther bit her bottom lip and nodded.

"Now you sleep good. None of those dreams tonight."

***

Beulah passed out towels and shook her head. "What in the world was you crazy folks doin', layin' out in the rain? Don't you know there's a storm comin'? I ain't never heard of such foolishness. Beulah Two, you go get ready for bed, darlin'."

Beulah Two approached her grandmother slowly with her hands held together behind her back. Her hair and dress were soaked from the rain, and she looked up with pitiful, pleading eyes.

Beulah smiled down at her with a fist propped on her hip. "Well, go ahead. Spit it out. Whatchu wantin'? I bet it's got somethin' to do with Jane Ellen, don't it?"

"Can she please sleep here tonight, Grandma? Please? For my birthday?"

Beulah looked to Kate, who looked to Malcolm. Beulah Two and Jane Ellen stared at him, too. Malcolm had already told Beulah about the incident at Kate's the night before and that they all needed to be more watchful than ever over the next several days. "I'll be here all night on the couch. It'll be fine. That is, if it's all right with you, Kate."

Kate nodded. "It's all right with me."

***

The dream found Esther quickly. St. Luke's was dark except for a single candle burning at the front of the sanctuary. There were voices, whispers, quiet at first, then louder, closer. Esther felt her way along the pews toward the sound. More candles caught fire on their own, adding light to the dark room.

Two men sat on a pew at the front of the church. They were talking in hushed, urgent voices as she approached them from behind. One of them turned to face her, and she was relieved to see it was Father Francis. He looked the way she remembered him before—happy, alive. He smiled as though nothing was wrong. As though he didn't know what had happened to him.

And then the other man turned, and it was the same man who'd been with Father Francis in St. Luke's that horrible night. He glared at her with narrowed, evil eyes and a mouth full of dingy brown teeth. His horrifying appearance forced a scream from her lungs, and suddenly she was at the back of the church again, facing the doors.

Run! she told herself. *Run!* But she could not bring herself to leave Father Francis alone. Not this time. This time, she had to save him. She spun around to go to him, but he was standing right behind her. His robe was wet with dark red blood, and his face was waxen white.

As if in slow motion, he reached toward her and draped his jacket across her shoulders. "It's too cold for you to walk home without a jacket." His voice was hollow, and Esther shivered. She wanted to look away from his icy gaze but instead reached out and touched his cold cheek.

"Father Francis?" Her teeth were chattering. "Who's watching?"

He removed her hand from his cheek and held it in his chilling grasp then turned and looked back at the man in the pew. He was staring at them, his eyes glowing red.

Father Francis squeezed her hand. "Happy Birthday, Beulah Two."

Esther gazed into his bloodless face until she understood. And then she woke up.

***

Malcolm had been asleep for over an hour when his cell phone rang on the coffee table beside him. He jerked awake and rubbed his eyes. Fumbling in the dark, he found the phone just as a clap of thunder reverberated throughout the house. "Hello?"

"They think he told me something!" Esther was almost breathless.

Malcolm sat up. "What? What are you talking about?"

"That night in the church, the man was staring at Father Francis and me. He must have thought Father Francis was telling me something about his confession!"

"I don't understand," Malcolm said, shaking his head in an attempt to wake himself up.

"In my dream he said, 'They're still watching.' They must know I always come home for Beulah Two's birthday. Anyone I knew in Memphis could've told them that. I've never missed any of her birthdays. Not one! They've been waiting on me. And they think I'm there."

"Esther, I'm in Beulah's house. Everything is fine."

Lightning lit up the living room, and another clap of thunder boomed in the distance.

"They're there, Malcolm! I know it. Please get Grandma and Beulah Two out of there! Please!"

The urgency in Esther's voice set him on edge. "Okay. Okay, I'll get them up and take them out to my place. I'll call you back." Malcolm hung up the phone and stuffed it in his jeans pocket. He found the light switch in the hallway and flicked it on.

On his way to Beulah's room, he passed Beulah Two's and noticed Jane Ellen sitting up in bed. She was holding her knees and rocking back and forth in her Snow White pajamas. As he got closer, he heard her soft sobs.

"Hey, Jane Ellen." He sat down beside her on the bed. "It's just a little storm. Nothing to be afraid of."

Jane Ellen looked up at him, and Malcolm saw the fear in

her wet eyes. "She told me she'd be right back."

"Your mom's going to come get you in the morning. But I can take you to her now if you want."

"Not Mama." Jane Ellen shook her head. "Beulah Two. She said she'd be right back, and she didn't come."

Malcolm stood and turned on the bedroom light. Beulah Two's bed was empty except for the crystal angel lying with its head positioned perfectly on the pillow. Malcolm's pulse quickened. He clenched his jaw and put his hand on Jane Ellen's shoulder. "Where did she go? When Beulah Two said she'd be right back, where did she go?"

Jane Ellen looked toward the window and pointed outside. "She saw something out there. I looked, too, but I didn't see anything. She said she wasn't scared and that I should stay here."

Malcolm hurried to the window and peered outside into the night. The rain poured down in heavy sheets, and lightning flashed in every direction, illuminating an empty yard.

Jane Ellen dropped her face into her hands and sobbed. "She said she'd come right back."

Chapter Thirty-one

Oh, don't you want to go to the gospel
feast, that promised land where all is
peace? Oh, deep river, Lord, I want to
cross over into campground.
-African American spiritual

Three patrol cars sat in Beulah's front yard with blue lights flashing. The rain continued to fall, but the worst of the storm had passed. Beulah, in her nightgown and robe, poured a cup of steaming coffee for one of the officers. He urged her again to go rest in her bedroom. She refused and instead retreated to the porch where she rocked rhythmically in the wooden rocker. The officer might have thought she was talking to herself, but Kate knew exactly whom she was talking to.

Kate and Truitt sat on the couch on either side of a sleeping Jane Ellen while Malcolm spoke with another officer out in the yard. Kate felt sick and watched the clock tick slowly. Then she stared at the phone, hoping it would ring, anything to bring an end to the merciless wait.

The front door swung open wide, and Malcolm entered, his skin and clothes soaked in rain from head to toe. Drops fell from his hair and nose creating a wet spot on Beulah's carpet. He looked at Truitt. "Will you take them to Modean's?"

Kate jumped to her feet. "Where are you going?"

"I can't just sit here. I'm going to look for her."

"But Sheriff Davis said—"

"I know what he said, and I'm going to look for her. Please take them to Mo's, Truitt."

"What about Ms. Beulah?" Kate asked.

He motioned toward the officer. "Drew will be here with her in the house, and another patrol car will stay parked out front. She'll be fine."

"Then I'm staying, too," Kate said with resolve.

Malcolm stepped toward her and leaned in close to her face. "Please, Kate. Take your daughter and go home. It'll be safer at Mo's. Please."

The standoff lasted only seconds before Kate conceded defeat with a nod, and Malcolm disappeared back into the night.

Truitt took Jane Ellen into his arms and covered her body with a blanket. He shook hands with Drew, the policeman, then ran with Jane Ellen through the rain to the Jeep. Kate followed but paused on the porch next to Beulah. She bent down next to her and took her hand. Soft tears ran from the old woman's eyes, leaving dark lines down her cheeks. She stared stoically into the darkness with pursed lips, her hands gripping the arms of the chair.

"Ms. Beulah?" Kate said softly. "Do you need anything?"

Beulah tore her eyes away from the darkness ahead. "I don't feel her."

A lump rose high in Kate's throat, and she felt her legs begin to shake. "Ms. Beulah, they're going to find her. They're going to bring her home."

Beulah squeezed Kate's hand and leaned toward her. "I think she's already there."

***

Malcolm crept along the rough dirt road, searching to his

left and right for any sign of where Beulah Two might have gone. His windshield wipers worked overtime but did little to help him see through the pouring rain. Still he drove on. At least five patrol cars were searching the area, three county and two troopers, but Malcolm knew it wouldn't be long before the decision would be made to suspend the search until morning. The thought terrified him. Daylight was still at least four hours away. Anything could happen in four hours.

He clenched his teeth in anger and determination. He had to find her. Fast.

After more than an hour had passed, Malcolm pulled his pickup to the side of the road. He opened the door and walked to the front of the hood as the rain beat down on him without compassion. He grabbed fistfuls of his hair and yelled at the top of his lungs. "Beulah Two!"

He beat the hood with his fists and kicked his tire over and over until he lost his footing and fell to the muddy dirt road. "Please," he begged. "Please, just let me find her. Please help me. I have to find her."

When he raised his head, he was not alone. A man stood in the middle of the road just beyond the headlights, his face shielded by the darkness. Malcolm considered the distance to his rifle, still in the truck, but somehow didn't feel the need to run for it.

Slowly, Malcolm pushed himself up from the ground. When he took a step toward the stranger, the man walked off the dirt road and into the woods.

"Hey!" Malcolm yelled. "Stop!" He grabbed a flashlight from his toolbox and ran after him, his heart hammering away in his chest.

In the thickness of the trees, Malcolm spun around, shining the flashlight in every direction until he spotted movement several yards ahead. In a flash he took off after it. Branches and limbs reached out and tore at his flesh. He tasted blood on his lip, but he didn't even bother wiping it away.

The trees broke into open air and Malcolm noticed the rushing sound of the river beneath him. He was standing on the Old River Bridge.

Malcolm shined the flashlight's beam in front of him, illuminating the rusty metal covered in forty years of graffiti. The light found the man on the other side, silent and still, and staring at Malcolm as though he was waiting for him. Lightning flashed, and Malcolm caught a glimpse of his face. His hair was dark and wavy, and his eyes seemed sorrowful, like he knew something Malcolm did not.

The shrill scream of a siren filled the air, and Malcolm glanced behind him. When he looked back, the man was gone. "Hey! Do you know where she is? Please help me!"

Malcolm started out across the bridge. It creaked beneath his feet, and he remembered just a year before a teenage boy had been spray-painting obscenities on the railings when he'd fallen through to the river below and barely lived to tell the tale. The incident had made all the papers and prompted the city to hang the sign posted in front of him.

Historic Old River Bridge: Danger. Do Not Cross.

But Malcolm pressed on, one foot before the other, slowly, cautiously.

Another bolt of lightning shot across the sky. Malcolm glanced down at the river below and caught a glimpse of white near the bank. He gripped the railing and leaned over, hanging the flashlight low and aiming its beam until the light found what he was looking for. A short gasp broke from his lips. A body, small and unmoving, was caught up in debris at the river's edge.

Malcolm ran. Fearless, he tore across the unsteady bridge, past the place the mysterious man had been standing, and down the riverbank to the water's edge. The night's rain made the current stronger than usual, but he plunged in up to his knees.

Her white nightgown clung to her body, lying face down in the water and bobbing with the moving current. He rolled her onto her back and pulled her into his arms. Her eyes were closed, her lips blue, and her mouth slightly open.

"No, no, no, no," he whispered. "Beulah Two."

She didn't move, her body limp and cold. Malcolm carried her from the water to the riverbank and put his head to her chest. He heard nothing but the beating rain and the sound of the river rolling past.

***

The police officer reclined at the kitchen table with his radio while Kate and Beulah held hands on the porch and rocked side by side. Truitt and Jane Ellen had left for Modean's hours before, but Kate couldn't bring herself to leave Beulah alone, despite Malcolm's clear instructions. So she'd stayed and rocked.

They hadn't seen a flashing patrol car creep past the house in nearly an hour. Drew, the officer inside, offered no information if he knew any, and so they waited as the rain hit the tin roof above until, finally, headlights appeared in the yard.

Kate jumped to her feet. "It's Malcolm."

Her heart pounded as Malcolm opened the screen door to the

porch, his red eyes swollen, his bottom lip quivering.

Beulah did not move when he knelt and put his hands on her knees.

"She's gone, ain't she?"

Malcolm nodded, his gaze on the floor.

Kate doubled over, struggling to catch her breath and feeling she would vomit. Malcolm's body quaked with sobs. He lay his head in Beulah's lap, and the old woman stroked his wet hair, her face calm but somber.

And then she began to sing.

"Deep river, my home is over Jordan. Deep river, Lord, I want to cross over into campground. Deep river, my home is over Jordan. Deep river, Lord, I want to cross over into campground. Oh, don't you want to go to the gospel feast, that promised land where all is peace? Oh, deep river, Lord, I want to cross over into campground."

The policemen who had gathered in the yard took off their hats and lowered their heads. Raindrops mixed with their tears. The thunder and lightning had passed, and the rain was slowing. Malcolm raised his head and pushed himself to his feet. Beulah reached for his hand.

"Somebody needs to call Esther."

Chapter Thirty-two

*See, I am sending an angel ahead of you
to guard you along the way and to bring
you to the place I have prepared.*
-Exodus 23:20, NIV

The Millsville Farmers' Market opened for business at 7 a.m. on the dot, but as usual, the throng of customers, men and women of all ages, shapes, and sizes, began arriving at 6:30. They had waited all winter for the moment when finally they could peruse the booths and stands for what was arguably the best produce in the state. They were restless and ready to make their move when at long last Mayor Mills hobbled to his feet and opened the gates. The crowd charged inside, scurrying in every direction, some polite, some not so polite, but all in a desperate dash to score the best the market had to offer on its opening day.

At 7:02 a.m., Virgil Wilson's strawberry stand was surrounded. At warp speed, the determined patrons filled paper bags, baskets, crates, and anything that would hold the plump, red berries. Virgil raised his cane high into the air amid the chaos. "Now, just slow down. Slow down. I only got two hands! Good Lord almighty!"

Other customers searched out fresh summer fruits and vegetables—asparagus, zucchini, broccoli, carrots, cucumbers, raspberries, green beans, peaches, mushrooms, okra, potatoes, and blueberries. It didn't take long before baskets were overflowing and the pace slowed, the urgency of competition waning. Folks began to mingle, content with their purchases.

Some talked about the unseasonably warm weather. Some gossiped about Reverend Mackey Johnston's rumored prison stint. Others shared their disappointment over the absence of the Market Queens on this, the opening day of the market. The pink booth sat empty. No twins in tiaras. No vegetables, jams, flowers, or any items for sale. Only the picture of a little girl mounted on the wall beneath a large yellow and white ribbon.

***

The funeral home delivered Beulah Two's body to Millsville Baptist Church at 7:45 a.m. for the 9 a.m. funeral. Malcolm sat alone in his black suit and gray tie in the front row next to Beulah Two's small pink casket and remembered when Anna's casket sat in its place just two years before.

Beulah had asked him to lead the service, and he'd agreed, but he had yet to think of anything to say. He couldn't remember getting dressed that morning—how could he come up with a proper memorial speech? He was numb on the inside and out and longed for a solitary place where he could go and crumble into the millions of pieces that were barely holding themselves together.

He turned at the sound of footsteps behind him, and he had to glance twice to recognize his visitor. Esther's eyes were wet, her nose and cheeks red, but she looked well, healthier than he'd ever seen her. She wore a long black dress and matching cardigan and held a damp handkerchief in her hand.

She sat down beside him and stared at the casket. Then she slid a tiny red box toward him on the pew. "I bought it for her birthday. I was going to send it but decided I'd rather give it to her in person."

Malcolm opened the box to find a silver chain with a bell charm in the shape of an angel. He jiggled it side to side, and the bell softly chimed. "It's beautiful. She'd have loved it."

Esther shook her head. "I know what you think of me, Malcolm. And I don't blame you. But I loved her." Tears poured from her eyes, leaving streams of mascara down her cheeks. "I was a horrible mother. I know I was. But I was making things right. I was going to make her happy. I swear."

Malcolm placed the necklace back inside the box and set it beside him. He scooted closer to Esther and put his arm around her. She closed her eyes, rested her head on his shoulder, and wept.

"I know you were."

Esther's sobs echoed through the sanctuary. Then she stood, picked up the red box, and reached for Malcolm's hand. "Will you help me?"

Malcolm hesitated only a moment before taking her hand. Together they lifted the coffin's lid and slipped the chain around Beulah Two's small, perfect neck. Esther carefully positioned the angel bell in front then leaned over and kissed her forehead. "Happy Birthday, honey. Sorry Mama was a little late with your present."

Malcolm closed the lid as the funeral director, Mr. McDonald, entered with two large baskets filled with magnolia blossoms.

"Excuse me, Pastor. The flowers are here. Is it all right if we go ahead and get them set up?"

Malcolm nodded. "Sure."

"All the ones with magnolia blossoms go in front by the casket," Esther told him. "Magnolias were her favorite."

Mr. McDonald smiled and glanced at Malcolm. "Ma'am . . . they're *all* magnolias. A whole truckload full." He shook his head. "I've been doin' this for thirty-five years, and I've never seen anything like it."

Four men entered the sanctuary, carrying as many arrangements of the white blossoms as they could hold. They set them down on the stage then went back for more.

***

By 9:05 a.m., not another soul could fit inside the sanctuary. Every pew was packed, every inch of standing room taken. People even spilled out the doors. Mr. McDonald scurried about, unfolding extra chairs to seat as many as he could in the parking lot. When he ran out of chairs, he passed out paper fans to help combat the June heat.

The church's air conditioning hadn't worked in years. The front and side doors were open and fans blew at full speed, partly in an effort to contend with the high temperatures, and partly to battle the overwhelming smell of magnolia. The flowers, ranging from gigantic bunches to single stems, filled the entirety of the stage and overflowed onto the floor, each bloom emanating a powerful, lemony aroma that hung thick in the sweltering heat of the sanctuary. Next to the closed coffin sat a tall white easel with a large, framed, black and white photograph of Beulah Two, reclining in her Grandpa Curtis's decrepit fishing boat, her eyes affixed longingly toward the sky.

Nina began the service with "Amazing Grace" then moved on to "It is Well with My Soul," and Beulah sobbed aloud during the last verse, as did many in the crowd. Kate slipped her arm around Beulah's shoulder and held her tight while Esther held Beulah's hand from her other side. Jane Ellen colored on her construction paper and glanced up at her mother. Kate gave her a reassuring smile, and the little girl continued filling in her hand-drawn heart with reds and blues.

***

When the song ended, Nina and the piano player took their seats, and all eyes fell upon Malcolm. He stood and walked to the podium next to Beulah Two's casket, cleared his throat, and looked out over the crowd, scanning the faces until he found Kate.

She wore no makeup, and her hair was pulled back into a loose bun. Her eyes were pink and swollen and looking to him to say something, anything to bring comfort. To her. To all of them. He unfolded the obituary in his hand, cleared his throat again, and began to read.

"Beulah Maxine Jones, known as Beulah Two, was born on June seventh, two thousand and five, in Memphis, Tennessee, and died on June seventh, two thousand and fourteen, near her home in Millsville, Arkansas. She was the daughter of Esther Mae Jones, granddaughter of the late Maxine Mae Jones, and great-granddaughter of Beulah Macon and the late Curtis Macon. Beulah Two loved puzzles, the river she was raised near, baking with her great-grandmother, playing with her best friend, Jane Ellen Canton, and most of all, looking for angels the rest of us could not see. She was loved by all who knew her, and during the time she spent among us, she made us, and the world, better."

Malcolm took a deep breath and looked up. Tears streaked every face he could see, as well as his own. He folded the obituary with trembling hands and tucked it away in his jacket pocket.

"Beulah Two was my friend. We met when she just six years old. She had just come home to be with Ms. Beulah again after living through worse circumstances than most adults in this room could bear. But that darkness she came out of, it didn't break Beulah Two. It didn't make her bitter. The darkness, as horrifying as it had been, only made her appreciate the light, and long for the light—something I could never learn to do. She saw hope when I lost it. She found good in the dead center of evil." He looked from face to face. "I couldn't find good even though it was all around me. She loved those who hurt her the worst. I turned my back on those who had done nothing but love me."

The sobs were forming in the pit of his stomach and clawing their way to the surface. "Beulah Two taught me that, sometimes, unthinkable things happen to good people, but that life doesn't have to end there. She showed me that life can still be beautiful, even after coming face to face with the darkness. Somehow, in nine short years, Beulah Two learned to see the beauty in an ugly world—a world where she never really belonged. She was too good, too precious to live anywhere but where she lives now—in a place where evil does not exist, where she doesn't have to imagine the angels, where she can reach out and catch a star instead of a lightning bug, where she's with her Grandma Maxie and Grandpa Curtis, and my Anna." His voice broke, and he wiped at the tears on his cheeks.

"Beulah Two was . . ." Malcolm noticed the mass of people

crowding the doorway and stirring. "She was . . ."

The group parted and a man stepped inside and stood in the center of the aisle. His eyes met Malcolm's—eyes Malcolm had seen before. In Beulah's yard. The man who'd been looking for Esther.

Malcolm's heart pounded. He stood tall and tightened his jaw as the man walked down the aisle toward him.

Sheriff Davis sprang to his feet in the back row with his hand on his gun. "Stop right where you are, son!"

Some people gasped, some escaped out the doors, but the man kept walking. Sheriff Davis drew his weapon, and several women screamed, but the man kept walking until he reached Beulah Two's coffin.

He stared at it and ran his hand alongside the smooth wood. Sheriff Davis stepped into the aisle and crept toward him, his gun pointed at the man's back. "I said stop right there. Turn around and put your hands behind your head."

Malcolm gripped the pulpit and stole a quick glance toward Kate, who was clinging to Jane Ellen. He looked back at the man, and for a moment Malcolm saw something reminiscent of sadness in his face.

With his hand on Beulah Two's coffin, the man asked, "Is this the girl?"

The veins in Sheriff Davis's neck and temple protruded, and his face and the top of his bald head were bright red. He held the gun steady. "On your knees now."

"Yes," Malcolm said. "That's Beulah Two."

The man blinked down at the coffin. "She came out of nowhere when we were waitin' down by the river. She wasn't even scared. I asked her where her mama was, and she wouldn't tell me."

Esther trembled violently, and she held tight to Beulah's arm.

"I grabbed her and held her over the bank to make her scared enough to talk, but she just . . . looked at somethin' behind me. Just like the last time I saw her." The man gazed at Malcolm with wild, searching eyes. "She saw it. What I feel but can't ever see . . . She saw it."

Malcolm studied the man's face. He was scared, even repentant. His moment with Beulah Two had changed him, and he wanted answers. He wanted to know what she knew.

"I looked back to see if I could see it, too," the stranger explained, "and I dropped her. I didn't mean to, but I dropped her in the water. The current was movin' fast, and she was gone."

Beulah and Esther sobbed together, and Sheriff Davis forced the man to the floor from behind and handcuffed him as the crowd of spectators gasped. Two more officers hurried inside to help escort the man out.

On the way back up the aisle, the man glanced back to Malcolm and yelled, "She saw it! Preacher, she saw it! What was it? Tell me!"

The people were mumbling and crying and rustling in their seats. Malcolm pried his hands off the podium and finally exhaled. He nodded at Nina, and in an instant she was on stage with the pianist, calling out hymn number seventy-five, "Oh How I Love Jesus." By the third verse, the crowd had settled and reluctantly sang along.

***

The graveside ceremony was brief, just as Esther had requested. The heat was unbearable, and Beulah was lightheaded and weak. Kate fanned her with a paper fan throughout the outdoor service and was relieved when Malcolm said the final amen. Her arm ached from all the fanning, and Beulah appeared more ill by the minute. Truitt and two funeral home attendants helped her from her seat and into a waiting, air-conditioned car with Esther by her side. Most of the mourners followed suit and escaped the heat inside their cool vehicles, while others mingled in small circles and talked in whispers about the man who'd crashed the service and was surely Beulah Two's killer.

Kate found Jane Ellen with Modean and Nate and bent to her level. "Hey, honey. How about riding home with Aunt Mo and Nate? Mommy needs to help out here for a bit."

Jane Ellen nodded.

"You know it's okay to be sad, Jane Ellen. Beulah Two was your friend. It's all right to miss her."

"I do miss her, Mama." Jane Ellen smiled. "But I'm not sad. Beulah Two told me a buncha times that she wanted to be in Heaven with all the angels. And now she is. Right? That's what Malcolm said. He said she doesn't have to imagine them anymore."

Kate pulled her daughter in a tight embrace. "Yes, honey. That's exactly where she is—with the angels."

Modean took Jane Ellen by the hand and led her toward Nate's truck.

Kate waved. "We'll see you at Beulah's."

She wiped her wet cheeks and made her way underneath the blue funeral tent with the velvet-covered chairs still lined up in neat rows. Most of the people had wandered elsewhere, and she stepped over to the coffin, alone. A familiar feeling came over her—a memory of the day they'd buried her mother not far from the very spot where Beulah Two would be laid to rest. She remembered the cold rain that soaked her to the bone. The sickness that overwhelmed her body and spirit. The feeling that nothing in life would ever be the same. The longing to be nowhere else but in Gray's arms.

She looked toward the sky. There were no storms in sight, though her heart ached as it had that rainy October day. She wrapped her arms around her waist and once more longed for arms to hold her, but arms that did not belong to Gray Canton.

She approached the small, pink casket and leaned close until her lips almost brushed against the wood. "Tell Mama I miss her, Beulah Two. And tell Anna . . . she'd be proud of him."

***

Malcolm watched Kate walk to the cemetery gate and then retreat inside the church. He removed his jacket and leaned against a tall willow near Anna's grave, his white dress shirt drenched in sweat. Beulah Two's coffin sat nearby on steel beams, waiting to make its decent into the earth.

He remembered the day they'd lowered Anna's body into the ground. He had sat near the fence as the workers had arrived with the backhoe and watched as they'd dug the deep opening and covered it again with the same red dirt over the top of her.

He glanced at Anna's picture, her never-changing face. She always smiled back at him, the same as on the day he'd taken the photo in the field where Nate proposed to Modean—the same field where they'd shared the lightning bug picnic. He thought of the last time she'd smiled at him, on the stretch of highway near the big oak tree when she'd ran her hand across her stomach and told him he'd have been a wonderful father.

Tears stung his eyes, and then he saw him—five graves away, leaning against a tree of his own. Malcolm squinted. He'd convinced himself the man was a figment of his imagination, an apparition his mind invented to help him cope with finding Beulah Two's body. But there he stood. The same build. The same face. The same dark, wavy hair. His presence—his existence—was undeniable.

Malcolm walked toward him, and the man furrowed his brow. He glanced behind him, then back to Malcolm with an air of surprise.

"You were in the woods," Malcolm said.

The man nodded. "I was."

Malcolm stared into the man's mysterious, yet gentle, eyes. And all at once, he knew.

Malcolm looked around at the remaining people left wandering about the cemetery, talking among themselves and visiting graves. "Can they see you, too?"

"I didn't know you could see me until you walked over just now. It isn't up to me."

"But Beulah Two could see you."

The man smiled broadly. "Yes. Sometimes, Beulah Two could see me."

"But how? Why her?"

He shook his head. "I don't know. Like Ms. Beulah always says, Beulah Two is special."

Malcolm lowered his head and tried to suffocate the sobs fighting their way out. The man put his hand on Malcolm's shoulder, sending a surge of energy down the side of Malcolm's body.

"It isn't for me to reveal the things of Heaven, but I can tell you this. I have seen her there."

Malcolm looked up and caught his stare, the word *there* searing into his heart and imagination.

"I was there when she saw him for the first time. He held her as long as I've ever seen him hold anyone."

Malcolm felt his legs go weak beneath him.

"I once told Kate, we can't understand his ways. Even others like me can't understand sometimes. But when you're given a view from there, only then can you see how every move of his hand is flawless—how everything, even what looks like madness to you, comes together in meticulous perfection."

Malcolm shook his head. "But we don't have a view from there. We can't see what you see."

The man's bright eyes seemed to glow. "But that's what makes you remarkable. We believe because we see with our eyes. We touch him, talk to him just like you and I are talking now. But you . . . you believe in things you can't see . . . that you've *never* seen. We don't understand the notion of faith, because what's known to us has always been known. But you believe in things only hoped for. We marvel at you."

Malcolm looked over his shoulder at Beulah Two's coffin. "She's happy, then?"

"She was fishing with Curtis when I saw her last, telling him all about Beulah and the magnolia cake and the angels that helped her fly."

Malcolm let his tears flow freely, and the man stepped toward him again.

"And Anna . . ."

Malcolm froze at the sound of her name.

"Would you like to know what Anna was doing?"

Malcolm's heart was thrashing within his chest, and he felt he could no longer stand. But he somehow managed a nod.

"She was building sandcastles on the beach with your son. He loves the water, just like you. Though it's been a while since you've waded in, hasn't it?" The man's eyes brimmed with compassion. "Down here your reality looks like a ruined puzzle, all scattered and broken on the ground. But there, Malcolm, *there* every piece finds its place, and the picture it completes . . . your mind can't conceive of it."

Malcolm wiped at his eyes and swallowed hard and wondered how all this was possible. "So, will you go? Since Beulah Two is there, now, will you go, too?"

"I wasn't here for Beulah Two." The man redirected his gaze past Malcolm toward the church.

Malcolm turned his head and saw Kate helping Mr. McDonald load flowers into Debbie's van for delivery to Beulah's.

"She is like her father, you know?" the man said. "Stubborn and strong."

"You're here for Kate?"

"Malcolm, I was here long before Jackson Boudrow became pastor of the church. I was here when Kate was born. I was here when Jackson left this Earth to go home. I was here the moment you laid eyes on her, just over there next to Ruth's grave. But I was sent for many moments and many reasons. Today, I'm here to bring comfort. I don't know why I was revealed to you, but be sure, he didn't do it for me. He did it for you."

Malcolm shook his head. "But I've done all I could to push

him away. I've ignored him. I threw hymnals at him."

The man smiled. "I heard about the hymnals."

"So why then? Why does he still care about me?"

"You're no prodigal. You may not have talked to him out loud, but you couldn't keep your spirit from crying out for him, and he heard. We all celebrated when Anna came home, but he cried with you. We come and go as we're told. We move in and out of lives and circumstances, but he's never left your side. Not once. Not for a moment. That I know. Hymnals or no hymnals."

Kate groaned from the parking lot, and Malcolm looked back over his shoulder and watched as she knelt to the ground. A large, blue flowerpot lay broken at her feet, soil and flowers strewn about. Kate bent to clean up the mess and rescue what was left of the delicate blooms.

"You're right," Malcolm said. "She is strong. So much stronger than me."

"No moment of your life happens by chance," the man said. "Not a mosquito bite. Not a fall. Not one victory or crash, or birth or death. Not one encounter. Not a broken flowerpot. You may not understand, but understanding isn't required of you. Only faith."

Kate picked up the last flower from the mess at her feet and brought it close to her face to breathe in the fragrance. Malcolm smiled.

"Only faith," he repeated. When he turned back, the man was gone. He scanned the cemetery, but there was no sign of him.

Malcolm looked toward the sky and imagined Beulah Two lounging in her Grandpa Curtis's fishing boat. He hoped she caught a big one.

Chapter Thirty-three

Long stormy spring-time, wet
contentious April, winter chilling
the lap of very May; but at length
the season of summer does come.
-Thomas Carlyle

Kate slid a pale blue lily into Modean's soft curls and secured it snuggly with a bobby pin. She stepped back and examined her work. "Ferfect."

Modean reached up and patted her new accessory. "Are you sure it ain't too much? I don't wanna overdo it."

Kate held up a mirror, and Modean smiled in spite of herself. "Oh my. It's beautiful."

"*You're* beautiful," Kate said. "Now hurry up. There's not much time."

"Wait!" Modean cried. "Something borrowed!"

Kate looked around for anything that would fit the bill. "How about my earrings?"

"You know my ears ain't pierced!"

Debbie stuck her head inside the tiny room. "It's time, ladies. Let's go, or we'll miss it!"

"We need something borrowed!" Kate said.

Debbie bit her lip then reached in her pocket and pulled out a stick of chewing gum. "Here. Chew this."

"Huh?" Modean took the gum and looked it over.

Kate snatched it from her hand and quickly unwrapped it. "Open up."

Modean opened her mouth wide, and Kate popped the gum

inside.

"It's borrowed. Now chew."

"Well, don't that mean I gotta give it back?" Modean asked.

"C'mon, c'mon," Debbie said. "The music's startin'."

The sun had almost set as Kate hurried outside and down the steps of the rented Winnebago. She reached for Modean's hand. "They're playing your song, Aunt Mo."

Modean emerged in her ivory dress, holding a bouquet of white roses and blue lilies. Just beyond the trees, the melody of the wedding march floated toward them on the warm wind.

"Violins!"

Kate smiled. "Now, go on. Follow Jane Ellen's petals."

Modean pulled Kate into her arms. "Thank you, honey."

Kate kissed her cheek then hurried her on her way, through the trees, and into the open field lined with hundreds of candles that flickered along her path. Three violin players drew their bows across delicate strings, their beautiful music rising high into the air above the field. At the sight of her, a hundred guests stood to their feet.

Esther sat with her boyfriend, Marcus, clutching his arm and leaning into his chest. He kissed the top of her head and pulled her nearer. The twins, Ella and Emma, yanked tissue after tissue from matching purses and dabbed at their wet cheeks.

Truitt met Modean with a proud smile, took her arm in his, and led her down the petal-covered pathway to the place where Nate had proposed and where he stood waiting for his bride under an archway made of willow branches.

Malcolm stood beside Nate with a Bible in his hand. He hadn't spoken in public since the day of Beulah Two's funeral nearly a month before. Since then he'd mostly been hiding away in his house and working overtime in Nate's wood shop. Church services at Millsville Baptist continued as they had for years—singing, testimonies, prayer, dismissal, but all without Malcolm. Even Kate hadn't laid eyes on him since the funeral. As she took her seat in the back row next to Beulah and Delta, she couldn't help but steal a glance.

Malcolm was dressed in a tan-colored suit and a baby-blue tie. His hair was damp with sweat from the blazing Fourth of July sun, but loosely styled to precision. His face had more color than she remembered, undoubtedly the result of hours in the sun, and the dark circles under his eyes had vanished.

Delta bumped her shoulder hard, and Kate twitched her head, averting her eyes.

"Hard not to look," Delta said. "That is one handsome man."

"One *good* man," Beulah added.

"If you'd have been payin' attention, you'd have seen him watchin' you walk all the way down here," Delta said.

Beulah nodded. "Mm-hmm. He sure was. And I'm sayin' it's about time she start payin' attention."

"Mm-hmm," Delta agreed.

Kate shushed them as Truitt and Mo reached the front and Truitt placed Mo's hand into Nate's. The ceremony was beginning.

The vows were brief but as beautiful as the setting. The candles danced in the dimness of the evening, providing perfect illumination for the open field. Nate had just finished saying "I do" when Debbie stood and waved her hands in a desperate attempt to secure Malcolm's attention.

Malcolm looked up, and Debbie pointed at her cell phone and motioned him to speed things up. He turned his attention back to the couple and talked faster.

"Modean, do you take Nate to be your wedded husband, to have and to hold, from this day forward, for better or worse, for richer or poorer—"

He glanced at Debbie again. She was still standing, cell phone to her ear. Her eyes were huge, and she moved her arms in large, exaggerated gestures then held up her watch.

"In sickness and in health, to love and to cherish, 'til death do you part, or the Lord comes for his own?"

Modean nodded and squeezed Nate's hand. "I do."

Debbie jumped up and down, and Malcolm spoke so fast the words were almost jumbled.

"Then by the power vested in me by the state of Arkansas and Almighty God, I now pronounce you husband and wife. Nate, you may kiss your bride."

As Nate leaned in and gently kissed Modean's lips, the deep blue sky erupted with a boom and lit up with colors. Debbie exhaled in relief and collapsed into her chair, and Modean threw her hand to her mouth. She, along with everyone else, stared up at the fireworks—everyone but Malcolm.

***

Malcolm studied Kate's face beneath the light of the erupting sky.

When at last the heavens went still and the "oohs" and "aahs" fell quiet, Malcolm stepped forward. "Ladies and gentlemen, I present to you Mr. and Mrs. Nathaniel Bell."

The guests broke into applause and cheers, and Susie hopped atop a chair. "And don't forget!" she shouted. "Reception at my place! Everyone's invited!"

As the crowd cheered and formed a line to congratulate Mo and Nate, Malcolm wasted no time in getting to her. He'd spent the greater part of the month alone, thinking about her and what he would say when the moment came. And there she was, only footsteps away.

Ella and Emma materialized in front of him. "What a beautiful service, Malcolm!" Emma said.

Ella took his arm. "And might I say you look exceptionally handsome in that suit. Sister and I were just talking about it."

"Yes, we were," Emma said. "Exceptionally handsome, we said."

Malcolm patted Emma's arm and slipped out of her grasp. "Thank you, ladies. If you'll excuse me a moment—"

A heavy hand came down on his shoulder just as he was making his getaway. Malcolm turned to find Sheriff Davis standing behind him in khaki pants and a short-sleeved button-up and tie.

"Nice service, Pastor. Can I talk to you a minute?"

Malcolm glanced toward Kate. She was walking away toward the trees with Jane Ellen and Beulah. He sighed. "Sure, Sheriff."

The sheriff motioned to Esther, who was standing nearby with Marcus, and she joined them. Marcus excused himself and went to help Kate escort Beulah to her car. The old woman clung to his arm and looked up at him with starry eyes.

The sheriff shook Esther's hand. "I wanted a moment with the two of you to fill you in on what I know. Demarius Reid, the man who showed up at the funeral, is finally talking, and you were right, Esther. Reid told us the man with Father Francis in the church the night he was killed was a guy by the name of Lamar Jones. Jones was a crackhead and part of Reid's inner circle who survived a gunshot to the chest and suddenly found Jesus. Well, Reid heard Jones was headed to the church to confess his sins—sins that undoubtedly involved Reid, and he had to make sure that didn't happen."

"Reid killed Father Francis?" Esther said.

"He hasn't officially confessed, but he will. The two men who came to town with Reid have been detained and they're singing like birds. One of 'em was there that night in the church in Memphis, and he says Reid was the one who shot the priest. He also said Reid took out Jones the next day."

"But why were they after Esther?" Malcolm asked.

"Jones told Reid that Father Francis was whispering to her at the back of the church, and Reid was convinced it had to do with Jones's confession. To make matters worse, Jones's cell phone was missing. He told Reid he'd given it to the priest as a sign he was done with the life he'd been living—to show he was making a clean break. But Reid believed the phone contained an incriminating video of him and assumed the priest would turn it over to the police. When he figured out Esther had the phone, he went after her."

Esther's forehead creased. "But Father Francis didn't tell me anything about the confession. He'd never do that. And that phone in his jacket—I tossed it back in Memphis."

The sheriff shook his head. "Yeah, but Reid didn't know that. And he couldn't take any chances. After Malcolm told us about you ditching the phone in the alley, Memphis police recovered it."

"Was there a video on it?" Malcolm asked.

"Oh yeah," the sheriff said. "I can't share the details with you, but I'll tell you this. If Reid thought Esther had it, or even knew of it, it's no wonder he didn't want to give up 'til he found her. That video alone could put him away for the rest of his life, or longer."

"Just tell me he's not getting out," Esther said.

The sheriff gave her hand a squeeze. "He's not getting out. Thanks to Beulah Two, he'll never see the light of day."

Malcolm shook the sheriff's hand. "I appreciate all you've done, Sheriff."

"I wish I could've done more." He extended an arm toward Esther. "Can I take you to your car?"

Esther nodded and walked with him.

Malcolm watched them walk away, his mind reeling. When Delta and Debbie ambushed him, he jumped, his body jerking violently.

Debbie didn't notice his surprise, or didn't care. "Can you believe how perfect that turned out?" she asked. "I was coordinatin' with Bob down at the ball fields. He's the one always in charge of Millsville's Fourth of July fireworks display. I did most of the flowers for his mama's funeral last year, so he owed me one. Still took some convincin' though."

"Well the timin' couldn't have been better!" Delta exclaimed. "Just right on the money. Don't you agree, Malcolm?"

Malcolm walked sandwiched between them, their arms locked with his, toward the trees and dirt road where the guests had parked their vehicles.

"Yes, ladies. I agree. It was perfect timing."

"There's somethin' to be said about timin'," Debbie said, shaking her head.

"Absolutely!" Delta said. She let go of Malcolm's arm and stepped in front of him. "You wouldn't want to mess around and let an opportunity pass you by. Would ya, Preacher? You know what they say. Timin' is everything."

Delta and Debbie stood cross-armed and glared at him. His eyes went wide before he gently parted them to make his way through.

"Well, it was good talking with you, ladies. But I really have to get to the reception now."

"Timin', Malcolm! It's everything!" Debbie shouted as he walked away.

***

By 11 p.m., the party at Susie's was in full swing. Guests ate and laughed together while old '70s rock tunes blared, the only selections available in Susie's jukebox. Nate and Modean shared a plate of fried shrimp and hushpuppies then left their table to slow dance on the makeshift dance floor. The rowdy crowd quickly joined in.

Outside on the square, Truitt and Vaughn sat on a bench next to the fountain and the statue of Colonel Trampus Mills. Vaughn lay with her head in Truitt's lap, looking up to a sky growing cloudier by the second. "I can't believe you grew up in this place. It seems so magical . . . Like an old movie, or a sixties TV show."

Truitt laughed. "Now that I think about it, it was sorta magical."

Vaughn sighed. "I don't ever want to leave here."

"Me neither." Truitt held out a hand and pulled her up to

sitting, then he slid off the bench and onto one knee. "Let's stay here together," he said before slipping the diamond from his pocket and onto her finger. "Vaughn Spencer, you're perfect. And I've got more flaws than I can count, but the thing is . . . I'm crazy in love with you. I'm askin' you to stay here with me forever. Right here in this magical little town . . . as my wife."

Vaughn took his face in her hands and her eyes filled with tears. "Yes. Yes! Yes!"

She wrapped her arms around him and they stood, and kissed, and danced around the square to the muffled music coming from inside Susie's.

They both jumped when they heard a cough, and Boyd strode toward them.

"Truitt, could I have a word with you?"

Truitt stole another kiss from Vaughn and then backed away from her. "If I'm not back in five minutes, call 9-1-1."

Vaughn laughed as she followed Boyd around the dark corner of a nearby building.

***

Truitt met Ella and Emma on the sidewalk as they headed toward their car. "Calling it a night so soon, ladies?"

The twins giggled.

"You caught us, Dr. Truitt!" Emma confessed. "Yes, we really must be getting home. Ella is just a big old grizzly bear in the mornings if she doesn't get her sleep."

Ella batted the air. "Oh, you hush, Emma DuBois."

"I wondered if I could show you something," Truitt said. "It'll only take a second."

The twins swapped curious looks then said in unison, "Why certainly."

Truitt motioned to Boyd, who stood waiting in the shadows of the building. He approached holding a small, white and gray kitten with piercing blue eyes and filthy, matted fur. The twins gasped.

"Boyd found her a few days ago behind his office. Looks like somebody abandoned her. He's been feedin' her, but she's needin' a real home. I told him I might know of just the place."

Emma hesitated only a moment before she stepped forward and took the kitten from Boyd's arms. The tiny kitten nestled close to her chest and purred wildly, and Emma rubbed her cheek against its dirty, fuzzy head as a tear rolled from her eye.

Ella nuzzled the kitten with her nose and sniffled. "What do you think, Sister?"

Emma wiped her eyes. "I think we'd better get her some tuna! Poor thing's starving to death." The twins wrapped the kitten in Emma's silk scarf and climbed inside their enormous Lincoln.

"Bring her by the clinic on Monday, and I'll check her out!" Truitt called before they drove away.

Boyd nodded at him. "You did a good thing there."

Truitt reached out his hand, and Boyd stared at it a moment before taking it. The two men shook hands on the sidewalk as the first few drops of rain began to fall.

***

Beulah sat alone at a booth watching Esther and Marcus dance, and Delta sat down next to her.

"You know, Ms. Beulah, I'll be needin' somewhere to stay 'til I find a place of my own."

Beulah snapped her head toward her. "You mean, you're movin' back here?"

"I think Esther will be just fine at my place in Houston by herself. That is, until Marcus finishes med school next year. Then I imagine she'll follow him wherever he goes for his internship. But don't you worry. That girl's gonna be well taken care of."

Beulah laughed. "I sure never woulda thought this town was big enough for you."

Delta laughed, too. "Me neither! But I'm happy here. And I would appreciate a place to stay . . . just for a while."

Beulah wrapped her arm around Delta's waist. "Girl, you can stay with me as long as you want to. That house been so quiet lately. It'll be nice to have some company. I get tired of bein' alone."

"Well, we're gonna fix that." Delta patted Beulah's hand then held it tight. "Two alones make one big together."

***

Boyd found Debbie rearranging a vase of flowers on a table that had been knocked over by some boisterous wedding guests. He took her by the hand and pulled her onto the dance floor as Ronnie Van Zant sang "The Ballad of Curtis Loew" on the jukebox.

"Boyd, everybody's watchin' us," Debbie said, smoothing her hair and looking around.

Boyd smiled. "Let 'em watch. They're gonna be watchin'

for a long time."

Debbie threw her arms around his neck. "You mean, you ain't gonna get tired of me and run off?"

Boyd kissed first one cheek, then the other. "Not a chance, Debbie Williams. I ain't goin' anywhere." And he lifted her off her feet and spun her around the floor.

***

Malcolm scanned the tables at Susie's but didn't see Kate anywhere. He sat down at the bar, and Susie handed him a Dr. Pepper.

"Good service, Malcolm. Those fireworks were really somethin'."

Malcolm managed a smile and nodded.

Modean sat down next to him. "She already left."

Malcolm gazed at her.

"Well, you ain't showed your face around here in weeks. I know you didn't come here to be around all these people just for me and Nate."

Malcolm smiled and his face flushed. "You look beautiful tonight, Mo."

"Oh, hush. I ain't been beautiful in forty years."

Nate approached them from behind and put his hands on each of their shoulders. "Not married two hours, and already somebody's moving in on my wife."

Malcolm stood and hugged him. "Congratulations, Nate."

"You were right. Time wasn't up for me. I got more places to go, starting with Hawaii." He reached for Modean's hand. "And somebody to love."

Malcolm patted his back. "I'm happy for you two."

Nate glanced at Mo, and she nodded. "I think . . ." Nate said. "*We* think . . . it's high time you start taking your own advice, Preacher."

Malcolm considered playing dumb but knew it would prove futile with his present company. He sighed. "I tried to talk to her tonight, but—"

"Well, you can't just give up!" Nate said. "What're you planning on doing? Sitting here at this bar all night? That won't get you anywhere. Get up and keep moving. That's what you told me to do. And that's what I did."

Malcolm took another drink of his Dr. Pepper. Nate was right. He couldn't give up. In an instant he was on his feet. "Where is she, Mo?"

Modean shrugged. "She said she had some stuff do to. That's all I know."

As Malcolm hurried out the front door, she called out to him, "Be careful! I hear there's a storm comin'!"

Chapter Thirty-four

I would hurry to my place of sheter,
far from the tempest and storm.
-Psalm 55:8, NIV

Malcolm drove through the wind and rain until the mounting storm forced him home. He walked through his door discouraged and soaked to the bone. Kate hadn't been at her house, or Modean's, or Debbie's shop, or Beulah's.

Maybe he was wrong. Maybe they all were wrong. Maybe he'd made too many mistakes, hurt too many people. Kate was good. So good. And good was the last thing he deserved. How foolish he'd been for entertaining any other notion.

He flipped on the light switch next to the door, but the room remained dark. He tried the switch in the kitchen to the same effect. He ran his hands through his dripping hair and sighed.

He rummaged through a kitchen drawer until his fingers found a flashlight. A quick search above the refrigerator produced a myriad of white candles, leftovers from weddings performed in the church. He threw them into a plastic bag and made a dash out his front door. The rain beat down upon him until he reached the doors of the church and shoved inside.

***

Kate turned the windshield wipers on full speed. Still, the driving rain made it almost impossible for her to see the road ahead. She was exhausted from the long day, but there was one thing left to do before calling it a night.

She glanced at the flowers sitting in the seat next to her. In lieu of tossing the bouquet to a pack of anxious, single ladies, Aunt Mo had placed it in Kate's hand after the ceremony.

"I know I'm s'posed to throw this thing, but I want you to have it," she'd said. "Just promise me you won't tell Delta. She's been eyeballin' it all night."

Kate had known exactly what to do with Aunt Mo's flowers. She'd already separated the roses and lilies into two bunches, one for her mother's grave and the other for Beulah Two's. It made sense for them to be included in the day. Both would have been overjoyed for Mo. Kate liked to believe they knew, somehow, and had celebrated the occasion together.

Kate squinted to see better through the windshield. She'd scoured the weather forecasts for days in preparation for Mo and Nate's outdoor ceremony, and not once had rain, much less severe weather, appeared in a single forecast. The window was streaked and blurry, and she decided it was time to find new wiper blades. And weathermen.

She came to a stop next to the cemetery gate and looked out among the tombstones. Angry gusts forced the trees to bend and writhe, submitting fully to the authority of the wind that took no mercy on them. The morning light would expose the evidence of their struggle, the scars of their battle. But they would be standing—tall, and strong, and better for the fight.

Lightning cracked and thunder exploded throughout the cab of the Bronco. Kate looked down at the bouquet again and sighed, wondering if maybe she should deliver the flowers the next day instead.

She'd just turned the car around when lightning struck overhead, and a heavy limb from a tall oak fell onto the Bronco's windshield, cracking it from one side to the other. She slammed on her brakes, her view out the windshield fully blocked by branches and leaves, and came to a stop in the church parking lot. Her hands trembled and her heart pounded. She gripped the steering wheel until her knuckles were white and willed herself to breathe.

"Remember, if you run into those storms, don't be afraid to stop and find a place to rest. Eventually the clouds will pass, and you can start again."

Her mother's voice was so clear, for a moment it felt like she was back there, looking down at the hospital bed as Ruth took her hand.

Kate looked up at Malcolm's tiny house just ahead.

"Find a place to rest."

With her heart still thrashing about in her chest, she took a deep breath and jumped from the Bronco into the storm. The wind whipped her long hair, stinging her skin, and her blue, strapless dress was doused in an instant. She took off her heels and ran barefoot across the parking lot to Malcolm's door and knocked, then pressed herself against the door underneath the narrow overhang. She knocked again, harder this time, and yelled his name, but the house was quiet, no light shining from within.

As she turned back toward the Bronco, she noticed a faint glow emanating from the sanctuary of the church. Instead of running to her car, she ran toward the light.

***

Malcolm had located every candlestick he could from the

various closets and junk drawers in the church building and situated them around the sanctuary. By the time he lit the last candle, the room was aglow.

The side door opened, and he looked up to see Kate standing there, soaked to the skin and shivering. A clap of thunder echoed behind her as she pulled the door closed against the force of the mighty wind.

"Kate! What are you doing here?"

She wrapped her arms around her waist. "I was driving by the cemetery when a tree limb fell on my car."

He retrieved a choir robe from behind the piano and wrapped it around her shoulders. "You shouldn't be out in this weather. It's crazy out there."

Her body's shivering slowed, and she pulled the robe tighter around her. "It wasn't supposed to rain."

"I looked for you tonight," he said. "At Susie's."

"I left early and went to Margie and Levi's. Gray's in town for the fourth."

Malcolm felt like he'd been punched. "Oh. I didn't know—"

"He'd called and asked if Jane Ellen could spend the night at his parents', with him and his wife. I'd told him I'd bring her by after the wedding." She blinked. "Did you say you were looking for me?"

He turned and picked up Jackson Boudrow's Bible off the stage, where he'd been reading. "I wanted to give you this. I was stupid to try to hold onto it. He was your father, and it should stay in the family . . . for you, and then Jane Ellen. I shouldn't have kept it from you the way I did."

Kate shook her head and waved the Bible away, her wet hair soaking the back of the robe. "No. Mama gave it to you because she knew exactly where it belonged. Mama could always see things I couldn't. Sort of like somebody else we knew."

Malcolm lowered his head. "I miss that little girl."

Kate felt in the pocket of her dress and pulled out a wet puzzle piece. "I was hoping I would see you tonight, too. Beulah Two gave this to me the night of your birthday. I was wondering if you could tell me why."

Malcolm took the piece from her hand. The picture appeared to be of a portion of a tree with a bright blue background. And on the back, in Beulah Two's messy handwriting, was the word *Kate.*

Malcolm's eyes widened. He rushed to the stage and pulled out a picture frame from behind the podium. He knelt and slid the backing out from behind the glass then gently laid the puzzle on the stage floor, completed all but for one piece.

Kate stepped closer to view the stunning landscape of tall mountains, soaring cedars, and blue sky. "Did Beulah Two do this?"

"She gave it to me as a birthday gift." He pressed Kate's puzzle piece into the empty space with a soft *thud.*

Malcolm stood and looked up toward the ceiling with his hands on the back of his head and almost laughed. "She knew," he said. "Beulah Two knew. Just like you said, she could see what we couldn't."

***

Malcolm walked off the stage in the candlelight, his eyes fixed on hers, until they met face to face at the altar.

Kate tried not to catch her breath aloud when he took her

arms firmly in his grip.

"Beulah Two could see that I needed you, Kate. I loved Anna. I will always love Anna. But you're the piece that makes my heart whole again."

Kate's eyes stung with tears. "That's what Beulah Two thought, and what she wanted. But what about you?"

His expression held the same familiar level of intensity she'd come to know, but instead of resentment and rage, his eyes burned with determination and fervor.

He leaned toward her. "From the second I first saw you that day in the cemetery, I couldn't get you out of my head. I wanted to. I tried to." He slid his grasp higher up her arms, then back down again. "Kate, I'm tired of pretending I don't love you. Because I love you."

He kissed her long and slow, until she was positive joy so deep and pure had never before existed. It rained from her eyes, down her face onto the choir robe and she prayed she was not caught up in a dream.

When he pulled away, they stood forehead to forehead, their eyes closed, their pounding hearts piecing themselves together to make a picture as beautiful as any of Beulah Two's puzzle scenes.

He wiped her tears with his thumb then looked up, his gaze focused behind her. Kate looked over her shoulder and then back to him, her brow furrowed.

He took her by the hand. "Come on."

In an instant he whisked her onto the stage and behind the heavy dark curtain that hung along the back of the sanctuary. Kate held to his arm as the curtain closed behind them, blocking all traces of light and leaving them in complete darkness.

He placed her hand onto a smooth, wooden railing. "It's a staircase," he said. "Follow me. One step at a time."

Kate had climbed up and down those steps a hundred times as a girl, even after her father's repeated appeals to the contrary. It had been built in the '60s for use in the church's Christmas plays. The steps led to a platform high above the stage—a place for the angel to appear to wide-eyed shepherds below—though it hadn't been used for a play or any other purpose in nearly thirty years.

Kate climbed the stairs with caution, and yet she'd never felt more protected in her whole life. Malcolm walked ahead of her, leading the way, holding her hand. When they reached the platform, Malcolm leaned forward and took the mammoth curtain in hand. In one powerful move, he spread back the heavy covering to reveal the sanctuary.

Kate placed her hand over her mouth. The room of candles had been pleasant from below, but from above, each flame seemed an individual soul—living, breathing, dancing to its own distinct, silent song. They burned bright, reaching toward the ceiling and the night and beyond.

"It looks so different from here," she said.

Malcolm ran his hand along her arm and looked below. "A view from there," he whispered.

Kate nestled her face against his chest, and he wrapped his arms around her as thunder rolled, this time far in the distance.

"Sounds like the storm is passing," he said.

As if Ruth Boudrow were sitting on her favorite pew in the sanctuary below, Kate felt her mother's voice rise to meet her on the platform. *"Don't be afraid to stop and find a place to rest. Eventually the clouds will pass, and you can start again."*

Kate smiled. "Until the next one. And then what will we do?"

Malcolm breathed in, his eyes shining, dancing in the flickering light.

"There'll always be storms. But when they come, you'll be held until they pass, and he'll send the sun in the morning. He always sends the sun."

THE END